# SONG
## OF THE
# CURRENT

# SONG
## OF THE
# CURRENT

## SARAH TOLCSER

**BLOOMSBURY**

LONDON  OXFORD  NEW YORK  NEW DELHI  SYDNEY

Bloomsbury Publishing, London, Oxford, New York, New Delhi and Sydney

First published in Great Britain in June 2017 by Bloomsbury Publishing Plc
50 Bedford Square, London WC1B 3DP

First published in the USA in June 2017 by Bloomsbury Children's Books
1385 Broadway, New York, New York 10018

www.bloomsbury.com

BLOOMSBURY is a registered trademark of Bloomsbury Publishing Plc

A CIP catalogue record for this book is available from the British Library

ISBN 978 1 4088 8900 8

Typeset by Westchester Publishing Services
Printed and bound in Great Britain by CPI Group (UK) Ltd, Croydon CR0 4YY

1 3 5 7 9 10 8 6 4 2

In memory of Grandma Barbara

# CHAPTER
# ONE

There is a god at the bottom of the river.

Some folks will tell you that's just a story. But us wherry folk know different. When the reeds along the banks whisper that a squall is rushing across the marshland, we listen. When the tide flows up from the sea, flooding the river with muddy brown water, we know enough to watch.

The god in the river speaks to us in the language of small things.

That's how my father knew something was wrong even before we rounded the bend into Hespera's Watch.

"Caro, take the tiller." Pa leaned over the stern to dip his hand in the river.

Our wherry was loaded up with timber for the lumberyard in

Siscema. The boat rode low in the water, so he had no trouble reaching the surface. A tiny wake curled after his fingers, forming a wobbly line of bubbles. The sun had disappeared below the moss-draped trees, and the river grew stiller by the moment.

He pulled his hand back as if it had been stung.

I sat up straight. "What was that?"

"I don't rightly know." He looked as if he wanted to say more, but he only added, "He's unsettled tonight."

He meant the god in the river. Everyone knows it can be bad luck—even dangerous—to speak of a god by name. The wherrymen usually call him the Old Man.

"Fire," whispered Fee. The frogmen aren't a people of many words.

Pa turned to her. "You feel it too?"

Fee perched on *Cormorant*'s cabin roof, her webbed toes spread out upon the planks. Her skin was the slick greenish-brown of a river bullfrog. With yellow eyes that protruded from a bulbous forehead, she stared unblinking at the water. The hem of her linen dress was shredded, threads trailing away behind her.

It's said that many thousands of years ago, time out of mind, the god in the river fell in love with a sailor's daughter. Their children became the frogmen. The land folks wrinkle their noses and call them dirty, but inlanders are ignorant about many such things.

I sniffed. "I don't smell any smoke."

As I spoke, the wind shifted and an acrid smell poisoned the air. Any moment now we would come into sight of Hespera's Watch, the first town south of the Akhaian border. I gripped the tiller so tightly my knuckles turned pale.

*Cormorant*'s stiff black sail swung halfway out on the starboard side. The heat of the day still warmed her planks, though the sun was gone. I spread the fingers of my free hand upon the decking, as if peace could somehow seep from her into me.

The god in the river doesn't speak to me like he does to Pa. Not yet. "The day your fate comes for you, you'll know," Pa always tells me. "The way I knew when it came for me."

Well, it seems to me my fate might hurry up a little. Pa was fifteen when the god in the river first whispered his name. I'm two years older, and I've yet to hear anything. But I keep my ears open, because I'll inherit *Cormorant* someday. Eight generations of Oresteia captains have plied their trade on these rivers. All of them were favored by the god.

We slipped onward through the shadowy water. The trees fell away, and the port of Hespera's Watch was before us. Or would have been.

"Xanto's balls!" I swore, my eyes stinging. I grabbed the sleeve of my sweater, holding it over my face.

Smoke poured from the warehouse roofs. The masts of sunken ships stuck up like dead tree trunks in the ugliest, most desolate swamp. This part of the river wasn't deep, so a few of the wherries were sunk only to their cabin tops. One had been ready to sail—the gaff and boom floated, sail billowing between them, under the surface. It looked like the dress of a drowned woman. Coals smoldered orange on the blackened posts, and bits of ash drifted on the air. The docks were gone.

"Those wherries—" Dry coughs racked me. I returned the sweater to my mouth and drew in a blessedly clean breath that tasted of yarn. No matter how I squinted at the wreckage, I was unable to make out any of the boats' names. "Pa, those wherries don't belong to anyone we know, do they?"

*Cormorant*'s sail gave an angry clap, making me jump. In my shock, I'd loosened my grip on the tiller. I tore my gaze away from the debris, hastily straightening our course.

Pa hadn't even noticed my steering lapse, which wasn't like him at all. "Give the dock a wide berth." He squeezed my shoulder. "We don't want to run up on any wreckage. Find a spot on the bank, near to the road as you can get, and head up into the wind."

"We're anchoring?" My mind leaped to our second cargo, the crate of muskets roped to the deck and surreptitiously covered by a tarp. We never stopped in towns when we were smuggling. "I thought we were making for Heron Water."

Pa rubbed the stubble on his chin, surveying the ruins. "A wherryman always helps a wherryman in need."

The sight of those lonely wrecks made my skin crawl. Where had all the people gone? I didn't need the god in the river to know something was very wrong.

Pa and Fee went forward to drop the sail. Pushing the tiller over, I steered *Cormorant* in a slow arc until her blunt white-painted nose pointed into the wind. She inched through the water, easing to a stop. Pa paid out the anchor rope, and we went about our ordinary tasks of stowing and settling the wherry.

Smoke permeated the air belowdecks, making the cabin seem even more cramped and close than usual. Pa shrugged on his good wool overcoat, arranging the collar so it fell just right. His somber manner heightened my worry. He only wore that coat to temple, or to pretend he hadn't drunk too much the previous night.

Candlelight flashed on something metal at his waist—his best flintlock pistol.

I paused with my hand on the locker door. "Weapons, then?"

"Better safe than sorry," he said gruffly.

I grabbed my leather-sheathed knife from the locker. Stuffing it in my pocket, I bounded up the cabin steps.

We rowed the dinghy ashore and walked into town, our footsteps scraping the gravel road. It was the only sound but for the mournful murmur of reeds along the riverbank. Pa kept glancing apprehensively at the river. Fee's head was cocked toward the water, listening with that elusive sixth sense I would've given anything to possess.

I swallowed down my envy, goose bumps prickling my arms. It was spring in the riverlands, and the temperature still dropped after sundown, but the chill I felt was mostly inside me. Why hadn't the god in the river protected the wherrymen whose ships had been sunk? And what did Pa and Fee know that they weren't telling me?

We found the dock inspector standing beside a pile of crates, surveying the docks with reddened eyes. From the haphazard way the boxes were stacked, it seemed they'd managed to salvage at least some of the cargo from the fire.

"You're a lucky man, Nick," he greeted Pa, as they clasped hands. "If you'd a been here two hours ago, I reckon that'd be your boat at the bottom of the river. Ayah, along with the rest."

Pa kept his voice low, out of respect. "What happened?"

"Eleven wherries sunk." Smoke trailed in a thin curl from the dock inspector's pipe. His voice was calm enough, but I noticed his hand trembled. "The ship come down from Akhaia. *Victorianos*."

"The name don't strike a bell," Pa said.

"She were a cutter. Speedy looking, with six four-pounders. They had 'em loaded with fire rockets."

I glanced up the river, almost expecting to see the ghost of the cutter rounding the bend. There was nothing but the trees' dark shadows, lengthening across the water. Looking at the charred masts, a pang of loss pierced me. Wherries weren't just cargo ships. They had personalities. They were homes.

I turned back to the dock inspector. "A cutter like that is wasted on this part of the riverlands," I said. "She can't use her speed proper with all these twists and turns, and her keel's too deep to get into the best hidey-holes. She belongs on the sea. What were they doing up here?"

"Trying to destroy the docks?" Pa asked. "Or one of the warehouses?"

The man shook his head in bewilderment. "Far's I can tell, neither. They aimed at the wherries first. Three of 'em were loading. The cargo all went up. Then the docks caught, and the fire spread to the first warehouse. We managed to get a bucket line going, but two boys were badly burned fighting the fire." He gestured at the stack of crates. "This is all that's left of the cargo."

The dock inspector looked so solemn, I knew there was more.

"How many killed?" Pa asked softly.

"Only two. The Singers were asleep aboard *Jenny*."

"Current carry them." Pa pulled off his woolen cap, smoothing back red hair streaked with silver.

"Current carry them," I echoed in a whisper, clenching my hands into fists. The ragged edge of one bitten nail dug into my palm. I couldn't imagine who would do something like this. The burned skeletons of the wherries poked out of the still water, where several wooden casks and crates bobbed.

We had anchored in a graveyard.

"Hair like weeds," Fee whispered, swiveling her eyes toward the dark water.

Before I had a chance to ask what she meant, a voice sounded behind us. "Nicandros Oresteia, captain of the wherry *Cormorant*?"

I wheeled around. An army officer stood on the dock, his knee-length blue coat covered in road dust. He was lit from the back by the last rays of the setting sun, so I couldn't see his face.

Pa and I exchanged glances. My pulse fluttered nervously.

The man spoke again, his voice carrying across the water. "I'm looking for the captain of the river wherry *Cormorant*."

Pa slowly turned. "I'm him."

"By command of the Margravina of Kynthessa, I'll need you to come with me now."

I sucked in a sharp breath. He wore a longsword and two pistols. He had drawn none of the weapons, but he didn't have to. They were easily visible on his belt, a silent threat.

"Really," Pa said, equal notes of teasing and disbelief in his voice. "Didn't think the Margravina knew my name to command me. We ain't acquainted."

Slowly I moved my hand, the one the commander couldn't see, toward my pocket, where my knife was stashed. I'd grown up on tales of Oresteias making mad, reckless escapes from men in uniform. I was ready.

Pa shook his head at me, and I paused, my hand hovering.

"I am Commander Keros," the stranger said, "of the Margravina's Third Company. I'm authorized to speak as her voice, as I'm sure you well know. Will you be so obliging as to come along with me to the harbor master's office?"

Then soldiers marched onto the dock behind him, and I knew he wasn't asking.

I spoke up. "You don't really think *we* had anything to do with this."

"Of course not, girl." The commander glanced at me the same way I might look at a minnow or an ant. He directed his words to my father. "I have an offer I wish to discuss with you, Captain. In private."

"But I'm—" I started.

Pa jerked his head toward town. "Go up to the Spar and Splice, Caro. I'll meet you there."

Before I had a chance to protest, they whisked him up the blackened cobbles, pressed between the commander and the soldiers. I wasn't fooled by his casual saunter. His shoulders were stiff as he burrowed his hands into the pockets of his overcoat.

I watched until my father was out of sight. It had happened so fast. My fingers twitched, brushing the outline of my hidden knife. They'd let him keep his pistol, I reminded myself. He couldn't be in *that* much danger.

"Well," I said to Fee, then grimaced. I'd intended to sound confident, but it had come out as almost a shout. "Let's go."

Hespera's Watch had but one tavern, the Spar and Splice. Its roof tiles were singed, but it was otherwise undamaged by the fire. I took the steps two at a time, barging through the door. Fee padded along behind me, her knobby elbows gleaming green in the lamplight.

A floorboard creaked under my battered canvas deck shoe. I glanced down, and realized I stood in a puddle of water. It trailed down the hall, staining the planks and soaking the woven rug.

Light flickered from an open door. I heard hushed voices, both male and female. Curiosity pulling me closer, I peeked into the room. Something long and lumpy was laid out on a bed, shrouded in a wet linen sheet. At first I didn't realize what I was seeing, until my gaze fixed on the boots sticking out from under the sheet.

I swallowed. I'd only known the Singers to shout hello to. Mrs. Singer had had lovely hair, long and straight. It spilled out from under the sheet now, like a black jumble of eels, drip, drip, dripping.

*Hair like weeds.* Remembering Fee's cryptic words, I pictured Mrs. Singer's hair tangled with the slimy green reeds at the bottom of the river, drifting in the murky current.

A shiver went through me.

Averting my eyes from the bodies, I stumbled down the hall to the barroom. I'd never seen a dead person before. My heart hammered in panic. *Stupid.* It was stupid to be afraid. Corpses couldn't hurt anyone.

Fee touched my shoulder. "Strong."

I nodded, inhaling deeply to steady my nerves.

Tension lay over the crowd in the barroom like a held breath. People huddled and whispered in small groups, occasionally slamming mugs on the bar. I could almost smell the shock and anger above the stale scent of spilled beer. There were many women, and one small boy, who stared with saucer-shaped eyes as his mother held on to his collar. It was not uncommon for wherrymen to sail with their families aboard. Two frogmen sat at a corner table, mottled heads leaning together as they croaked in their own language. On any other night, Fee would have hopped over to join them. Tonight, she only stepped protectively closer to me, her wary gaze darting around the barroom.

Someone whistled. "Ain't you Nick's girl?"

Thisbe Brixton was in her thirties, with a thick blond braid down her back and a tattoo of a serpent winding around her forearm. The sun had bleached the hairs on her arms white and creased the skin at the edges of her eyes. I was momentarily overwhelmed with relief to see someone I knew—until it hit me that Captain Brixton's wherry must be among the sunken boats.

I elbowed my way to the bar. "Why are there soldiers here?"

"Don't know." She beckoned the bartender over and ordered two mugs of the strong dark beer they favored in the northern riverlands. "They arrived right before you did."

"They wanted to talk to Pa." My voice sounded hollow. I was shaken, still remembering the disconcerting stillness of the dead bodies and the brusque way the soldiers had hauled my father away. "Said it was about a job."

From the red rims of Captain Brixton's eyes, I could tell she had been crying. "I don't like any of this," she muttered.

I curled my hand around the cool mug. Despite the horrible circumstances, I couldn't help feeling pleased she thought me old enough to order a drink. I'd always admired Captain Brixton. Her wherry was one of the few crewed only by women, and she carried the prettiest pistol I'd ever seen, engraved with a pattern of swirls and flowers.

"Thank the gods your pa's here," she said. "We're putting together a crew to hunt down those bastards what did for the Singers."

The old man beside her shook his head. "We are *not*."

"Oh, stuff it, Perry. The time to act is now." She banged a fist on the bar, setting the mugs clattering.

If someone sunk *Cormorant*, I reckon I'd be raging to charge off and fight too, four-pound cannons be damned. Something like excitement stirred recklessly inside me. I shoved it down. People were dead. Pa was in trouble.

I turned to the old man. "Your wherry too?"

"Ayah," he said, "though we fought like hell to save her."

I couldn't believe he'd lost *Jolly Girl*. Captain Perry Krantor had been sailing her since before Pa was born. She was a lovely old boat, with a cheery red-painted deck and a weather vane at the top of the mast carved like a windmill. As for the captain himself, he'd been a friend of my grandpa. It was too awful to take in.

"Was the damage bad?" I asked. "Can she be raised?"

"Bless you, Caro," he said, and my heart ached at the way his sun-spotted hands trembled around his mug. "I don't know as she's a total loss, but that'll be for the assessor to decide. And the salvagers. We sent off a runner to Siscema. On a gods-bedamned *horse*." He twisted his lip to show what he thought of a wherryman stooping to send word by road. "Not a boat left bigger than a dory."

I suddenly saw *Jolly Girl*'s weather vane, warped and blackened, paint curling from the heat of the fire. My fingernails bit into my palm.

"Reckon you and your pa don't get down south much these days, eh?" Captain Brixton said. "Well, I do. Heard of this *Victorianos*. Her master is Diric Melanos, and we all know who that blackguard runs with." She spat on the floor.

I didn't know. She was right—we didn't get down south much.

Seeing the question in my eyes, she leaned in close. "The Black Dogs."

"Black Dogs?" My head shot up. "This far up the river?"

Everyone knew to steer clear of the Black Dogs, an Akhaian mercenary crew—pirates, really—whose fast ships terrorized the Neck, the long saltwater bay in the southern riverlands. Now I knew why Captain Krantor wasn't keen on putting together a crew. Standing against the Black Dogs was a good way to get yourself dead.

"Pirates," hissed Fee. She dipped a long green finger into her beer and pulled it out again, examining the bubbles on her fingertip. Captain Brixton paid this no mind. Wherry captains were used to the frogmen's odd mannerisms.

"There's something gods-cursedly fishy about this whole

business. They didn't even take nothing." Captain Brixton took a big pull from her half-empty mug. "First Black Dogs, and now soldiers."

"You ought to slow down, is what," Captain Krantor told her.

"And you ought to mind your own business, old man."

I pushed my beer away, untouched. If pirates had set fire to those wherries, they might attack others. My thoughts leaped to *Cormorant*, anchored alone and unprotected out there on the river. Those pirates hadn't been looking to capture prizes or coin. Their purpose was to destroy, and with six cannons they were well equipped to do it.

"Black Dogs." My throat was hoarse. "I have to tell Pa."

# CHAPTER
## TWO

Only one guard was posted outside the harbor master's office. Not much older than me, he slouched on a bench on the porch, picking at a hangnail. I strode past him.

"Hey!" he cried belatedly, leaping to his feet with an armored clatter. "You're not supposed to—"

I banged through the screen door. "Pa!" I gasped, out of breath. "It's the Black Dogs."

Pa sat in a spindly-legged chair, arguing with the harbor master across a cluttered desk. "Now look here, Jack—" He broke off, turning at the sound of my voice. "What?"

Commander Keros stood behind the harbor master, arms folded. The last of the sunset slanted in through the blinds, lighting up dust motes on the air and sparkling on his sword hilt. The office was lined with glass-fronted cabinets stuffed with curios from around the riverlands.

"I—I heard the news in the tavern," I stammered, suddenly embarrassed by the weight of the strangers' eyes on me. "Captain Brixton says the ship belonged to Diric Melanos."

Pa's head snapped up. He recognized the name even if I didn't.

The commander's mouth tightened. "A fish story from a bunch of wherrymen. They don't know what they're talking about."

I heard the scuff of heavy boots behind me. Two soldiers stood on either side of the door. Startled, I stepped back, bumping the glass cabinet and causing the articles inside to shift with a rattle.

"Those wherrymen are my friends." Pa cut a grand figure with his long red hair and his shirt laid casually open at the collar, exposing the faded tattoos on his chest. "I trust them more than I trust the likes of you."

Commander Keros turned to me. "What do you mean barging in here, girl? This is a private meeting."

Pa sat up straight. "Whatever it is you have to say to me, my daughter can hear it."

"This girl is your daughter?" The commander studied me in a way I was, unfortunately, plenty familiar with. I tried to ignore the prickly feeling as his eyes crawled over me.

My mother resembled a classical bronze statue, tall and stern. She gave me her brown skin and long, slender neck, but the freckles and the auburn shade of my tightly coiled curls came from my father. In the coastal cities, it's common to see folk with mixed heritage. But in the inner riverlands, especially here, near the

Akhaian border, my appearance stuck out. The commander looked back and forth between the two of us, like we were a puzzle to be figured out.

Pa ignored him. "Melanos and the Black Dogs, this far north?" He shook his head. "It don't make sense."

Drawing a rolled-up parchment from inside his coat, the commander tapped it in his palm. "As I was saying, Captain Oresteia, there is a certain ... shipment ... resting in the warehouse. We want you to deliver it to Valonikos."

The Free City of Valonikos, an independent city-state to the northeast, was a week's journey by wherry. I was familiar with the run, which traversed two different rivers, but it wasn't one we made very often. Pa preferred to work the route between Trikkaia and Iantiporos. The money was better.

"That's the pitch?" Pa's eyes flashed with anger. "That's all you got to say? Looks to me like eleven friends of mine got burned out because the Black Dogs were looking for this shipment of yours. Didn't expect me to put two and two together and make four, did you now?"

It was the harbor master who spoke. "Run the shipment to Valonikos, and the smuggling charges go away. It's the best deal I'm prepared to—"

"What charges?" I interrupted. "What's going on?"

The harbor master narrowed his eyes. "Don't bother playing innocent. That crate you're hauling is filled with muskets and enough shot to make trouble."

Smuggling was a time-honored tradition in the riverlands. We dabbled in it, as did plenty of other wherries. Certain men would pay good coin to have an undocumented cargo transported across the border, no questions asked. It wasn't as if those muskets were going into the hands of criminals—their destination was a group of Akhaian rebels, exiled from their country for printing a pamphlet the Emparch hadn't liked. Pa had a soft spot for them, and often smuggled them supplies and packets of letters from their homeland.

"How do you know about—" Cheeks flaming, I balled my hands into fists.

Of course. While Fee and I were in the Spar and Splice, the commander's men had been stomping their muddy boots all over *Cormorant*. They had no right to board our wherry without permission.

Pa's face was tight around the jaw. "Maybe I broke some rules with those crates, Jack," he said. "But you be breaking some yourself with that search and seizure."

I stepped forward. "This is blackmail."

Commander Keros ignored me. "Captain Oresteia, I'm prepared to give you a letter of marque," he said. "Authorizing you to use any and all force necessary to get that shipment up to Valonikos."

"A letter of marque?" Pa's voice curled up.

"Ahem." The harbor master turned red around the edges. "The fact is, you are the only ship in Hespera's Watch that wasn't destroyed by the fire."

"Begging your pardon, Jack, but *Cormorant* is a wherry. We're equipped to haul cargo. How d'you want me to stay clear of the Black Dogs? Outrun 'em? Such an endeavor would require more speed than we have. Not wishing to be impolite, of course. But you catch my meaning."

"I think I know what a wherry is, thanks, Nick."

My curiosity getting the better of me, I turned to the harbor master. "What's the cargo?"

It had to be something important. Something dangerous. Why else would the Black Dogs leave their territory in the southern waters to come all the way up here? And why would the commander go to all this trouble, searching our wherry and trying to intimidate us with soldiers?

The harbor master shuffled his sheaf of papers. "I can't say."

"Then I can't run it to Valonikos. Caro's right." Pa flicked the papers. "You ain't meaning for us to have a choice, are you? It's bad of you, Jack." He looked at the harbor master. "How long you been knowing my father?"

"Your father would never have touched them smuggled guns, an' you know it."

Pa laughed. "I know my father was very good at what he did. I'll say no more than that."

I bit back a smile. My grandpa had been a notorious smuggler, but of course the harbor master had never caught him.

The harbor master's lips pulled to one side. I could see Pa hadn't exactly endeared himself with that comment. "You'll take this crate to Valonikos."

Pa could handle old Jack. It was the commander I was worried about. He had the air of a man not used to being denied.

"I've already got a cargo," Pa said evenly. "Got a full load of timber for Siscema. Or have you confiscated that as well? You won't, for you haven't got the crane and levers to unload it, not with the docks in ashes. Nor have you the right. The paperwork on that timber is in perfect order." He tapped the table. "As for this crate of yours, maybe a few years ago. Not now. I got my daughter with me, Jack."

I bristled at that. Pa always talked about the Oresteias' proud history as smugglers and cannon dodgers and scalawags. We were the perfect wherry for the commander's cargo run. A tiny thread of indignation twisted in my chest. I couldn't hear the god at the bottom of the river yet, but I reckoned I could throw a knife as well as anyone. I wasn't a child.

"Pa, I think—"

He quelled me with a stern look. "'Fraid it's a no go. I don't deliver cargo unless I know what it is, especially something that brings danger to me and my crew. You want someone who'll take your coin in the blink of an eye with no questions, you ought to talk to Bollard Company."

The Bollards were a powerful merchant family with a reputation for being somewhat ruthless. I reckoned they could afford to take on a contract like this—they had buckets of money and owned dozens of ships. More importantly, they had cannons.

Pa's grip tightened on the arms of the chair. "I'm a free wherryman," he said, and I knew he was preparing to stand up and leave. "I don't have to run your errands for you."

The commander smiled. "I'm sorry to hear that."

The soldiers seized Pa's arms, dragging him up out of the chair, which toppled with a bang. He kicked the shortest man, attempting to sweep his legs out from under him. But he might as well have been trying to knock over a tree.

"Pa!" I lunged forward, my hand hovering over the hilt of my knife.

My father jerked in the hold of the soldiers, his muscles straining. He blew strands of hair out of his reddened face. "Caro! Stay out of it!"

The commander waved to his men.

"It's too bad we couldn't come to an arrangement," he said calmly as they shoved Pa out the door. "But fortunately there are eleven wherrymen in the Spar and Splice who currently find themselves without wherries. One of them will agree."

"No!" My voice cracked. The idea of someone besides us sailing *Cormorant* made me sick. She was our home. "You can't! She's *ours.*" My mind raced with all the things that could go wrong. The Black Dogs might sink her. I might never see her again.

The commander turned to me. "What's your name, girl?"

"Caroline." I glared fire at him. If he called me "girl" one more time . . .

"Put that knife away, Caroline."

I stared down at my hands in surprise. I hadn't realized I'd unsheathed the blade. Everything had happened so fast. My shock was so great, I stepped backward. My legs hit the chair, and I dropped into it.

A commander of the Margravina's army. And I'd pulled a knife on him.

But he didn't seem as if he was about to hang me. Or arrest me. Indeed he did not seem to regard me as a threat at all. The commander glanced in the glass above the harbor master's desk, straightening his uniform coat. He looked almost bored by the proceedings.

Returning the blade to its sheath, I sprang up. "What about my father?"

"Your father will be conveyed to one of the prison ships in Iantiporos." He opened the door. "He will be assigned an advocate, as is his right under the law."

"This isn't fair." I followed him onto the porch. I'd heard gruesome stories of those ships, where hundreds of men lay in chains and filth awaiting trial for crimes against the Margravina. "You had no gods-damned business boarding our wherry without our leave."

"Vulgarity doesn't impress me," the commander said. "I don't tolerate it from my young soldiers, and I don't care for it from you either."

Well, I wasn't one of his soldiers, so he didn't have a say.

The men marched Pa around the corner of the building. Fee jumped off the railing and scrambled after them. As soon as they were out of my sight, a pang of uncertainty pierced me.

The commander was already at the bottom of the porch steps. "What about *Cormorant*?" I called, anger thickening my voice.

"Your wherry is under impoundment. It will be confiscated and put under the control of the harbor master."

A wherry was a "she," not an "it." I burned with resentment. "What about me and Fee? Where are we supposed to go?"

"I'm afraid you'll have to take that up with your father. It was he who made the choice, not I."

"You didn't *give* him any choice." I jogged to keep up with his long strides.

"I might remind you, Miss Oresteia, that smuggling is a crime in these waters." He raised his eyebrows. "And since it is perfectly obvious that you and the frogman were complicit, one could say you're getting off easy."

"What if I pay the fine?"

He stopped. "Very well." I could tell from his voice that his temper was growing short. "If you can produce sixty silver talents and pay them to the harbor master, you can have your gods-bedamned father and your gods-bedamned boat."

He knew I didn't have that much money. He was toying with me. I swallowed around the bitter lump in my throat.

The commander smirked down at me, as if I were a clump of dirt under his boot. "Good day."

The beginning of an idea is like the wake behind your boat when you first shove off from the dock, nothing but little bubbles twirling in a lazy circle. But then it deepens and picks up speed, until there's a frothy white wave trailing away from your stern. My idea started like that—a tiny flicker of bravery that grew.

"Commander Keros!" I ran to catch up. "Wait!"

"What is it now?" he barked, voice crisp and commanding. I realized he'd been holding back before, but now his patience seemed to have worn through.

"I'll deliver your cargo." There was no way he couldn't hear my heart pounding. "I know the way to Valonikos like the back of my hand," I said. "And I know *Cormorant*. I've been sailing her my whole life. I reckon that makes me a better bet than any of those other captains." In truth, I wasn't sure of that at all.

"Well." The commander's gaze swept over me. I held my breath. "Then I suppose, Miss Oresteia, we shall need a contract."

The harbor master looked up from his account books in surprise as we reentered the office. The carpet was still rumpled near the door where my father had fought back against the soldiers. I dragged my eyes away, settling myself stiffly in the chair. Then I remembered how Pa had sprawled, as if he didn't care. I forced myself to lean back until my shoulder blades touched wood.

The commander drew a fancy piece of parchment from his coat pocket, unrolling it flat on the table. "This is a letter of marque, Miss Oresteia. Do you know exactly what that entails?"

Numbly I shook my head.

"The Margravina is the ruler of Kynthessa—"

"I know that," I snapped. "I'm not an idiot."

He went on. "A captain with a letter from the Margravina in her possession cannot be detained or questioned. Anything she does, any action, even murder or an act of piracy, it is understood that she does in the service of the Margravina." He tapped the parchment. "You're a privateer now. If anyone gives you trouble, you're to show them this letter."

I thought of the Black Dogs, in that cutter with the four-pound cannons. If I showed them a piece of paper, they'd likely laugh in my face. And then shoot me. But I kept that thought to myself.

"You'll deliver the crate to the Akhaian Consulate in Valonikos. Upon completion of your contract, you shall be paid ten silver talents."

Ten silver talents was an incredible sum of money, far more than a cargo of one crate was worth.

"And if I do this," I said carefully, "if I take this shipment to Valonikos, no questions asked, et cetera, whatever. If I do this, you'll let Pa go free? Drop all charges?"

"You're not exactly in a position to bargain here."

I heard Pa's voice in the back of my head. *You're always in a position to bargain. If they think you're not, all the better. You've already got them.* I shrugged. "Fine. I guess we don't have a deal."

The commander's jaw twitched. "This shipment must be on the wherry and out of Hespera's Watch within the hour, either with you or another captain."

I gripped the chair arms. "You wouldn't dare." But I knew he would. Deep inside me, a small voice wondered if *Cormorant* wouldn't be safer in the hands of Captain Brixton or Captain Krantor.

"Calm down, Miss Oresteia." He sighed. "Finding another crew would take time. Attempting to reason with your unreasonable father would, again, take *time*. Time is what I don't have."

"Why don't you take the box yourself, if it's that important?"

"My men and I are bound across the border for Akhaia," he

said. "There's . . . unrest in the capital. We go to look out for the Margravina's interests there."

"The box isn't one of her interests?"

"Young lady, we're soldiers, not carters or wherrymen," he said dismissively, as if a carter or a wherryman was a person far beneath the commander of a military company. A person of little consequence. He shrugged. "We all do as we must."

I understood his meaning. He was telling me our conversation was at a close. Now I must do what I must.

"The Margravina wants me in Akhaia, not squandering precious hours in this dirty little town," he said. "Your terms are acceptable. If you deliver the crate to the dock inspector in Valonikos, your father will be a free man. For the time being, he shall remain here in the harbor master's custody."

The harbor master finished scribbling out the contract and blew on the ink to dry it. He offered the sheet of parchment to me. I dragged it across the table.

"Can you write your name?" The commander pressed a pen into my hand.

I glared at him. "Of course I can. I might not be a *commander* in a very fine coat, but I'm not stupid."

From the sharp look he gave me, I knew I had annoyed him. He must have been eager indeed to be rid of me though, because he said nothing.

Pa says you should read every word of a contract at least twice, but the language was flowery and included many clauses that went off on endless tangents. I exhaled. *Calm. Like the river.* I tried to visualize water flowing peacefully among rocks and reeds, but my emotions were as riotous as ocean breakers. The words swam before me like black spiders on the parchment. I gave up and signed "Caroline Oresteia" next to the $X$ at the bottom.

And then it was done.

# CHAPTER
# THREE

A wherryman, Pa says, follows no man but the river. A wherryman is free.

As I stepped onto the harbor master's porch, I knew it wasn't true. The scroll I held clutched in my hand told me that. It weighed me down.

"I shall escort you to the docks, of course," the commander said. He didn't look as if he wished to escort me any more than I wished to be escorted by him. I reckon he was itching to be off already with his company, going to their important duties in Akhaia.

"I'm not likely to get far, even if I leave now. The wind was all but dead when we put into Hespera's Watch."

He frowned. "Was it?"

A fresh easterly breeze cooled the sweat on my forehead. "That's funny," I said. "The wind's changed. This wind is blowing out of the east, from the sea."

For a moment I thought I could smell the salt on the air. But that couldn't be. Hespera's Watch was far inland.

I lifted my head to look squarely up at the commander. "I'm not leaving without saying good-bye."

I was sure he would deny me, but he did not. "Your father is in the brig. I'll expect you to return in five minutes."

I found Fee outside the brig, squatting with her webbed toes spread in the grass. Her eyes glowed dimly in the dark, two glassy orbs.

"I'm going to Valonikos." I hardly believed the words myself. "You'll come with me? Please?"

In the riverlands it's considered good luck if a frogman takes a fancy to your wherry. Fee was loyal to *Cormorant*, having sailed with us for many years, but her contract was with Pa, not me. I honestly didn't know what I would do if she said no. Wherries can be sailed single-handed, but they are designed for a crew of at least two.

She hopped up and nudged me with her shoulder, touching me just above my elbow. The frogmen aren't a tall people.

"Help," she said.

"Thanks, Fee," I told her. "I can't do it without you."

The brig was a dank low-ceilinged shanty. I almost bumped my head on the lantern that hung from a beam. The place reeked of sweat and mold, and I doubted the packed straw on the floor was clean. Rusted iron bars split the right side of the room into two cells. The first one was empty. Pa sat on a three-legged stool in the second cell, his coat unbuttoned and trailing around him.

At the sound of the door swinging shut, he looked up. One eye was reddened, but other than that he seemed perfectly at his leisure. Relief rushed through me. I ran to kneel beside his cell, not caring if the damp rotted straw stained my trousers.

"Pa, don't be mad at me." The words tumbled out. "I told the commander I'd do it."

His fists gripped the bars. "Caro, no. *No.*"

Tears burned my eyes and throat. "They were going to send you to a prison ship. And take *Cormorant* away ..." I explained what had happened. As I finished, my voice trailed off into the silence of the dark room.

Pa rubbed his chin, his face unusually still. I steeled myself for a scolding. I'd been reckless. I was gambling with both our lives, and with *Cormorant*. But he said nothing.

"You don't think I'm ready." I dared to whisper my doubts aloud. "You said when my fate came for me, I'd know." I lifted my chin. "What if this is it?"

He exchanged glances with Fee. "Oh, Caro. Of course you're ready." He looked down at his hands. "Perhaps it's me that's not ready."

"That cutter doesn't know the riverlands. But I do." I sniffed. "I reckon almost as well as you do. I know you were trying to protect me, when you told him you wouldn't run the cargo." I touched my pocket, where I'd tucked the letter of marque. "But I can do this."

"It ain't exactly the easiest run." Pa sighed. "But I suppose it's too late now. You already signed the contract?"

I nodded.

"You read it from front to back, I hope?"

I rolled my eyes. "*Pa.*"

The commander rapped sharply on the door. My five minutes were almost up. I scrubbed my eyes with my sweater, so he wouldn't see I'd been crying.

Pa glared at the door. "Ayah, let him barge in! I'd like to give him a piece of my mind, I would." His glance flickered toward Fee then back to me. "Caro, listen. The thing you got to know about gods is, they can be tricksy. Don't be in a rush for your fate to come a-visiting. It might not be what you expect, is all."

"What do you mean?"

"A god will do what—" He hesitated. "What he wants. A god won't be forced, nor hurried." He sounded as if he wanted to say more, but he just shook his head. "Well, what's done is done."

I wasn't sure what to make of his words.

"No more tears, girlie. You're an Oresteia." Pa grabbed my hand through the bars, giving it a shake. The clenched feeling in my chest lightened. "Deliver that crate. Take the river route north, past Doukas. Don't mess with Iantiporos or the channel. That part of the coast is full of pirates. And don't tie up in any towns. If you need help," he added grudgingly, "send to your mother's people."

I raised my eyebrows. Pa didn't always get along with them.

"Well, as a last resort anyhow," he said. "Listen, that letter of marque? You're not to use it unless it's an emergency. Draw as little attention to yourself as possible. Flashing that letter about ain't going to do nothing but get you dead, no matter what that commander says."

I kept nodding, though his words streamed over me like rain. Doukas. Hide the letter. No towns. Overcome by the shock of this evening, I could barely take it in.

"You can do it, Caro," Pa said firmly. "You mark this: I'd rather have *Cormorant* in your hands than any one of them wherrymen in the Spar and Splice."

"Even Captain Krantor?"

"Ayah, even him. He ain't an Oresteia. You are."

A memory swam to the surface. I was seven years old, listening to Pa tell stories as my legs dangled off the cockpit seat. I could feel my hair pulled tightly into two little poufs on either side of my head. We were going up Nemertes Water, the sea wind buffeting my face.

A gull perched on the rail beside me, its feathers fluffed up. With one gleaming black eye, it stared at me.

"Your great-grandma once smuggled four barrels of rum through the Siscema harbor master's back garden," Pa had said, his hand draped loosely over the tiller. "Because she was bold enough. My pa faced down a gang of river bandits with naught but a knife and a frying pan and lived to tell the tale, and how?" Pa pointed at me. "He was bold enough. During the war, it were folk like the Oresteias and the Krantors who took their wherries through the blockades. And you know why?"

I'd heard this story many times. "Because the Oresteias were bold enough."

He poked me, making me giggle. "Ayah, right you are."

I closed my eyes on the memory, the world whirling around me. I knew how to read a depth chart, how to reef and stow the canvas. I had the skills, but I had never sailed *Cormorant* without Pa. Was I bold enough?

"The wind's changed," Pa said, bringing me back to myself.

I didn't ask how he knew, stuck inside this tiny cell with only the one closed window. The god at the bottom of the river told him things like that.

Pa relaxed back against the wall, closing his eyes. "And so it comes," he whispered. "I can't stop her."

Before I had time to ask what he meant, Commander Keros loomed in the doorway. "Time to go."

I stumbled out into the smoky evening, Fee padding along at my left elbow. Her presence was like the calm after a rough storm. At least I wasn't completely alone.

Outside the Spar and Splice, I saw the silhouettes of several wherrymen gathered in the street. Someone had lit a pipe, its ashes a lone smudge of light, while other men talked in hushed voices. For a moment, I let myself imagine that Captain Krantor or Captain Brixton might intervene. We all had pistols, and there was power in numbers. We could rush the brig. Rescue Pa.

I felt the letter of marque stuffed in my pocket and knew it was a foolish hope. The wherrymen had their own troubles. As for myself, I'd signed a contract. I was going to Valonikos.

The dock inspector had loaded the crate into a dory, along with a basket of provisions. "My wife baked that bread fresh this

morning. There's coffee too, and what little butter I could scrounge."
He pushed off from the stump of the dock, pointing the boat
toward *Cormorant*. The commander sat on the back thwart, looking bored.

Walking back to our dinghy, Fee and I were quiet. She never
said much anyway, and I was too busy sifting through all the worries and questions in my head. The dock inspector's dory was
already waiting, bobbing idly in the shadow cast by *Cormorant*,
when we rowed up. I ignored it while I noted the placement of the
ropes and equipment on deck, and went below to inspect both
cabin and cargo hold. Nothing seemed amiss. Still, the idea that
someone had been rummaging aboard our wherry without our
leave bothered me.

The men fastened ropes around the crate and hauled it up on
deck. It didn't look like anything special. It was simply a rough
wooden packing crate with a canvas tarp draped over the top.

I pretended to bump my hip against the edge of the box. It
didn't shift. Whatever was inside was heavy.

Perhaps it was gold. A crate full of treasure was certainly
enough to bring the Black Dogs calling. But I remembered what
Thisbe Brixton had said. *They didn't even take nothing*. Not gold
then.

"You're not to open it," the commander said sternly. "In fact, it
will be better for you if you never touch it. Do you understand?"

"So I'm not ever to know what it is I'm carrying?"

"Miss Oresteia, you signed a contract."

Had that been in the contract? I supposed I should have read it more carefully, but it was too late to haggle about that now. The commander bid me a curt farewell and descended into the dory without another word. But the dock inspector paused at the top of the rope ladder.

He grabbed my wrist in a strong grip. I gasped.

"Diric Melanos is a killer," he said in a low urgent whisper. "And a traitor. You be on the lookout. *Victorianos*, out of Iantiporos. White sails she has, and blue paint. She were running only the main and one staysail when I saw her." He let me go. "Current carry you."

CHAPTER
**FOUR**

In spite of everything, my heavy mood lifted as the wind filled
*Cormorant*'s sail.

"We'll make for Heron Water," I told Fee. "We can stop there
for the night."

Heron Water was a marshy lake several miles downriver. The
narrow dike leading to the lake, too shallow to accommodate anything bigger than a wherry, was nearly hidden by trees, making it
a popular spot for smugglers to hole up. The pirates on *Victorianos*
mightn't even know about it—they certainly wouldn't be able to fit
through the entrance.

Glancing over my shoulder, I realized the town of Hespera's
Watch had nearly disappeared astern. I squinted into the dark,
searching the rooftops for one last glimpse of the brig. It was six

days from here to Valonikos. Maybe more, depending on wind and weather. Pa might be two weeks in the harbor master's cramped lockup, with nothing but a bed of itchy straw to sleep on.

And that was if nothing went wrong. A moment ago I'd felt almost exhilarated to be captaining *Cormorant* on my own. Guilt welled up inside me. This cargo run wasn't supposed to be fun. Our situation was deadly serious.

Night sailing can be dangerous. It is sometimes done, of course, for why else are the noses of wherries painted white? The northern stretches of the River Thrush are perilously narrow, with bends and twists to challenge the best helmsman, but you couldn't ask for finer weather than tonight. The breeze was steady, and the fast-moving clouds did not block the moonlight. I could see well enough, and Fee even better. Night vision is one of her people's most prized abilities.

Three hours passed without incident, until finally my stomach growled, and I remembered we'd never had supper. It must be nearly midnight. Flexing my cramped hand, I handed the tiller off to Fee and dropped through the cabin hatch.

*Cormorant*'s small living area was split into three sections by great beams, curved like the bones of a whale. The two forward cabins had canvas curtains that could be closed for privacy, but we mostly left them open to give the illusion of more space. Pa's bunk, in the bow cabin, was the largest. My bunk was in the middle section, nestled against the starboard side. Across from it, Fee's hammock hung from the ceiling.

The common area had a table with a bright checkered

tablecloth, built-in benches, and a leaf that could be unfolded to make room for company. On the port side, a tiny sideboard was wedged amid a wall of cabinets. The iron stove squatted there, its pipe traveling up through a hole in the ceiling. She was a simple boat, but she was shipshape.

Two fish, already gutted and filleted, lay on the sideboard. At the sight of them, a bolt of raw emotion shot through me. Pa had caught the fish this afternoon. We should have been eating supper together in the homey lamplight of the cabin.

I melted butter in the frying pan, sprinkled bread crumbs on the fish, and laid the limp strips in a row. The pan hissed.

*Cormorant* gave a wiggle, as if someone had joggled the arm of the person at the tiller. I gripped the edge of the sideboard. Fee was as good a helmsman as Pa. That wasn't like her.

A frog chirp sounded from outside. Trouble. I snatched Pa's extra pistol from the locker and lunged up the steps.

Moonlight shone on Fee's round eyes. She silently lifted one long finger and pointed.

A ship, laid up alongside the bank on the starboard side. Her ghostly white sails were furled and lashed down for the night. Not a wherry—she was nearly twenty feet longer and her mast was set farther back, in the dead middle of the ship.

A cutter.

"Check," Fee whispered, slinking forward. She padded around the edge of the cabin and disappeared.

My hand began to sweat on the tiller.

They might be asleep, or drinking and gaming belowdecks,

but they would certainly have posted a watchman. Like any wherry traveling at night, we had hoisted a lantern up one of the stays. By a fantastic stroke of luck, our sail blocked it from the cutter's view. If I changed course and hugged the port side of the river, perhaps the man standing watch wouldn't notice us. On the other hand, we would look as if we were trying to avoid being seen. Which would give them a reason to chase after us.

I made my choice, angling to port. The overhanging trees cast long shadows on the water. A wherry, with her black sails and low profile, might drift by unnoticed among those shadows. We might sneak past and into Heron Water. It couldn't be far now.

Fee slipped back along the deck. From her face I already knew what she had seen.

"Them," she whispered.

I glanced to starboard. We had drawn even with the stern of the resting cutter. The wind gusted, causing our rigging to creak. I held my breath.

For a few long heartbeats I thought we were going to slip past them. I thought the man on watch hadn't seen our white nose slicing through the water.

I was wrong.

"Sail, ho!" The shout rang clear across the water. A bell clanged, pealing over and over in the dark. "Wherry coming down! Wherry!"

"You there, up sails!" This voice was rough and commanding. I wondered if it was the notorious Captain Melanos. "To the cannons! Muskets!"

Everything on *Cormorant* was made of wood, canvas, or rope.

If one of those fire rockets hit us, she'd go up like kindling. Just like *Jolly Girl*. Just like *Jenny*.

"Fee, take the tiller!" Crouching on the starboard deck, I loaded Pa's old pistol.

A sharp crack rent the air. The noise rolled over me, and with it a wave of nervous excitement. For several seconds, I knelt in stunned stillness, before I realized they'd missed.

I aimed my pistol amidships and squeezed the trigger. The gun kicked, its backlash reverberating up the bones of my arm. I didn't think I'd hit anything. All I could see were the wraithlike shapes of the sails as the cutter's crew worked to raise them.

Now I knew the silliness of Pa's story about my grandpa. It might have been true or just a fish tale, growing bigger and longer in the telling, but it didn't matter how bold I was—for fighting pirates, a pistol was far superior to a knife and a frying pan.

"Roll out those gods-blasted cannons and don't be all night about it!"

Whirling across the cockpit, I took aim at the lantern swinging from *Cormorant*'s forestay. I shot it out with a bang on my first try. Broken glass tinkled as it hit the deck.

A real pity, that. Had our lives not been in dire danger, I would've paused to admire that shot.

The muskets rang out again, three in a row.

My right shoulder stung. "Ow!" I yelped, clapping my hand over the wound.

The wind shifted on my face as we went around a bend, out of sight of the cutter for the moment. I held my shoulder and tried to calculate in my head. How many minutes for them to get their sails raised? How long until they caught up? Blood ran hot and slippery through my fingers.

I turned to Fee. "Watch for Heron Water," I said under my breath. "Maybe we can give them the slip."

We were close. Usually I marked the way into the marshy lake by the line of trees and the white farmhouse squatting in the fields beyond. But it was so dark I was terrified we'd miss the turn. Or had already missed it. A mistake now would mean death.

The moonlight revealed a gap in the riverbank, where the fuzzy tops of cattails made dark spots against the reeds. Cool relief trickled through me. "There!"

Fee put the tiller hard over and we turned, bubbles rushing in a whirl against the rudder. Water slapped the hull. Above us tree branches hung low over the narrow dike. I leaned out and watched the bank slide by mere inches away.

Branches scraped the top of our sail as I hurried to haul in the mainsheet, forgetting my wound in my rush to gather in those handfuls of rope. The top spar lodged among the trees, and we lurched to a stop twenty feet from the main river. Broken clumps of leaves and twigs dropped to the deck.

Fee and I exchanged fearful glances. We were stuck.

"Hush," she whispered, releasing her grip on the tiller. She slid to the floor of the cockpit. I did the same. The trees swallowed up our black sail, drenching us in shadow.

I heard the cutter first—the creak of her boom and the rattle of rope against wooden blocks and tackle. Then I saw her high bowsprit, pointing through the air like a finger. I sucked in a panicked breath. Now her hull was in sight, moving past us for what felt like forever, though it must only have been seconds. She couldn't have been more than eighty feet long.

As the cutter's bulk streamed away, moonlight flashed on the letters painted across its wide transom. In blue outlined with gold, they read, *VICTORIANOS*, and underneath in smaller print her home port, *IANTIPOROS*.

The ship passed that close. It seemed the thrum of beating drums accompanied it, a threatening rhythm. After the stern of the cutter had been swallowed by the dark, I realized it was just my own heart.

I was so badly shaken my teeth chattered. I peered up into the tree branches, which were hopelessly tangled with our mast and halyards.

Fee shrugged. "Mess."

It was that.

"Well," I said, "at least we're not dead."

"All right," whispered Fee, nudging my uninjured arm.

"I know it's all right." I examined the bloody hole in my sweater. "It's just they might have killed me."

It was only a graze. Once when I was little, I'd tried to grab the anchor rope as it dropped and it had burned the skin clean off my hand. This seemed no worse. Already the pain was fading. As my panic receded, something else was rapidly taking its place.

Anger.

Wiping blood on my pants, I caught up a lantern from the

cockpit floor. My trembling hands struggled with the flint, but finally it sparked. The lamp, encased in painted glass, was meant to be a signal during foul weather. It cast an ominous pool of red light as I strode around the cabin roof. Leaves and sticks littered the deck, dislodged from the trees above when our mast and gaff had struck. I kicked them out of my way.

The crate, blanketed with canvas, loomed up in the circle of lantern light. What was in it that men would kill for? Warily I stepped closer, as if the box might suddenly pop open and monsters or Black Dogs or other nameless terrors might pour out.

"Forbidden," Fee warned at my shoulder.

I hesitated. The blackness around us was quiet but for the chirping of crickets and frogs. The wind tickled the leaves above.

I had half a mind to throw this gods-damned crate overboard myself. We'd never asked to be involved in any of this mess—me, or Fee, or Pa, or the Singers, current carry them. The Black Dogs thought people like us were expendable, and so did that commander. Well, this was my wherry. This was my life, and I was taking control back. *Now.*

I ripped off the canvas tarp. It fell in a crumpled pile.

Wood scraped on wood as I tugged at the lid of the crate. It toppled over onto the discarded canvas. I lifted the lantern.

"Oh," I breathed, because I couldn't think of a single intelligent thing to say.

There was a boy in the box.

# CHAPTER
# FIVE

The light hit him and his eyes snapped open.

I yelped. Fumbling at my waist for Pa's pistol, I pointed the barrel at his head.

The boy squinted up at me with light blue eyes, dazed by the glare of the lantern. Wincing, he rubbed the back of his neck as he uncurled himself from the bed of packing straw. I realized he was my age, or perhaps a little older.

He spat out a mouthful of dust. "Put that ridiculous thing down." Brushing a clump of straw from his chest, he tossed it aside.

I glanced at Fee, whose eyes were wide as she peered down into the crate at the boy.

He had strange foreign coloring, with a bluish cast to his skin that made it seem almost translucent. His curls were black or dark brown—I couldn't tell the difference at night. Among them something sparkled in the lamplight. A tiny garnet he wore in his earlobe, I realized. His clothing was fancy, all rich colors and swirling brocades, and he wore a loose jacket, knotted at the waist with a tasseled silk rope.

"Who are you?" he demanded.

I took an inadvertent step back. My anger had fizzled away into stunned confusion. "Caroline Oresteia," I answered automatically, then cursed myself for it. It was my place to ask the questions. I drew myself up, trying to sound commanding. "Who are *you*?"

He rolled his eyes upward, as if asking the gods for patience. "I mean, who is your father? Who are his people?"

"His name is Nicandros Oresteia. This is his wherry." What a snobbish thing to ask. Pa says only a fool looks at a man's name before he looks at the man himself.

"A wherry?" The stranger's lip curled. "Why have you been entrusted with this task?"

Annoyance leaked into my voice. "I was given this crate and a letter of marque by the harbor master in Hespera's Watch."

"Very well. And how many men do you have?"

"Men?" I echoed, beginning to think we were having two different conversations, in which neither of us understood what the other was saying.

"Men. Soldiers. Guns." He gripped the edge of the crate and surveyed the deck, clearly unimpressed with what he saw. "It's not just *you*, is it?"

"Oh, ayah, I've an entire company of the Margravina's best infantrymen stuffed in the cargo hold." I felt as if the gods were having a bit of fun with me, and I didn't like it. I kept the pistol leveled on him. "You still haven't told me who you are."

"My name is—" He hesitated. "Tarquin," he finished, rather grandly for someone sitting in a packing crate. "Tarquin Meridios. I have the honor of being a courier for the Akhaian Consul."

Too much honor, if you asked me. I failed to muffle the laugh that escaped. His stiff manner of speech was so at odds with our surroundings. Who exactly did he think he was?

He glared. "Take me to your father at once."

"He's in the lockup in Hespera's Watch."

"Worse and worse," he grumbled. "This isn't Valonikos. Why am I awake? This looks like the middle of nowhere."

"When people are trying to kill me, I like to know why."

"This box," he explained slowly, "was enchanted by a powerful shadowman to make me sleep the whole journey to Valonikos. You broke that enchantment when you opened the box . . . very stupidly, I might add."

He surprised me by lunging to his feet. I took a step back. He was taller than me by nearly a foot.

"Didn't I tell you to put that contraption away?" he demanded, glancing at the gun.

"Sorry if I'm not accustomed to having boys hatch out of packing crates," I snapped. "Maybe it happens all the time up north, but it never happens here."

"As if I travel like this on a regular basis," he muttered, shaking out his clothes. It didn't do much good. They were badly rumpled and full of straw. "And don't say 'hatch.' I'm not a chicken."

"That's what it looked like." I felt overwhelmed by the whole situation. "Listen, can't you just . . . I don't know . . . get back in?"

"No, I can't get back in." He spoke in a sarcastic tone, with the crisp accents of a northerner. "Unless you're a shadowman."

"Of course I'm not."

"Of course you're not." He mimicked me. "Well, it can only be done by a shadowman. They should have told you to never, under any circumstances, open the box."

I didn't have a retort for that. He seized on my silence, narrowing his eyes. "I see that they did. Only a great fool disregards advice given by his betters."

"I am not a fool," I said, "and what do you mean, *betters*?"

Above us a tree branch creaked loudly, startling us both into silence.

A chill crawled down my neck. The night takes small noises and amplifies them. The shadows turn tiny bugs into monsters. I forced myself not to glance over my shoulder into the dark.

Fee jerked her head toward the river. "Scout," she whispered, slipping over the side of the boat with a soft splash.

Tarquin stared after her. "I've never seen a frogman before." His lip curled. "I didn't expect it to be so . . . green."

The wind stirred the branches again, making them rattle against our mast. Tarquin's eyes met mine in the circle of lantern light, then darted away to peer intently into the night that crowded around us. Somehow I knew the noise had unsettled him too.

"Let's talk inside," I said in an undertone, gesturing with the lantern. I realized how unwise it was to be standing in the light. *Victorianos* had gone down the river, but they might come back. Even now they could be anchored outside the dike, listening to the rise and fall of our voices. Anyone raised on the river knows how sound carries across the water at night.

He nodded. We were suddenly in complete sympathy.

Which he spoiled as soon as we entered the cabin.

"Ugh, what's that foul smell?" He covered his nose with the embroidered sleeve of his robe, shrinking back against the steps.

Billowing smoke filled the cabin. "The fish!" Grabbing a towel, I waded through the smoke.

In our clamor to escape the Black Dogs, I'd forgotten the fried fish. It was ruined now, blackened and stuck to the bottom of the pan. As I unlatched the portholes, swinging them outward on their hinges, my stomach wailed in protest.

"This is a large boat." Tarquin's muffled voice was scornful. "Why is the cabin so cramped?"

"This is a working wherry. Most of the space is for cargo." I scraped sticky black crud off the frying pan and set it to soak in a bucket of water.

Unsurprisingly, he didn't offer to help. He watched me, breathing into the collar of his robe, which had been punctured by bits of straw. It must have itched, because he absently rubbed it back and forth. Under the robe I could see a triangle of bare chest. He slouched over, shoulders hunched, trying to keep his head from hitting the swinging lantern.

"There's a clean shirt in there, if you'd like." I nodded at the locker. "My pa's not as tall as you, but I guess it might fit all right."

I halfway expected him to make a rude comment, but he only wrinkled his nose at the neatly folded clothes. They were the plain woven shirts of a wherryman.

I studied the stranger as he rummaged in the locker, wondering what message he carried, that the Black Dogs wanted him dead so badly. And why was he in a packing crate, of all things? It was a cursed peculiar way to travel—I couldn't imagine the bruises he must have.

"Why don't you make your frogman clean that up?" He fastened the last button, waving a hand dismissively at the frying pan. "We have things to discuss."

"She's not *my* frogman."

"Are you sure?" Pa's shirt hung loosely on his thinner frame, but the cuffs stopped inches above his wrists. "I'd always been told that in the riverlands they keep frog people for servants."

"Fee's been working this boat since I was nine years old," I said. "Not as a servant—as part of our crew. I can't *make* her do anything. She does as she wishes. I thought you said you were a courier. Haven't you ever been out of Akhaia before?" But they had frogmen in Akhaia too, along the waterways. Hadn't he been *anywhere*?

He flushed red but said nothing.

This talk of frogmen made me worry about Fee. I bit my lip, trying to remember how long it had been since she dove into the water. Surely not more than a few minutes.

"Did you know you're bleeding?" Tarquin said in a bored voice.

"Of course I know." I examined the hole in my sweater, where a dark bloodstain blotted the wool. In truth I had forgotten. I grabbed the bottom hem and started to pull it gingerly over my head.

"Turn round," I ordered him.

"Excuse me?"

"I need to take my shirt off. Turn *around*." The shirt I wore underneath was so threadbare, it was almost see-through. There was no way I was letting him get a peek. Of anything. And I didn't want him smirking about how poor we were. We were working people. There was no shame in that, but I felt a rush of embarrassment anyway.

He faced the wall. "While you're seeing to that," he said, fiddling with the jewel in his ear, "I shall require you to tell me everything leading up to the moment you opened the crate."

I sighed. "Can't you talk like a normal person?"

No one I knew spoke like that, all convoluted and formal. Not even my cousins on my mother's side, and they were city girls who lived in a fine town house.

Again he tugged at his ear.

"Why do you keep doing that?" I asked. "Touching your earring."

He brushed it with a fingertip. "It marks me as a member of a great Akhaian house," he said. "A house which you no doubt will not have heard of."

I snorted. "Probably not."

Opening Pa's medicine chest, I removed a tin of salve and a roll of bandage. As I cleaned the bloody graze on my shoulder, I related the tale of what had happened that night, beginning with us coming around the bend into Hespera's Watch and ending with the Black Dogs.

I tugged my sweater back on, grimacing as it snagged on the bandage.

"All right, I'm done." I took down Pa's brandy bottle and set two glasses on the table. My insides still felt shaky from our near escape. "You want a drink?"

Tarquin, who had been surprisingly quiet during my story, shrugged. I took that as a yes. He accepted the glass, pulling it across the table. I noticed dark smudges under his eyes, which struck me as strange. Surely an enchanted sleep would mean plenty of . . . well, sleep.

I swallowed the brandy down, its rich flavor burning my throat. Immediately I felt emboldened. No one gets drunk after one sip of liquor, so it was likely bravado or my own imagination. I didn't care.

"Now it's your turn." I slouched sideways in the booth, kicking my feet up on the bench. "Why were you in that box? Why are the Black Dogs after you?"

"I shall tell you my story," he said, "for although you are both rude and unladylike, it seems I'm stuck with you on this floating piece of junk. I suppose I'll need your help."

"Stuff it," I said. We glared at each other in mutual dislike from opposite sides of the table.

"Very well." He drew his finger down the glass but did not drink. "Let's talk plainly. What do you know of Akhaia?"

"I know the capital is Trikkaia," I said. "I know there's a shop in the market there that sells the best fish stew in the northern riverlands." The truth was I'd never explored beyond the docks and the market district.

"That's almost nothing." He twisted his hand in his hair, rumpling it up. My ignorance seemed to dismay him. "What do you know about the Akhaian succession?"

"Um." I had only the vaguest idea what a succession was. Something to do with royalty. And heirs?

"It's all so clear." He sprang up to pace the cabin. "The pirates that attacked you must have been hired by the Theucinians."

I failed to see what was clear about any of this. "What's a Theucinian?"

"You don't know?" Tarquin halted, whirling to stare at me. "I thought . . ." For a moment he appeared stricken, which made him look younger and more uncertain. "You said this wherry was chosen by the Margravina's man. I assumed he told you."

"Told me *what*?"

"The news I'm taking to Valonikos." An odd look flickered across his face. "The Emparch of Akhaia has been murdered."

# CHAPTER
## SIX

"Murdered," I repeated flatly. "The Emparch of all Akhaia. Pull the other leg, why don't you?"

Tarquin's jaw tightened. "This is *not* a laughing matter."

Akhaia was a fading empire. When the Margrave of Kynthessa had declared his province independent from the Emparchy, he'd launched a long bloody conflict now known as the Thirty Years' War. In the two hundred years since, several other territories had broken away to form smaller republics and city-states. But despite its decline, our neighbor to the north remained formidable. As the largest country on the continent and the birthplace of our culture, Akhaia cast a long shadow.

I leaned forward. "Why do these Theucinians want you dead? What is it you're carrying—a letter or something?"

"Yes." He stared hard at the lantern, its wavering red light reflected in the darks of his eyes. I got the sense he was trying to decide exactly what to tell me. "After Valonikos seceded from the Emparchy to become its own city-state, certain distant members of the royal line continued to reside there. In exile, of course. The Emparch has"—he corrected himself—"*had* no use for them. Not until now. The message I carry is vital to the future of Akhaia."

When he stopped, I gestured expectantly. "Well?"

"Well what?"

I ground my teeth. "What's in the letter?"

"It's a secret, obviously." Tarquin drew himself up. "If I told every common river laborer my business, I wouldn't be much of a courier, would I?"

In my extreme curiosity, I was willing to ignore the slight. "What happened to the Emparch?"

"He's been assassinated." His voice was hoarse. "By Konto Theucinian, who by the grace of the gods was once born the Emparch's own cousin."

"Once?"

His nostrils flared. "A man who murders his own blood has no honor. He is not a man. The Theucinians have always been bitter because their line didn't inherit the Emparchy in the Succession of 1328. Preposterous, of course."

He dropped into the seat opposite me, downing his drink in one swallow. "I don't know how long they've been planning the coup, but Konto Theucinian has attacked the palace and seized the throne."

I remembered Commander Keros's haste to get to the Akhaian capital. This had to be what he was talking about when he said there was unrest. But if word of the Emparch's murder had already trickled south, why were the Black Dogs so intent on hunting down Tarquin? His news wasn't exactly a secret. Something was missing in his story—and that wasn't the only thing bothering me.

"You're the one they sent?" I eyed him doubtfully. With his high and mighty mannerisms and that silk robe, he would stick out like a sore thumb in the riverlands. Not to mention he didn't seem very experienced. "Surely you can't be the consulate's best."

"I don't know what *you'd* know about it," he muttered. "It's due to the influence of my father that I have a diplomatic posting, despite my youth."

"Who's your father?"

"He's on the Emparch's council. I"—his voice cracked—"I don't know if he made it out of the palace." His hand trembled on the checkered tablecloth. He saw me looking and pulled it into his lap.

We sat in silence as the lantern flickered, long enough for it to feel awkward. Much as it annoyed me to admit, he was right. I wished I'd never opened the box. Pa and I were smugglers, but it wasn't as swashbuckling as it sounded. Sometimes we buried a shipment in a hidden cache or gave a tariff agent the slip in the dead of night, but most days we just sailed from port to port. Nothing had prepared me for being in a scrape like this. The commander should've taken Pa's suggestion and given the crate to the Bollards—I was in far over my head.

"All right." Taking down a chart from the shelf, I unrolled it and spread it on the table. "This is us." I jabbed my finger on the snakelike line that marked the River Thrush. "And this is the Free City of Valonikos."

Tarquin waved his hand. "I have no intention of going to Valonikos. Not now that I'm awake."

"Oh, well, la-di-da." I was nearing the end of my patience. "Where do you intend to go, then?"

"Casteria."

He traced the River Thrush on the map until he came to the fork, where he drew a line not up the River Kars toward Valonikos, but down through Nemertes Water, past Iantiporos. He didn't stop until he got to the Neck, the great narrow bay that lay many miles to the south.

I flattened my palms on the map. "No."

"This is a different matter. Just as important." He squeezed his glass, knuckles whitening. "You *have* to help me. I'm an agent of the crown."

"Not any crown of mine. I have to deliver you to Valonikos." Pa's freedom depended on it. On me. "I've got a letter of marque from the Margravina says I'm to take you there and let no one get in my way."

"So?"

I crossed my arms. "You're getting in my way."

"But everything's changed now. When the shadowman enchanted that box, he didn't know—" He abruptly shut his mouth.

I'd heard of the shadowmen who live in the north, whose lineage is full of secrets they mostly keep. The stories say they can pluck horrors and illusions from the dark, and twist your dreams into bone-chilling nightmares. It is whispered that they were descended from the god of the night, just as the frogmen are children of the river god. I had never seen a shadowman. Only very rich people could afford their services.

A shudder ran through me.

Tarquin noticed. "You're not scared of shadowmen, are you?"

"No," I lied.

"Magic doesn't make a man evil," he said. "It's just a skill. It isn't inherently good or bad. It's what's in his heart that makes him evil, the same as anyone else." He leaned across the table, the lantern casting weirdly shaped shadows on his face. I stiffened. "Are you afraid of the dark?"

I stared him down. "Of course not."

"Then you have no reason to fear a shadowman. They work the magic of light and dark, sleep and awake." His voice took on a lecturing tone. "But that's all they can do. Misdirection and shadow and sleep, and so on. Their power is passed down from long ago, time out of mind, when gods spoke and walked abroad among men."

*They still do*, I wanted to say. *I thought everyone knew that.* But I reckoned we'd had enough bad luck. I wasn't about to bring more of it down on us by speaking of the river god out loud to a stranger.

Outside, the wind whistled through the treetops. A spattering of rain blew in the open cabin window and the candle in the lantern guttered low.

Wood slammed on wood, causing us both to jump. Fee's long-toed feet appeared on the steps. "Gone on," she said, shaking off water droplets.

"Do you think they saw us?" I asked.

"They shot at you. Of course they saw you," Tarquin said.

I shot him a rude look. As if I'd been talking to him. "I meant *Cormorant*'s name."

Surely it was too dark. I swallowed through a dry throat, remembering how I'd crouched in the cockpit and read *Victorianos*'s stern in the moonlight. It was impossible to know.

I turned to Fee. "A disguise might not go amiss."

"Tomorrow," she agreed.

"Very well," Tarquin said. "For now it's best we all get what little sleep we can. In the morning you can convey me to Casteria."

"Valonikos."

"Casteria."

I slid Pa's pistol a few inches out of its holster.

He was unimpressed. "Will you cease pointing that contraption at me? You won't shoot me. You don't want to damage your precious cargo, after all."

"Why do you keep calling it a contraption?" I asked. "Surely they have guns in Akhaia."

"Of course we do. But a blade is the weapon of a gentleman. It's the only honorable way to fight."

"Oh?" I looked pointedly at his waist. "I don't see yours."

"I left in a great hurry. I didn't have time to—" He closed his mouth and fell silent.

Grabbing the lantern off the table, I gave him a sharp look. I still suspected he wasn't telling me everything. But he was right about one thing—I didn't dare shoot him, not when Pa's freedom depended on his safe arrival in Valonikos.

I decided further investigation could wait till morning.

"You can take Pa's bunk." I nodded at the forward cabin.

That bunk was the biggest we had, although he would still probably have to bend his knees to get into it. I showed him the head, in case he needed to use it during the night, and got an extra wool blanket out of the locker. This I shoved at him, almost daring him to make a remark about its scratchiness. But he said nothing.

I stumbled through the motions of getting ready for bed, then blew out the lantern and dropped into my bunk.

*Cormorant* rocked reassuringly, water slip-slapping at the hull, as the occasional burst of rain sprinkled the cabin roof. I lay awake, uncomfortable with the knowledge that a strange boy was sleeping on the other side of the curtain. I couldn't see or hear him, but his presence seemed to fill the cabin. The wound on my arm throbbed. And worse, I felt the lack of Pa, a raw self-pitying loneliness that clawed at my chest.

It was a long time until my heart slowed enough for me to fall into sleep.

That night I dreamed of Mrs. Singer, the wherryman's wife who died on *Jenny*. I dreamed she lay still on a bed of coral, and that coral was brighter than anything at the bottom of the river. The reef sat on a patch of golden sand. Motes of light trickled down through the dark water.

Mrs. Singer lay with one arm dangling off the edge of the spongy coral. Slick green weeds wound around her face, weaving through the locks of her long hair. Fish swam above her, but they weren't like any fish I had ever seen. Their colors were brilliant—yellow, orange, and vivid blue.

Then Mrs. Singer opened her eyes and said my name.

# CHAPTER
## SEVEN

I awoke the next morning greatly relieved not to have been murdered in my sleep by the Black Dogs. Casting a glance at the closed curtain to Pa's cabin, I bound my hair with a red paisley scarf and slipped barefoot onto the deck.

Mist hovered over the riverlands. A dragonfly flitted in the air, its wings a flash of green among the shivering cattails. Fee perched on *Cormorant*'s bow, a faraway look on her face. Was she talking to the god in the river? As his descendants, all the frogmen had a connection to the god. Whether it was the same language of small things the wherrymen spoke of, or something far older and stranger, I didn't know. A pang of jealousy stung me.

Squinting at the peak of the mast, I surveyed the mess from last night. *Cormorant*'s halyards were still tangled in the branches, her deck scattered with twigs and leaves. Pa wouldn't approve of the way we'd left the sail in a heap. Together Fee and I unwound the ropes and lowered the mast to shake it free of the tree. I winced as sticks rained to the deck around me. We steered the wherry out of the dike and into Heron Water, where we anchored near the bank.

Fee scrambled up from the cargo hold, setting a bucket on the deck. "Paint." She pressed a brush into my hand.

Reluctantly I eyed *Cormorant*'s name, spelled out above the cabin door in light blue letters with red flourishes. "I hate to ruin it."

She shrugged. "Or die."

"I know, I know." I swiped the wet brush across the *C*, blotting it out.

As I put the finishing touches on the paint, Tarquin emerged, blinking in the morning sunlight. He gazed out at the lake in surprise. It had been too dark to see anything last night.

"I didn't know there were other boats here." He drew his brocade robe around him.

One vessel was anchored down at the far end of Heron Water, a finger of smoke curling up from her roof. I couldn't identify her—a houseboat, maybe? The other was a wherry, the *Fair Morning*. The wherryman's wife sat on deck in a rocking chair, smoking a long pipe. She and her daughter stared at us. I didn't know them, but I could tell they were wondering why we hadn't said hello yet. And what kind of idiots we were to get our mast stuck in the trees.

I set down the paint bucket. "Is that what all the Emparch's couriers wear?"

"It's a dressing gown." He saw my mystified look. "Sleeping clothes."

"Oh." My cheeks burned with embarrassment. Well, really. Why would anyone waste such an elegant garment on sleeping?

He rubbed the fabric between his fingers. "I didn't have time to change before I was forced to flee—"

"Flee?" Again his words caused an alarm bell to go off in the back of my mind. Something wasn't right about his story.

"I was rushing to get on the road," he explained hastily. He put his hands in his pockets and looked out at the flat land, the breeze stirring his curls.

The only white sails belonged to a two-masted schooner far away across the yellow-brown marsh. That didn't mean anything, though, since the River Thrush had many bends and places where lines of trees blotted the horizon. *Victorianos* was lurking out there somewhere.

The packing crate still sat on deck, its lid askew. I heaved it overboard with a muddy splash.

Tarquin followed me. "What are you doing?"

"The Black Dogs are looking for a wherry carrying this box," I said over my shoulder. "I'm going to sink it. And you're going to help me."

I slung the rope ladder over the edge of the deck and climbed down. At the bottom rung, I jumped off, landing thigh deep in the water. Mud squished between my toes.

He sighed. "You expect me to jump into that muck? There could be leeches. Or snakes."

I put my hands on my hips, squinting up at him. The crate bobbed in the water beside me. "Of *course* there are leeches. Most likely snakes too."

He spent far too much time removing his boots and rolling up the cuffs of his trousers, as I hunted along the shoreline for large rocks. By the time he inched down the ladder, I had piled up a collection.

"I aim to get rid of everything that might make this wherry stand out," I said. "Starting with this crate. And you."

"Well, you can't get rid of *me*." He waded ashore, mud sucking at his bare feet.

"But I can make you look more like a wherryman." This was the part he wasn't going to like. "Take off that robe and your trousers and put them in the box."

His nostrils flared, and he stepped toward me splashily. "Now see here—"

"Oh, honestly. I won't look." I studied him. "What you should do is cut your hair. And take out that earring."

"No."

"What do you care more about, your vanity or your survival?" I countered. "No one in the riverlands dresses like that. The clothes have to go."

His gaze flickered over me. "Your scarf is unusual for a wherryman's daughter. Made in Ndanna, I should guess from the pattern, and a particularly fine silk. I suppose we're not burying *that* in the mud."

I touched the scarf knotted around my hair. It had been a

present from my cousin Kenté, which was none of his business. "I'm not the one the Black Dogs are trying to kill."

Tarquin made all manner of unnecessary huffing noises as he pulled off his trousers. Out of the corner of my eye, I saw him balancing on one leg like a heron. At a glimpse of white under-shorts, my cheeks went hot.

"After I *just* finished getting all the gods-damned straw out of that robe," he muttered. Tossing the bundle of fabric into the crate, he raised his eyebrows. "All right?"

His letter from the consulate hadn't been in his trousers or his robe. He must have stashed it in Pa's cabin. I filed that information away for later.

I piled my rocks in the box and watched bubbles rise up from the water as it sank. When it was completely submerged, we waded back to *Cormorant*. I kept my eyes politely slanted downward. Things between Tarquin and me were awkward enough without me seeing him in his underwear.

"Ugh! There's a leech on my ankle." He pinched one end and began to lift. Its slimy black body stretched longer, but it didn't loosen its grip.

"Scrape, don't pull." I turned my foot over to find one of the creatures latched onto my big toe. "Like this." With my fingernail I removed it and flicked it overboard.

Instead of saying thank you, he let out a loud sigh. "I won't have any further conversation with you while I'm not wearing trousers. It's ridiculous."

Fee and I exchanged glances as he stalked up the deck, leaving wet footprints. He might have been a great deal more tolerable if he wasn't so obsessed with his own dignity.

I rummaged in the cargo hold until I found a sign, brightly painted with the name *Octavia*. Smaller letters underneath named the city of Doukas as our home port. I hung it above the cabin door, where it almost covered the slick new paint. Someone who inspected us closely would notice, but I figured if any of the Black Dogs were that close, we were already dead.

Tarquin clumped up the cabin steps. "There. Do I look like a *wherryman* now?" He spat out the word as if it were a curse.

The truth was he didn't, especially not with that haughty sneer on his face. His forearms were pasty white. I couldn't see his palms, but I knew they would be as smooth as mine were hard. He looked uncomfortable in Pa's clothes, and furthermore his boots were all wrong. They were knee-length, crafted from creamy soft leather, and the brass buttons were decorated with lions. I regretted not sinking them too, but we didn't have any others that would fit him.

"What are we going to do about those pirates?" he asked.

"There are lots of hidey-holes in these parts," I said. "Dikes and ponds and the like. Places only a wherryman would know about." Or a smuggler, but I didn't say that aloud. "Even if they do know, I reckon that cutter can't fit. Too deep in the draft."

"Can't you speak plainly?"

"The draft. A ship like that must be nine feet at least." He still looked confused. "Her *depth*. Our keel is only four feet deep."

"Must be nice," he said. "I bet they can stand up in *their* cabin."

I ignored that dig. "With any luck, we'll see the Black Dogs before they see us. I can't outrun them, but I know where to hide. And once we deliver the lumber—"

"What are you talking about? What lumber?"

"You're not my only cargo." I struggled to keep the annoyance out of my voice. "There's a shipment of timber in the cargo hold that's bound for Siscema."

"Can't it wait? My mission is far more important than your *logs*."

I glared at him. "After we unload the logs, we'll go a great deal faster."

He seemed to accept that, turning to examine the fresh paint on *Cormorant*'s cabin wall. "Why do you have a sign with another boat's name on it?"

"Smuggling," I said. It wasn't as if he could turn me over to a dock inspector. He needed me. "Sometimes a disguise comes in handy. Of course, anyone who knows her well enough won't be fooled."

Tarquin glanced over his shoulder at the *Fair Morning*, which had raised its big black sail, then back to *Cormorant*. "They look exactly alike to me."

I laughed. "Ayah, to *you*."

The woman on the other wherry gave us a cutting look as they glided past. No doubt they had heard the gunshots last night and seen me painting out *Cormorant*'s name, and decided we were scoundrels of the worst sort.

Tarquin pointed to the boat at the far end of the lake. "Is that a wherry too?"

Fee squatted on the cabin roof, her toes splayed out. "Pig man," she said.

I looked up sharply.

Some said the pig man was a god. If you caught him on a lucky day, he would tell you your fate. On the unlucky days, he sat at his stove on the roof of his rickety houseboat, smoking pork until it fell off the ribs. He went slowly up and down the river selling it, as well as bacon and salt pork, because even wherrymen tire of fish. Pa had purchased provisions from him many times, apparently all on unlucky days, because he'd never said or done anything remotely godlike. He was just old. And strange.

Likely the whole thing was a fish story, but if ever I had needed someone to tell me my fate, this was the day. And even if it wasn't my lucky day, the pork was delicious.

I climbed down into *Cormorant*'s dinghy and rowed across.

The pig man sat next to his smoker, his face hidden under a floppy-brimmed hat. It was impossible to tell if he had brown skin like my mother's family or was simply tanned that color from sitting out in the sun all his long life.

"How be you on this high morning?" the pig man called down as I tied up the dinghy.

"I'm for Valonikos," I said, heart skittering nervously. "To deliver a shipment."

"Foolish girl. 'Tis your fate that be pulling you down that river." He glanced at me. "Your fate . . . and that boy's."

I put my hand on my knife hilt. "What do you know about—"

I stopped. Surely it wasn't wise to say his name. "I mean, what do you know about my fate?"

"Salt pork today? Got a fine batch of salted smoked pork for the buying." He winked. "I be thinking your fate is far away from here, Captain Oresteia."

I wished he would stop being mysterious. "I'm not a captain," I said, passing him a handful of coins. "*Cormorant* is my father's boat. You know that as well as I do."

"You can't fight it." He grinned, showing all his white teeth. "Why is it every soul be always thinking he can fight it? Does a fish swim upstream against the tide?"

I wasn't a man or a fish, and I was beginning to weary of his knowing leer.

"It damn well tries," I told him. "Salt pork, please." I hesitated. "Is it true, what they say? That you're a god? Can you speak to the god in the river?"

He only laughed, bending to measure out the salt pork from his barrel.

I stifled an irritated sigh and glanced over my shoulder at *Cormorant*, uncomfortably aware of how vulnerable and shabby she looked. She was no match for the Black Dogs. But we couldn't just hide here forever. Somehow I had to get to Valonikos, or Pa would be stuck in the lockup and—gods forbid—I'd be stuck with Tarquin.

I stared into the murky reeds at the edge of the water. If there really was a god at the bottom, I could use his help right about now.

The pig man watched me with keen black eyes. I had the uncanny feeling he knew exactly what I was thinking.

"She a bigger, deeper god. The one who steers you." He spat over the side of the boat. "He don't be fighting her."

"I steer myself." The idea of the gods poking and prodding me about, like a piece on a game board, didn't sit well with me.

He flipped the bacon in his frying pan and cackled. "They all say that too."

I tried to look dignified as I climbed into the dinghy. "Good day, sir."

"Current carry you, Captain," he called after me, sounding just like any old river man again. It was as if our eerie conversation had never happened.

As I rowed back to *Cormorant*, I tried not to think about the pig man's unsettling words. I was an Oresteia. We belonged to the river. I didn't want another god messing around in my business.

Tarquin gave me a hand up from the dinghy. As I clambered onto the stern, I realized I'd been wrong about his hands. They were pale, all right, the hands of a man who had never worked long hours in the sun. But he had rough calluses across the tops of his palms, and he was strong.

Perhaps he wouldn't be completely useless after all.

As I raised the sail, I noticed him watching me. "What are you staring at?" I demanded, freezing with the halyard in my hand.

He flinched, peeling his gaze off my legs. "In Akhaia the women wear skirts."

"Well, bully for them." My cheeks and ears went suddenly warm.

"I wasn't saying it was a bad thing." He tapped his own knees in a way that made me think he was embarrassed.

"That's because you're staring at my legs." I bent to tie off the rope, resisting the urge to tug down the hem of my cutoff trousers, which had ridden up. He acted like he'd never seen a girl's kneecap before. It was nothing exciting. Nothing to *stare* at.

We got under way, water bubbling under *Cormorant*'s bow. I steered her down the dike and out to the river, the dinghy trailing behind us like a duckling paddling after its mother. Long after the smoke from the pig man's boat had disappeared astern, I sat chewing on my lip.

"Traveling by wherry is so slow," Tarquin complained from the seat opposite me. He rubbed his finger along the strip of wooden trim that edged the deck. I wished he wouldn't—flecks of paint were coming off. "I'm bored. Let me take a turn steering the boat."

He'd barely been traveling by wherry for half an hour. Too bad I'd thrown the box overboard, or I might've stuffed him back in.

"What direction is the wind coming from?" I asked.

"That way." He waved a hand, incorrectly, off the starboard bow.

"No, you can't steer the boat."

"What did I say wrong?"

"The wind is coming from dead aft." He stared at me blankly. "Aft is behind us," I said. A five-year-old child knew more than he did. "Why do you think the boom's so far out? The boom being that big piece of wood attached to the sail."

"Which one?" He must have seen the rude face I made, because he added, "I need to know these things, don't I? To blend in."

"The bottom one. The other is the gaff. The point is, a ship can't sail into the wind. The wind has to push the boat. Turn around."

The breeze ruffled his curls as he shaded his eyes to examine the sail.

"You see? That's where the wind is coming from."

Tarquin seemed to absorb this with a thoughtful look. To my relief, he didn't ask to sail again. Instead he turned to Fee, who sat with her knobbly frog legs dangling over the side, and studied her. "Is it true that frogmen can breathe underwater?" He directed the question at me.

I bit back my annoyance. "You know, you can ask her. She understands you just fine."

"Oh." He straightened, addressing Fee this time. "I apologize if I offended you, Miss . . . ?" He paused formally.

"Just Fee," she croaked, eyes scrunching up at the edges. Her long tongue snapped out to grab a fly.

Tarquin jumped back, startled, while I choked down a laugh.

The river was narrow here, with round hillocks of marsh grass crowding us on both sides. The only sounds were the wind whistling low and mournful through the weeds and the buzzing of insects. Downriver from us, the sails of other wherries floated like black triangles above the fields. The cutter was nowhere in sight.

Off the port side a fish jumped, sunlight flashing on silver scales. Wavelets lapped the shore, and somewhere a bee hummed.

*Small things.* I yearned to know what secret messages Pa heard in them. No matter how hard I listened, I could not decipher anything.

"What are you thinking about?" Tarquin asked.

"The pig man," I lied. "They say he's a god."

He sighed. "Ask yourself what's more likely. That an old man who sells meat off a houseboat is a god or that he's an old man who sells meat off a houseboat."

I wasn't convinced the pig man was a god either, but I certainly wasn't going to sit here and let Tarquin poke fun at him.

"Well, but he knew about—" I hesitated. "Look, it's just something people whisper, is all. The thing about gods is . . ."

He rolled his eyes. "Oh yes. A girl who lives on a wherry is going to tell me the thing about *gods*. I'm full of anticipation."

"The thing about gods is," I said, pointedly ignoring him, "they like to be a bit secretive about their business. And for your information, wherrymen are plenty acquainted with gods. There's one at the bottom of the river. Everyone knows that. All the captains in my family are favored by the river god."

Except for me. I squeezed the tiller, fervently hoping he wouldn't think to ask for particulars. I felt Fee's keen gaze on me, but she said nothing.

"Don't you think a *real* god has better things to do than skulk at the bottom of the river like a crocodile?" he persisted. "Or cook bacon, for that matter?"

"No wonder the consulate made you travel in a box," I snapped.

"You're not very good at diplomacy, are you? I doubt you'll have a long career as a courier. *If* you ever make it back."

He clenched his hands into fists. "Is that a threat?"

"It's an observation."

"Well, in Akhaia it's known that the gods who once walked among us have long since returned to their halls in the sky and under the earth." He put one boot on the cockpit seat, looking out at the flat land drifting by. "The only people who can speak to them now are the oracles."

"In words, maybe," I scoffed.

I'd seen the ostentatious temples in Akhaia, decorated with snarling lion heads made of solid gold. I suspected the Akhaian god was nothing like the river god.

"How else would you speak, other than in words?" Tarquin asked.

"The god at the bottom of the river speaks to us in the language of small things."

He gave a loud sniff to tell me what he thought of that.

The pig man had said my fate was far from here. I hoped he wasn't really a god, because that was just nonsense. I was Pa's first mate on *Cormorant*, and someday, after he retired, I would become her captain. Perhaps when the pig man had said "you," he'd meant Tarquin. *Your fate . . . and that boy's.* Those were his exact words.

Or maybe the pig man wasn't a god at all, but an eccentric old coot who sat on a houseboat and smoked pork.

And yet I couldn't stop thinking about what I'd been too unnerved to say to Tarquin.

*He knew about you.*

## CHAPTER
# EIGHT

As a wherryman's daughter I'm not supposed to admit this, but I think fishing is gods-blastedly dull. That was what I found myself doing the next morning. And I was not happy about it.

Like other unpleasant things to recently befall me, it was Tarquin's fault. By the time he dragged himself out of his bunk, Fee and I had been sailing for hours. He lounged on the bench cushions, the wreckage of his morning meal strewn about him. Sticky flatware lay in a lopsided stack on the tablecloth and a string of greasy drips trailed across the cabin floor. I didn't know one person was capable of making such a mess.

"I hope you don't think I'm going to clean up after you." I glanced at the sideboard. "Where's the rest of the pork? I left it right here."

"Oh. I . . . ate it for breakfast."

"All of it?" I stared in horror. "That was supposed to last for days."

"Nonsense," he said. "It was hardly enough for breakfast."

"It's not meant to be the whole meal. It's a treat. A luxury."

He snorted. "It was good, but not *that* good."

I stomped up to the deck. "Thanks to you, lunch is fish. Dinner is also fish. I hope you aren't stupid enough to ask what's for breakfast tomorrow." Opening the basket of fishing supplies, I fixed tackle to a line. "But as I suspect you might be, it's fish."

He followed me. "Look, I didn't know. Can't we stop and get more provisions?"

"Look around you," I said. "There's nothing for the next twenty miles."

Tall grasses stretched out on all sides. About half a mile ahead, a humpbacked ruin lay covered in green moss—an old manor house, perhaps, or the remains of a bridge. We'd spent last night hidden behind another such ruin, with *Cormorant*'s mast lowered and the curtains pulled tight to hide our lantern.

"There's not another pig boat or something?" he asked.

I cast the line over the stern. "And after you made fun of the pig man too. This is your fate catching up to you, is what it is."

Tarquin leaned out to survey the pile of rounded stones. "I wonder if that ruin dates back to the days when Kynthessa was still part of the Emparchy."

"I reckon so." I twitched the fishing pole. "This is where the patriots held the line, to keep the Emparch's army from sacking Siscema during the Thirty Years' War."

In those days, the Oresteias were blockade runners for the patriots. I tried to imagine these empty marshes crowded with Akhaian galleys and campfire smoke, the riverlands plunged into war.

"Patriots," Tarquin scoffed. "Traitors to a great empire, you mean."

"Ayah, Akhaia must be a wonderful empire," I said. "I guess that's why little bits of it keep cutting themselves off to become independent."

He pressed his lips in a flat line. "The Margrave was just as much at fault for that war as Akhaia."

"I heard the current Emparch exiled fifty men and women just for having political meetings," I shot back. "That was only last year, so you can't blame it on people who died long ago."

"Antidoros Peregrine and his revolutionaries had been a thorn in the Emparch's side for years." After a pause, he explained, "But it wasn't the meetings that caused the Emparch to finally lose his temper. It was that pamphlet he published—full of radical ideas about the rights of the common people."

"Have you read it?" I asked, irritated by his dismissiveness. *I* was one of the common people.

"Of course not." He waved a hand. "The Emparch didn't want it to cause an uprising, so he ordered it burned. But Lord Peregrine used to dine with us when I was a child," he mused. "Before he published his mad writings. I wonder what became of him."

I could have told him. Lord Peregrine was hiding out in Kynthessa. He and his friends were, in fact, the very same rebels whose muskets the harbor master had confiscated in Hespera's Watch. I certainly wasn't about to share that secret, since I suspected it would anger my passenger to hear we were running guns to people he considered traitors.

"Is your father a lord too?" I asked instead. "Or was he elected?"

"No one is *elected* in Akhaia," he said, as if it was a filthy word. "That would show weakness. He was appointed to the council by the Emparch, as is only fitting."

I guess he thought our Margravina weak then. Her title was inherited, passed down from the original Margrave who'd led the rebellion against Akhaia all those years ago, but she was really more of a figurehead these days. She presided over the senate, which was elected from among the people. The Free City of Valonikos had gone even further when it seceded from Akhaia, abandoning all hereditary titles. If Tarquin planned to continue talking like this after he got there, he'd offend everyone. I wondered if I should warn him.

"Ready?" Fee called to me. I jumped up, abandoning the fishing reel.

She put the tiller hard over and we jibed, the boom slamming across. I paid out the mainsheet as the sail filled with a snap. We began to heel over on the starboard side. *Cormorant* swept down the river, our wake bubbling behind us.

Tarquin gripped the edge of the cockpit, his knuckles white. "What's going on? I don't like that."

"A jibe," I said. "We switched the sail to the other side."

"Next time, please warn me," he said stiffly.

"Fee said 'ready.'" I knew he'd had no idea what she meant, but I was tired of his superior attitude.

I didn't see how a person wouldn't enjoy sailing on a fine day like this, when the clouds rode aloft like horsetails in the sapphire sky. Couldn't he feel how *Cormorant* moved, as if the wind challenged her to a race? I supposed he didn't appreciate good weather the same way as people who depend on it for their work.

We'd spotted no sign of Diric Melanos and the Black Dogs since the night they chased us. It was as if the cutter had vanished right into the air. As the day wore on, the only folk we passed were a pair of fishermen in a dory, bobbing among the reeds.

The sun dipped lower and trees sprang up on either side of the river. We glided through a tunnel of overhanging branches. I couldn't shake the mounting unease that prickled my neck. We were sailing blind now. If the Black Dogs were near, we wouldn't see them until we were practically on top of them.

Reaching over the stern to trail my hand in the cool water, I waited hopefully.

Nothing happened. The god in the river speaks to us in the language of small things. So the wherrymen say, but what did it mean exactly? I heard buzzing flies and splashing frogs and felt the gentle pull of the water on my skin. That was all.

Pa said the day my fate came for me, I would know. Annoyance stirred within me. He might have been a *bit* more specific.

Glancing up, I caught the flicker of motion behind the trees. A ghostly flash of white. Something tall.

A ship was sailing up the River Thrush.

"Come about!" I gasped, scrambling to my feet.

Fee pushed the tiller all the way to starboard, sending us into an uncontrolled jibe. *Cormorant* pitched, water sluicing down the deck, and the sail flopped back and forth.

Tarquin almost fell off the seat. "I told you to warn me!"

"Shut *up*." Frantically I scanned the riverbank for somewhere— anywhere—big enough to hide a wherry. "There!" I pointed to a stand of willow trees, their leaves dangling into the water like a lady's skirt.

As Fee steered *Cormorant* toward the trees, I ran to the mast. A wherry's mast can be lowered, through a system of winches, weights, and pulleys, to get through low bridges. But we had precious little time.

"Tarquin," I whispered. He didn't respond. "Tarquin!" I hissed louder, until his shoulders jumped. "I need your help." I gestured up at the peak. "Catch the mast when it comes down. *Quiet*."

To my intense relief, he instantly jumped up and did as I commanded. The mast came rattling down, weighted by the lead counterbalance at its base. Lacking experience, Tarquin let part of the sail sag into the water. I couldn't worry about that right now.

Without the sail, *Cormorant* lost speed, slicing through the water foot by foot, then inch by inch. Her bow disappeared, swallowed up by the trees. Branches trailed across her deck like long hair.

Her stern still hung out, visible to anyone on the river. Without thinking, I jumped overboard, my feet sinking into soft mud.

The water was little more than shoulder deep. Leaning hard on *Cormorant*'s hull, I shoved with all my weight.

Slowly, slowly she moved under the trees' veil, helped along by the last of her momentum. I glanced wildly down the river. *Cormorant* had a low profile and dark paint, but would the shadows be enough to hide us?

The approaching ship was still mostly concealed by the trees, but I could hear the creak-thump of her rigging and the swish of water streaming past her hull. Any moment she would round the bend. My chest tightened. I crouched in the water like a frog, with only the top of my head above the surface. The smell of mud and grass was thick in my nose.

The ship passed, her wake sloshing over me. My vantage point was too low to see much of her, other than a glimpse of blue paint.

Ten minutes slid agonizingly by before Fee's face appeared over the edge of the deck. Without a word she dropped the rope ladder.

"Was it—?" I felt for the bottom rung.

"Them."

I heaved myself up. Water streamed out of my clothes, pooling at my feet.

"This is intolerable." Tarquin sat in the cockpit, hands balled into fists. "They almost caught us." I realized he was shaking. "There *has* to be another way."

I felt suddenly weary. "This is the only way to Valonikos."

"You don't understand! You're not the one in danger!"

"Aren't I?" I pressed a hand to my bandaged gunshot wound. "I was shot because of you, but I guess that's slipped your mind." I noticed his eyes were cast down at the cockpit floor and demanded, "Why aren't you looking at me when I'm talking?"

"Because," he said stiffly, "your shirt is wet and I can see right through it. Though I suppose *manners* go unappreciated on this wooden bucket."

I slapped my arms over my chest and went down the ladder into the cabin.

"Wooden bucket," I muttered. How dare he accuse me of not having manners, when all he'd done all day was insult me? I jerked open the door of my locker, yanking out a towel.

And froze, my gaze drawn to the curtain separating Pa's cabin from mine. I glanced over my shoulder at the cockpit steps. Tarquin thought I was changing.

This might be my only chance.

Pulling open the drawers of Pa's desk, I rifled through the papers. Nothing—just old contracts and rolled-up charts. I lifted the straw mattress, feeling the slats under it. He hadn't hidden the letter there. I hoped I'd be able to hear Tarquin coming over the pounding in my ears. Whirling in a circle, I scanned the rest of the tiny cabin for anywhere he might have stashed the message.

But the letter wasn't hidden in Pa's bunk. Where could it be? Pa's clothes had no inside pockets to conceal something like that, and I knew every inch of *Cormorant*'s main cabin—it wasn't out there. Unless there *was* no letter.

Earlier when I'd said his name, Tarquin hadn't answered,

almost as if . . . An icy chill crept over me. Almost as if Tarquin wasn't his name at all.

A royal courier in an enchanted box. It sounded like a fairy tale because it was. A flicker of anger jumped to life inside me. I hated being tricked. Whoever Tarquin Meridios really was, he'd made me look like an idiot.

A creak on the steps alerted me. I flung the sheets back on the bed and softly slid the desk drawers shut. Heart thudding, I whipped my wet shirt off and whisked the towel around myself. I spun to glimpse Tarquin ducking his head to enter the cabin.

He bumped into me, and I almost dropped the towel.

"Why are you snooping around in my room?" He towered over me.

"It's not *your* room." I clutched the towel tight, acutely aware of my bare shoulders. Water dripped on the floor from my drenched trousers. "I was just—looking for a towel."

Tarquin skimmed his fingers across the bandage on my arm. "I—" He cleared his throat. I saw a flutter there. "I didn't mean to make light of your injury."

Something shot through me like a bolt of lightning. My cheeks burned.

He trailed his hand down the towel. I inhaled, immobilized by the shock of his touch. Then he leaned in, and I knew he was going to kiss me.

I slapped him across the face.

His hand flew to his reddened cheek as if he couldn't quite

believe what I'd done. That second of wondering hesitation was all I needed.

I yanked my knife from its sheath, spinning out of his reach. By the time he recovered enough to react, I was behind him. I grasped a handful of his shirt and twisted, holding him in place.

And pressed the tip of my blade into his back.

We stood frozen in a silent, tense stalemate. I felt the erratic up-and-down movement as he tried to get control of his breath. I hoped my knife hand wasn't shaking. The danger of my situation hit me all at once. He seemed sheltered and spoiled, but for all I knew it was an act. If he was lying about being a courier, he might be anyone.

"You realize I'm a lot stronger than you." His voice was steady. "And trained in hand-to-hand fighting. I can break your arm before you know what's happening. If I choose to."

"You realize this is a knife," I said right back, my heart racing at his threat. "I can gut you before you break my arm. If I choose to."

"You won't do it."

"I've skinned half a thousand fish," I said. "I'll skin you."

I couldn't imagine doing anything of the kind, but I'd never had a boy just up and try to kiss me like that, as if he was entitled to it.

"You're bluffing," he said.

Of course I was, but what about him? I studied him, my gaze lingering on his arms. Yesterday when he helped me out of the dinghy, I'd noticed his surprising strength. He might be telling the truth about having combat training. Whether he'd ever been in an actual fight . . . I was more skeptical about that.

Should I confront him? Accuse him of lying? Alone with him here in the cabin, I suddenly didn't feel safe. I almost resented him more for that than for lying to me. Cormorant was my home.

"Why did you do that?" I dug the point of the knife in.

"Ow! I thought you wanted to. You're the one who came into *my* room. With no shirt on. And then you looked at me like—I had the impression—Well, everyone knows girls from the riverlands—" He stopped.

"Everyone knows girls from the riverlands *what*?" I poked harder with the blade, hoping my voice sounded dangerous.

"Never mind," he muttered. "It wasn't gracious."

Damn right it wasn't gracious.

I was beginning to rethink my position. While it was true that I had him at a disadvantage, I was pressed up against his back. I could smell his scent and feel the damp warmth rising off the skin of his neck.

"I can't believe you thought I would—ugh!" I let him go, backing across the cabin.

"I'd heard the girls in the riverlands are more . . . experienced . . . than in Akhaia." He reached his fingers under his shirt, rubbing them together to confirm I hadn't cut him. "I guess not."

"I've kissed a boy before, if that's what you mean." As soon as the words were out of my mouth, I regretted them. I didn't have to explain myself to him.

"Then what are you so offended about?"

I held the towel to my chest. "Just because I've kissed someone else doesn't mean I'm interested in *you*!"

From the way he stared, I could tell this idea had not occurred to him. "Saying no is a perfectly acceptable option," he spit out. "One which falls rather short of pulling a blade on someone."

"I'm taking you to Valonikos because I don't have a choice," I said. "Not because I like you." He'd called me common, insulted *Cormorant*, and on top of that, now I was certain his story was a lie.

"I don't want you to take me to Valonikos at all!" His lip twitched furiously. "Haven't I been telling you that?"

I saw a guilty glint in his eye. "Why did you really try to kiss me?" I demanded.

"What?" He broke eye contact.

"You thought if you . . . you seduced me, I'd take you to Casteria, didn't you?" He said nothing. "*Didn't you?*"

"All right! I mean, that's not—" He exhaled. "The thought crossed my mind, yes. When girls think they're in love, they—"

"They what?" I brandished my knife.

"They are willing to do things they wouldn't usually do."

I shook my head in disbelief. He was disgusting.

"I—this—are the girls you know really that gullible?" I sputtered.

He eyed my damp trousers. "The girls I know are *girls*."

The words dropped between us, and even he seemed to realize they were too much. He stuck his hand in his rumpled hair.

I turned and stormed out of the cabin. Snatching a dry shirt from the locker, I flung it over my head and slammed the door.

Seeing the murderous look on my face, Fee scampered out of my way. In a fiery red haze, I paced back and forth among the fallen willow leaves that scattered the deck. I couldn't imagine how Tarquin could get it so wrong. As if I'd been thinking of *that*.

*The girls I know are girls.* It stung because he didn't know anything about me. When I visited my mother's family in Siscema, I put my hair up and wore dresses. I went to revels and bonfires, gossiping with my cousins. And last summer, I'd fooled around with a sailor boy. I wasn't naive enough to think it had been a great love affair or anything, but it had been fun. At least Akemé had made damn sure I wanted to kiss him first.

This couldn't be more different. I didn't trust Tarquin—and even if I did, he wasn't my type at all. He was a snob, far too concerned with his own honor. And he didn't know how to *do* anything. There was nothing attractive about a man who was almost helpless.

I was so deep in my thoughts, I heard *Victorianos* before I saw her. Her boom rattled as she came around the bend, and her ropes groaned and creaked. Men's voices echoed across the still water. Not daring to move, I watched in silence through the curtain of willow leaves.

So they were hunting up and down the river for us. My head felt giddy and strangely weightless. Diric Melanos might've been a blackguard, but he was a skilled captain. It had to be tricky, maneuvering a fast cutter like that through all these twists and turns. Long after the cutter passed, bound downriver, my heartbeat still fluttered.

"Blessings in small things," I whispered, wishing the river god would say something in return.

Dipping a bucket in the river, I rinsed the deck clean of debris. Willow leaves went splashing overboard in a satisfying waterfall. I stopped, focusing on the bucket in my hands.

I had an idea.

Refilling it, I strolled back to the cockpit. "Tarquin," I called, leaning down the hatch. "Come here. I've got something for you."

He approached cautiously. "I hope it's an apology," he said with a sniff.

I upended the bucket.

Cursing and spluttering, he splashed around in the puddle. Spitting wet hair out of his mouth, he glared up at me in silent rage. A slimy green weed dangled from his ear. His fine leather boots were soaked, and Pa's shirt was plastered to his shoulders.

Good. That ought to cool him off.

# CHAPTER
# NINE

"Why're we moving?" Tarquin barged up the cabin steps. "The Black Dogs are still out there!"

It is difficult to live on a small wherry with someone you're not speaking to. I wrapped my hand around the tiller, steering *Cormorant* into the middle of the river.

Over my shoulder I addressed Fee. "Tell our passenger we can't just hide forever. We're going to have to take a chance if we want to get to Valonikos."

Fee's eyes swiveled like globes. "Childish," she said.

I shrugged. She was right, but I didn't care. "I don't want to talk to him."

He scowled at me from the farthest corner of the cockpit. "I assure you the feeling is mutual."

He put his boots up on the cockpit bench. Flecks of dried mud fell off, dirtying the seat. He lifted his chin, daring me to make a comment.

I seethed in silence. He'd done it on purpose, because he knew it would annoy me. Tarquin hadn't taken well to having a bucket of water dumped on his head.

We'd waited a whole day, but the Black Dogs hadn't come back. I was itching to get under way. Every hour we lay low in those trees was another hour Pa would be stuck in the brig. The River Thrush was the only route to our destination.

We would simply have to risk it.

Consulting a chart, I concluded we should be just above Gallos Bridge. The late afternoon sun rode low in the sky. If nothing went amiss, I thought we could make it to the House of the Shipwright before dark.

The house was a wherrymen's tavern, set high above the water on rickety stilts. It squatted alone like a long-legged marsh bird, for there were no other buildings from here to Gallos. If the cutter had passed this way, someone there would know.

Soon the trees gave way to flat marshland and I tensed, scanning the horizon for white sails. I saw none. I relaxed, letting out a breath I hadn't realized I was holding. As we sailed on, a wooden structure appeared, no bigger than a dot. Three lights popped into existence one by one. Someone at the House of the Shipwright was lighting lanterns.

I glanced at Fee. "I'm going into the tavern to ask around." I couldn't bear a second agonizing day of not knowing where *Victorianos* was.

"I'm coming too," Tarquin—if that was even his real name—surprised me by saying.

I gritted my teeth. "You can't. The Black Dogs might be in there."

He rose to his feet, towering over me. "If I say I wish to go, I'm going. You wouldn't be trying to order me around if you knew—"

"Knew what?" I demanded, hoping to goad him into giving something away.

He wrestled down emotion until his face was smooth as the river at dawn. "Nothing." Unclenching his fists, he let his hands fall limp. "Just—my father is a very influential man."

Handing the tiller off to Fee, I descended into the cabin. Since many wherries employed a frogman, no one would spare a second glance for her. Tarquin was another matter. Everything from his manner to his coloring marked him as Akhaian—and not just Akhaian, but of wealth and breeding. I rummaged through *Cormorant*'s lockers. Scooping together a heap of old garments, I laid them on the bunk.

"I can't wear that." Tarquin flicked the flowered veil sitting atop the pile of clothes. "That's for an old woman."

"That's right." My lips twitched at the corners. "Because you're going to be dressed as an old woman."

"I won't."

"Oh yes, you will." I gestured at the clothes. "You can't go flaunting that stupid earring in there. That veil will cover your head much better than anything else we've got. If you don't like it, don't come." I smirked. "Or come as you are. The Black Dogs will recognize you right away."

"Oh, so you want me to be killed?"

I shrugged. "It would get you out of my hair."

He surveyed the frizzy curls trailing down my back. "I don't see how that could possibly improve things. I assure you, your hair is hopeless with or without me in it."

My mouth dropped open, but I bit back a sarcastic reply. Making him dress up like an old woman was revenge enough.

He grabbed up the dress, shawl, and veil, and ducked his head to enter the forward cabin. I shrugged on my oilskin coat, stuffing a knit cap over most of my hair. Its color and texture were uncommon enough to be memorable. That was the last thing I wanted.

Fee steered *Cormorant* into an empty berth. Judging from the boats, the crowd was mostly locals. Long, curved dories shared slips with smaller dinghies. At the end of the dock, a pair of frogmen, croaking back and forth to each other, unloaded a basket of wriggling eels. The only other wherry had a flag flapping at its masthead—a wine cask crowned with three stars, which I immediately recognized as the Bollard sigil. Throwing a wary glance at it, I hopped down to the dock.

"This isn't a very good disguise." Tarquin's voice came from the depths of the flowered veil. "How many old women more than six feet tall are we likely to see wandering around the riverlands?"

"I reckon just as many as eighteen-year-old boys with Akhaian looks."

He bristled and shot me a rude look. I had to admit he made an uncannily funny old woman, with his skirt swishing around his boots.

Making our way up the dock, we passed a pair of fishermen.

They smelled of sweat and the pungent river mud caked onto their thigh-length waders.

Tarquin wrinkled his nose. "Why must everything in Kynthessa be so filthy?"

I gave him a disdainful sideways glance. Doubtless he would find the cities in Kynthessa more to his liking. Most of the wealth was concentrated along the coast, where shipping companies controlled empires of trade. Bollard Company, for instance, had a whole fleet of brigs and barks and wherries. He couldn't possibly look down his nose at *them*.

On the other hand, I suspected Tarquin was better off with us. It was well known in these parts that, in addition to goods, the Bollards dealt in information. They could sniff out a secret a mile away.

Tarquin tugged at his shawl.

"Stop fidgeting," I hissed. We began to climb the stairs to the tavern. Fee padded behind us, trailing wet footprints.

"If we must do another caper," he said, "next time I want a better disguise."

"This is not a caper. My grandpa once impersonated a dock inspector and smuggled a whole shipment of whiskey into Iantiporos, right under the Margravina's nose. *That* was a caper."

"Hush." Fee gave both of us a stern look.

As we reached the top landing, I pulled open the screen door. The barroom was packed with fishermen and sailors, only a few of whom looked up to note our arrival. A barmaid, apron dashed with amber stains, made a circle of the room, lighting candles with a taper. Each table had an oiled checkered tablecloth, like the one in our cabin.

I let the door bang shut behind us.

Tugging my knit cap lower over my hair, I inspected the crowd. Pa never had trouble starting conversations with folk in bars, but he knew practically everyone in the riverlands. There was no one here I recognized. Perhaps I could ask the barmaid if the Black Dogs had been here.

A man pushed his way to the bar, jostling me. I pressed my hands over my pockets, because there's nothing a pickpocket loves more than a crowded tavern. Tarquin just stood there, which didn't surprise me, as he had no sense at all.

Someone grabbed me, encircling my upper arm with an iron grip.

I sucked in a sharp breath. Out of the corner of my eye, I glimpsed dark hair and a beard. He smelled of wood smoke and soap and something foreign.

"You best come with me," he said low in my ear.

"What if I don't?" My nerves were strung tight as a line with a fish on it.

The muzzle of a pistol dug into the small of my back. "Out." His beard tickled my cheek. "Onto the balcony. Quiet-like."

I did as he asked, hoping Tarquin wasn't about to choose this moment to say something stupid. Then I realized a second man had him by his shawl and was steering him outside too.

No one in the barroom seemed to notice our plight. Between my captor's coat and mine, the pistol was hidden from view. To everyone else, it must have looked like the four of us had simply met up and walked onto the balcony together.

As the door creaked shut behind us, I was relieved to see it had a screen. Surely the Black Dogs wouldn't murder us within view of everyone in the bar.

The bearded man bent his lips to Tarquin's ear. "Listen, son, I don't know what you're doing down here, especially dressed like that. But you need to be careful."

I jerked loose from his grip. Spinning around, I got my first good look at his face.

"Oh." All the fight went out of me.

His cloak was so dark red it almost looked black. Like Tarquin, in his ear he wore a jewel. His clothes were cut like a wherryman's but made of finely woven cloth, the garments of a rich man trying to hide who he is. But his dark hair and blue eyes betrayed him.

Antidoros Peregrine, the exiled Akhaian revolutionary.

"Ow! Call off your frogman!" Another man struggled through the door with Fee latched onto his arm.

"We're all right," I told her. She let the man go.

"I won't tell the Black Dogs who you are," Lord Peregrine said to Tarquin. "I didn't like your father, but the Theucinians are worse. I don't hold with murdering children."

Tarquin shoved his veil back. "I don't know what—"

"What I'm talking about. Of course you don't." He glanced at me. "It's Caro, isn't it? Forgive me for the guns. I had to make sure you would come quickly and quietly. We have no quarrel with the Oresteia family. I figure we owe you for keeping us supplied this last year."

His words reminded me. "Oh! I can't believe I forgot about the muskets." I rushed to explain. "They were confiscated by the harbor master in Hespera's Watch. It's a bit of a mess. I swear, Pa will make it up to you—"

He held up a hand. "No matter. You've more important things to worry about right now. Diric Melanos was in this very tavern yesterday."

Tarquin interrupted. "I know who you are. My father used to speak of you often."

Peregrine almost smiled. "I doubt it was flattering."

"It wasn't. But he respected you as an opponent. I remember you dined at our table once or twice when I was a boy. You're Antidoros Peregrine."

"You probably won't believe me, but I was sorry to hear of his death." Emotion flickered across his bearded face. "And Amaryah's."

I reached out without thinking to touch Tarquin's sleeve. He refused to meet my eyes, swallowing guiltily. He didn't look shocked to hear that his father was dead. In fact he seemed more offended than anything else. Perplexed by his reaction, I let my hand drop.

Lord Peregrine went on. "I heard everyone was killed in the coup. I suppose there's a grand tale behind how you came to be here in Kynthessa."

"There is," Tarquin said, and that was all.

Lord Peregrine gave him a respectful nod, acknowledging that he would not be hearing the story.

"But how did you recognize him?" I asked.

Lord Peregrine gestured down at Tarquin's too-short skirt. "The hood hides your face, but I wonder you didn't take more care about those boots." He raised his eyebrows. "Gold buttons? The mark of the mountain lion?"

Dismayed, I stared at the boots. He didn't mean *real* gold? I'd assumed the buttons were brass. I cursed myself for not throwing those boots overboard when I had the chance.

Lord Peregrine went on. "When I realized who you were, I knew I had to warn you. Melanos sprayed silver all about this tavern, telling loud tales about the wherry he was chasing." He raised his eyebrows. "Seems it gave him the slip, up near Hespera's Watch. But he left more than loose coin behind him. That man at the end of the bar—"

He gripped my arm before I could turn.

"Don't look," he hissed. "Just know this—he's dangerous. Every man on that crew is. In the skirmishes of '88, Captain Melanos made a name for himself as a privateer, that part's true enough. But then he went rogue. His crew's sunk fifty ships and killed hundreds of men. Mark my words, they don't sail for the Theucinians—they sail for themselves."

If he was a privateer, Captain Melanos must once have had a letter of marque. Just like I did. A funny unsettled feeling shivered through me.

"Who do you side with?" I asked. "The old Emparch or the Theucinians?"

"Neither," Lord Peregrine said. "The day of the absolute monarchy is past. We want Akhaia to be a republic, with a senate elected from among the people. But I don't celebrate this bloodshed. People I—" He bent his head. "People I knew are dead."

Tarquin's eyes flashed with anger. "How can you say that, when you were stirring up the people! You think there wouldn't have been blood in a revolution?" A muscle in his cheek twitched. "I don't understand how you can be a traitor to your own class."

"Son, my position as a lord provides me with power." Lord Peregrine set a hand on Tarquin's shoulder. "Power is a touchy thing. You can use it to crush those without it, or lift them up. It's a choice. I believe it's my responsibility to use the voice I've been given."

Tarquin shrugged his hand off.

"Just think on this," Lord Peregrine continued, unoffended. "The common people of Akhaia are like ants to Konto Theucinian, to be trampled under his boot heel. That doesn't have to be the way."

As Tarquin stared out at the darkening river, hands in pockets, I saw his throat bob. I couldn't say what he was thinking, because his face was painstakingly blank.

I turned to Lord Peregrine. "Where's *Victorianos* now?"

"Somewhere between here and the bridge, I expect. I heard they plan to go downriver tomorrow."

The House of the Shipwright was the last stopping place before Gallos. The drawbridge there was too low for the likes of *Victorianos* to pass through, and the men who worked the turnstile would have gone home for the night. Wherever they were, the Black Dogs were stuck there till morning.

"I must go," Lord Peregrine said. "Current carry you, Miss Oresteia, as they say here in the riverlands. Give my regards to Nick." He gave Tarquin a small bow. "Your Excellency."

I froze, unable to breathe.

Tarquin stiffened, his eyes flickering across to me. "She didn't know," he said in a strangled voice.

Lord Peregrine grimaced. "My apologies."

Throwing us a small salute, he shouldered through the door. I watched his dark cloak swirl around him as he slipped through the crowd and out a rear exit.

You didn't call a courier "Your Excellency." Even if he was the son of a nobleman. My mind spun, buzzing with suspicion . . . and a rising sense of dread.

The man at the end of the bar turned. He was a bald bruiser, with arms twice the size of my thighs. His leather gauntlets were scratched, and a blue tattoo curled across the stubbly skin of his head. A conspicuous lump under his jacket led me to believe he had a blade strapped to his back.

"I can explain—"Tarquin began.

I held up a hand. "Not here," I growled. "Go straight for the door. Keep your head down."

We almost made it out.

Muscles flexing, the bald man pushed off from the bar. As he jostled his way through the crowd, he slid one hand inside his coat.

Tarquin—I didn't know what else to call him—pushed up the sleeves of his dress. All pretense of his being an old woman had gone out the window. "If only I had a sword."

"Well, we haven't got a sword." The better for us, I suspected. His confidence probably far outweighed his actual ability with a blade.

Fee's lips curled back, showing small pointed teeth.

The tattooed man whistled a signal. A second and third man lunged out of the crowd, arrowing toward us. I didn't know if they were part of the Black Dogs' crew or simply bold river men lured by the promise of coin.

But Oresteias are bold too. I kicked over a table, halting them in their path. Empty mugs hit the floor with a clatter, and the candle landed on its side, where flames immediately began to lick up the checkered tablecloth.

"Fire!" someone yelled.

The tattooed man charged us. I picked up a chair and heaved it at him as hard as I could. It bounced off his head. Howling like an enraged bull, he stumbled into a table of fishermen and knocked their game pieces onto the floor.

The largest fisherman jumped to his feet, belly bulging under a wool sweater, and told him exactly what he thought. The tattooed man threw him aside, causing his friends to stagger up with shouts of protest. Meanwhile the flames had jumped to a second table. The barmaid shrieked.

Tarquin stepped between me and our pursuers, but I seized the collar of his dress, hauling him toward the door. We clattered down the stairs. Fee reached the bottom first, leaping them three at a time. Frog legs are an advantage when you're in a hurry.

"Fee, cast off!" I yelled.

She let loose the mooring ropes, and *Cormorant* drifted sideways out of the slip.

"Pierhead jump," I gasped, taking a flying leap. Dark blue water flashed under me.

I hit the deck running and went straight to the mast. Without the sail, we were helpless to steer. Out of the corner of my eye,

I saw Tarquin jump aboard. My breath heaving in my throat, I tugged down on the halyard. The black sail rose in jerky lengths until finally the blocks clanked together.

A gun went off. Splinters exploded from *Cormorant*'s wooden trim.

"The paint!" I shrieked.

Tarquin spun on the deck. "The paint? Really?"

But the paint was soon the least of my worries. The man with the tattoo leaped across the gap and landed on the deck. He leered, exposing two missing teeth. "Hello, love." He held a long, dirty knife.

I drew my own blade. It looked like a child's toy next to his.

A pair of oars lay stacked alongside the cabin wall. Tarquin grabbed one up, holding it like a spear. He shoved me roughly behind him. "Get back."

The tattooed man, narrowing his eyes, lunged toward him with the knife. Tarquin struck out with the blunt oar end, easily parrying the thrust. The man attacked again. Tarquin darted forward, moving so fast he was almost a blur. Wood slapped against flesh as he clubbed the man over the head. He howled, toppling overboard.

I realized my mouth hung open and promptly shut it. "You're *good*."

Tarquin grinned. Then he slipped on a wet piece of deck, and I felt less confident in him.

He recovered his feet. "I am the Emparch of Akhaia," he said, drawing himself up. "Did you think I wouldn't be good?"

# CHAPTER
# TEN

He tossed the oar down with a clatter. "You already knew. I may as well admit it."

I turned away and walked up the deck, trembling with anger. His betrayal lay like a hard stone on my chest. How could he not have told me something as big as this? It changed *everything*.

Tarquin followed me. "I said, I'm the Emparch of Akhaia."

"I heard you."

With Fee at the helm, *Cormorant* slipped downriver, picking up speed. A mist had begun to roll in, wet splotches of the first rain dotting the deck. Holding on to the forestay, I leaned out to scan the riverbank. Danger hung over us like the low, damp clouds. We had to find a place to hide.

"What *would* impress you?" Tearing off the flowered veil, Tarquin began to unbutton his dress. "I suppose it's impossible. I suppose it would require an encyclopedic knowledge of fish. Or ropes."

At least now I understood why the Black Dogs wanted to kill my passenger. I could not say I blamed them.

I whirled to face him. His shirt, sticky with sweat, clung to his shoulders. The discarded dress lay in a pile at his feet, and the red jewel shone in his left ear. *It marks me as a member of a great Akhaian house*, he'd said. Everything finally fit together—his formal manner of speech, his arrogance, and most importantly the Theucinians' desire to have him out of the way.

"Look, whatever-your-name-is—" I started.

A raindrop rolled down his forehead. "Markos. My name is Markos." He rubbed the bridge of his nose. "I'm—that is, I *was* the second son of the Emparch," he said, a strange note in his voice. "I was never meant to inherit the throne. But now . . ."

"Wait—the second son? Then why—" Horror trickled through me and I halted, immediately dreading his answer.

His voice trembled. "The man who slaughtered Loukas—my brother—was the captain of our guard. The Theucinians must have bribed him. Konto killed my father himself," he said in a rough whisper. "Slit his throat, in our private quarters. That's when I ran." He shot me a look, eyes gleaming. "I suppose you're going to call me a coward for that."

I should've said I was sorry for his loss. It was the polite thing to do, but my anger at him stopped up my throat, preventing the words from coming out.

"My father the Emparch was not a fool," he continued hoarsely.

"He knew the people were restless. He was preparing for a revolution. So he called his own personal shadowman, Cleandros, and instructed him to enchant five crates. Once the lid was closed, the person inside would fall into a deep sleep."

"Why are you telling me this?"

"Because. You should know."

I swallowed. He said that *now*. Now, when it meant nothing. After he'd lied and lied and lied some more.

"In case of an attack on the palace," he went on, "each crate was to be shipped in a different direction. But—" His voice cracked. "He never expected the attack to come from someone in our own family. The only ones who ever made it to the boxes were me and—" He hesitated. "And my mother. She was supposed to be sent to Iantiporos, to prevail on the Margravina for—for asylum."

"Amaryah," I said out loud, remembering. "That's who Lord Peregrine was talking about? Your mother?"

He sniffed. "He ought never to have spoken of her so familiarly."

"Why in the name of the gods didn't you tell him she's alive?" I demanded. "Don't you think that's a detail he might've wanted to hear?" Turning my back on the Emparch of Akhaia, I strode down the deck.

I heard his boots behind me. "I don't *trust* Antidoros Peregrine."

Fee blinked her yellow eyes as we stepped into the cockpit. She bowed almost to the floor. "Excellency."

"Stop that," I told her, climbing through the hatch. He didn't deserve that. He hadn't *earned* it.

Tarquin—or Markos or whoever he was—followed me into the dimly lit cabin, ducking his head to avoid the ceiling. "Well? I just told you I'm the Emparch of an entire gods-damned country. Aren't you going to say something?"

Raindrops formed a glistening mist on his black hair. I opened the locker and grabbed Pa's oilskin jacket. "Here," I said gruffly, throwing it at him.

He caught it. "You're taking this very calmly."

"No, I'm not." My voice was flat. "I'm furious. I knew you were lying about being a courier, but this"—I swallowed over the painful lump in my throat—"this is too big a secret to keep from me. Did you even think about *my* life?" I demanded. "Or Fee's? We deserved to know how much danger we were in. And it is a *lot* of danger."

A line appeared between his eyebrows. "You knew I was lying?"

"A real courier would be street smart. Accustomed to rough travel." I paused, hand on the locker door. "You acted . . . well, spoiled."

"That's what you really think of me?" he asked quietly.

I shrugged on my jacket. "'Why's everything so dirty?'" I mimicked. "'Why are there so many flies in the riverlands? I'm bo-ored.'"

"All right, you've made your point," he choked out, cheeks reddening. "Just . . . stop using that voice."

I slammed the locker. "I never asked to be involved in this! The man who gave me that box lied to me. And then *you* lied to me."

"My family has an estate in Casteria," he said. "When we get there, I can pay you. Gold, silver, whatever you like. In compensation for the extra danger."

I stared at him. "You really must be thick. We're not *going* to Casteria."

Markos straightened to his full height, his head bumping the ceiling. "Ow! Surely now that you know the truth about who I am, you can see it's important."

I only saw everything I cared about going up in flames. Taking him to Casteria would mean breaking my contract. Playing with my father's life. And for what? For Akhaia? It wasn't even my country. For *him*? He'd called my wherry a piece of junk, tried to kiss me without my leave, and to dig the knife even deeper, he'd deceived me.

"All I see is more secrets." I shook my head. "More lies."

We anchored in a swampy pond off the main river, lowering the mast to better conceal *Cormorant* from searching eyes. From the look of the sky, the weather was going to get worse before it got better. In the dark, Fee and I draped the waxed awning over the sail to protect it from the rain.

Markos hovered to one side of the mast.

"Me and Fee can do it by ourselves." I elbowed him out of the way. "Wouldn't want you to get your hands dirty, Your Lordship."

"That's actually not how you address an Emparch," he said.

I ignored him until he gave up and wandered off. Fee adjusted the awning, shooting me a disapproving glance.

"What?" I jerked the ties down harder than necessary. "I expected *you* at least to be on my side."

"No sides." She nodded at Markos's back. He stood alone, hands in pockets, watching the rain patter on the pond. "Sad," she said softly.

"If he wanted me to feel bad for him," I snapped, "he should've told me the truth."

Pulling up the hood of my oilskin coat, I made my way to the stern. Lord Peregrine had said the Black Dogs were somewhere between us and the bridge. *Victorianos* was scouring the riverlands for *Cormorant*, but we knew almost nothing about her. I didn't even know what Diric Melanos looked like or how big a crew he had. Perhaps in a dinghy identical to the hundreds of other dinghies in these parts, I could get close enough to find something out. At the very least, I'd know where they were moored.

Light rain fell around me, ringing the surface of the pond. A puddle was starting to gather in the keel of the dinghy. I untied the rope and clambered in, running out the oars.

The dinghy lurched, and I almost tumbled off the seat. Looking up, I saw the rope stretched taut.

Markos stood with a boot on the stern, eyebrows raised. In one hand he held a lantern and in the other, the rope. "Where do you think you're going?"

I gripped the oars. "Scouting ahead."

"Alone?" He wrapped the rope around his hand, preventing the boat from moving. "Have you any idea how dangerous—"

I glared at him. "I don't need your help, Your *Majesty*."

"Also wrong," he muttered. The hood of the oilskin jacket revealed only his profile, but his jaw was stubbornly set. "I am trying to be a gentleman. Will you please just let me?"

"What use do I have for a gentleman?" I tapped the knife at my waist. "I can take care of myself."

"Oh really?" He dropped into the boat, rocking it. "What are you going to do, start another bar fight?"

I clenched my hands around the oars. He was the very last person whose company I wanted, but I couldn't kick him out. He *was* stronger than me. That part hadn't been a lie.

"Douse that light," I ordered, raising my voice over the creak of the oarlocks. The dinghy glided out of the pond and into the river.

Without the lantern, my eyes adjusted to the dark. Clouds mottled the sky, and the water was flat as a sheet of glass but for the raindrops. I gave two short strokes with the starboard oar to point the bow toward Gallos.

Markos sat forward, drumming his fingers on the thwart. "The part I can't figure out," he said, "is what the Margravina's game is."

Sweat dampened my neck. "What do you mean?"

"Well, why send *you*?" He felt me stop rowing, and sighed. "Xanto's balls, will you keep going? It's not an insult. I only meant the Margravina might easily have ordered the commander to bring me to Valonikos himself. But clearly she had other priorities."

"I don't presume to know," I panted, "what the Margravina is thinking. Because obviously I've never met her." How he could think about politics, when any minute we might come upon the Black Dogs, was beyond me.

He shifted awkwardly on the seat.

"You've met her." I rolled my eyes. "Of course you have. What does she look like?"

Markos's lip twitched. "Like an old bat."

I snorted, and we shared a glance that was almost friendly. "What I don't understand," I said, "is how she knew you were in the box."

He shrugged. "Her spies, probably."

"She has spies in Akhaia?"

He waved a hand. "Everyone has spies. I think she's playing both ends against the middle," he said thoughtfully. "Likely she wants to see if Konto is more favorable to her as Emparch than my father was. So she can decide whose claim to support." He spat over the side of the boat. "We'll see how she likes dealing with him. I wish her no joy in it."

I rowed without speaking for several minutes, lulled by the rhythm of the oars. A cloud moved over the moon, making it more difficult to see the shoreline.

"So you've been running guns to rebels." Markos hesitated. "Didn't you ever stop to wonder what Peregrine was going to do with them?"

"He's a philosopher, not a fighter." I focused on the oars as his reproachful gaze burned into me. It didn't help. "Perhaps he just wants to defend himself."

"I don't really believe you're that naive," he said softly. "Words can be weapons too. You're supporting a dangerous revolutionary."

"It's not my place to care what he wants the muskets for. When we run a cargo, it's just a job," I lied. "Nothing more."

"You're sympathizers." He was sharper than I'd given him credit for. "That's why you and your father were smuggling the muskets." He sounded more wistful than angry. "You hate everything I stand for."

"Not *hate* exactly . . ." I paused, water dripping from the end of the oar blades. "Lord Peregrine was exiled from Akhaia for writing a book about the rights of people like me. Would it really be that strange if I did sympathize?"

It was too dark to read his expression. "If it had been Antidoros Peregrine who murdered my family, instead of Konto Theucinian, I wonder if you'd still be sitting here saying that."

An uneasy shock rippled through me. The truth was I'd never thought much about the consequences of those muskets. I still believed Markos was wrong about Lord Peregrine, but he was right about the guns—if people had come to harm because of them, I would be partially to blame.

We were coming up on Gallos Bridge. I put a finger over my lips to signal for quiet.

Looming over the dock was the cutter *Victorianos*, her bundled-up sails stark white against the dark sky. The rainy chill sank into my bones.

Gallos was barely a town, just a cluster of houses around the bridge. The dock was deserted, all the boats closed up with canvas awnings to keep the rainwater out. A lone lantern dangled under the eaves of the dock inspector's shack.

Silently, I rowed closer. None of this was *Victorianos*'s fault. Indeed she was a lovely thing, with sleek, graceful lines. As we passed under her bow, I could see she was clinker-built, like *Cormorant*, out of curved overlapping planks. Her bowsprit loomed over my head, much bigger than it looked from across the water. If three of me lay end to end, we might be the same length as that bowsprit.

A pool of lamplight spilled out of a porthole near her stern. It flickered, disappearing entirely, then burst back to life. Men, I realized, walking up and down in one of *Victorianos*'s cabins. What interested me was that the window was open, and through it I could hear voices rising and falling.

I turned to Markos. "I'd pay a silver talent to hear what they're saying."

We bobbed in the shadow of the dock. I half rose, peering over the other boats at the cutter's dark hulk.

Markos hauled me down. "If you think you're just going to waltz down the dock into their hands, I won't allow it."

"Not on the dock," I whispered. "Under it."

"Isn't that going to be disgusting?"

"Very."

"As in, leeches and muck and eels?"

"And spiders," I said.

He surprised me by removing his oilskin jacket. "Fine. Then I'm going with you." As he unlaced his boots, he grinned up at me. "Someone's got to keep you from doing something dangerous and stupid."

His smile went through me like a flash—I hadn't been expecting it. Had I unfairly judged him? Certainly growing up in the Emparch's court, he would've learned to conceal his feelings. Maybe the arrogance was a mask he hid behind.

I made the boat fast to a piling. Stripping off my shoes and sweater, I placed them in a heap on the seat, oilskins on top. Then I wrapped my arms around the piling and hoisted myself onto it. Behind me, the dinghy rocked.

My legs curled around the muck-coated post. It was, as Markos said, disgusting. There's nothing slimier than a wooden piling that's been in the water for twenty years. And I'd seen spiders the size of my hand under docks. Steeling myself, I dropped silently into the water.

Hand over hand, we felt our way along the dock with only our arms and heads above water. Rain pelted the boards above us, dripping through the cracks to land with a splat on my face. The smell of mud and fish was strong.

I wouldn't let myself *think* about thinking about dock spiders.

Presently we found ourselves even with *Victorianos*'s stern, where her great rudder rose up out of the water. From our vantage point under the dock, I could barely see the bottom of the porthole. Light played on the water as it lapped the pilings.

I tapped Markos on his bare shoulder, gesturing with my chin toward the cutter. We inched closer, treading water under the porthole, just beyond the slanting lamplight. I forced my breathing to slow. The hot pounding of physical exertion faded away, and in the new quiet, I found I could understand their voices.

"She ain't faster than *Victorianos*." I heard the clink of glasses. I bobbed closer, careful to stay in the shadow of the piling.

"'Course she ain't. One of you asses probably missed her when you were supposed to be on watch."

"I think you should tell Theucinian to go rot," drawled the other man. "Let's head back out to sea. These rivers are slow, and the flies are bloody murder. I vote we go back to Katabata."

*Katabata.* It sounded vaguely familiar, like I'd seen it on a chart somewhere. I filed the name away.

"Good thing I be captain," the first man said. "You don't tell an Emparch to rot."

With that, Captain Diric Melanos crossed in front of the window, and I saw the face of our enemy at last. In profile, at least, he did look a bit dashing. He wore a brocade waistcoat and a tricorn hat, and a scar marred his cheek under his right eye. A proper pirate ought to have a pointed beard or an earring, but he had neither. Lord Peregrine had called him a brash young man. Young to him, I guess. He looked about thirty.

"Even if I could do," the captain said, "there's still the matter of *that* one. I daren't go against him."

"Ayah, he gives me the willies, and no mistake."

"Hush."

The light shifted and changed again. The men's voices moved farther away, where I couldn't make them out. There was a creak and a soft thump. A door closing.

Someone else had entered the cabin.

The voices drifted back toward us. "—Meet up with Philemon. See if he's had any better luck."

I'd never heard of Philemon, but if they were on their way

to meet up with him, he wasn't on *Victorianos*. Did the Black Dogs have a second ship out looking for Markos? For our sake I hoped not.

"At least we managed to burn the one anyway," Captain Melanos said. "I reckon we should make for Casteria next."

"No." The third voice was high and oily. "We need the boy."

I heard a sharp gasp beside me. Light shone through the cracks in the dock, striping Markos's frozen face.

"Cleandros," he whispered.

# CHAPTER
# ELEVEN

I grabbed his arm underwater. "The shadowman?"

Markos jerked away, lips trembling with emotion or cold.

The Emparch's shadowman was a traitor. And he wasn't just some hazy threat, miles away in Akhaia. He was *here*. He knew Markos's face. My breath caught. We were in darker trouble than I'd ever imagined.

"Ayah, well, we been up and down this stretch twice," Captain Melanos was saying. "That wherry's disappeared."

"I told you. They've passed us." That was the oily voice Markos had named as the shadowman Cleandros.

"How, I ask you, when we've twice the speed? Reckon they're holed up somewhere. They'll know every bedamned dike and pond along these waters." I heard the clunk of a glass hitting the table. "Wherrymen know these things."

"We've wasted enough time. Tomorrow we go through the bridge," Cleandros said. "We'll look for them up the River Kars."

"We ought to burn these wherries, is what. Drag their wives out. Show 'em the cannons. Someone knows something."

"You were a fool at Hespera's Watch," the shadowman said. "Lighting that fire only angered every man on the river from here to Iantiporos. It was nothing but inefficient, needless waste. A gamble, and now you see what it got you. No one will tell us anything."

"I *know* that boy was there. Can't you fish for him with your magic again?"

"For the tenth time," the shadowman snapped, "it won't work. Wherever he is, he's no longer in the box, so I can't feel him. The magic itself is the only thing I can trace. Please cease your tiresome questions. We got the Emparchess. We'll find him."

Markos stiffened with a jolt, water swirling around him.

"What was that splash?" The shadowman's voice carried across the water. He must have been standing at the window.

"Frogs. Fish." Captain Melanos sounded unconcerned.

A beam of brighter light fell on the water between the cutter and the dock. Someone had lifted a lantern. I shrank back into the shadows, holding my breath. Fear made me grip the slippery post.

We needed to get out of there. This wasn't one of Pa's stories about the bold Oresteias of long ago. This danger was real. If they caught Markos, they would murder him. Not liking someone was one thing. It didn't mean I wanted him killed.

*At least we managed to burn the one.*

A horrible thought ricocheted through me. They didn't mean *alive*, did they? I saw a beautiful lady wrapped in a silk dress, twisting and turning against the flames, banging on the inside of the box with frantic fists—

I squeezed my eyes shut, trying to force the image from my mind. I hoped the Emparchess had been asleep when she died, like the unfortunate Singers.

Shaking Markos, I whispered, "Come on."

We swam back to the other end of the dock without speaking a word.

"My mother." He hauled himself into the dinghy. Water trickled down his legs, pooling in the bottom of the boat. His lips were pressed together so hard the color had gone out of them. "By the lion god . . . I knew my father and brother were dead," he said through chattering teeth. "But I thought—she can't inherit the throne," he choked. "She wasn't even a *threat* to them."

With shaking fingers I pulled on my clothes. I was glad of my thick-knit fisherman's sweater, for wool warms even when it's wet.

Markos sat with his clothes in a heap in his lap. Panicked, I seized both shoulders and shook him. "Markos. Pull yourself together."

The rain came down harder, falling through the beam of the lantern at the end of the dock. I shoved Pa's oilskin jacket at Markos. He managed to get his arms through the sleeves, moving like someone half-dead. I tugged the hood up, covering his face.

We were stupid to ever have come here.

I ran out the oars. On *Victorianos*, no one gave any sign that they had heard us. I stretched back and pulled as hard as I could. The dinghy leaped, almost lifting out of the water, as we shot away from the dock.

Once we reached the murky dark of the opposing riverbank, I didn't stop. I rowed so hard it sent up a swirling wake behind our stern. My heart pounded and my blood sang hot. The rain fell in torrents, trickling down the collar of my jacket and into my sleeves. The knit cap kept my ears warm, but my fingers were clammy and half-numb.

It had been foolish to get in the water, when we had no way of getting dry. It wasn't so bad for me, but Markos did not have the exercise to warm him. His lips looked blue as he shivered on the thwart across from me, but the rest of his face was in shadow.

He said nothing, not even when we reached *Cormorant*'s hiding place. Lurching to his feet, he attempted to feed the rope through its rusted ring on the stern. He missed. The dinghy bumped the hull of the wherry.

Fee appeared in the cockpit, eyes wide. She took the rope from Markos and tied it off so quickly her hands barely seemed to move. As he climbed over the stern, she touched his arm, concern shading her face. He shrugged her off. I watched him descend into the cabin, his hair plastered to the back of his neck.

"We saw *Victorianos*," I explained. The darkness nestled inside me seemed too big for words. I lowered my voice. "We heard them talking. It's bad. The Black Dogs killed his mother, and the Emparch's shadowman is in thick with those Theucinians."

There wasn't much more to say. Climbing forward, I stood

with my hand resting on *Cormorant*'s mast. Now that the danger was over, my whole body shook. I closed my eyes.

*God of my father. God of my ancestors. Carry the Emparchess on your current. Help us. Help us. Help us.*

When all was quiet except for the sprinkling rain, I strained outward with my whole being. The world became the space between my breaths. I listened so hard I thought the blood vessels in my ears might burst.

And heard—

Nothing. Rainwater dripped from the leaves, and a fish flipped over on the surface of the pond with a soft plop. Unseen creatures splashed along the bank. If this was the language of small things, it wasn't something I could understand.

Eight generations of Oresteias were favored by the river god, so why not me? Was it something I'd done? A tear squeezed out of my eye to spill hotly on my arm.

Back inside the cabin I changed into dry clothes, wrapping a blanket around my shoulders. Rain battered the windows. For the first time since my fingers closed around that blasted letter of marque, I felt truly hopeless.

The curtain dividing Pa's bunk from the rest of the cabin was pulled all the way across. Fee fixed a mug of tea with a dash of brandy and knocked on the beam next to the curtain. Tilting her head to one side, she chirped.

Markos didn't answer.

I propped my head up, watching the tea grow cold on the table. I uncorked the brandy bottle and took a chug. My throat burned, but the heat was only superficial. It did nothing to thaw the chill in my heart. Fee slipped up the steps to go sit in the rain, leaving me alone. Frogmen aren't bothered by being wet the way human people are.

The clock had ticked almost to midnight when the canvas curtain slammed across, rattling its rings. I jumped at the sound.

Markos slid into the bench across from me, a bundle tucked under his arm. Noting his red-rimmed eyes and clenched jaw, a wary fear crept through me. Something about him put me in mind of a rope stretched taut. Sooner or later, everything meets its snapping point.

"I just wanted to thank you for conveying me this far." He took a ragged breath. "I'm leaving. For Casteria. Tonight."

I snorted. "What are you going to do, wade there?" I rubbed my aching temples. "What's so important about Casteria?"

He was quiet for a moment. "*If* I were to tell you, would you consider taking me there?"

"No."

"What if someone's life depended on it?" He added, "Not mine."

I bristled at that. "What do you mean, 'Not mine'? Do you think I would let you die, just because I don't like you?"

"I don't think that," he said quickly.

"Yes, you do." I was determined not to let him see how his words had hurt me. "Or you wouldn't have felt you had to say it."

It was true I hadn't been very nice to him, but I was still responsible for him. He didn't know the riverlands, and he wasn't good at—well, anything. If he left *Cormorant*, he'd likely end up lost in the marshes. Or killed.

"What is this anyway?" I seized the bundle, dragging it across the table. He reached out to stop me, but I was too fast. I flicked the rope that bound it together, and the knot fell apart. "That's not even a real knot."

I unrolled the bundle, revealing two shirts, a loaf of bread, and Pa's flintlock pistol.

My mouth fell open. "How *dare* you steal from us?"

"I—I'll reimburse you, of course," he stammered. "For these things, and for—for the oilskin coat."

I stared incredulously at him. "You can't *take* the oilskin coat."

"It's raining."

My throat tightened. "You think I care about this—this stuff?" I swept the bundle onto the floor. "What about my *father*? How can you be so selfish—"

"*I'm* the one being selfish?" he roared, lunging to his feet. "They burned my mother alive!"

I was certain he could hear the rapid thump of my heartbeat. "Your parents are dead." My voice was suddenly thick. "My pa isn't. I made a promise. I'm taking you to Valonikos."

He loomed over me. "So that's it, then." Muscles stood out in his hands as he gripped the table. "You don't intend to let me leave."

An uneasy feeling skittered through me. Tension breathed in the air between us. I swallowed. "No."

We both dove for the gun at once.

He beat me to it, yanking it out of my reach. "I told you I need to get to Casteria," he panted as he scrambled to his feet. "Perhaps you'll take me seriously now."

I took a step back. Out of the corner of my eye, I caught a glimpse of green on the cabin stairs.

Markos reacted immediately, pointing the pistol at my head. His blue eyes were like ice. "Sorry, Fee. I don't want anyone to get hurt, but you'd better keep out of this." I inhaled, my breath a strangled gasp, as he stepped toward me. "Or I *will* have to shoot her."

Coming that close was a mistake. I kicked him between the legs. He grunted, grabbing himself with one hand. I seized the barrel of the pistol, jerking it away. He made an off-balance pass at the gun and missed, hitting me hard in the face.

Reeling back, I slammed into the sideboard.

Markos lunged after me, but I twisted to the side. The latches rattled as he hit the lockers. I sidestepped across the cabin, putting the table between us. Snarling, he advanced on me again, only to be brought up short by Fee's knife, its point hovering between his ribs.

She shot Markos a reproachful look. It was the same one she gave me when she was disappointed in me.

I wiped blood from my lip. "Nice try." My breath was coming hard.

His eyes widened in shock at the sight of the blood. I supposed he'd never hit a girl before. Too *ungentlemanly*.

He inhaled through his teeth. "A man of honor wouldn't do that," he muttered, adjusting his trousers. "It wasn't a fair move."

"Ayah?" I glanced at Fee. "Well, *I* try never to get into a fair fight." And I was not a man of honor. Not even close. I swung the flintlock open. "The gun's not loaded. And there's a safety lever, which means even if it were loaded, it can't be fired."

His chest heaved. "Is there *anything* I can say that will convince you to take me to Casteria?"

"Yes," I said, my throat knotting up. "Tell me the truth."

"Caroline, please." A strange ripple of surprise went through me. It was the first time he'd ever called me by my name, his accent rolling the *r* in a way that made it different from how everyone else said it. "What is it you want most in all the world?" he whispered, studying my face. "Is it coin? Your own ship? I'll give you anything."

I swallowed hard. "The. Truth."

Fee cocked her head, chirping encouragingly at him.

Markos's eyes met mine. He took a deep breath.

"I swear on the lion god, everything I am about to say is true. My name is Markos. I am the Emparch of Akhaia." His voice broke. "My eight-year-old sister is in Casteria, and I will do anything to get to her before the Black Dogs do. I will kill anyone who stands in my way." Tears shone in his eyes. "Even you."

I stared at him, my heart sinking. I saw *Cormorant*, dilapidated and rotting in a shipyard. I saw Pa struggling against chains as the Margravina's men hauled him away. I saw his beard growing longer, as he waited first days and then weeks. Waited for his daughter, who would never come for him.

I saw all these things, and still the choice wasn't hard. I slumped into the bench. Across the cabin, Fee lowered the knife. It wasn't even a choice.

"Oh gods, Markos." Propping my elbows on the table, I dropped my head into my hands. "You're such an idiot."

"What does that mean?" Markos asked. His damp hair clung to his head, emphasizing his hollow eyes.

I lifted my head. "It means we're going to Casteria."

He turned abruptly to face the wall. For several long seconds he didn't say anything, as his shoulders moved up and down.

"Thank you," he finally managed, drawing an unsteady breath. "You asked for the truth. There's only a little more to the story of what happened that night in the palace. With my father and brother dead on the floor, I ran to my mother's rooms. My sister was already there. We traveled through a secret passage to the wine cellar where the boxes were kept."

From the way he choked out the story, I knew it was difficult for him, but I couldn't help interrupting. "If Cleandros is a traitor, why didn't he just kill you all then?"

"Our family had several escape plans. The only explanation is he didn't know which one we would choose. Of course, he would have known the moment the crates were sealed and the magic activated." Tugging the jewel in his ear, he continued. "I helped my mother and sister into their boxes, one stamped for Iantiporos and the other for Casteria. My mother's maid was the one who stayed behind to have the servants load the boxes onto a cart bound for the docks. You know," he said after a pause, "it's only just now occurring to me to wonder what happened to her."

"Likely she was killed," I said sourly.

"You think I'm unfeeling." His voice was thick. "But I thought only of my sister. My—my only hope was that she wasn't important enough to the Theucinians, being the youngest child and a girl."

"Markos." Icy dread sliced through me. "Captain Melanos asked if they were going to Casteria next."

"That's why we need to leave now." He stared out the window into the dark. "I have to get there first."

Was it even possible? The Black Dogs, believing we'd somehow slipped past them, were going to hunt for Markos up the River Kars. If we made it to Siscema, we could offload our cargo at the lumberyard and pick up a good bit of speed. We might run down through Nemertes Water to the River Hanu, and then south to the Neck.

Maybe. If everything fell together perfectly.

When we blew out the lantern it was long past midnight, but I couldn't sleep. I heard Markos in the forward cabin, flinging his weight around on the mattress.

I sat upright, swinging my legs over the edge of the bunk. Moving the pillow to the opposite end, I flopped down with my head against the timber that divided my cabin from Pa's.

I rapped softly with my knuckle.

"I'm sorry about your mother. Did—did you love her very much?" I squirmed, the words sounding uncomfortable and false to my ears.

"Of course I didn't love her."

That sounded like the Markos I knew, both in the tone and general horribleness of the sentiment. Taken aback, I hesitated. "Well, if you want to talk . . ."

"I don't," he said in a strangled gulp.

"It's just you sound upset."

"I'm not upset, and I don't want to talk about it." His voice wavered. "Go away."

Some minutes later, he spoke again. "Once my mother did her duty to my father and gave him two sons, she went to our summer house in the mountains. She only visited a few weeks out of the year." The rhythm of his words was slow and measured, as if he recited the story of someone else's life. "My father didn't take an interest in me until my eighteenth birthday. It's ironic, really—I look just like him. You'd think that would matter to my father," he said, his voice still strangely devoid of emotion, "but it didn't. To him I was just the spare. The only purpose of a second son, you see, is to take the first son's place, if necessary. That isn't to say he neglected me," he hastened to add. "He hired the very best people . . ."

Hiring the best people didn't sound like love. It sounded kind of sad.

"I am perfectly aware you think I'm cold," he said. "But how do you mourn someone you didn't really know? I miss the *idea* of my mother and father, but I miss my old life more." He exhaled. "That's selfish, isn't it?"

"I think," I said carefully, "your parents were who they were. You can't feel guilty about that. It's not your fault."

"I don't think I ever knew what it was to love someone, until Daria was born."

I realized it was the first time he'd spoken his sister's name. His voice had softened, making him seem sympathetic, almost likable.

"My brother, Loukas, was many years older than me." He laughed bitterly. "Gods, I was *desperate* for him to pay attention to me. I was always—always running around after him. He mostly ignored me." He took a rasping breath. "Perhaps we were a cold family. But I couldn't be cold to Daria." He sniffed. "Why are you being nice to me? You've made it clear what you think of me. You don't have to pretend."

"Because," I said, "you were crying."

The cabin was so pitch dark I couldn't have seen my own hand in front of my face. It was easy to feel alone in that kind of dark.

"I was not." I heard a muffled thud. If I had to guess, he'd punched the pillow. "If I was, that would be stupid, wouldn't it? Crying because I *don't* feel anything for them."

"I said a prayer to the river god for her," I whispered. "For your mother."

After that, so much time went by that I began to think he was asleep. I was drifting off myself, eyes heavy and sandy. *Cormorant* gently rocked and creaked at anchor. Out on deck, I thought I heard Fee softly whistling a song.

"You say your god in the river talks to the wherrymen?"

"I'm not sure anymore," I whispered, so low he couldn't hear me. A hot tear escaped the corner of my eye, running down my temple and onto the pillow.

"I envy you," he said quietly. "I wish Akhaia's god talked to me."

I don't know whether he fell asleep then, but I did. My sleep was not restful. The pillow felt like a rock under my head, and I dropped in and out of fitful dreaming.

It began with one image that flashed over and over. My hand, skimming along the smooth rail of a ship. From the roll of the deck, I knew we were at sea. I smelled rope and tar and brine.

In a fine waistcoat and a shirt with billowing sleeves, I walked the deck. I wore a three-cornered hat and a matched set of gold pistols with engraved bone handles.

The ship was the cutter *Victorianos*. I hadn't recognized her at first with her square topsail unfurled, and three foresails bulging out above the bowsprit. She was running before a following sea, her bow slicing the water with a slip-splash, slip-splash. My heart sang with the waves.

Gulls circled and dove around the cutter. One landed, gray wings flapping, on the rail.

It swiveled its head and looked right at me.

And whispered my name.

# CHAPTER
# TWELVE

As we lowered *Cormorant*'s mast to go under Gallos Bridge, the old man on the toll boat watched us through his foggy cabin window. Wet clouds hovered low over the marsh, spitting out cold raindrops.

"Who's that?" Markos stared, his eyes hollowed from lack of sleep.

"That's the man who works the toll boat."

"What does he *do* there?"

I shrugged. "Collects the toll. If it's dark he makes sure the lamps are lit. If it's a big ship, he gets them to move the bridge."

"Is that what *Victorianos* had to do?"

"Yes. They attach a team of horses to the turnstile, and it spins the bridge so the ship can get through."

He looked up at the bridge with a new appreciation. "It's too bad our mast comes down. I should've liked to see how they do it."

The toll man came out of his cabin to stand at the rail. Smoke curling from the end of his pipe, he gave me a nod. "There was a cutter come through at morning tide as was looking for a wherry." He spoke in the rolling tones of an old man who has seen all manner of things come up and down the river and won't be bothered or hurried by any of them. "A wherry called *Cormorant*."

I tried to sound casual, despite my buzzing ears and racing heart. "They said *Cormorant*? The last I seen of *Cormorant* was up at Hespera's Watch." I stretched over the side, dropping a coin in the toll man's net. "Must be four days ago."

"Them brigands been a-roaming the river. They was searching the wherries at the docks. His eyes settled on Markos. "Asking questions about a boy. But I guess you missed all the ruckus."

Abruptly turning his face away, Markos picked up a rope end and began to coil it around a cleat. I winced. He was doing it all wrong.

The toll man blew out pipe smoke. "I told 'em, I says, 'I ain't seen any such boat.' But I don't think folk here will look kindly on them Black Dogs if they come back." He pulled his oilskin coat aside to reveal the pistol tucked in his belt. "We looks after our own in Gallos."

"Current carry you, sir," I called.

As we slipped under the bridge, Markos and I exchanged grave glances. The smell of wet moss and muck surrounded us, water droplets falling with little *plink*s from the stone overhead. Then light poured over us, and I blinked. *Cormorant* had cleared the bridge.

"Up mast!" I called out. "Up sail!"

When the wind filled the sail again, I snatched the halyard from Markos's hands. "Don't touch the ropes."

"I was only—"

"Making a mess." He'd wrapped it in big, sloppy circles around the cleat. I sighed. "Look, just don't—don't touch anything."

"Do you think he knew who we were?" Wiping his hands on Pa's trousers, he nodded at the bridge as it retreated astern.

I looked grimly at Fee. "I know he did."

"What?" His voice jumped up an octave. "Is that why he showed you the gun? As a threat?"

"That pistol wasn't for us. He was showing me he knew who we are, and he isn't going to tell."

"You're sure he knew?"

"I've been sailing up and down this river since I were the size of a minnow," I said. "He knows my face and he knows *Cormorant*, even without her name. And he also knows if Pa isn't with us, there must be trouble. You heard him." A lump swelled up in my throat. I looked back, but the toll boat was out of sight. "He said we look after our own."

It rained the rest of that day and into the night. I didn't mind—the gray weather echoed my mood. Markos made himself scarce, only coming out of the cabin to pick listlessly at his meals.

I spent most of my time brooding alone on deck. Drops pattered on the water, ringing its surface, and thick fog hung over the riverlands. With the hood of my oilskin jacket pulled down low, I watched Fee squat by the tiller, rain streaming down her slippery face. Occasionally she tilted her head, chirping at the river. Once again I wondered what she heard that I could not.

I curled my hands around my warm coffee mug and stared into the muddy water as if by doing so, it might reveal its secrets to me.

It didn't.

*The day your fate comes for you, you'll know*... But the more I watched and listened, the more my doubts solidified into certainty. Coldness settled in my heart.

The god at the bottom of the river speaks to wherrymen in the language of small things. And to the Oresteia family, always. Every one of them, going back to our blockade-running days.

Except me.

It hurt, like a gaping black hole had opened up in my stomach. There have always been some wherrymen who sail without the favor of the river god, but everything is harder for them. And I knew for a fact that other captains talked about them behind their backs. The river had always been my home. If I didn't belong here, where else would I ever fit in?

The next day dawned chilly and wet. Inside the cabin, Markos stared blankly out the porthole, eyes bruised and reddened. I didn't think he'd slept. Through the curtain I'd heard him rolling and sighing all night. Finally he had lit a lamp. I'd turned over to face the wall and tried to ignore it as he flipped the pages of a book until morning.

"It's cold." I tossed one of Pa's pullovers at him. "Here."

He obviously hadn't looked at himself in the glass, or he would have seen the white dusting of salt where tears had dried on his face. He had hardly spoken a word all day yesterday. I didn't mind, because I hadn't been much inclined to talk either. Something bigger hung over us than the storm clouds.

Markos fingered the sweater in his lap. A minute went by before he spoke. "It wasn't only because I wanted you to take me to Casteria."

I gulped a mouthful of coffee, burning my tongue. My eyes watered.

"You know. That night. I didn't just try to kiss you because I wanted you to change your mind about Casteria. I... misinterpreted the situation." He halted. "What I mean is, you were standing there in my cabin—" He cleared his throat. "That is, I really did want to—"

"I don't want to talk about it," I snapped.

He spoke loudly over me. "I'm trying to apologize."

"Oh." We fell into an awkward silence. He pulled the sweater over his head, mussing up his black hair. If it had been Pa and I sitting in the cabin on a rainy day with the stove going, I might have called it cozy, but with the two of us it was just tense and sad.

I broke the quiet. "How could you think that? I only just met you."

"Probably because I *wasn't* thinking." He mumbled something.

"What?"

Markos looked away, but not before I saw his cheekbones and the tips of his ears redden. "I said, 'And I thought you were pretty.'" He fiddled with his hands. "I... imagined some things that weren't there."

If he had said there was snow falling through the roof of the cabin, I wouldn't have been more shocked. *Pretty*. After he'd spent the last three days insinuating that nothing on this wherry was good enough for him, including me.

He went on. "I suppose you might wash more, but there is a certain . . . rural . . . charm about you. And you're very . . ."

I narrowed my eyes. "You should've stopped while you were ahead."

"I was going to say capable."

That wasn't at all what I'd expected. I stared at him. "Who ever tried to kiss a girl because she's *capable*?"

He shrugged, giving me a lopsided smile. "My world is full of useless people."

"Oh." I was certainly a great conversationalist this morning.

"I jumped to conclusions about who you were," he went on. "Conclusions that might not have been true and were likely hurtful to you. I *did* hope to manipulate you. I've been thinking about what Lord Peregrine said. A person who holds a position of power ought never to use it to take advantage of others." He swallowed. "I'm sorry."

I sensed he wasn't finished.

"I feel so backward here." He watched the rain pelt the cabin window. "The only thing I know how to be is an Emparch's son. I know everything I do seems wrong and stupid to you."

He had a strange look on his face, as if he hoped I would deny it but was already resigned to the fact that I would not.

I almost felt bad now for dumping the bucket of water on him.

But I remembered how he'd put his hands on me, and how angry and ashamed it had made me. And then how ashamed I'd felt for *being* ashamed, because he was the one in the wrong.

"I reckon we'll make Siscema by noon," I said, hoping to steer the conversation in a less embarrassing direction. I was sure he could hear the apprehensive patter of my heart. "You can stay in here if you want. I won't think less of you if you don't want to go outside in bad weather."

"Now there's a lie. Yes, you will."

I shrugged. "I was only trying to make you feel better."

"There's one more thing I wanted to say." He squared his shoulders. "Having resided on this boat for several days, I can see now that it's not a piece of junk. It's very good at . . . the things it does."

I glanced sharply at him. He was clever enough to figure out that complimenting *Cormorant* was a sure way of getting back into my good graces, but I saw no guile behind his tired eyes. I decided to accept his awkward speech for what it seemed to be—a peace offering.

"Thanks for that, at least." I paused for a moment. "Where do we go from here?"

He looked into his coffee, as if the solutions to the problems that haunted us were at the bottom of the mug. "I think that's up to you."

"On the lightship at the Neck," I said slowly, "they put out different colored lights to warn ships of the weather. One yellow lamp means the day is fair. A red lamp means conditions on the sea are bad."

"What are we?"

"Two yellow lamps," I said. "Sail with caution."

We made Siscema just after noon. The rain had stopped, but clouds hung low over the land, as well as the smoke from hundreds of chimneys. Siscema was bigger than Hespera's Watch or Gallos. Lying as it did at the place where the River Thrush and the River Kars joined, it was the most important port in the northern riverlands. The city was a cobblestoned maze of alleys and walled gardens. Its docks were a sprawling hodgepodge, with barrels and crates stacked everywhere. Wagons rolled in and out of the riverside warehouses, and the smell of tar and sawdust lingered.

I steered *Cormorant* into an empty slip at the lumberyard. Surrounded by the familiar port sounds of clanking cranes, screeching gulls, and creaking rigging, we waited for the dock inspector to unload our cargo. There was no sign of *Victorianos*.

I had other reasons to keep an eye out. I was known to too many people in the city of Siscema. People I would rather not be seen by.

Markos watched a group of sleek black birds duck and glide among the buoys.

"Cormorants," I said.

"They ride low in the water, like the boat."

I was pleased he'd noticed. "She does look a bit like a big black cormorant, don't she?"

Markos had lost some of the shadows under his eyes. He'd emerged on deck with his hair damp and face pink from fresh scrubbing, looking much more like his usual self.

Of course, his usual self was still annoying. But he seemed more relaxed as he sat with his legs dangling off the cabin roof, the collar of Pa's shirt stirring in the breeze. Perhaps he and I had come to a wary understanding, or his grief had simply broken him down.

"Will you stop looking over your shoulder? You're making me twitchy," he said.

"We might be waiting for hours. What if the Black Dogs show up?" I was reluctant to tell him the Black Dogs were only half of what was on my mind.

"We could just forget about the logs," Markos suggested.

"We'll go twice as fast without them." I chewed on my lower lip, biting off a tiny patch of skin. It was a bad habit, but I was so nervous I couldn't help it. "Why must the dock inspector be so cursed slow?" I gestured at the other wherries. "I wish we could just skip this line and get out of here."

"Of course! Caroline, I've just had a thought." He jumped down. "Your lip is bleeding."

"Yes, thank you. That's not very helpful." I sucked the offending lip into my mouth, tasting the metallic tang of blood.

"That wasn't it. The letter of marque! I only wish we'd thought of it an hour ago."

"You think that'll do any good?"

"Do you think a Margravina's ships wait?" He looked down his nose in scorn. "Because an Emparch's certainly don't. Where do you keep it?"

I drew it from the upper pocket of my oilskin coat. The ribbon was crushed and the parchment dog-eared, but it was still a letter of marque.

"You there!" There was an authoritative snap to Markos's voice as he called to the dock inspector. "We're on the Margravina's business."

Unbelievably, the dock inspector stopped what he was doing and came right over. Perhaps the trick was confidence. Markos assumed people would obey him at once, and so they did.

I supposed I was the exception.

The dock inspector had a grizzled beard and skin darker than my mother's. He wasn't anyone I knew. Siscema was a large port, with many wherries coming through every day—and seagoing ships too, up Nemertes Water from Iantiporos.

"I have the honor of being Tarquin Meridios. I am a courier with the Akhaian Consulate," Markos said, offering the squashed scroll to the dock inspector. "I have a letter of marque."

I watched the man's brown eyes skim the contents. "This is for the wherry *Cormorant*." He lowered the letter.

"This is the wherry *Cormorant*."

"Ain't what the paint says," he pointed out, eyes flicking up and down from the paper to the boat. "Says this be the *Octavia*."

"Our business requires the utmost secrecy. Captain Oresteia, will you please produce the ship's papers for this man?"

I ducked into the cabin to grab them from the waterproof box where Pa kept his important things. With unsteady nerves, I passed them to Markos, who in turn handed them to the dock inspector. He wasn't going to go for this. I just knew it.

"And here's the contract for the timber," I spoke up, suspecting Markos wouldn't know to ask for it. With a bored half-lidded glance at me, Markos extended a hand palm up. I placed the paper in it.

"As you can see," Markos said, "we are bound for the Free City of Valonikos with all swiftness on the Margravina's business. We must discharge this cargo immediately and make way."

The man tilted the paper into the sun. There was a design woven through the parchment that I hadn't noticed before.

"It bears her mark and seal," he admitted with a bewildered shake of his head. He was probably wondering why a courier would be aboard a cargo wherry, but was too awed by the letter to ask. He whistled to his men.

As they rolled back the hatch on the cargo hold and brought in the levers and crane, I asked Markos under my breath, "Who is Tarquin Meridios anyway?"

He grinned. "I made him up."

"I am not saying you have a future as a criminal and scalawag," I told him, "but that was mightily well done."

A lone seagull fluttered down from the sky, lighting on a dock post. It tilted its head to one side and squawked at me.

Looking up, I froze. A woman strolled down the dock in the company of a robed man who carried an account book. Two bodyguards shadowed them, men with studded leather armor and swords.

"Gods damn me." I jerked Pa's pistol out of its holster.

"Who's that?"

I seized Markos's sleeve. "Listen. The Bollards got their fingers in every pie. Goods, money, rumors. Everything. I can't let them find out who you are. Get down in the cabin and *hide*. Smuggling compartment on the starboard side. Go!"

"Bollards? Why—"

There was no time to explain. They hadn't seen us yet, but it was a matter of moments. I stuffed the letter of marque in my pocket and shoved him belowdecks. "Go."

The woman on the dock wore a gold doublet with puffed slashed sleeves. Above her shrewd brown-skinned face was a red silk turban dotted in a gold pattern. A fine engraved watch and a set of matched brass keys hung from a chatelaine at her waist. The etching on the device depicted a wine cask crowned with three stars.

Most people knew her as Tamaré Bollard, negotiator for the Bollard merchant family. Unfortunately, I knew her by a different name.

I lowered my pistol. "Hello, Ma."

# CHAPTER
# THIRTEEN

"Caro? Why've you painted out *Cormorant*'s name?" was the first thing she wanted to know. "Your pa in trouble for smuggling again?"

Pa always says the closer a lie is to the truth, the better, so I seized on the opportunity she'd handed me.

"Ayah," I said. "When is he not? He reckoned he'd lay low for a spell. It's just me and Fee. I'm bound for Valonikos to pick him up."

I realized she was staring at my hand, where I still clutched the pistol. I slid it casually into my belt. "There were a man hanging round before," I said by way of explanation, my neck prickling with chilly nerves. "I didn't like the looks of him."

"You come down from Hespera's Watch?" Ma leaned against a

dock post. "We've been hearing strange rumors. Of trouble in Akhaia and . . . other things. Don't know what to make of them."

I admired the row of earrings running all the way up her lobe. She also wore a sparkling stud in the left side of her nose. I didn't doubt they were real gold.

"No," I said, cool as a trout's belly. "I mean, we *were* in Hespera's Watch. But that was days ago. I heard pirates burned them out. The man at the toll boat at Gallos Bridge said so, but I thought he was pulling my leg."

Ma looked troubled. "I don't think he was."

"Is something the matter?" I was glad I'd hidden the letter of marque. There was no easy way of explaining that to my mother.

"Couldn't rightly say." She shook off her worries. "But of course you'll come up to the house for dinner."

"I . . . uh . . . I need to catch the tide up to Doukas," I lied. I wasn't going north toward Doukas but south, through Nemertes Water.

"Avoiding your ma, now, are you?"

I tried not to squirm like a bug being prodded with a stick. "It's my first run without Pa. I wanted to be fast."

"You can catch the morning tide and be there by noon, Caro. As you well know." She jumped down onto *Cormorant*'s deck, waving a hand to dismiss her attendants. "Now cast off and go to the third dock. We've a berth open. You shan't have to pay the docking fee."

Just like that, I was trapped.

As we guided the wherry to the Bollard dock, Ma crossed her legs, reclining on the cockpit seat. Fee glanced apprehensively across at me but said nothing. Myself, I tried to avoid looking at the cabin hatch. I hoped Markos had the good sense to heed my instructions and hide, but with Ma's eagle eye on me, I dared not check. After we finished stowing everything, I joined my mother on the dock, leaving Fee to stand watch.

Ma stuck tight by my side as we strode up the busy street. I knew there was no dodging her. She was sharper than a knife—and right now, just as dangerous.

The Bollards commanded a vast trading empire, that much was true. But like I'd told Markos, they had their fingers in many pies. Officially the family preferred to remain neutral when it came to politics, but I knew we traded in secrets as well as cargo. Markos's identity was a particularly priceless morsel of information.

"I don't like the idea of Nick letting you go off on your own," Ma said, ducking around a wagon full of barrels.

"Ma, I'm seventeen. Someday it'll be my wherry."

She pursed her lips to show what she thought of that. "Yes, well. Nothing's decided. You're still young. What was the trouble?"

I hesitated. "It don't seem like the kind of thing he would want you knowing about." That was the truth. Sort of. "No offense, of course," I added, realizing how fortunate it was that she didn't know Pa had been smuggling muskets to Lord Peregrine's rebels. She would've pitched a fit.

She snorted. "Of course."

But she seemed more annoyed at Pa than me, which suited my purposes just fine. "How is business?" I asked as a diversionary tactic.

It worked. "In fact, Bollard Company has come into a number of lucrative arrangements recently." Ma veered off into a long and dull explanation of shipping contracts.

The Bollards love to talk about themselves. They think they're the best thing since bread and jam. It was why they didn't understand Pa. They couldn't see why a man would want to work the river as an independent wherryman, when he might ally himself with a powerful merchant house instead.

The Bollards owned and managed many ships, both on the river and at sea, but they hired other people to sail them. They fancied themselves a cut above a mere wherryman.

Perhaps they were. It was a Bollard discovered the sea route to Ndanna and first circumnavigated that great continent. Becoming useful to the family was not a choice—it was expected. My mother wanted me in school, learning rhetoric or navigation or something. She thought I could do better than a shabby old wherry like *Cormorant*. It was a source of constant friction between us.

Obligingly, every summer since I could remember, Pa had packed a knapsack and dropped me off at the Siscema docks to spend a month with my mother. But she invariably found herself occupied with family business, so I just ended up getting into trouble with my cousins instead. There were two close to my age—Kenté and Jacaranda. That was part of why I'd wanted to avoid going up to Bollard House. I'd be sorely tempted to spill everything to my cousins, but I couldn't.

The stately Bollard town house was situated in a row of identical, connected four-story houses. Folks in town called it the Captain's House, for it had belonged to Jacari Bollard himself. It was larger on the inside than it appeared from the outside. It went on and on, ending in a garden and a mews and a cellar with its own loading dock. Over the front door was mounted the family crest: a wine cask with three stars in an arc above it.

In the entry hall, presiding over visitors with his stern brow and tall hat, was a painting of the great explorer Jacari Bollard. He peered down at me as I wiped my muddy boots on the mat, doubtless wondering how one of his descendants came to be captaining a lowly wherry. He looked exceedingly upright and noble—no smuggling for Captain Bollard, no sir.

Under the portrait sat a polished case full of curios. The original charter for Bollard Company was kept there under glass, along with a sextant and several maps in the classic style, with monsters and serpents scrawled around the edges.

An old warning of danger. Here be drakons.

Ma signaled to a servant to take my oilskin jacket. "Of course you'll want a hot bath. I'll send up a maid."

This was my fate laughing at me. The captain of a wherry doesn't expect to be whisked up to the bath like a naughty child, not after I'd been shot at by pirates and set a tavern on fire. I hoped Markos didn't take it into his head to do something stupid while I was gone.

After the maid left, I piled my hair on top of my head so it wouldn't get wet and sank into the steaming copper tub. As I sculpted handfuls of bubbles into lopsided towers, I could almost pretend everything was as it should be. I wondered if my infamous ancestors—the blockade-running Oresteias or the intrepid Captain Bollard—had ever paused in the middle of their adventures for a long bath. Likely not.

But my life was suddenly a cursed mess. I rested my head on the rim of the tub, trying not to think about Pa, or Markos, or the Black Dogs. I did not succeed.

The dress the servants carried in was made from stiff blue brocade with a starched panel in front. It was cut low and topped with a jacket in a lighter blue that belted at the waist, puffing out over my skirts. The jacket sleeves were gathered with ribbon bows and a spill of lace. I would've liked to find a place in that sea of fabric to stash my pistol, but the servants annoyingly refused to turn their backs for more than a few seconds. I was forced to leave it behind.

So it was that I found myself herded down to dinner. The Bollard dining room was a wood-paneled hall with many tables. My mother and the elder members of the family sat at the head table, raised on a platform. The room was full of wine, olives, and loud talk. Silk curtains wove in and out of the rafters, creating a billowing ceiling.

The paintings were all of ships, each with a brass nameplate at the base of the frame. There was the *Magistros*, our flagship of the last century, a three-masted bark. And the *Nikanor*, lost at sea off the Tea Islands long ago, and in the most ornate frame of all, *Astarta*, which had been Captain Jacari Bollard's own ship.

All that history staring down at me, and who was I? Just a wherryman in a heap of trouble.

Ma's eyes skimmed over my town dress, lingering on my hair, which was pulled neatly back. "Much better," she said.

Which was pretty rich of her, if you ask me, because she hadn't bothered to change into skirts. She was still in the same doublet and turban she had worn on the docks. Ma was a woman who had made many unconventional choices in her life. I'd never understood why she was forever insisting that I dress properly and act more ladylike.

My uncle Bolaji was seated beside her. He was the head officer of Bollard Company, a broad man with a reddish-brown complexion who wore his black beard in three twists.

"The Black Dogs are not a respectable crew. I don't like to bargain with such men," he grumbled. Then he saw me. "Hello, Caroline. I trust your father is well."

I stiffened at his words. "He—he is, thank you," I managed to stammer. Black Dogs, at Bollard House?

"And yet they say a wise man gets more use from his enemies than a fool from his friends." Ma raised her eyebrows at Uncle Bolaji, downing the last of her wine.

He sighed. "You were correct not to turn them away. It is also said that a sailor must know the direction of the wind before he can set his sails." They exchanged significant glances. "If the rumors we've heard are true, the wind has changed. Find out what you can."

Ma stood. "I'm sure you'll want to sit with your cousins, Caro. I have business."

As a little girl, I had always resented those words. Tonight, as I watched Ma leave the dining room, they stirred a powerful curiosity. What business did she have with the Black Dogs? Was *Victorianos* even now sitting in the harbor? Captain Melanos's men might be searching the docks.

I headed to the lower tables, weaving a path through the laden servants. Spotting my cousins Kenté and Jacaranda, I stopped and broke into a grin.

Heads together, they leaned over a tray of bread, hummus, and dates. Jacky was a year older than me and Kenté a year younger. I had spent many weeks with them at Bollard House over the summers. Jacky was my mother's cousin's daughter. In truth I wasn't sure how Kenté and I were related, but all the Bollards called one another "cousin." As children we'd climbed on shipping crates in the family warehouses and spent hours balancing on the dock posts, making up stories about the ships that puffed slowly up and down the river. Though my feelings about being a Bollard were complicated, I loved my cousins.

"Current carry you," Kenté said as I joined them, the gold stud in her nose twinkling in the candlelight. "I thought you weren't coming till summer!"

She wore her hair parted into four sections and twisted up in braids. Her dress was green and gold striped, and very handsome indeed. It showed off even more chest than mine, which was saying something, but this was Siscema. They did things differently in town.

"Current carry you." It felt like days since I last smiled, but with my cousins it was impossible not to. The ominous sense of danger that had been constantly humming around me lifted a little.

"I don't see your father," Jacky said.

"It's just me and Fee." I dropped into a chair. "I'm making my first run up to Valonikos as captain." I decided to leave it at that, lest they guess I was hiding something.

"Are you? Well done, Caro!" Kenté poured a glass of wine nearly to the top, shoving it across the table.

"Ooh, wait till Akemé finds out he missed you." Jacky poked me in the shoulder. A sly smile stole across her face, which was a lighter shade that came of there being Akhaian blood in her branch of the family.

I took a date, hoping they wouldn't notice me blushing. "He's not here?"

Akemé was the sailor boy I'd slept with last summer, in what was my first and so far only experience of that kind. My cousins knew all—well, most—of the details of the encounter, and were determined to never let me forget it.

"Apprenticing in Iantiporos. With his father." She batted her eyelashes at me. "I'll tell him you sent him a kiss."

"Jacaranda Bollard, you wouldn't!" Kenté squealed, sloshing wine over the rim of her glass.

"Oh yes, she would," I said. "Listen, you girls know anything about these Black Dogs?"

Kenté always knew the good gossip. As I expected, she seized on my question, her eyes narrowing. "I know they came into town an hour ago on that sloop *Alektor*. Down the river, from Doukas. Your ma's put the captain to wait in the Blue Room."

An hour. While I was luxuriating in the feel of hot water on my skin. How could I be so stupid? And how many ships did the Black Dogs have out looking for us? I'd never heard of a sloop called *Alektor*. I needed to get back to the docks and warn Fee and Markos.

"I heard Diric Melanos is the handsomest outlaw on the high seas," Jacky said.

I almost snorted. How legend exaggerates. "He's not here, is he?"

"No, more's the pity."

"What do they want?" I asked Kenté, my heart thumping

erratically. I ripped off a chunk of bread and swiped it across the plate, scooping up hummus and oil.

"To negotiate." She shrugged.

Ma was the chief negotiator for Bollard Company. That didn't tell me much. "D'you know what about?" I asked with my mouth full, trying to sound as if it didn't matter a bit to me.

"They're looking for someone on a wherry."

"Oh, ayah? Do the Bollards be stooping to bounty hunting now?" I demanded, with more snap than I'd meant.

"It's something to do with a stolen cargo."

My fingernails dug into the table. The filthy liars.

"How do you always know everything?" Jacky asked her.

For a flash of an instant Kenté's face took on an odd glow. "Such is my fortune," she said, candlelight playing on her brown skin and amber eyes. "The shadows favor me." She laughed, and I realized she was only joking.

I leaned closer. "What do you hear of a cutter called *Victoria-nos*, out of Iantiporos?"

"Nothing at all. Why?"

I chewed in silence. The Blue Room was the Bollards' second-best sitting room. I needed to somehow scheme my way in and find out what was going on.

"They say Captain Melanos captured a hundred ships, you know," Kenté said. "During the skirmishes of '88, when he was a privateer for Akhaia."

Jacky laughed. "They also say the *Nikanor* was sunk by a great sea drakon, don't they?" She nodded at the painting on the wall. "But that's just a fish story."

Kenté looked sharply at her. "How do you know?"

"Because there's no such thing as drakons, of course."

A shiver went unbidden down my neck. Everyone who's ever read a story knows there is no better way to ensure that you are swallowed up by a drakon in the last chapter than to say there's no such thing as drakons.

I knew Kenté was thinking the same thing, but she didn't say it. Instead she dropped her voice low. "I know a story that has a drakon in it. It begins like this: Long ago, time out of mind, there was a girl who loved secrets. Fortunately for her, she lived in a great old house that had many of them. Late at night she used to creep like a ghost down the servants' passage. It so happened that in this particular passage, there was a particular knothole next to a chimney. When she put her eyes and ears to that knothole, she could see and hear all that went on in the parlor beyond. It came to pass that one night—"

Jacky rolled her eyes. "I don't believe there's any drakon in this story. You're just making it up as you go."

Kenté stuck out her tongue, but her eyes crinkled as they met mine. A thrill ran through me, for I understood it wasn't a story at all. Her words were for me.

I shoved my chair back. "I'm going to the washroom, girls."

Kenté tapped the side of her nose with her finger.

There are many secrets in Bollard House. Lucky for me, Kenté knew most of them. She was right about the servants' passage. I opened the door a crack and slipped through. The narrow hall had whitewashed walls and low-hanging rafters, a poor reflection of its fancier companion running parallel along the front of the house.

Stacked crates and barrels lined the hall, all stamped with the Bollard cask and stars. This end of the passage was deserted, for most of the servants were occupied with dinner.

And in that way I was able to put my eye to the knothole by the chimney and spy on my mother's meeting with the Black Dogs' man.

Likely this was the very same Philemon that Captain Melanos had mentioned. He didn't look like much to me. His beard was straggly and unkempt, and he kept pausing to wipe the sweat from his forehead with a striped handkerchief.

"We heard about a massacre at Hespera's Watch." Ma pushed a glass of wine across the table.

The man smirked. "Only two people were killed, so it can hardly be called a massacre." I itched to punch his ugly face. The Singers were real people—good people—and he thought the whole thing was a joke.

My mother waited with folded hands. "I heard the Black Dogs were responsible."

"Diric Melanos took a contract from the Theucinian family to seek out and recapture a certain crate of stolen goods. By any means necessary, love." He took a gulp of wine and grunted. "It's good."

A look of disdain, promptly hidden, floated across my mother's face. She was probably thinking this man a waste of a fine vintage. The Bollards were particular about wine.

"Why don't you tell me what you're seeking?" Ma poured herself a glass.

"Our quarry is a wherry. Called *Cormorant*."

I rocked back on my heels.

Ma didn't react. Didn't even blink. I shook my head in awe. I was seeing why she was the Bollards' best negotiator. So the man on the toll boat was right. The Black Dogs did know *Cormorant*'s name—not just *Victorianos*, but this other ship, this *Alektor*. And now Ma, too, knew they were looking for us.

"There are thirty wherries tied up at the docks," Ma said. "Do you plan to set fire to them as well? Because I can tell you that if you do, you will never have the help of the Bollards." She sat back in her chair. To someone who wasn't paying attention, she might have seemed relaxed, but she was like a cat debating the right moment to pounce. "Philemon, is it? Do you mind if we talk plainly?"

"I love plain talk," he said with a leer. I almost felt sorry for him.

"Some of those wherries you put to the torch at Hespera's Watch were Bollard ships."

"Now, t'weren't me done that. It were Melanos. He's young and he overdoes things."

"Nevertheless." Ma leaned closer. The man Philemon grinned, thinking she flirted, but I knew she was moving in for the kill.

"If we assist you in locating this wherry, this *Cormorant*," she said, "naturally any fees we are paid would be in addition to the restitution the Black Dogs will already be paying Bollard Company for the destruction of its property. I believe it was four ships sunk, which brings the amount you owe to a quarter million." She smiled, running her finger along the curved handle of the decanter. "Pending a ruling by the assessor, of course. And so, how much in addition to that sum were you looking to pay us for our assistance?" She tilted the carafe in his direction. "More wine?"

Philemon blinked.

I crept away from the knothole, my head buzzing with thoughts. So some of the sunken wherries were Bollard owned. Well, if anyone could get money off the Black Dogs, it would be Ma. She could squeeze coin out of a rock.

I suspected she was just stalling Philemon. She had no intention of helping him with his search—not when she knew *Cormorant* was right here. As soon as Ma got out of this meeting, I was in for a very firm interrogation.

Carefully I closed the door to the servants' passage, listening for the soft click of the latch. I dared not stay another minute in Bollard House. I couldn't outlast a questioning by my mother. She'd find out everything. I had to sneak upstairs, change back into my clothes, and escape at once.

I almost made it to the staircase before my uncle's voice in the entry halted me. I dove around the corner, flattening myself against the wall.

Another visitor had come late to Bollard House. One I knew all too well.

## CHAPTER
# FOURTEEN

Markos wore a coat I'd never seen before. Dark blue with gold trim, it cut away at the waist and fell in a set of long tails to his knees. A row of shiny buckles marched down his chest.

"Current carry you on this fine evening, sir." He snapped his feet together and bowed.

With a small wave to dismiss the butler, Uncle Bolaji backed into the hall to allow Markos entry. "Yes, yes. I bid you welcome to Bollard House."

"My name is Tarquin Meridios." He stepped in from the misty drizzle, drawing himself up to his full height and removing Pa's oilskin hat. His hair rippled back in crisp waves from his forehead. "I have the honor of being a courier for the Akhaian Consulate. I heard this was the house to come to. For you see, I have need of a ship posthaste."

"Indeed I may be able to find passage for you on one of our ships," my uncle said. "But why did you not come to our offices? We have premises in Broad Street, much closer to the docks."

"Alas, due to my circumstances I have come late to Siscema. For that I make apology, as well as for my disarray."

Markos gestured to his clothes. I sniffed at the suggestion that there was anything wrong with the way he was dressed. He still wore Pa's shirt and trousers, but that jacket was finer than anything we had aboard *Cormorant*. I saw Uncle Bolaji glance at it, clearly marking the quality.

"I was to bring a set of documents to my colleagues in the city of Valonikos," Markos said. "By a series of misadventures, including but not limited to the theft of a fine horse by a band of brigands, I was forced to barter passage on a local wherry. But now I have need of greater speed."

His lip twitched when he got to the part about the brigands. He was enjoying this. He would've been having a lot less fun if he knew one of the Black Dogs was sitting on the other side of the door, not twenty feet away.

"Your coming at this hour is unfortunate, for our representative is currently meeting with another client. In fact, I was just about to join them." Uncle Bolaji scratched his head. "Perhaps you wouldn't mind waiting in the hall until we're through with the other business?"

"That would be more than adequate," Markos said. "You have my thanks."

I marveled at how adeptly he'd slipped back into formal speech.

When we first met, I'd thought he was hopelessly stiff. But now I realized his manners were like a costume that he could put on or take off—an ability that certainly had its advantages.

"Unless . . ." My uncle paused. "Would you like to join the family at dinner?"

I couldn't let him stay here, where Philemon might spot him. I edged out from around the corner.

"That won't be necessary. I've already—" Markos glanced up and saw me. I shook my head vigorously, and his voice trailed off into an awkward cough. "That is . . ."

I swept in, skirts swishing around my legs. "I will take him into the dining room, Uncle, if you want to go in there with Ma."

I seized Markos's arm. He immediately lifted it, as town men do when they escort a lady. I set my other hand on his jacket sleeve and tried my best to simper up at him. I don't think I succeeded, because he swallowed down a laugh and stared hard at the floorboards.

"Caro." My uncle raised his eyebrows. "I thought you were at dinner."

"I had to fetch something," I lied. "Anyhow I reckon he'd like to sit with folk his own age. Wouldn't you?"

Markos looked back and forth between the two of us.

"Only till I get back." Uncle Bolaji glanced at the door to the Blue Room. "For I would like to press him for news of Akhaia. If you don't mind, young man. We've heard only rumors."

"I can tell you what I know," Markos said, "although it won't be much, I'm afraid. I've not been back to Akhaia for weeks. But I too have heard grave news."

"Well, then. You must join me at my table upon my return. For now I shall entrust you to the girls and be on my way." He smiled. "I'm sure no young fellow would mind that, eh?" He disappeared into the Blue Room, leaving us alone in the hall.

I dragged Markos through the nearest door. As it turned out, it was a coat closet. The room smelled of cedar and camphor and was barely big enough for the two of us to stand in, squashed as we were between rows of overcoats.

"What are you doing here?" I demanded.

"Ow! Let go of my sleeve." He jerked his arm away. "I thought you were in trouble when you didn't come back. When were you going to tell me?"

"About what?"

"You know what." When I didn't say anything, he prodded me. "This house? Your mother? You were so angry at me for keeping my identity from you, yet you never mentioned a word about any of this. I had to hear it from Fee."

I spoke through clenched teeth. "My identity isn't going to get us killed."

"Your identity could save us. These people have ships—"

"Markos, you can't be here," I cut in. "You shouldn't have left the boat."

"Fee's there. It'll be safe."

"I meant *you* won't be safe. The Black Dogs are here! Their captain is in this house as we speak. Down the hall, in the sitting room."

"What do you mean, Black Dogs? That cutter's nowhere to be seen."

"Philemon," I said, watching his eyes widen with recognition. "There's another ship. A sloop."

"What's a sloop?" he asked. I bit my tongue so as not to say something rude. He continued in a whisper, "Might it be a black boat with two sails, a regular one and a front one? There's one like that across from us. *Alektor*. It came into port after dark."

"Ayah? Well, look who knows everything. Did you know it belonged to the Black Dogs?"

"You're sure?"

"Absolutely sure," I said. "It's like the toll boat man said. They did see *Cormorant*'s name that night, but they can't tell one wherry from the next. That's why they've asked for the Bollards' help. Listen. We've got to get out of town now. Ma knows. She knows it's *Cormorant* they're looking for."

A crease appeared between his eyes. "She didn't tell them you were here?"

"No."

"So we're safe, at least for now."

"I'm not sure," I said. "Ma won't let them hurt me. But I don't know what she'll do if she finds out who you really are. She won't allow us to leave this house, that's for certain. Not until they figure out what to do with you."

"Xanto's balls," he swore. "Who are these people?"

"The Bollards are a great merchant house," I said defensively. "We didn't get to be a great merchant house by angering the Emparchs of powerful countries."

"I'll be burned before I hear you call that impostor an Emparch!" His voice went up two or three notches.

"Will you shut up?" I hissed.

He pinched the bridge of his nose, leaning on the coat rack. "What are we going to do?"

I opened the door a crack so I could peer through. "You'll have to sneak back out."

"By the lion god," he said, "I wish I'd known all this before I came up here."

"Ma took me by surprise," I admitted. "I couldn't get away. I was just about to give them the slip."

"You were going to give them the slip, were you?" His eyes gave me a quick up and down. "Not before you took a bath, changed into a nice dress, and ate a perfectly luxurious dinner. At least I expect it must be luxurious, in this house. While I was smashed into a smuggling cupboard, naturally."

I felt slightly guilty about that. "Did you get something to eat?"

"I was reduced to eating common street food."

I rolled my eyes, my sympathy evaporating. I liked street food.

"Where's your hair?" He stared at me by the shaft of light that fell through the crack in the door.

My hair was stuffed into a black lace net, secured with a velvet ribbon. I thought it was very smart, but Markos was looking at me like I'd grown a second head.

"I put it up. Never mind that." I plucked at the stiff fabric of his jacket. "Wherever did you get this?"

"I purchased it in a shop," he said, disdain curling around the word, "but it fits well enough in spite of its low origins."

I wondered where someone would buy clothes if not in a shop. Steeling myself, I asked, "How much did you spend?"

The sum he named, though less than I'd feared, was much more than Pa would've allowed me to spend on a single article of clothing. My eyes were drawn to the handsome stripes of white tape and gold lace lining the lapels, crisscrossed by brass buckles. I would have liked a coat like that. It was a man's coat, but fitting, after all, for a wherry captain.

I shook my head. I didn't know what had gotten into me— fancying myself a captain. I was Pa's first mate. If we succeeded in disentangling ourselves from this mess, likely he would sail till he was seventy, as his father and grandfather before him had done.

A pang of hurt stabbed me in the heart. Better that way. The most I could aspire to be was a mediocre wherry captain, now that I was sure the god in the river didn't want me.

I peeked out the door. "The coast's clear. Go straight back out the way you came. Quickly."

"What about you?" Markos asked as we slipped into the entry hall.

There was no way I was leaving Pa's pistol behind. "I've got to get my things. I'll be right behind you."

The sitting room door opened and voices spilled out. Before we had time to hide, Ma, Uncle Bolaji, and the Black Dog Philemon were upon us.

When Philemon spied Markos, a keen look crossed his face, like a wolf whose ears have pricked up because it smells prey. "Who is that?" he asked Uncle Bolaji, halting with his hat halfway to his head.

"Oh, that fellow. Courier from the Akhaian Consulate."

Philemon seemed very much like he wanted to linger, but the butler had already pressed his coat into his hands. He threw one last hard glance over his shoulder, then drew on his overcoat and went out into the mist.

Uncle Bolaji frowned at me. "I thought you were bringing him into the dining room."

"Oh. Well . . ." I tried to pick an excuse from the many that tumbled through my head.

"That was my fault, sir." Markos spoke up behind me. "You see, I have an interest in old maps." He gestured at the glass curio case. "I told Miss Bollard I wished to inspect your collection. It is a fine one."

I inhaled sharply. I knew why he'd called me Miss Bollard. It fit with the pretense that we didn't know each other, and yet something in my very being rebelled against it. I didn't want to be disloyal to Pa.

"Those are originals." Uncle Bolaji stroked his beard with pride. "That is the chart on which Jacari Bollard marked out the trade route to Ndanna." He pointed under the glass. "And there is the chest he used to bring back the tea leaves he presented to the Emparch."

"Indeed? Do you have many other artifacts from *Astarta*?" The Southwest Passage was a significant achievement in naval exploration, but it surprised me that Markos knew the name of Captain Bollard's ship. Lately he was surprising me a lot.

I remained silent as we returned to dinner. When I chanced a look in her direction, Ma's eyes skewered me. She shook her head, and I understood it was only because of Uncle Bolaji that she wasn't lighting into me right now.

Markos dropped back. Under the clamor of the dining room, he whispered, "Was that him?" He jerked his head toward the front door. "The man who just left?"

"You've never seen him before?" I asked.

"Of course not. Should I have?"

I whispered, "Then why did he look like he recognized you?"

"You're seeing monsters everywhere, Caro. He's Akhaian. I'm Akhaian. That's likely all it was."

I didn't think so. I had never met the Margravina, but Pa had a miniature of her in his desk, a souvenir of her golden jubilee. A man from Akhaia would know what his Emparch looked like, and Markos had already told me he resembled his father.

Uncle Bolaji turned. Realizing Markos's head was bent scandalously close to mine, I stepped away. "Go with my uncle," I said under my breath.

"How are we getting out of here?"

"I'm working on it," I muttered.

Perhaps Markos was right. I was seeing monsters and pirates and drakons everywhere. I heard them in the screech of the fiddle as a man took it from a velvet case and tuned it. Panic caught in my throat. The sense of merry warmth and safety in the dining room was an illusion. Outside, danger scratched at the windows of the house.

My cousins' table was deserted, scattered with empty glasses. I spotted Jacaranda dancing with a young man, but Kenté was nowhere to be seen. At the head table, Uncle Bolaji was deep in conversation with Markos. I could tell Ma was listening, but she twisted the stem of her goblet around in her hands and did not speak. I snagged a glass of port off a servant's tray and sidestepped closer, pretending to watch the dancers.

Markos leaned over, addressing my uncle. "I should very much like to beg the privilege of a dance with your daughter."

Uncle Bolaji laughed. "She's a bit old for the likes of you, isn't she?" Which was true. His daughter was over thirty.

"Ah. I meant the young lady I met at the door."

"Oh, you mean Caro? She is a daughter of this house," Uncle Bolaji said, "although not my daughter." He nodded at me. "By all means, you may ask her."

That was smart of Markos, to mistake my identity on purpose. It never occurred to my uncle that we had met before tonight. Plucking the glass from my hand, he bowed politely and led me onto the floor.

I set one hand on the shoulder of his new coat. He was probably the tallest boy I'd ever danced with. As he curved his hand around my waist, above where my skirts billowed out, my breath felt strangled. I reminded myself it was just a dance. Perfectly respectable. Markos waited, counting the beats, then swirled us expertly into the pattern of dancing couples.

"I wish you had told me yourself." His fingers tightened on mine, but not in a romantic way. In an annoyed way. "You let me believe you were a common wherryman's daughter, when in truth you belong to a great merchant family."

"I am a common wherryman's daughter." I hurled the words sarcastically back.

He'd never heard the condescending way some of the family spoke to my father. Or how they smiled indulgently at *Cormorant*'s chipped paint. No matter how much I enjoyed visiting, I wasn't certain I would ever truly belong in this house.

"The Bollards don't approve of Pa, you know," I said under my breath. "Or me."

"That's not what I see. Not at all."

"They like who they *want* me to be," I countered. "They like my mother's daughter, the one who wears dresses and talks proper. But that's not really me. I'm a smuggler. And a sailor."

"Our family name is who we are." His shoulder went rigid under my hand, and I wondered if he was thinking of that jewel in his ear. He swallowed. "It means everything."

Maybe that was true for him. But he would never know what it was like to be torn between two families. Two futures. I bristled at the speculative way he was looking at me. I guess he'd revised his opinion of me, now that I was descended from someone famous. Good for him. But nothing about me had changed. Not one gods-damned thing.

"I like my pa's name fine," I said. "I live with him because that was the agreement they made."

Easier than admitting my mother had been more interested in shipping contracts than little girls. She was so often out of town, negotiating deals for the family. Ma had pushed for me to be raised at Bollard House, but Pa put his foot down. Despite their differences, you had only to meet my parents for five minutes to know there was a mighty spark between the two of them. They just couldn't live with each other on a very small wherry.

"What man lets his wife leave his home to go work in trade?" Markos asked.

"This house was built on trade," I reminded him. Because lashing out any other way would've made people stare, I squeezed his fingers until he winced. "Anyway, what makes you think they're married?"

"Oh." His cheeks colored.

"For eight generations the Oresteias have plied their trade on these rivers," I snapped, anger and pride boiling inside me. "They been working wherries since long before anyone ever heard of Jacari Bollard. So you riddle me this: What makes the Bollards *great* and the Oresteias common?"

Of course I already knew the answer. It was money.

"I've upset you. But Caroline," he said, rolling the *r* with his accent, "I didn't mean to insult your father's family, and you practically bit my head off just now. Don't you think—perhaps—it's possible you took it that way because of certain unresolved feelings on your part?"

"Stop it." I let go of his hand and stepped back, awash with conflicting emotions. It was happening again, as it always did. Bollard House twisted things up. "I didn't sign on to be picked apart like a beetle under a glass. Not by the likes of you."

Great-Grandma Oresteia, who once smuggled rum right through the harbor master's garden, would not have let him needle her like that. But things were so muddled right now. Markos didn't realize his words had tweaked all my doubts, bringing them to the surface to float around me like laughing ghosts. I had never felt less like an Oresteia. And yet calling myself a Bollard would've felt like a betrayal of my father.

Across the room, Uncle Bolaji and Ma were in deep conference with the other people at their table. They weren't looking at us. "Come on." I tugged Markos out by the sleeve. "We're going."

In the quiet hall, the lamps flickered in their sconces. A lone parlor maid carrying a basket of rags scurried along the carpeted runner. She barely glanced our way.

I fetched Markos's hat from the rack and shoved it into his hands. "Follow the edge of the house to the left until you come to an alley. At the end of it, you'll find a garden. Hide there." I pushed him out the front door. "I'll meet you just as soon as I can grab my things and get away."

As the door latched behind him, my distinguished forebear stared down at me with disapproval from his gold-framed portrait. Lamplight glistened off the stroke of black oil paint that formed the curve of his whiskers.

"Oh, shut up," I growled over my shoulder.

# CHAPTER
# FIFTEEN

Booted footsteps rang out on the polished floor. It was Ma, in the company of Uncle Bolaji. They were deep in whispered conversation, their faces grave. I flattened myself against the glass curio case to let them pass.

Ma barely glanced at me, but hissed out of the corner of her mouth, "Bed. *Now*. And don't you dare set one toe out of that room. I'll be up shortly."

Uncle Bolaji paused. "Where's that young courier?"

"A messenger boy come from the docks, and he had to leave straightaway," I said without hesitation. Lying is easy as peas and pie once you become accustomed to it.

"Ah. Pity. I've just thought of something else I wanted to ask him about—Never mind, then." He strode past me. "We should discuss sending an envoy at once, though it turns my stomach to curry favor from the murderers of children. The Emparch's daughter was eight."

My heart lurched in my chest, until I remembered Markos hadn't even wanted me to know his sister was alive. My uncle had likely made the assumption she'd been killed along with the rest of his family, and Markos had not corrected him. Or perhaps he'd even suggested it himself to put the Bollards on the wrong track.

"We might push for a revision of the Agreement of '86," Ma said. "The savings from the tolls alone . . ." Their voices drifted away down the hall.

I remembered what Markos had said about the Margravina—that she was playing both ends against the middle. If I knew Bollard Company, they would do exactly the same.

I crept up the stairs to the fourth floor rooms where the girls slept, under the eaves with slanted ceilings. I scratched on Kenté's door, then let myself in without waiting.

"Did you find out what you wanted to?" She was seated upon a velvet stool, turning her head back and forth. Her eyes met mine in the mirror.

"I did," I said.

"We're going out." Jacky set one last pin in Kenté's braided hairstyle and examined her work. "Of course you'll come with us."

"Where are you going?"

"To a party. You can borrow a dress from me if you lace your stays in tight enough." She glanced calculatingly at my midsection. I wasn't wearing stays, and she knew it.

"I can't go," I said. "I've got to be on the river by five. I'm going down through Nemertes Water, and you know the tide don't wait."

"True enough," Kenté said. "The current carries us all. Only I thought you said you were going to the Free City."

I tapped the side of my nose with my finger. "And that's a secret for you. So we're even."

She pouted. "But it's not very fun, is it? You just got here."

Every moment I stayed, I ran the risk of being nabbed by my mother. And Markos was waiting. I said my farewells and slipped down the hall, regret pulling at me. My cousins blithely assumed I'd be back this summer. They had no way of knowing that by then I might be dead at the hands of the Black Dogs.

I turned. "Good-bye," I whispered at the closed door.

Back in my room, I had to contort myself to reach the laces of that stiff dress, but I dared not ring the bell for the maid. She would want to oil and braid my hair, help me wash up, and all manner of nonsense I didn't have time for.

A creak on the landing warned me of Ma's approach.

The maid had laid something on the bed that looked like a bolt of lace had gotten in a fight with another bolt of lace and lost. Mouth pulling to one side in disgust, I flung the gown over my head just as I heard footsteps outside the door. I blew out the candle and dove under the covers.

The door banged open. "All right, Caro, what's this business with the—" Ma's strident voice trailed off.

It was impossible that she couldn't hear the hitch in my breath and the hammering of my heart. I let my lips part slightly, relaxing my fingers where they lay curled on the pillow.

She stood there so long that after a while I thought I must be imagining it. Surely she had crept from the room and gone. I breathed steadily, willing my muscles to go slack. Finally I heard the soles of her boots brush the rug, followed by the whisper of the door hinges.

What was the meaning of it—and why hadn't she shaken me awake to question me? With Pa, I knew where I stood. But she was ... different. Sometimes I wished she wasn't so good at the bargaining table. I was never quite sure what she was feeling or thinking, and I was her daughter. Ma's mind was constantly ticking, looking for angles and upsides and ways for Bollard Company to get ahead. To her, revolution in Akhaia meant potential business opportunities.

One thing was certain. I couldn't trust her with this secret.

A change in the shadows made my eyes snap open. I sat straight up in bed, hand scrabbling on the bureau for my pistol.

Markos squatted on the window ledge, blocking the moonlight. His long coat trailed behind him.

I kicked aside the sheets. "How did you get in here?"

He jumped lightly down. "I saw you cross in front of the window, before the light went out. So I climbed up the trellis." I could tell he was very pleased with himself, despite the grass stain on his jacket. "What are you *wearing*?"

I'd forgotten about the monstrosity of a nightgown. "Never mind," I growled, crossing my arms over myself. "I thought I told you to wait for me in the garden."

"You said you were right behind me. That was half an hour ago. I got worried."

"I'm fine, but we must leave Siscema at once. Turn around." I cast around the floor for my clothes. "Bother it. The maid's taken my shirt. And my underthings." My hand came to rest on a pile of bunched-up fabric. "Wait. She's left the pants. Blessings in small things."

The ridiculous nightgown hung off my shoulders, its lacy yoke ruffling down my front. I grabbed the hem and twisted it into a thick bunch, shoving it down the back of my trousers. Taking the pistol from the bureau, I shrugged into my oilskin coat.

"All right, you can turn around," I said. "But know that if you laugh, I won't hesitate to shoot you and give your body to the Black Dogs."

Markos's profile was outlined by the faint light from the window. "Caro, are you sure we're doing the right thing? The Bollards are a rich and powerful house. They can help us. Why are we running?"

"The Bollards care about profit." I raised my eyebrows. "How much is an Emparch worth to them, I wonder?"

Uncle Bolaji seemed to disapprove of the Theucinians' bloody coup, but Ma had been her usual pragmatic self. I didn't think the Bollards cared who held the throne of Akhaia, as long as the Emparch was favorable to trade.

"You don't trust your own mother?" he asked.

"She's a Bollard first and a mother second." I balanced on the end of the bed, shoving my right foot into my boot.

"That's not a very nice thing to say."

I smiled in the dark. "She wouldn't agree."

The floorboards creaked as he walked to the window. "Do you think we might pass by the Akhaian Consulate on the way back to the docks? I have an idea."

I eyed the trellis below the window. It had supported Markos's weight, so I guessed it was sturdy enough. I would hate to escape from the Black Dogs only to fall to my death from a fourth-story window. "It better be something useful."

The light from the gate lamp made his eyes shine. "Are guns and blades useful?"

I didn't know what to make of this Markos. He seemed to be savoring this adventure. Even more surprisingly, he wasn't bad at it.

As I swung my leg over the windowsill, I said something I would never in a thousand years have anticipated. "Lead the way."

A damp mist still hovered low over the city. The Akhaian Consulate was dark except for a light in one upstairs window. Under the peak of the roof, a giant stone cat's head jutted out. Lamplight fell through its carved fangs to cast gruesome shadows on the wall.

"Are you going to be Tarquin Meridios again?" I whispered.

"No, of course not. Anyone who really works here will recognize me immediately." Markos glanced at the cat's head, then swept his gaze down. He looked as if he was measuring something. "Every consulate is supposed to have a safe house. There'll be a secret door somewhere. With the Emparch's seal on it."

I nodded toward the front entrance. A guard was posted there, musket strapped to his back. "Careful."

Markos ducked into the narrow alley. He examined the cornerstone, running his hand across the surface. Feeling along the wall, we crept toward the back of the building.

He stopped. "It's here."

It looked like scratching on a brick to me. He pushed, and the wall descended inward with the creak of rusted gears. I held my breath, hoping the guard wouldn't come around the corner to investigate the noise.

Markos fumbled inside the opening. "Oh, excellent," he said. I heard a snap and the smell of sulphur—an alchemical match. He held a candle lantern aloft, beckoning to me.

I swallowed at the sight of those stairs leading into a mouth of blackness, but followed him down. The flickering light illuminated a tiny round room.

Swords and axes hung from hooks on the walls, along with one wicked-looking curved weapon I could not identify. A number of boxes rested on tables around the edges of the room. At least one had coins stuffed into it. More weapons were scattered on the tabletops, and bundles of fabric too. A ghostly gray layer of dust covered all.

Markos went straight for a pair of short swords. "A cache of weapons and other useful things," he explained, sliding one of the blades out of its sheath to examine it. Seemingly satisfied, he hooked the sheath to a broad leather belt. "Placed here for just this contingency." He buckled the other sword to the left side of the belt. "It doesn't look like any of this has been touched for a hundred years."

I spun, taking in the wealth around us. "It's wonderful."

"Do you see anything you want?"

"I'll stick with Pa's pistol, thanks. I know how to use it."

"I think you should take a sword," he said. "In case."

"I'd rather take a dagger. I can throw a knife. Pa has me practice."

He flipped a dagger over in his hands. "How good are you?" he asked, tossing it to me. "Could you kill a man with a knife?"

I caught it. The scabbard had a pretty pattern of vines and scrollwork. "I've never tried."

Could I? I prided myself on my accuracy with a knife, but there had never been a flesh-and-blood person at the other end. Pulling the blade out a few inches, I traced the curlicues along the handle. I wouldn't dare throw something this fine, when I mightn't get it back. I buckled the knife to my belt, but knew I would never use it except as a last resort.

Markos dropped three coins into my hand with a lopsided grin. "For your father. To repay him for the coat."

Rifling through a small chest, he tugged out a scarf. He draped it around his shoulders in the old-fashioned style and fastened it with a gold pin in the shape of a wreath.

I eyed it dubiously. "Isn't that going to get in your way if we end up in a fight?"

He glanced down at himself, lips tightening. "You're right." He unwound it.

"Wait, what's that?" A glint of gold had caught the light. I shoved the rest of the clothes aside. At the bottom of the chest was a set of gold pistols with engraved bone handles. They were nestled in a velvet case, one pointing left and the other pointing right.

I touched the barrel of one of the guns. The metalwork was exquisite. I could pick out flowers and flourishes and a lounging mountain cat, its tail curved around the handle. The cat was set into a circle with words running around the outside in a script I could not read. Its eyes were tiny gems.

"That's the royal crest of Akhaia," Markos said.

I wished he hadn't told me. I didn't feel fit to carry a set of pistols like that. "These weren't meant for me."

And yet there was something familiar about them. Something I'd seen before. Shock running through me, I remembered my dream—walking the deck of the cutter *Victorianos* as she raced the waves. My hand had trailed down the rail, the wood smooth under my fingers. Seagulls circled and dove around me. On my head I wore a three-cornered hat and at my waist—a set of matched gold pistols.

Exactly like these.

I stumbled back, my breath tight in my chest.

Markos, busy examining the pistols, hadn't noticed. "Well? Aren't you going to take them?" He looked expectantly at me. "You're a much better shot than me."

"It's not—not right." I wetted my lips. "They're so much fancier than your swords."

Coincidence. That's all it was. Only oracles dreamed true dreams. I'd been thinking of the Black Dogs when I fell asleep two nights ago. Letters of marque. Privateers. It had all gotten jumbled up in my dream somehow. Surely lots of people had gold pistols. Well, lots of rich people anyway.

"Caro." He tilted his head. "I'm the Emparch. All these things belong to me. I'm *giving* them to you."

Another compartment in the chest held a crisscrossing leather harness, meant to be worn under a man's jacket. Strapping it on, I adjusted the buckles down to the smallest hole. I lifted the pistols from their box, still feeling strange about it.

Oblivious to my hesitation, Markos moved on. He brushed the dust away from a glass on the wall, leaning in close.

"This is the first decent mirror I've seen in ages," he said. "My hair is a dreadful mess. I don't know how people manage without a valet." He sighed. "You're going to make fun of me for that, aren't you?"

"Yes."

There was nothing the matter with his hair. It looked exactly as it always did. All at once my fingers got a strange twitch, as if they might reach up and touch it.

I jerked away. "Your hair is fine." I picked a string of beads, pretending to admire it. "Don't fish for compliments. It's not becoming."

"A man who fished for compliments from *you* would find himself with an empty hook and no dinner," he grumbled.

I clapped my hands. "Markos! You sound like a wherryman."

"Oh, shut up." I saw him trying to hide his smile.

I turned from side to side to see my image in the glass, admiring the way the lamplight sparkled on my new pistols. Free of the net, my hair bounced around my shoulders, a mass of reddish-brown corkscrew curls. I leaned closer to examine my face.

Markos noticed. "You know, the girls in Akhaia put juice from the orangeflower on their freckles to fade them."

It was just like him to pick the one thing I was self-conscious about. Some girls had a dusting of dainty freckles, but mine were big and blotchy.

"Ayah? Do they be wearing fine hats too, and sitting all day indoors?" I rolled my eyes. "I work on a wherry. In the sun. Orange-flower won't do anything."

"I didn't mean you don't look nice," he muttered.

A shadow blocked the arched doorway.

A man in sailors' clothes stood on the stairs. He grinned, revealing a rotted tooth. Light from the sputtering lantern shone on his long, curved blade. He certainly didn't look like he worked for the Akhaian Consulate.

"So it is you. Philemon did be thinking it was." Boots scraping heavily, he stepped down. "You have the Andela look about you, to be sure."

Markos's face froze. "I don't know what *you'd* know about it," he snapped with scorn, drawing both swords in one sweeping motion.

The man laughed. Markos's snobbish remark had only confirmed he was exactly who the Black Dogs suspected. He truly was an idiot sometimes.

My new pistols weren't loaded. I slowly snuck my hand around my belt, reaching for the dagger.

The man gestured with his blade. "Try it and I'll gut you like a trout."

Time seemed to slow as I calculated—the length of his sword, the number of steps to cross the small room, how long it might conceivably take to gut someone like a trout.

Everything happened at once. The man lunged, light flashing on steel. The gilt and lace trim on Markos's coattails darted out into the dark like twin serpents striking. He jumped between me and the pirate. Before I had time to be afraid for him, the man was down on the floor, clutching his throat.

Blood spurted from his neck, pooling in a widening circle on the stones. His slick red hand twitched and fell away, limp. I didn't know where to look. It was so messy.

Markos straightened, a dark-stained blade in each hand. A metallic smell filled the room.

"You know," I said, my voice sounding high and disconnected, "I much prefer pistols."

The rushing in my ears grew louder, and I stumbled. The floor lurched alarmingly toward me. Something clattered on the stones.

A warm, painful grip encircled my arm. Markos dragged me up so hard my jacket bit into my underarms.

"Ow," I said vaguely from what seemed like ten miles away. My ears roared.

"You were going to faint." His fingers twisted into my coat sleeve. "Why didn't you tell me you aren't good around blood?"

"How am I supposed to know that? I've never seen so much blood in my life." I swallowed, letting my eyes go unfocused so I wouldn't have to see the blood spray on his shirt. The hot buzzing in my head began to fade.

"Better?" He loosened his hold.

I pulled away, fixing my jacket. "It just seems to me you might've killed him in a less disgusting way."

I refused to look at the dead man as I stepped over his leg. Bracing myself against the wall of the staircase, I gulped in cool river air. I was not feeling dizzy. I *wasn't*. That kind of thing only happened to town girls. Behind me I heard a swishing sound. Markos, wiping his swords on the dead pirate's clothes.

"I didn't expect you would faint," he said. "You're not afraid of anything."

"I didn't faint." My cheeks burned. "I'm not *afraid*."

"Many men get sick after they kill for the first time," he said. "Many warriors."

"Did you?"

"I've never killed anyone." His voice shook. "Till now." The fabric of his jacket stirred. I knew he was glancing over his shoulder at the dead man.

"I did not need to know that," I muttered.

Markos brushed at the cuffs of Pa's shirt, which only smeared the blood specks. "I don't feel ill," he said, a look of distaste crossing his face. "Just . . . dirty."

The fear I didn't have time for earlier came rushing in, making my heart flutter. "What are we going to do with the—with him?"

Inhaling, he turned his back on the dead man. "Leave him here, I suppose. With the door closed, it's not likely they'll ever find him."

When someone next opened the secret room, there might be only a dusty skeleton left. I shivered, and not from the night air. It seemed a gruesome fate.

On the way back to the wherry, we kept to the shadows. If Philemon had thought to send someone to the consulate, he likely had men all over the city looking for us. The scent of the river was potent at night and somehow still wild in spite of the urban surroundings. We followed it to the harbor, finally rounding the corner of the last warehouse.

My throat almost closing in panic, I frantically sought *Cormorant*. She lay at rest in the Bollard docks, the familiar curve of her bulk rising out of the dark water, exactly where I'd left her. One lantern winked high up in her stays.

I exhaled in relief. "Fee!" I called softly as we boarded.

In the dark, we loosed and raised the mainsail. Markos helped, with Fee tapping his hand to give him wordless directions. Not fifty feet away from us lay *Alektor*. I was too scared to breathe.

"Caro!"

Ma jogged down the dock, followed by her two bodyguards. Was this why she hadn't woken me up—because she intended to search *Cormorant* herself, behind my back? All I knew was I couldn't let her stop us. I undid the last mooring warp.

"Caro, what's all this about a stolen cargo? How did you get mixed up with the Black Dogs? Wait!"

I cast off. *Cormorant* slipped out of her berth, moving sluggishly.

Ma strode along the dock in her tall boots, keeping pace with us. She lifted her head, and her eyes seized on Markos. "Who are you, really?" she demanded.

I knew he thought I was making a mistake. Yet he stood back and said nothing, deliberately leaving the choice to me. For one desperate moment, I hesitated. It wasn't too late to throw her a rope. To turn back. The Bollards had schooners and barks and brigs—large seagoing ships, armed with long nines. I only had a wherry.

"I can't tell you," I said. But there was one thing she could do. "Send a ship to the harbor master in Hespera's Watch. They've got Pa locked up on smuggling charges. He'll explain everything."

"Hespera's Watch? You said he was in Valonikos. Come about, Caro!" She stopped. There was no more dock.

"I'm sorry, Ma," I called softly across the lengthening gap. I didn't dare say more. Behind her lurked *Alektor*, dark and silent in her berth.

"Hey!" a man yelled. "Who goes there?"

"A lookout. On the dock," Markos whispered, eyes widening. The expanse of water between *Alektor* and *Cormorant* grew, but not quick enough.

"Gods damn me." My sweaty hand gripped the tiller.

"Alarm! Alarm!" The man scrambled to his feet, reaching for his musket. "There's a wherry left its mooring!"

I shoved Markos hard. "Get *down*."

He dropped to the cockpit floor. My heart thumped a hectic rhythm. We were still in range. I ducked my head and clung to the tiller, bracing myself.

Waiting for the shot.

Sound carries far at night across still water, even at a distance. I heard the unmistakable scrape of a knife blade against a sheath, followed by a gargling cry and a heavy splash.

My mother's voice rang out. "Anjay, Thessos! Quickly now. Get rid of that body."

# CHAPTER
# SIXTEEN

The sun on my face stirred me awake. I blinked, trying to clear the fuzz from my head. I lay in my bunk, fully dressed and very much wrinkled. Across the cabin, Fee was curled in her hammock.

Waves gently slapped the hull. As I eased myself out of my bunk, everything came back to me. Our frantic escape from Siscema. The harrowing night sail, terrified the Bollards or the Black Dogs would catch up to us any moment. Anchoring in the tall reeds on the shore of the widening river, too exhausted to go any farther.

And the dreams.

I'd dreamed of the dead Mrs. Singer again, fish flitting around her. I was growing to despise that one. But to my relief this time there was no possibility of it being a true dream, because there had also been talking seagulls and dolphins. And a snake—no, bigger than a snake . . .

I rubbed my forehead. I couldn't remember.

Somewhere a bell clattered rustily. I went barefoot up to the deck. The river was so wide it looked like a lake, but I knew we were really anchored in an inland sea, the water brackish. Just off the stern, wavelets splashed a leaning wooden post. Two rows of posts exactly like it marked out a channel, while seagulls wheeled and cawed above the marsh grasses.

Nemertes Water. We'd come upon it in the dark.

I'd always loved the feel of my toes curling on *Cormorant*'s planks. It made me feel closer to her. But I was a bit guilty about leaving everything a mess last night, so I went to work stowing and tidying the deck.

I didn't notice Markos until he was almost upon me.

"You look like a pirate princess." He leaned against the cabin, shirt collar unbuttoned and flapping in the wind.

I still wore the lacy nightgown tucked into trousers, with a scarf wrapped around my hair. "There's no such thing."

"Yes, there is," he said. "There's a story about one. Arisbe, Princess of Amassia. Amassia That Was Lost."

"Oh, I know that one," I said. "The island prince promises his daughter's hand in marriage to an Emparch in a faraway castle, but the sea is angry, for that was a girl the sea god had claimed for herself. So there's a great war, with pirates and swordsmen and magic crocodiles and, oh, I forget. And in the end, doesn't the sea take revenge by destroying the city?" I shrugged. "It's just a legend."

"Some of the people in it are real figures from Akhaia's history."

"They are?"

"Don't you know anything?" He threw my old mocking words back at me with a grin. "What makes you so sure it's a legend?"

"Because all sailors tell tales like that, but not one of them's ever seen the ruins of Amassia That Was Lost. It doesn't exist."

Hands in his pockets, he wandered up the deck. "And yet there really was an Emparch called Scamandrios the Second who had a wife from an island country. Actually, they were the first of my family's direct lineage to rule Akhaia. When he died young, that same wife ruled as regent for many years. She's one of the most famous Emparchesses in our history. Our version of the story doesn't have any magic crocodiles in it though."

"Likely Pa added them. They're always popping up in his stories." A wave of hurt washed over me. I swallowed, turning away from him to unlace the sail cover.

"It's going to be all right." Markos cleared his throat. "You said yourself that your mother is very influential. She has to be able to do something."

If anything happened to Pa, it was Markos's fault. I knew he realized that. It lay unspoken between us, a looming shadow.

I changed the subject. "I don't like that Arisbe story."

He rolled his eyes. "Fine, I'll bite. What's wrong with it?"

"The ending." Starting at opposite ends, we undid the knots lashing the sail down.

"She marries an Emparch," he said. "She rules Akhaia."

"Everything she knows is destroyed! The sea god drowns her family. But, all right, it must not be a big deal because she marries an *Emparch*."

"It's a cautionary tale," he said. "A warning about the dangers of defying your fate."

"As if Arisbe was the one who arranged that marriage! The story is about a lot of people fighting over her, but she's the one who pays in the end."

He shook his head. "You have so many opinions about things."

"Thank you," I said, though I suspected it hadn't been a compliment. Together we hoisted the sail, hauling until the blocks clicked together.

I gave one last pull on the halyard, trimming the slack. "Watch," I commanded. Markos leaned over my shoulder as I wrapped the halyard around the cleat in a figure eight motion. I twisted my hand, catching the rope end under itself, and pulled the loop to tighten it. "That's how you cleat off."

"It looks so simple when you do it," he said.

"That's because it is."

"You only think so because you were raised on a boat." He dropped cross-legged onto the cockpit seat. "This all seems like a foreign language to me."

The sail flapped as the wind filled it. I steered *Cormorant* between the nearest two posts. "Markos." I hesitated. "Last night. When I . . . got dizzy . . ."

He smirked. "When you fainted, you mean."

"I did not." I took a deep breath. "The truth is, I could've been nicer to you. When we first met. I . . . I made fun of you a lot. I wouldn't blame you for mocking me."

He acknowledged me with a small nod. "We're stronger together than apart. Don't you think?"

It wasn't what I had expected him to say, but he was right. Our adventure in Siscema had changed things between us. "Ayah," I said. "I reckon I do."

"Well. That's why I didn't make fun of you."

I was afraid to bring up the next subject, for fear of upsetting him. "That man you killed last night . . ."

He gripped the edge of the seat. "What about it?"

I noticed he'd said "it," not him. "Do you . . . Well, do you want to talk about it?"

"No." He rubbed his forehead. "Yes. I don't know. I hate that I did it. It's not a pleasant feeling, watching someone's life gush out of them like—"

I swallowed convulsively.

He winced. "I didn't mean to say 'gush.'" Straightening, he stared at something over my left shoulder. "There's a boat coming," he said sharply.

She was a sloop, narrow and graceful, beating up Nemertes Water at a good clip with a jib and staysail billowing out before her. I read the name in gold letters: *Conthar*. An oddly shaped object, covered with a piece of canvas, sat near the rail. I caught a flash of metal at its base.

A cannon. My mouth went dry.

As the sloop angled closer to us, I saw a woman hanging onto the forestay. "Hellooooo!" she shouted.

Markos stiffened.

Across the water, I heard the woman arguing with a man who sat on the cabin roof. "Well, they ain't answering," she said. "It's not her. Look at the name. *Octavia.*"

"That's Nick's boat."

"Look at it through the glass, old man." She shoved a spyglass at him.

"My eyesight is fair enough." He pointed his pipe at us. "That's *Cormorant* or I'm a marsh goose."

I recognized his voice. As they sliced across *Cormorant*'s bow, well ahead of us, I waved.

Markos hissed, "What are you doing?"

I ignored him. "Is that Perry Krantor?" I hollered across the water. "Captain Krantor of the *Jolly Girl*?"

"How be you on this fine morning, Caroline Oresteia?" he called back.

The man on the wheel turned away from the wind. *Conthar* spun in a circle, dropping astern, but in a moment she had caught back up. Her crew let fly the jib and let the mainsail luff, to keep pace with *Cormorant*. I could see their faces now. The woman was Thisbe Brixton.

"I didn't know that sloop," I said.

"Borrowed." Captain Brixton leaned over *Conthar*'s starboard side. "We're bound upriver. Twenty of us, stout wherrymen all. We're going to do for those bastards what set fire to Hespera's Watch."

"You're going to take on the Black Dogs?"

"Ayah." Her long braid whipped out in the wind. "We couldn't touch 'em on the sea, but we ain't on the sea. These are the riverlands. We know these waters better than they do."

"They gone up the Kars," I called. "That's what I heard anyhow. And best watch out. They got friends —the sloop *Alektor*."

Captain Brixton's eyes settled on Markos. "Who's that? He looks like someone . . ."

"Just a cousin," I said, hoping she didn't know much about my family. He certainly didn't look like me or Pa, or indeed any of the Bollards. I cursed myself for not thinking of a better lie.

Captain Krantor removed his pipe from his mouth and gave me a sharp look, but he didn't say a word.

"Have—have you any word of Pa?" I held my breath.

He shook his head. "He be in the harbor master's lockup."

I exhaled. Thank the gods. He was safe enough for now. Hopefully Ma would be successful in springing him from the brig.

Captain Brixton snapped her fingers. "I thought of it. He looks like the man on the cent piece."

I opened my mouth to say the cent piece had a tree on it.

She anticipated me. "Not ours. The Akhaian one. They're not called cents, they're called something else, but anyhow they've a young man on them. And you look like him."

Markos smiled uncomfortably.

"Of course, that's not likely where I know you from." She laughed. "It's just a bit of whimsy. Pay me no mind."

"What news of your wherries?" I called, before Captain Brixton could explore any further down that tributary.

"I'm forgetting you left that very night," Captain Krantor said. "Finion Argyrus come up himself from Siscema. No finer salvagers than Argyrus and Sons, to be sure. If anyone can raise those boats, Argyrus will!"

"You don't get the best of a wherryman that easy, eh, boys?" Thisbe Brixton shouted. "Ayah, and didn't the Old Man send us for vengeance?" I saw Markos glance at Captain Krantor, but I knew that wasn't who she meant.

A ragged cheer rose up from the men.

Captain Brixton threw me a farewell salute. "Current carry you, Oresteia!" *Conthar* sheeted in and shot away, whisking toward the northern end of Nemertes Water. I wished I was going with them.

"I shouldn't be on deck," Markos said.

"They're on our side. You look like the man on the Akhaian cent piece, do you?" I hit him on the arm. "I knew we should've kept you dressed like an old woman. Gods damn me."

"My grandfather's on that coin." He rubbed the crease between his eyes. "How much does a wherry cost?"

"Why—"

He just looked at me. "You know why. This happened to them because of me." His shoulders were hunched, as if the burden weighed heavily on him. "I should make restitution."

I didn't want to make him feel worse, but I had to be honest. "It's not about how much they cost," I said. "You're not a wherryman. You won't understand."

"So make me understand."

"I can't." I dug for the words I wanted. "To a captain, a ship is ... more than just something that carries cargo from place to place. To someone who loves her, it don't matter if she's old. Or her decks aren't tidy. Or her paint is chipped."

I placed my palm flat against the warm deck. "When you see her, with her sails standing high against the sky, it's like being punched in the chest. For a moment you can't breathe. Her beauty strikes you that hard. You understand the life in her, and it calls out to you. That's when you know you love a ship. *That's* when she's yours."

"And that's how you feel about *Cormorant*."

"She's not just a boat," I said around the lump in my throat. "She's my home. She's everything."

I spread my hand wide. I felt her every creak and movement. I felt her spirit, the little quirks that made her *Cormorant*. That made her ours and no one else's.

"I would like to pay them, just the same," Markos said. "Someday."

Nemertes Water was dotted with ships. I sighted at least six wherries, a long topsail barge, and one seagoing bark, but there were also pleasure boats and fishing boats and all manner of small craft. Strangely, being on the open water felt safer and more dangerous at the same time. I could clearly see every ship up and down that blue stretch. None of them were *Victorianos* or *Alektor*, blessings in small things.

But I also felt naked. We were exposed on Nemertes Water. If the Black Dogs appeared, there was nowhere to hide.

"Are we close to Iantiporos?" Markos asked.

I pointed. "It's on the other side of those cliffs. If we sailed a little farther to port, you'd be able to see the pillars of the senate building. It's one of the wonders of the modern world." Knowing how he disapproved of Kynthessa's democratic government, I was surprised when he did not interrupt with a disapproving comment. "Beyond Iantiporos is the sea."

"Can you take this boat onto the sea?"

"She does all right on the Neck. But on the open sea?" I shook my head. Wherrymen were superstitious about the ocean. It was not the realm of the river god. "Out there you need a deep keel. High rails. More canvas."

Turning to Markos, I had an idea. "You want to try sailing?" For some reason, I found myself hoping he would say yes. "This is a big bay. You can make mistakes here."

"Me? I—you'd let me sail?" I saw a glint in his eyes. He set his hand tentatively on the tiller. Fee let go, scooting over on the bench.

"Well, that's no good," I said right away. "Grip it. She's made of wood. You can't break her." I pointed to the posts marking the deepest part of the water. "Just stay in the channel."

He closed his fist around the handle.

I bounced up out of the cockpit, climbing onto the cabin roof. The sun had come out and the water was blue, capped with lacy white-tipped waves. With two hops, Fee joined me.

"Don't just leave me!" Markos looked panicked. "The post is getting close. What do I do?"

"You're going to jibe."

"What?"

"That thing you don't like, when the sail slams all the way across."

He almost let go of the tiller. "We'll tip over."

"She's twenty tons. It's impossible to tip her."

"I doubt the Royal Society of Physics would agree," he said between tight lips.

"It's impossible to tip her in fair weather," I amended. "Now, when I tell you to shove the tiller over, you're going to do it decisive-like."

He sat on the edge of the seat, glancing up at the sail. "Now?"

"Wait."

He gave me a dirty look. "I am perfectly aware you're doing this just to torture me." The piling slid closer. I could see barnacles on the crooked post and, below, seabirds perched on the wet rocks. His voice rose. "We're going to hit."

"We're not. Wait . . . wait . . . now!"

Markos shoved the tiller hard over. The boom and gaff slammed across with a wooden thunk. He half ducked out of instinct, though the boom passed several feet above his head. The sail snapped, then filled.

I trimmed the sheet a bit. The wind was coming more across our beam now.

"I didn't know she could fly like this!" Markos shouted. *Cormorant* was heeling a good bit to port, but for once he didn't complain about the tilt.

"She makes a good speed when she's empty of cargo. She don't point as well as that fast cutter might, but she does all right for herself."

"It's fun!" he yelled.

I wanted to tell him it wasn't fun—it was work. But I found I couldn't. A fair day with a fresh wind has a magic of its own. Of course a wherryman finds beauty in the work, or he wouldn't be a wherryman.

Flopping on my stomach, I rested my chin on my arm. Above us, seabirds dipped and reeled. The wood of the cabin roof warmed me through my shirt. Salt was on my skin and in the air. I inhaled, closing my eyes and savoring the briny tang of it. For a moment I thought I understood . . . something.

*The god at the bottom of the river speaks to us in the language of small things.* I listened, but whatever elusive whisper I'd almost heard was gone before I could snatch at it.

Markos pointed. "Look at the birds."

Four seagulls perched in a line along the curved deck of the wherry. "Oh, the gulls," I said. "They do that sometimes."

Maybe it did look strange to someone who wasn't used to it. Another gull landed, wings flapping. When I moved, all five birds swiveled their necks to fix me with their beady eyes.

"Caw," the closest gull said solemnly.

"They look like they're watching you," Markos said.

I laughed. "Shoo!" I waved my arms at the birds and they scattered, which was fortunate, because everyone knows gulls will shit all over your deck.

It seemed like no time passed before we were at the mouth of the River Hanu. I reluctantly rolled myself to a sitting position. The channel narrowed as Nemertes Water drained into the river, and on top of that the tide was rushing out, revealing mudflats on either side. It was a job for an experienced sailor.

"Almost," Markos said, relinquishing the tiller to Fee. His hair was mussed from the wind. "Almost, I thought I understood."

"What you meant, before." He ran his hand along *Cormorant*'s trim. "The life in her."

Standing to stretch his stiff legs, he froze. He squinted at the cabin roof, voice darkening. "What's that?"

I spun, whipping out my pistol. I heard the whisper of steel as Markos drew his blades.

The air before us began to shimmer. I blinked. It had to be a trick of the light. The image of the river and the mud and the afternoon sky seemed to melt away and flutter to the deck, like someone throwing off a silken cloak.

My cousin Kenté sat on the cabin roof.

"Now that," I said, my voice an uncertain croak, "was unsettling."

# CHAPTER
# SEVENTEEN

"Stay back," Markos warned. He grabbed my wrist, forcibly moving me behind him. "She may not be what she seems."

"Let go of me." I tried to wrestle out of his grip, but he held on.

"Only one manner of creature can completely hide itself like that." He didn't take his eyes off Kenté. "Caro, it's a shadowman."

"Don't be stupid. That's not a shadowman." The idea was so ridiculous, I wanted to laugh. "That's my cousin Kenté."

"Is it? Then how did she get here?"

Kenté uncrossed her legs and stood, smoothing her skirts. She wore the same green-and-gold-striped dress from dinner last night. "Easy as peas and pie," she said. "Perhaps I wished to know the secret of why my cousin was in such a hurry to slip away from Siscema." She studied Markos. "I seem to have found you."

He advanced on her, brandishing his blade. "I know an illusion when I see one. If you're Cleandros, I'll gut you right now, you traitor."

She gulped, eyeing the sword. "I would greatly prefer that you *not* gut me." She held up her hands. "Caro? A little help here?"

My mouth felt as dry as if I'd been chewing rope. Could a shadowman really mimic my cousin, right down to her twisted hair and upturned nose? He couldn't possibly know what she looked like. I shuddered, a horrible image crawling over me like icy fingers. My cousins, laughing as they wandered innocently across the dark cobbled street on their way to the party . . . while the shadowman lurked, watching them.

I shoved my Akhaian dagger against Kenté's throat—or the shadowman's. "Where is she? What have you done with her?"

Her amber eyes widened. "This," she said, "is an awful lot of blades. I'm Kenté, I swear!" She nodded toward Markos. "But he has the right of it. I'm also a shadowman."

"What do you mean, you're a shadowman?" I demanded.

"The god of the night has had her finger on me since I was a little girl," she said. "How else do you think I know so many secrets?"

I almost believed her. Kenté was indeed sneaky—and besides, if this was Cleandros in disguise, come to murder Markos, why hadn't he done it already? He might have stuck a knife in his back anytime today.

"When last we spoke," I said, "you told me a story. What kind of creature was the story about?"

"That's easy. A drakon. Though I never did get to that part."

Satisfied, I put the dagger away. "It's Kenté." I raised my eyebrows. "What are you doing here?"

"I've got a nose for trouble." She pushed Markos's blade out of her face. "And you two seem to have a boatload of it. As for how I got on board, like I said, that was easy enough. I cloaked myself in an illusion and followed you to the docks. Then I stowed away in the cargo hold." She brushed her dress. "Which, by the way, is very full of sawdust."

I felt somehow lighter now that she was here. It might almost have been one of our childhood adventures. Two girls, conspiring under the tented covers. Only we weren't children anymore—the danger was real.

"We ought to put you ashore," I told her.

She pouted. "You two look like you're having shenanigans. And I want in." She waggled a finger at me. "I came for the fun of it. But you're going to keep me because I can help you."

Curse her, she was right.

"How did you do that?" I asked. "The illusion. If you're a shadowman, shouldn't you only be able to work your magic at night?"

"It's simple. If I make the illusion at night, it will last during the day. Unless I end it, like I just have."

I noticed Markos staring at Kenté. My cousin was no prettier than me, although her dress displayed a good deal more cleavage.

I smacked him on the arm. "You might keep your eyes up here."

"I wasn't—" His cheeks flushed red.

"You were."

"Maybe a little," he muttered.

"But how did you come to realize you have shadow magic?" I asked Kenté, ignoring the sharp way her eyes darted between Markos and me.

"Something inside all of us is always calling out to the world." She shrugged. "That's what magic is: when something in the world calls back."

It wasn't an answer, but Kenté's cryptic words sparked recognition in me. Calling out to the world was exactly what I'd been doing, only the river wasn't saying anything back.

She went on. "I've been able to do little tricks as long as I can remember. I used to think I was just good at hiding, until . . ." A strange note came into her voice. "Three years ago I heard the god of the night call my name. Since then I've only gotten stronger. I can make the shadows come or go. I can see flashes of Jacaranda's dreams when she sleeps. I'm sure I could do so much more with the proper training, but . . ." She sighed. "I don't want to disappoint my parents."

"Is there a—a school for shadowmen or something?"

"The Academy," Markos said, rubbing his earring absently. I suspected he didn't even notice when he was doing that. "In Trikkaia."

I understood what Kenté had left unsaid. The Bollards hadn't the least notion why anyone might not want to be a member of a merchant company. My cousin was expected to make an advantageous marriage and go into the family offices. Her parents weren't likely to approve of her skipping off to a school of magic. It wasn't that the Bollards didn't believe in gods or magic—they were just too practical to put much stock in such things.

"Now." She grinned. "You must tell me how you came to be mixed up with the Black Dogs."

All at once Fee sprang to her feet, dropping the tiller. Her rubbery lips stretched into a sneer. She put me in mind of an animal with its hackles raised.

I lunged for the tiller, steadying *Cormorant* before she sailed into the mud. "What is it?"

She squatted on the deck, peering over the lee side, where *Cormorant*'s shadow made the water dark. Markos's hand had flown to his sword hilt, while Kenté merely watched with bemused interest. My pulse pounded hot in my ears, sweat dampening my forehead. Fee would never just drop the tiller like that. Not unless something was wrong. I squinted into the river, but it was too murky.

Fee hissed at the water. "Monster," she whispered.

Keeping a hand on the tiller, I leaned out. Nothing moved under the water.

"Her." Fee hugged herself tight. "*Her.*"

"There's nothing down there." I reached out to touch her shoulder.

Her eyes flashed. "Not right." She flinched away, as if my fingers were fire. "Not here."

"What isn't right?" I asked, aware of Markos's and Kenté's gaze fixed curiously on me. It had seemed—but that couldn't be it. That made no sense. It seemed like Fee was afraid of *me*.

She scuttled back. "Her," she muttered, shaking her head over and over, and refused to say more.

Once again I glanced at the dark ripples. I saw nothing, but shivered anyway.

"Don't you wonder what's down there?" Markos grasped a stay and leaned out to gaze into the water. I wished he wouldn't. Fee's strange behavior had set me on edge. *Monster*. I couldn't help picturing a great tentacle suddenly popping out of the river to grab him.

"Nothing's there," I repeated.

Images jumped into my head. Something massive stirring in the depths. Fish darting in and out of a barnacle-crusted ruin. A woman's long hair floating. Swallowing, I focused my eyes on the river ahead.

"So many mysteries in the world," Markos mused. "For one, what do we really know about the gods?" He nodded at the water. "Why does yours speak to you, while Akhaia's keeps silent? He must be a powerful god indeed."

Whatever was down there was *not* the god in the river. Fee wasn't afraid of him.

"What makes you say that?" My mouth was dry.

"Well, look at all this luck we've been having."

I should've admitted the truth to him—that our luck had nothing to do with me. But I told myself my pride couldn't take the hit. That was a lie. A person can live without pride. It's just not very comfortable, is all.

That night we moored on the bank of the River Hanu, where the gleaming mudflats and sea of marsh grass had given way to rolling hills dotted with rocks. We'd made excellent time that day, what with the fair wind, and hadn't seen a sign of the Black Dogs. While we sailed, I had recounted for Kenté the story of our journey, ending with the escape from Bollard House. It was hard to believe that was only the night before. It seemed like a dim memory. If the weather stayed fair, in two days we would reach the Neck. From there it was only half a day's sail to Casteria.

I bolted the cabin window, drawing the curtains across. "Well, we've had no sighting of *Victorianos*."

"That's a good thing." Kenté saw my face. "You don't think that's a good thing?"

I dropped onto the cushioned bench. "We know she went up the Kars. It's *Alektor* I'm worried about."

"What worries you?" she asked.

Unrolling Pa's chart of the lower riverlands, I spread it on the table. "Where is she? Perhaps Philemon went to look for us in Iantiporos?" I trailed my finger down the map. "Thinking we mean to hide ourselves there, or apply to the Margravina for help?" I shook my head. "I don't like this."

"The pirates who are trying to kill you have disappeared without a trace," she said with amusement, "and you don't *like* it."

I shrugged. "I just don't."

Markos sat with his back to the wall, fingering his sword hilt. He stared ahead with a moody expression, refusing to participate in the conversation.

Kenté snapped her fingers. "I just remembered! I brought something. It's in the cargo hold."

Markos watched her scamper up the steps. Lowering his voice, he said, "It still seems like too much of a coincidence to me. Are you certain you trust her?"

"As if she were my own sister," I said, instantly regretting my choice of words.

He pressed his lips into a white line but said nothing.

Kenté returned, dragging a brocade shoulder bag. She rifled inside it. "Courtesy of the Bollard cellar." With a flourish, she produced an amber glass bottle. "And now we drink."

"Oh, well done!" Kenté always had been remarkably good at sneaking drinks. Now I knew why. I grinned, taking the bottle. "Long live the Bollards!"

I divvied out the mugs, carelessly splashing three fingers of rum in each. Fee dipped a long finger into hers, then stuck it in her mouth. Markos was still brooding on the opposite bench. I pushed a mug across the checkered tablecloth at him.

He took a gulp, then coughed. "What is this swill?" he managed, spluttering.

"Rum. The sailor's drink."

"I suppose *some* might call that rum," he said. "It tastes as if it was distilled in a slimy barrel with an old shoe at the bottom. It's vile."

It was, a bit. But I didn't dare admit I agreed.

"What happens when we get to Casteria?" Kenté asked.

Out of the corner of my eye, I saw Markos shift, likely bristling at the word "we." Perhaps I was asking too much of him. It was only over the course of days and several narrow escapes that he'd come to trust me. He didn't know Kenté like I did.

After a long hesitation, he said, "My family owns an estate in Casteria that my grandfather used to keep for fishing. Since his time, the house has fallen into disuse. My father . . ." He paused, a tremor in his voice. "My father had no interest in sport. However, we still own the property, which is maintained by a small staff. That's where my sister, Daria, was sent. The instructions specify that the box shall only be opened by the Emparch or his representative."

I noticed the way he lingered on his sister's name. For his sake I desperately hoped she had made it to Casteria—and that, unlike Cleandros, the servants there were trustworthy.

"At least we have some assets." He ticked them off on his fingers. "Kenté's magic, Fee's extraordinary eyesight, my skill with a blade, and Caro's—well, your knowledge of generally unlawful behavior."

"Plus three pistols," I added. "And you'll have your swords."

"What do I get?" Kenté asked in a fake wounded tone.

"Shadows."

She made a face at me and turned to Markos. "What will you do after you rescue your sister?"

"I hadn't dared to think that far ahead." He sipped his rum. "It tastes better if you don't smell it." He twirled the glass slowly on the table. "It's my hope that some of my father's advisers also escaped. They all knew we were to meet in Valonikos in case of . . . well, in case something like this ever happened."

"The Free City is lovely," I told him. "It rises up on a big hill. The houses are whitewashed brick. There are porches with pink flowers spilling over them, and rooftop gardens. And temples with red domes."

"The Free City," Markos repeated. "My father hated when people called it that."

"He would," I muttered. "Seems to me Valonikos is doing perfectly fine without an Emparch. Did you know their Archon is elected by the people?" Even here in Kynthessa, cities were ruled by Archons appointed by the Margravina. Though the senate made most of the decisions, she still held on to a significant amount of power.

"All very well for them," Markos sniffed. I hoped he wasn't about to get all stuffy again. "Akhaia is three hundred times the size of the Free City. It requires the stability that comes from a strong ruling class. If we turned around and handed all that power to the people, like Antidoros Peregrine wants to do, it might have disastrous consequences."

He *was* going to get all stuffy. I rolled my eyes. "You sound like you're reciting from a book. What do you think? Not your tutors. You. Markos."

"I *can* think for myself, you know," he said sourly.

"Oh really?" I teased him.

"A toast to Valolikos, then," he announced, "just so Caro will cease pestering me about it." He lifted his glass, finishing off the last of his rum. His eyes crinkled at the edges. "You know, this is the lightest I've felt in days. I actually feel like we might make it."

"That's because you're drunk."

"I'm not drunk."

"You are too." Kenté grinned. "You said 'Valolikos.' I heard you."

"I didn't. Valonikl—Valol—*damn*."

We all dissolved into snorts of laughter. "You're a bad influence on me, you know." I eyed the half-empty bottle. "The both of you."

Kenté wiggled her eyebrows, furtively gesturing toward Markos under the table. I elbowed her hard.

"Well, I'm to bed," she announced, sliding out of the booth. "Come on, Fee. Let's fix me up a hammock."

The gods preserve us from meddling cousins.

At once Markos and I leaped to our feet. "I'm just going to—" He grabbed the rum bottle.

"Right," I mumbled, my cheeks flushing as I bent to gather up the dishes. Kenté tapped one finger on the side of her nose before ducking through the curtain into the next cabin.

Markos watched her go. "You're different with her."

It seemed ridiculous that I had never noticed what a strikingly handsome combination blue eyes and black hair were. My heart was going at a frantic pace. I didn't know where to look.

"She's my cousin." I pretended to arrange the dirty dishes.

"My cousin tried to assassinate me, so . . ." He shrugged.

"Ayah. Your life is kind of a mess, isn't it?"

"It is. It really is." He paused. "Caro, I've been thinking about what's going to happen when we get to Casteria."

I felt ashamed for having been laughing only minutes ago. And for thinking—well, whatever I'd been thinking.

"If . . ." He took a deep breath. "The shadowman's magic . . . it's only broken when someone opens the box. What if everyone who knows Daria's in there is dead?" He set his hand on my sleeve, and sparks rocketed through me. "Caro, if something happens to me and I don't make it, you have to get her out. Promise me."

"You're going to make it."

He wouldn't let go of my arm. "Promise."

I didn't see how I was supposed to make it out alive if he didn't. We were on the same boat. We'd likely live or die together. "All right, I promise."

"Listen. In Valonikos there's a house." He spoke in a rush. "In Iphis Street. Go to that house and ask for Tychon Hypatos. His family are cousins to us. He's a very wealthy man. He can help Daria."

"Markos, stop it," I whispered. He was talking as if he was already dead.

"You need to know. In case." His hand curled warm around my arm. "Now. What is his name?"

"Tychon Hypatos. Iphis Street. I'm not going to *need* this."

"I hope not." He released me. I expected him to step back, but instead he inclined his head toward me.

We were only inches apart. It would have been easy to lean my body against his. Easy to mess up his hair and press my lips to that triangle of soft skin at the base of his neck. Images jumped unbidden into my mind: Markos, pushing me up against the locker and kissing me over and over until we were both breathless. Hands under clothes.

The rum and my embarrassment made my face burn. How can you ever be certain a person is thinking the same thing you are? I heard his uneven breath and saw the jumpy way he glanced away from me, and I knew at once that he was.

"I'm going on deck," I blurted out, shouldering past him to escape the warm, cramped cabin.

Air was what I needed. Fresh air, to calm the buzz of the rum in my head. And in other parts of my cursed body.

Maybe I wasn't the right girl for this kind of adventure. In the stories, the heroine is a lady locked in a castle. Or a common girl with dreams of being special. Or a servant who meets a handsome boy who will take her away from all this.

A heroine is always someone who wants out.

Well, I didn't. I wanted Pa back. I wanted to inherit *Cormorant* someday. So I didn't have the favor of the god in the river. So what? I could still be a wherryman. This boat was alive beneath my boots, a friend and a home. I already had the life I wanted.

I didn't want to be swept off my feet by some Emparch, to have everything else in my life seem smaller and emptier by comparison. At the end of this, I would deliver Markos to Valonikos. Or we'd all be run through by the Black Dogs. Either way, I'd never see him again. Sixty years from now, I'd probably be an old woman knitting in her chair, telling the tale of the one exciting thing that happened in her life.

Suddenly I didn't want that either.

*Current carry you*, the folk of the riverlands say. It is many things. A greeting. A benediction. An acknowledgment that the river continues to flow around us, no matter what happens.

To me, tonight, it felt like a warning.

# CHAPTER
# EIGHTEEN

"You know, Bollard Company has a branch in Casteria." Kenté perched on the cabin roof, legs dangling. Her skirts flapped in the wind as we tacked up the Neck.

They ought to have called it the Spine, for that was what it looked like on the map, a narrow bay with many short, bony tributaries. Leaning posts marked out a channel between the cliffs, which were dotted with caves. So far we'd seen nothing suspicious, but I was still wary. In the northern riverlands, you can see sails moving far away, but here a ship might hide among the rocks. Rumrunners and pirates made these waters perilous.

I knew what Kenté was going to suggest. "No."

"Caro, they can help us. Don't you think you're in a bit over your head?" She must have registered my stubborn glare. "A bit! I just meant a bit."

"You didn't hear Ma and Uncle Bolaji. D'you know what their first thought was, when they heard Markos's family was murdered?" I demanded. "Getting a better *trade* agreement."

I glanced at the cockpit, where Markos sat across from Fee, staring determinedly into the distance. He had taken one of his swords out and was slapping the broad side against his knees. *Tap. Tap. Tap.*

I lowered my voice. "So, yes. I was afraid Ma would hand him over to the Theucinians. The Bollards are—" I stopped, not wanting to offend her.

Kenté's nostrils flared. "You think we're no better than the Black Dogs."

"That's not what I was going to say."

She shook her head. "You got the same problem as your father, Caro. You're too independent."

"A wherryman follows no man but the river," I said. "A wherryman is—"

She waved a dismissive hand. "That's your pa talking, not you. Your mother killed a man to protect you, no questions asked. Any of us would've done the same. We're family."

But Markos wasn't a Bollard. I watched him turn the sword over, sunlight glinting up and down the blade, and sighed. Since two nights ago, when we'd drunk Kenté's rum, our interactions had been excruciatingly polite.

Which was awkward on a boat the size of *Cormorant*. His legs were so long, our knees bumped under the table at meals. When he'd reached for his mug at breakfast this morning, his hand had brushed mine, causing both of us to drop into a squirming silence.

It wasn't even like anything had *happened*, but the tension of the almost-kiss thrummed between us.

I startled as Kenté scrambled up, whistling an alarm. "What?"

"Trouble, I think." She stood with one arm wrapped around the mast, skirts whipping out to the side. "You said you were looking for a cutter or a sloop? One's coming up the Neck."

My whole chest twisted. "What colors?"

"White sails, black paint. She's not flying any flag."

I jumped down into the cockpit. Bracing my elbows on the stern, I shook Pa's brass spyglass out of its bag and extended it. "It's *Alektor*, all right."

I lowered the glass. On the horizon, the city of Casteria was a blur. The Black Dogs would be upon us before we could reach it. It wasn't a guess. It was a certainty.

*Cormorant* was pitched far over, beating up the Neck as fast as she ever could. I trusted Fee's skill at the helm, but a wherry was built for hauling cargo. The sloop made better headway against the wind than us. She was just plain fast, crashing along with mainsail and jib close-hauled, and a triangular topsail wedged between the gaff and the mast. We couldn't outrun a boat carrying that much canvas.

Markos took the spyglass. "They followed us!" He stood so close behind me, I felt the warmth radiating off him.

"They can't have," I said too loudly, to cover the jangling of my nerves. "We'd have seen them." I exchanged sober glances with Fee. They would be on us within half an hour.

"They know what you look like," Kenté pointed out. "You and Markos should hide. Fee can sail. There are plenty of frogmen in the riverlands, and there's a chance they'll mistake us for a different wherry."

My mind raced. *Alektor* had been berthed right across from us in Siscema. Philemon would know the wherry *Octavia* left port three nights ago, but other wherries might have departed overnight too. Perhaps he didn't know which one carried the Emparch.

"Get down." I seized Markos's shirt, dragging him to the cockpit floor. Belowdecks would be better, but *Cormorant* was my wherry. There was no way I was going inside. I sat cross-legged, sweat dampening the back of my shirt. We'd be safe enough as long as we stayed low.

Markos clutched one of his swords in his lap. "What's your plan?"

"Haven't got one. You?"

"I was hoping you knew some kind of sailing trick," he said.

"Not a lot of tricks to sailing. Ships carrying more canvas go faster." I was thinking as hard as I could and coming up with nothing. "Kenté, can you do an illusion or something?"

"Not in the middle of the afternoon." She wrung her hands. "I need the dark."

"We don't have any extra sails, do we?" Markos asked me.

"Where would we put them?" I snapped. "Do you see a bowsprit?"

"You know I haven't the faintest idea what a bowsprit is."

We had no choice but to fight. I folded and unfolded my fingers, trying to calculate how long it would be until we were in range of their muskets. I hated this—the waiting. *Cormorant*'s bow was like a knife, slicing the thick damp air.

I glanced up at the pointed tip of the sail and realized with surprise that I couldn't see it.

"Fog," Fee said.

I popped up on my knees, then onto my feet. *Alektor* had completely disappeared into the gray mist.

Markos joined me, shivering. "Does bad weather usually come up this fast?"

"It can, this close to the sea." It was odd though. The day hadn't even been cloudy.

"Are we? Close to the sea?"

"Of course. The Neck is saltwater."

A wet chill lay over the water. I could still see the chop of the waves and feel the wind on my face, but the land had vanished, and so had much of the Neck. I lifted the big clapper bell we used to ring out our position in foggy weather.

"Is that a good idea?" Kenté squinted into the murky fog. "Won't they know where we are?"

"Would you rather get run down by a barge?" I clanged the bell. The Black Dogs were the least of my worries right now. We were far more in danger of running into a post or those rocks. "Dead by pirates or dead by shipwreck is still dead."

Distantly I heard the sounds of other vessels—bells small and large, and one blaring horn. That was likely to be a seagoing ship, far out. It was hard to tell the direction of noises in a fog. If one of those bells was the Black Dogs, I didn't know which.

Fee's fingers tightened on the tiller. "Can't see," she whispered.

The posts marking out the channel were wraithlike in the fog, but I could see them. How was it that she, with her sharp eyesight, could not?

Fee's long tongue darted out to lick her lips. She shook her head in defeat. "Anchor."

If we anchored right there in the middle of the channel, a bigger ship might plow over us. The fog was thick, but I was sure we'd sailed in worse.

I pushed the bell into Kenté's hands, and she glanced up, startled. "Ring this on the count of sixty," I said.

A strange sense of exhilaration ran through me as I took the tiller. My worries about *Alektor* trickled away. I was at the helm of *Cormorant*. It felt right. Far off our starboard bow, a post stood in the mist. I adjusted course, pointing toward it.

Markos leaned out to peer around the cabin. "Fifty," he counted. "Fifty-one. Fee thinks we should drop anchor."

"It's all right. I know where I'm going."

"Caro, be reasonable. I can't even see your hand on the tiller, and it's three feet away." His voice rose. "We'll run into the piling or the cliff or . . . or . . ."

"I can do it."

He and Kenté exchanged dark looks as she struck the bell. "*How* are you doing it?"

The post looked like a tall, thin ghost in the fog, but I could see waves striking its base. "It's not that thick."

"It *is* that thick." He sounded exasperated. "It's all just gray, as far as the eye can see."

"Hang on, I've got to turn here." I glanced up at the sail. "Post coming up."

Markos gripped the cockpit trim, knuckles pale. His eyes dropped to meet Fee's as she held on to the edge of her seat, her body braced. None of them trusted me. I ground my teeth. Well, all right. If this was the way they were going to be, I'd do it alone.

"Come about!" I called out, and Fee roused herself to help guide the boom over, flinching as she tightened the sheet around the cleat. I didn't know why. I wasn't going to hit anything.

"It's letting up," Markos said many minutes later.

I wiped sweat from my neck. Behind us fog hung like a great cloud descended from the sky, but ahead sun rays pierced the gray. Instead of only one post, I could see three. Markos was right. The fog was lifting. As I watched, a tiny gust of wind rippled the waves.

"I suppose that was your god at the bottom of the river," Markos said. "Telling you where the posts were?"

I wished with my whole heart that it was true, but I'd been listening for small things this entire journey, and all I'd heard was a lot of nothing. Besides, it couldn't have been the god in the river—or Fee would have been able to see through the fog too.

My chest clenched. "The god in the river tells me nothing."

He gave me a quizzical look.

And so here we were. It is a scary thing, giving your truth to someone. But beyond that, I was reluctant to say it out loud, as if doing so would somehow make it final.

"Markos." I paused, biting my lip. "I don't hear the god."

"But you said all the Oresteias are favored of the god. You said—"

My ears were warm. "I didn't lie, exactly." I wished I could sink to the bottom of the Neck. "The god in the river does speak to the Oresteias in the language of small things." My voice wavered. "Just . . . not to me."

"What about the fog?" He studied it, a thoughtful line appearing between his eyes. "That was obviously river magic. Magic of some kind anyway." He turned to Kenté. "It wasn't you, was it?"

She shook her head. "A shadowman works the magic of dark and light, sleep and awake. Not weather."

"Shadowmen can make illusions," Markos pointed out.

"True, but then it wouldn't *feel* like a fog." She shivered. "This one seemed cursed damp enough to me."

The lower end of the Neck still lay in cloud. *Alektor* had been swallowed up. Meanwhile, off our bow, the city of Casteria sprawled along a white line of beach, close enough that I could clearly pick out individual buildings. The afternoon sun shone on the great stone arch of the Archon's estate, while tiny sails dotted the harbor. We had made it.

I jumped up, passing the tiller to Fee. "I'm going to—to get the sail ready."

I didn't have to do anything to the sail, but only Fee knew that. She watched me scramble out of the cockpit, a strange look on her face. Sympathy—and something else I couldn't name.

My eyes stung. I didn't want her feeling sorry for me.

"If you don't hear the river god, why didn't you just say so before?" Markos persisted. I heard his boots on the deck behind me.

I walked faster. "Because I didn't want it to be true." Tears hovered in my eyes, but I fiercely blinked them away. "I'll still get you to Casteria. We're almost there, and I didn't need any god to do it."

"I know you will," he said. "Caro, if what you say is true, this only means you're more talented than I thought. If these other sailors hear the river, then how good must you be, to come so far without that advantage? It's nothing to be ashamed of."

"I'm not ashamed," I lied. "I don't want to talk about it."

"All right," he said slowly. "I only wanted to ask ... are you sure? What if this fog is a sign? What if the god *is* speaking to you?"

He was wrong. He had to be. Pa said the day my fate came for me, I would know, but if anything, I felt more uncertain than ever.

"You don't even believe in the gods," I said.

"I've always believed in the gods. I just didn't believe they speak to us." Hands in his pockets, Markos scrutinized the fog. "Until now. You're the one who made me reconsider. All that talk about your language of small things and your river god and your pig man. Why are you so reluctant to see that this fog is magic?"

I wished he would drop the subject. I'd been so close to accepting my fate, but now he was threatening to make me hope again. And I didn't want to hope. Not when there was no point.

"I've tried and tried to hear the god." My fingernails bit into my palm. "I can't. Markos, you don't know how it feels to think all your life that you're meant for something special, and then find out you're ... not."

He just looked at me.

"Oh," I whispered, realizing what I'd said. "I didn't mean—"

"Never mind."

"Look, Markos," I said. "You can't fix this for me, but we can still put things right for you. We'll get you and your sister to Valonikos. We'll get your throne back."

The moment the words were out of my mouth, I wanted to take them back. I hadn't meant *we*. Perhaps someday he would raise an army and march on Akhaia. But I would not be there.

He gave me a half smile. "You think you can do just about anything, don't you?"

If I did, it was only right. I was descended from blockade runners and explorers. Boldness was twice in my blood. I felt it singing through me as I stood on deck, the wind tangling my hair. We passed fishing boats and bobbing crab traps, until finally Fee steered us past the red buoy marking the entry to Casteria harbor.

Kenté let out a whoop. "We made it!"

I saw before they did.

My knees buckled and I swayed, reaching out to hold on to the forestay. It wasn't fair. Not after we'd come all this way.

Tied up at the dock, her sails furled and stowed, was *Victorianos*.

# CHAPTER
# NINETEEN

"You know this is a trap, don't you?" I watched Markos pace the cabin. "It's a trap for you, and your sister's the bait."

His fingers flexed on his sword hilts. I knew from the stiffness of his face that he was barely containing his emotions. "I don't care. I have to get her out." He punched the locker. "*Damn*."

"I understand, but—"

"Oh, excuse me." He shook his fingers out. There was a red mark across his knuckles. "I wasn't aware your entire family was recently murdered. Don't you dare tell me you understand," he said hoarsely. "She is all I have left."

"Well, *I* wasn't aware you had recently lost all your sense," I snapped. "If you ever had any. What exactly do you plan to do?"

"Cleandros is a traitor." He lifted his chin to stare ahead. My rage tended to boil hot, but his was ice cold. "I will challenge him to single combat."

I'd suspected it was going to be something noble and stupid like that. I bit my lip to keep from making a sarcastic comment.

At my silence, he narrowed his eyes. "What?"

"I didn't say anything."

"You were thinking it," he said. "Very loudly, I might add."

"It's just . . ." I hesitated. "If you think the shadowman or the Black Dogs are going to fight fair—"

He spun, gilt-trimmed coat swishing around his legs. "You think I'm naive." His cheeks reddened. "Foolish."

"Look, if we do things the way you want to do them, you're going to be killed!" My throat suddenly ached. "And I don't want you to be killed. Or am I not allowed to say that?"

When he spoke again, his voice was steady and quiet. "I have to go. If you don't want to come with me, I understand. Thank you for everything." He stuck out his hand. "I hope we can part as friends."

I sighed. "As if I would just leave you."

"And why shouldn't you?" He swallowed. "I've brought nothing but trouble to you and your family."

I paused, considering his words. I'd promised to take him to Casteria, and here we were. Why shouldn't I cast off and turn *Cormorant* right around? Akhaia wasn't my country. This didn't have to be my fight. But as I looked at him, everything that had happened since we met came flashing back, starting with me opening the box and ending with his words on Nemertes Water. *We're stronger together than apart. Don't you think?*

I couldn't leave him to face the Black Dogs alone.

Shrugging, I said, "Have it your way. Fee, let's get the sails ready. Kenté, untie us."

Markos's voice wavered. "Really?"

"No, not really." I swatted his outstretched hand away. "You can be thick sometimes. Did you think I would just shake hands and leave you to go up there alone? And get yourself killed, most likely," I added.

Kenté glanced out the window, where amber rays of late afternoon sun slanted low over the city. "If we're doing this, best make our move now."

I knotted a scarf around my hair. "We're doing this."

"What's the plan?" she asked.

"Not ending up dead." The rest we could figure out on the way.

As we hurried up the dock, I examined the cutter out of the corner of my eye. She seemed deserted, which made me nervous. I looked back at *Cormorant*, my love for her plucking at my heart. I hated leaving her unattended. Maybe Fee should stay behind—but no. If there was trouble, we'd need all the help we could get.

"Tell me everything I need to know about the shadowman Cleandros's magic," I ordered Kenté, as we stepped off the dock. The busy street was dotted with market stalls and buckets of fresh fish.

"It's still afternoon. We need to get to Markos's sister before the sun goes down."

"What happens after—Oh." I realized what she meant. "You're saying if it's dark, he'll know when we open the box. Can you tell if he's already opened it?"

"It's not like that." She pursed her lips. "It's not my magic. For him, it's like—like a bubble popping in the back of his head. Markos, for example. He would have known the second Markos woke up." She glanced at him. "You ought to be grateful. Caro probably saved your life when she opened that box. After the magic was broken, he couldn't sense you anymore. He didn't know where you were."

"Can *you* feel every piece of magic you've ever made?" he asked.

"I daresay I can if I try. I've left them all over the place. There's one right now in the corner of Bollard House's best sitting room. I put it there to cover the shards of a vase I dropped last week. I might feel that when I'm strong enough."

"Strong enough?" Markos asked.

"When it's night. In the night, I can *feel* things around me. The shadows. People sleeping. Their dreams and fears. Sundown is when my powers start to come alive, but the darker it gets, the more everything . . . shifts into focus."

"Why are you asking all these questions?" I demanded of Markos. "I thought you knew all about shadowmen, being from Akhaia."

"Very few people know all about shadowmen. They mostly keep their own secrets."

"Your father had a shadowman at his court," I pointed out.

"I don't know what Cleandros did for my father." His face assumed a guarded look. "I've come to suspect he was particularly talented in the magic of sleep—for one, look what he did with the boxes. But it was more than that. After I turned eighteen, my father permitted me to sit in on his council meetings. I saw things happen that I found ... strange. A man would express strong opposition to something my father suggested, but then he would suddenly ... I don't know, give way."

I stared in horror. "You think Cleandros controlled their minds?"

"Not controlled, exactly. A tired man is confused. Forgetful. Susceptible to suggestion. I don't claim to know everything about the magic of the shadows, but I know that, above all, it's about trickery."

I turned to Kenté. "Have you ever done that?"

She smirked, sunset light sparkling on her nose ring.

"Have you ever done it to *me*?"

She ignored the question. "What Markos says is essentially correct. A shadowman cannot set a man on fire. But he can manipulate his dreams to make him *believe* he's on fire. Riddle me this: Which is more dangerous?"

"It seems to me a useless magic," I said, "if you can't even do it in broad daylight."

"I certainly stowed away on your boat easy enough." She pressed her lips together, and I saw the thin line of sweat above them. "He'll start out weak, but as it gets darker, his powers will grow. Until midnight, when they're at their strongest. We must hurry."

"But you're a shadowman too. You can fight him." At least I hoped she could.

"Don't forget, I have no training."

As we wove through the streets of Casteria, I felt naked. Foreboding crawled down my neck, making my heart beat faster. We had seen nothing of the Black Dogs, but they might be anywhere, watching us.

The oldest estates in the city were built into the side of a hill, across which the streets ran in tiers. Every now and again, a set of steps led down through the cluttered houses to a small dock or private beach. The nicest houses were smashed right in alongside the hovels, the only difference being that they had a stone gate or a garden with sculpted trees.

Markos came to a halt outside a peach-colored house, nodding at the lions' heads on the gate. "This is the place."

He stepped onto the front walk, but I grabbed his jacket, hauling him back. "Were you going to just stroll up to the front door?"

"Right." He grimaced, looking a little sheepish. "Let's do things your way."

"Keep walking. Don't even look at the house," I whispered without moving my lips. The street was empty, but I didn't know who watched us from behind the curtains of those houses. "There'll be a back door, for servants and tradesmen."

We skirted the edge of the garden and ducked down the next alley. There, as I'd suspected, we found the back entrance, an unassuming wooden door.

I tried the knob. Unlocked.

The door swung inward, revealing a kitchen with a massive brick oven. The fire had not been lit. As my eyes adjusted to the dark, I saw that the wallpaper was peeling. Dirt from many muddy boots had dried on the floor, and a stale smell lay over the place. Meeting my eyes, Markos shut the door softly behind us.

I didn't think it mattered. "Markos, no one's lived here for days." I nodded at the moldy cheese on the table. "Look at the food."

"I'm telling you, she's supposed to be here!" Blade drawn, he moved down the hallway, peeking in the doors. Finally he shook his head. "There should be servants—a whole household. My family owns this house. And they *dare* just up and leave?"

I was wary of the mess on the shelves. Porcelain dishes lay shattered everywhere. This place had been turned over. I carefully swiped my fingers over the shards of a broken wine bottle, rubbing them together.

"I don't like this," I murmured. "I don't like this at all."

Markos slapped the wall. "Those were meant to be loyal men. I suppose that's what you get, hiring Kynthessan servants . . ." He glanced at us. "Sorry."

"Perhaps they heard the news about the Emparch." Kenté studied the mess. "And fled in fear."

"We have to search the house." He straightened. "Look for a chest. Large enough for a child."

It didn't take long. The other doors led to a small library, a bedroom suite, and a root cellar that was completely dark except for the dim glow of one dirty window. We found no Black Dogs hiding in the closets, to my relief.

"It's not a very big house," I said. "For an Emparch." I had expected something more grand. Bollard House was easily twenty times the size.

"It's only a fishing retreat." Markos rubbed the bridge of his nose. "What do we do now? If the servants took her with them, how am I going to find her? Gods damn me, I wish we'd chosen *any* other manner of escape. Anything but these cursed boxes." I laid my hand on his sleeve, but he shrugged me off. "I can't—" His voice broke. "I can't bear not knowing what happened to her."

Fee whistled from the kitchen.

I burst through the door. "What's—"

She nodded at a wooden chest, in the back corner next to a sack of potatoes. We'd missed it the first time. Someone had thrown soiled dishtowels on top, nearly concealing it from view.

Sweeping the towels to the floor, Markos pulled out his sword and hacked at the leather straps holding the chest shut. The first strap gave, snapping. He sawed easily through the second, and bent to grip the chest lid.

Outside the window, the sky over the rooftops of Casteria blazed sunset orange. One last bright beam hovered on the horizon. As I watched, it winked out.

"Markos, wait!"

He opened the box.

Huddled inside was a little girl. For one frozen, horrible moment I thought she was dead. Then her thin shoulder moved, and she uncurled herself.

Her eyes went round. "Markos!"

I swallowed down sudden emotion at the way his smile lit up

his face. He lifted his sister from the crate, clutching her hard to his chest. She wore a gauzy nightgown spangled with stars, and had the same jet-black hair as Markos, except hers was stick straight. The poor thing had bruises up and down her arms.

She looked up at him as he brushed straw from her gown. "I had the worst dreams."

Markos's eyes met mine over her head. He knew what he had done. "I'm sorry," he said hoarsely.

Kenté stared at Daria like she was death come to snare us. "He'll have known instantly. We have to go."

Markos hoisted his sister out of the box, setting her on the table. "Daria, this is Caroline. You must do everything she says. If she tells you to run, you run. If she says hide, you find a small place and crawl into it. Do you understand? If she says to duck—"

"I duck." The girl rolled her eyes. "I'm little, not stupid."

"Daria. This is serious."

"She can't run in that." I gestured to the floor-length night-gown. "She'll trip."

Markos made a face. No doubt he desperately wanted to make a comment about how I was always spoiling nice things, but he took the knife I offered and cut off Daria's gown at her knees.

I tried to remind myself that my part in this adventure was to be the one with knowledge of pistols, knives, and generally unlaw-ful behavior. But it was hard when my heart wanted to get all warm at the gentle way he dealt with his sister.

A door hinge creaked. My breath catching in my throat, I ran into the hall.

Diric Melanos braced his arm across the front door, blocking it. He wore a navy blue coat, strapped with gun belts. I didn't doubt he had at least ten weapons on his person.

"You must be the wherry girl," he said, a grin crawling across his scarred face, "that I keep hearing so much about." Boots falling heavy on the floor, he stepped down from the threshold.

Cleandros the shadowman entered, trailing black robes with gilded stripes. I'd only ever heard his voice, but I knew him at once. He was not as old as he sounded—there were only little tufts of gray in his dull brown hair. He looked altogether mild mannered and boring, like a teacher or a clerk. Several pendants dangled about his neck on long chains.

The rest of the Black Dogs trickled in behind him. Five— ten—fifteen men, armed with cutlasses and pistols.

My whole body hummed with danger. We were like the crabs in the traps floating in the harbor.

Stuck.

## CHAPTER
# TWENTY

Daria looked back and forth between Cleandros and her brother. "That's Father's friend."

"He's not our friend," Markos said, hands on sword hilts.

Cleandros surprised me by ignoring him. "One whom the shadow has called, I greet you," he called to Kenté. Then he nodded to Captain Melanos. "Kill the Emparch, the child, and the river rat. But bring the shadow girl to me." He focused on Kenté again with a smile that felt like spiders on my neck. "What are you doing away from the Academy? Does the headmaster know where you are?"

She lifted her chin defiantly, but her voice wobbled. "I don't answer to your headmaster."

"What's your name, girl?"

Kenté looked down her nose at him, which was a very Bollard thing to do and also a good trick seeing as the shadowman was taller. "Never mind."

I didn't like being called a river rat, nor did I like the shadowman's tone. I drew my weapon. So did Diric Melanos, only his was a Bentrix volley gun. It had five barrels, and I had to assume all five were loaded.

He waggled a finger at me. "Don't even think about it."

Why shouldn't I? Oresteias are bold. We don't take kindly to being murdered. After all, hadn't my grandfather fought off bandits with only a knife and an old frying pan? I had two shots and two daggers. That was four men I could take out before they cut me down.

Markos was thinking along the same lines. Jaw twitching with anger, he drew his swords and stepped in front of Daria.

"Well?" Cleandros turned to Captain Melanos. "Tell your men to kill him."

"That bunch of riffraff? Please." Markos sneered. "Try. I shall enjoy cutting their heads off, but none more than yours." He drew himself up, and in that moment I saw the Emparch he would be.

Diric Melanos's eyes swept from Markos to Daria. "What about the little girl?" he asked. I reckon killing children didn't go along with his swashbuckling image of himself.

"I took you for the terror of the seas," Cleandros snapped, "not a sniveling weakling."

Kenté pressed close to me, whispering, "Get ready to run on my mark."

The pirates' lantern whisked out. The room went dark, but not very. I could still clearly see everyone—Markos brandishing his swords, Cleandros and Captain Melanos, and the pirates arrayed behind them with cutlasses drawn.

Sucking in an unsteady breath, Kenté took a step back.

Cleandros laughed. "All you can manage, is it?" He fingered something around his neck. It was a locket, an odd-looking brass one with eight or twelve sides. "An admirable attempt. With training, you could be very powerful. Come, child, I've already told you, *you're* not in any danger. Indeed the headmaster will be very pleased with me for bringing him such an intriguing recruit."

"I won't abandon my shipmates," she declared.

His fingers moved. "So be it."

Cleandros disappeared.

I fired at the spot where he had been, only to hear oily laughter from the other side of the room. I took an uneasy step back and fired my second pistol, accidentally hitting a pirate in the thigh.

That's when they rushed us.

Markos sprang in front of Daria and me, his blade blocking the nearest Black Dog's cutlass. He spun through the men, ducking and slashing. It was clear he was accustomed to using two swords at once, because they moved like they were part of his own arms.

"Kenté!" I yelled, pulling a cushioned bench over on its side. She grabbed Daria, and we dove behind it. With shaking fingers, I reloaded, while Daria crouched on the floor beside us. "Stay right there," I ordered. I popped back up, pistols in both hands, and fired.

Diric Melanos spotted me. Lunging between two of his men, he seized me, wrenching my arm as he dragged me out from behind cover. I struggled, kicking out at any part of him I could reach.

With a shrill squeak, Fee launched herself in the air. She landed on his shoulders, knife between her teeth.

He swatted at her, but her bare toes dug in.

That was diversion enough for me. Luckily Pa taught me how to throw an elbow. It met Melanos's chin with a good hard smack. He swore. I wrestled free and grasped Daria by the arm, yanking her up.

Suddenly Markos cried out, touching his hair. His fingers came away bloody, as uncertainty rippled across his face. Cleandros must have either swung or thrown a dagger. How was Markos supposed to fight him when he was invisible?

"Let's go!" I scrambled backward down the hall. We needed to get out of there.

Blood running into his eyes from a deep cut on his face, Diric Melanos raised his gun.

Many men favored a Bentrix volley gun for their handsome carved bone handles and ability to fire five rounds of shot at once, but Pa only ever carried a one-chambered flintlock pistol. He said the volley guns were inaccurate.

The shot scattered in all directions, ricocheting off the walls and splintering a mirror. None of the bullets hit us.

One of the Black Dogs dropped, blood spurting out of his leg. I shook my head. *Fool.* You couldn't fire a gun like that in close quarters. He was going to kill us all.

My eyes seized on the cellar door, and I remembered that dingy window, up high. If we barricaded the door behind us, it might buy us more time.

As I wrenched open the door, a damp, earthy smell rose up from the cellar. I pushed Daria down the set of flagstone steps set in sod. Something blurry ran past me, bumping my arm. I tightened my fingers on my pistol, until I realized it was Kenté, half-wreathed in shadows. Fee joined us, her knife dripping blood.

Booted footsteps echoed on the floor of the hall behind us. Dropping to my knees, I aimed my pistol at the door.

Markos skidded into view, almost toppling me. "Oof!"

As I recovered my balance, he shut the door and let the bar slam down, locking it. We clattered down the short staircase.

"It's a dead end!" There was panic in Kenté's voice.

I nodded toward the back of the cellar. "Look."

A yellowed rectangular window, coated in spiderwebs, spread lengthwise along the ceiling. Nimbly Fee leaped to the top of a rickety pile of boxes. She rattled the window and then, finding the latch stuck, broke the glass with the blunt end of her knife.

She wriggled through. "Safe," she croaked from the other side.

Someone banged on the door.

"Daria first," I gasped. Markos lifted his sister into Fee's waiting hands. Her stocking feet disappeared through the window.

"Come on." He beckoned Kenté over. Stowing her dagger, she allowed him to boost her up. "Caro, you next."

"No, you." I glanced over my shoulder. The pirates were hacking at the door from the other side. "You're the Emparch."

The door buckled. I heard the Black Dogs cursing, followed by a gunshot. The shouting stopped.

"Markos, come *on*!"

He exhaled, tension releasing from his shoulders, as if all the fight had left him. His throat bobbed as he swallowed. "No."

I realized what he meant to do.

"But you're the heir to Akhaia." I refused to let him sacrifice himself. "You're more important than your sister."

His eyes flashed with intense emotion. "You still don't understand. *Nothing* is more important."

"We can all go," I insisted. "If we go now. Fee and I will pull you up."

"If I stall them, the rest of you will have a chance." His trembling hands hovered over the hilts of his swords. "Get to the boat. Take her to Valonikos. To the house we spoke of."

"Markos—"

"The name. Quickly, tell me the name again."

"Tychon Hypatos." My lips were half-numb. "Iphis Street. But—"

"You made a promise," he said.

"This isn't what I meant!"

"You think they'll ever stop searching for me?" He looked fierce. "You have no hope of making it to Valonikos, Caro. *None*.

Not if I'm with you." I reached for his sleeve, but he flinched away. "I'm the one they want. Those two people on the wherry already died for me. I suppose you thought I didn't regret it, but I do. I can't imagine if—"

"Markos—"

"Stop. Arguing. For once in your life, stop." His voice shook, and I knew he was afraid.

Time slid to a halt as we looked at each other. A million thoughts reeled through my mind. One of them had to be the right one. The one that would stop him from doing this.

"Oh, hell." He strode toward me as the door groaned on its hinges. "I'm going to die anyway."

He hauled my face close. I twisted my fingers into his hair and slammed his mouth down on mine.

It was a kiss that raged like battle, exhilarating and immediate. His lips tasted of salt. My racing heartbeat throbbed in my ears. I wanted more of him. I grabbed the front of his shirt in my fist, to pull him closer—pull him with me.

He broke the kiss and staggered back. I felt the absence of him on my lips, a coldness that threatened to burrow deep inside me.

"Wait." I found my voice. "Markos, wait—"

The door burst into splinters. He drew his two swords. "Go! Get out of here."

Hoisting myself onto the window ledge, I could not help looking back.

"Don't," he said without turning. And then they came rushing at him with swords and fists.

I didn't want to see.

With a ragged breath, I turned away and let Fee pull me through the window. Tears blurred my eyes. You don't leave behind a member of your crew. Any sailor knows that. You just *don't*.

I straightened, stashing my pistols. The others stood in the cobblestoned alley, watching me expectantly. The blue of early evening was upon us.

"Where's my brother?" Daria's voice was shrill.

I grabbed her hand. "Your brother," I growled over the ache in my throat, dragging her down the alley, "once told me he would do anything to save you."

"Where are you going?" She tried to pull away. "We have to wait for Markos," she screamed. "Let *go*!"

"He's not coming." I rubbed my eyes with my sleeve. "Hush! Markos said if I tell you to run, you run. Well, I'm telling you now."

We raced under the shadows of the eaves, ducking around puddles of refuse and piles of rank fish bones. Bumping into a lamplighter carrying a long pole, I stumbled. He cursed after me, but I could not stop. Above us lights winked on in the hillside houses. Somewhere people were sitting down to supper, while I struggled to breathe around the pain in my chest.

Markos was an excellent swordsman. Perhaps . . .

I shoved the thought away. The Black Dogs had outnumbered him. There were too many of them. I knew it. Markos had known it.

The alley ended. I glanced frantically left and right.

"Which way?" gasped Kenté.

A group of seagulls scattered into the air, squawking. Their cries drew my eyes to the right, where I caught sight of the masts far below us.

"There!"

We clattered down a stone staircase set into the hill. Glimpsing the harbor, I almost wept in relief. I heard no commotion behind us. No gunshots. As we raced down the dock, Daria tripped, but I pulled her up. Her pale face was stained with tears. Markos may have given us just enough time.

I halted.

Five men stood on the dock between us and *Cormorant*. Three of them held blades and one had dual pistols stuck in his belt. The fifth was the pirate Philemon. *Alektor* had arrived.

We were cut off.

A week ago, if you asked me, "Would you die for *Cormorant*?" I might have said yes. It was what happened in all the stories. A captain went down with her ship. But now I didn't hesitate. Didn't think about it for a second.

Markos had traded his life for ours. I knew what my sacrifice had to be.

I turned my back on *Cormorant*.

"Leave her," I said.

CHAPTER
# TWENTY-ONE

There is a reckless freedom in leaving behind everything you know. As I ran down the dock, tugging Daria behind me, it thrilled in my veins.

Markos was gone. *Cormorant* was gone. But I was alive. I was an Oresteia and I was bold. My brain sharpened and my blood surged.

I knew what to do.

A cutter does not carry a large crew. Only one man was left to stand guard near *Victorianos*. He sat on a dock post, boots dangling. His musket leaned against a stack of barrels, too far away to be of any use to him.

He didn't even see us coming.

Yanking out my knife, I flung it at the guard. I heard a wet thunk and a grunt, but I was already running up the gangplank.

"Kenté, pull it in!" I panted. Wood scraped on wood as she obeyed me.

The cutter had an open deck with two hatches leading below. She was steered by a tiller, much bigger than *Cormorant*'s. "Get back there," I ordered Daria, pointing. "Don't touch anything."

I couldn't think about Markos. Or the man I might have killed. Or *Cormorant*.

To anyone who grows up around boats, it is sacrilege to cut good rope, but I didn't hesitate. I ran along the port rail of the cutter, slashing the mooring warps. *Victorianos* drifted out of her berth.

I began to desperately heave up the mainsail. It weighed too much, but just when I thought I might burst into frustrated tears from the effort, I felt Fee beside me. The gaff climbed to the peak. Hands shaking, I looped the halyard around the wooden cleat.

"Foresail?" Kenté gasped, out of breath.

"Do it," I said.

The Black Dogs had seen the cutter's sails go up. They started to run, shoving wherrymen and dock workers out of their way. I took a flying leap off the hatch cover and into the stern. We had only moments before they drew their muskets.

The little girl stood where I had deposited her, next to the tiller. "Move," I said brusquely, regretting my tone.

She scuttled away, just in time for me to grab the tiller and slam it hard over to one side, right where she'd been standing seconds before. The cutter, still pointed into the wind, floated backward. Gritting my teeth, I leaned on the tiller. I pumped it toward me and slammed it over once more.

One of the Black Dogs raced down the dock. Kenté had pulled in the gangplank, but he geared himself up to jump. We hadn't drifted far enough. He might make it.

Fee stretched her lips in a ferocious grin, hopping onto the rail. She balanced there, knife in hand.

The man's arms and legs churned, and his body lifted into the air. In that moment, Fee looked over her shoulder at me.

I let go of the tiller. "No, don't—!"

She leaped.

They collided in midair and, tangled together, they fell. There was a splash, and the white churning of water. Then I saw nothing but the gentle waves.

"Fee!" I screamed, my voice breaking. "Fee!"

But neither she nor the pirate resurfaced.

Slowly, slowly, *Victorianos* began to turn. High up, the edge of her sail flapped. Kenté climbed onto the hatch cover and leaned on the boom, pushing it over on the starboard side. I pumped the tiller again, and this time the sail shuddered. The wind caught it and with a nice slapping noise, it filled. I felt the pull on the tiller as the ship picked up speed. The canvas tightened.

I glanced wildly behind me. "We have to wait for Fee."

"Caro, she's gone." I hated the sympathy in Kenté's voice.

Bubbles popped up behind our rudder, growing into a rolling wake. Kenté made the mainsheet fast. The Bollards might not be a wherrying family, but they knew something about boats.

We were off and on our way, beating up the Neck. Behind us shots reverberated across the water, though we were well out of range. "Duck your head," I told Daria just in case. "Better yet, lie all the way down on the floor."

She dropped like a rock, obeying immediately. She listened better than Markos, I had to give her that.

*Markos.* There was a gaping black space where he used to be. I wanted to scream in frustration, to fall to pieces, but I couldn't. Not if I wanted to live.

I was afraid to even think about Fee. It was too new. Too fresh. Stinging tears crowded my eyes. Pa, *Cormorant*, and Fee—that was the patchwork that made up my life. One missing piece I could handle. Now everything was full of holes, the shreds flying tattered on the wind.

Which had picked up.

Far astern, *Alektor* moved away from the dock. But this time I didn't need strange fogs. I knew she couldn't catch us, for *Victorianos* simply flew. She crashed through the water, her bow throwing up white spray. This was the kind of sailing she was built for.

Kenté squinted astern. "I don't *think* they're gaining."

"I'm not going to crowd on sail," I said. "Not unless I have to. This ship is a lot more than what I'm used to."

"Cleandros shouldn't have been able to disappear like that. Not moments after sundown." Kenté shook her head. "He should have been too weak, like I was. Did you see that thing around his neck?"

"You mean the locket?"

"It must be some kind of—of shadow box or something. He disappeared the moment he opened it. That's so clever." She rocked forward, dropping her forehead into her hands. "And I'm so stupid. Why didn't I ever think to do that? There's dark inside the box even if it's light outside."

"You're being stupid *now*," I said. "How were you to know? It's like me telling Daria to go aloft and reef that sail and expecting her to know how. He was an Emparch's own royal shadowman."

"I was a fool to think I could help you." She picked at a fingernail. "Fee and Markos fought them. *Died* fighting them." A tear rolled down her cheek, blending with the spray. "I did nothing."

I had other things to worry about. Rain began to spatter down on the deck, the drops big and angry. It was going to storm.

"We're in for a blow. Take Daria into the cabin. I don't want her catching cold."

"I want to stay here!" Daria was wide-eyed, hair plastered to her forehead like so many wet snakes. Markos had hated when *Cormorant* sailed with any kind of tilt, but his sister seemed exhilarated by how the cutter pitched over on her side, battling the waves. "I'm not going to catch cold."

In the excitement of our escape, she had ceased crying. I suspected her brother's death hadn't truly sunk in yet.

"Go through those lockers," I told Kenté. "We'll be needing oilskins. Cold weather gear."

"You might take a reef," Kenté suggested, squinting up at the sail. A wave broke across our bow, sending bucketfuls of ocean sluicing along the deck toward us. I paid it no mind. My boots were already soaked through.

"Not yet." I was afraid to stop.

"Is this the way to Iantiporos?" Daria scrambled to her feet, scrutinizing the misty cliffs. "Mother's in Iantiporos."

Horrified, I raised my eyes to meet Kenté's. "I can't," I mouthed. It was too much. I was barely holding myself together.

Kenté unfolded her legs, holding out a hand to Daria. "Let's go down below and explore, shall we? We can pick out a bunk."

I was glad the wind and waves were loud. If she cried when Kenté told her, I did not hear it.

Truth be told, I was relieved Daria was belowdecks and out of my sight. I couldn't imagine finding out you were the only surviving member of your whole family. She'd want someone to hug her and make hot chocolate and tell her it was going to be all right.

Well, I couldn't do that. Not when she was the reason Markos and Fee were dead. Perhaps it was selfish, but I'd lost everything for her and she didn't even know it. A stinging bolt of pain went through my chest. It would never be all right again.

Oh, Markos.

The Emparchy of Akhaia was inherited through the male line. As a cousin, Konto Theucinian's claim to the throne hadn't been legitimate before, but it was now. What Markos had done, exchanging his own life for his sister's, was so infuriatingly noble and stupid.

My throat ached, but it felt more like sickness than grief, like I should be in bed with my neck wrapped in a flannel and smeared with liniment. I wanted to cough and faint and throw up all at once.

The weather didn't help any. *Victorianos* plowed through the whitecaps, heeling far over to starboard. Sailing *Victorianos* was not like sailing *Cormorant*. She fought me for control, as I wrestled with the tiller, trying to keep us on course. I almost imagined she was being fussy because she couldn't believe someone as small and insignificant as me had been bold enough to steal her.

"All right, *Vix*," I said out loud, because "*Victorianos*" was a mouthful. It seemed much too formal for an outlaw ship like this. "You aren't going to get the better of me. You got to get used to that fact right now. I'm taking you down the Neck and out to sea. And you can't stop me."

The clouds broke apart, displaying faint stars, as if the sky winked at me. In that moment, I swear I felt the sea grow calmer and the wind slacken. But it was just wishful thinking.

The next two hours proved it. A bank of dark clouds rolled in and the wind kicked up. Rain battered the deck, as my hand grew numb on the tiller. The oilskins from the cutter's lockers were meant to fit grown men, so they were far too big for me. Water ran down the gaping collar and into my sleeves, plastering my clothes to my upper body.

Eventually we passed the lighthouse at the end of the Neck. We were in the open ocean. I came about for the last time and slackened the sails. At this angle, I didn't have to fight the wind and the water so much. Finally the slant of the deck lessened, and I felt like *Vix* wasn't straining against me anymore.

To look upon the sea and try to understand it is to try to know the unknowable. It can't be done. Gazing out into the sea's vastness, I felt a hole at the bottom of my heart. And yet I thought the sea understood that. It knew emptiness. It knew despair. It echoed mine, throwing it back at me with the splash of the waves. Everything was rolling and lashing and gray, gray, gray.

*I* felt gray. I was shivering and soaked. Fee was dead and *Cormorant* was gone. I wished Pa was here, but I'd messed that up too—the Margravina's soldiers would lock him up in darkness and squalor on a prison ship, and it was all my fault. Why hadn't I told Ma the truth? Why had I been so foolish to think I could do this alone? The salt spray on my cheeks blended with my tears, erasing them like they were never there.

I'd been given one simple task—deliver the stupid crate to Valonikos. Now the true Emparch of Akhaia was dead, and I was tangled up in it. They should've sent someone the gods actually cared about. Any wherryman would have been better than me.

I screamed into the night. The sea swallowed my scream, taking my rage and grief into itself. I screamed so hard, my voice cracked and my eyes felt like they might explode.

Then I heard it—a rumble from the depths.

We weren't alone. Something was out there.

An enormous head burst through the roiling waves, sending gallons of spray flying. It was tufted with what looked like wet feathers, and clumps of barnacles clung to its long, scaled neck. With it wafted a strong, snaky smell.

So great was my shock, I let go of the tiller.

It was a drakon. At least, I thought it was. I'd never even seen a picture of one, for the people who write the natural history books say they are only legends. But it couldn't possibly be anything else.

*Vix*'s sails clapped and groaned in warning. I quickly corrected our course, pulse racing.

The drakon opened its giant mouth and roared at me, its head streaming water and its teeth like swords. I was mesmerized by the purple sheen on its scales. It shook its spiny mane, foam and droplets flying everywhere. There was something wild and beautiful about it.

Suddenly I didn't care if I made it mad. I didn't care if it ate me, if it wrapped its great tail around us and dragged us to the bottom of the sea like the ship *Nikanor*.

Let it come.

I screamed back, a roar of defiance to match the drakon's.

"Caro!" Kenté jumped in front of me, aiming a pistol at it.

I seized her arm. "Wait! Don't."

"Have you lost your mind?" she demanded. "That's a drakon."

She struggled with me, but I was stronger. I held her back. "And you're going to take it on with a pistol?"

Out of the corner of my eye, I watched as the monster kept pace alongside *Vix*. I couldn't remember whether or not you were supposed to make eye contact with a drakon. Far astern I could dimly pick out three lumps that looked like islands—the loops of its tail sticking out of the water.

"It'll wrap itself around us and sink us." Kenté's voice rose. "It wants to eat us."

"No," I said, surprising myself. I didn't know how I knew. "It's not bothering us. The last thing we should do is provoke it. If we pay it no mind, maybe it'll go away."

"All right," she said doubtfully, lowering the pistol.

The drakon gave a mournful roar, diving headlong into the surf. Its long body swished there under the water, kicking up bubbles. I couldn't say why I'd stopped Kenté from shooting it, only that it had felt important.

I had stared a sea drakon in the face and lived. How many people had ever seen a drakon? Not just in a fish story, told by some old wherryman about his brother's aunt's cousin. *Really* seen one. I wondered what it meant—that the drakon had chosen to surface for me. Did such a creature have intelligence, or was it merely a wild animal, like a fish or a snake or some unholy combination thereof?

"I figure we should take it in turns." Kenté stared uneasily over the rail. "I'm going to get some sleep now, and then later I'll come relieve you." Tearing her gaze away from the sea, she shuddered. "Though I can't say as I'll be able to sleep. Not with that thing out here."

"I think it's gone," I lied.

After Kenté disappeared belowdecks, the hours blended together. I couldn't see the drakon anymore, but I sensed it was still there, undulating just under the surface. Its presence was strangely comforting. Almost, it seemed like it was keeping me company. I knew from the constellations which way was north, but it was unnerving to steer blindly into black sky and black sea.

"Tychon Hypatos," I whispered through chattering teeth. "Iphis Street. Valonikos."

A light appeared, off the port bow. It was a dim yellow pinpoint, flickering on and off. I squinted hard at it. There was nothing there. I was so tired and cold, I was hallucinating a speck of lamplight in the dark of night.

The light stopped flickering, and then I remembered there was a lightship that sat anchored outside the shoals off Enantios Isle.

I was not mad. It was a real light, on a real ship, with a real man inside who was probably drinking hot gin beside his stove. The light sparked something deep inside me that was not quite hope. Long after we passed the ship, I kept glancing over my left shoulder at it, a winking reminder that some things in the world were still steadfast.

Kenté climbed through the hatch, carrying a lantern.

"I think that's the Enantios lightship," I said, sniffling. I rubbed my nose on my sleeve for the hundredth time, the raw skin burning. "I'll look at a chart to make sure. But we must be a third of the way to Iantiporos."

"You need to get some sleep." She closed her eyes. When she opened them, the pool of light cast by the lantern had doubled in size.

"I didn't know you could do that."

"It's not very good." She cupped her hands around it. "It hasn't any warmth to it. It's more like the absence of shadow around the lantern than an actual light. You reach into the dark and you *twist*, and shove it aside . . ." She shook her head. "You haven't any idea what I mean."

"No." I was too tired to say more.

"Go to bed, Caro."

I uncurled my stiff fingers from the tiller, flexing them against the sudden sharp pain. "Have you ever sailed by yourself before?"

"I grew up in Siscema. Of course I have." I stared at her until she admitted, "In a dinghy. But there's no one out here but us, and I daresay I can read a compass as well as you." She set the lantern down and took the tiller.

I peered into the dark water. The drakon seemed to have gone. Surely there must be a meaning lurking behind it—a sign of some kind. Of good or ill, I did not know.

At the top of the ladder, I stopped. "Kenté? Thank you. For everything."

I stumbled to the cabin, pausing to reassure myself that Daria was all right. Curled up sleeping in one of the bunks, she looked heartbreakingly tiny. I shed my wet clothes and found a blanket to wrap around myself. It was scratchy and smelled like rank male sweat, but it was warm.

Too numb to sleep, I stared at nothing, waiting for the tears to come. But they did not. Perhaps they were all used up.

In spite of everything, warm brown spots crowded the edges of my vision. My head nodded to my chin. I fell sideways into the nearest bunk and surrendered to sleep.

When I woke, the first thing I saw was a man squatting on the opposite bench, watching me.

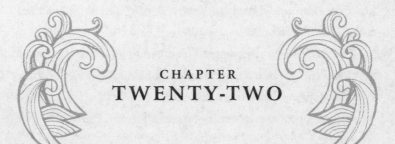

# CHAPTER
# TWENTY-TWO

I shrieked, scrambling for my knife.

The man sat at the galley table, picking dirt from under his fingernails with a blade. His hair was whitened either by sun or age—sun, I thought, for his skin had no wrinkles except around his eyes—and he wore it twisted into locks and tied with a red-striped head wrap. Tanned golden brown all over, his cheeks were blotched with sunspots and freckles. He wore a vest with no shirt underneath, displaying hairy muscular arms covered in tattoos.

"Good morning, Captain." He grinned, showing a missing tooth.

"Xanto's balls!" I clutched the blanket to my chest. "Who are you?"

"I am Nereus." He raised the hand with the blade. "Please sit. I have fried you an egg and made coffee."

I *could* smell the food. I was sorely tempted. "Where did you come from?" From the movement and the waves slapping the hull, we were still on the ocean. I dug in the blankets, finally locating my dagger in its sheath. "How did you get on this ship?"

The man who called himself Nereus looked disappointed. "Oh, come now. Is this how you treat every man who makes you breakfast? Let's not go pulling knives."

"*You* have a knife." I bundled the loose end of the blanket, throwing it over my shoulder like an old-fashioned toga. "And strange men aren't in the habit of making me breakfast."

He flipped his knife in the air, caught it with a flourish, and put it away. "Now. Why do you not eat? The little one eats."

Startled, I leaned out of the bunk. Daria sat cross-legged on a bench, casting shy glances at the mysterious sailor as she sliced up an omelet with a fork.

"Daria," I said, "don't eat that. *I'll* make you breakfast." I turned to the man. "You weren't here last night," I insisted, brandishing my dagger. "Where did you come from?"

The other hatch on deck led to the cargo hold. Perhaps he had hidden there, but why hadn't he shown himself yesterday? If he was a Black Dog, he could have easily overpowered us during the storm.

"Ah." As he sipped from his mug, I glimpsed an obscene mermaid tattoo on his forearm. "The coffee grows cold. Eat up, little one." He winked at Daria. "There is nothing like hot food to convince us that all *may* not be lost, ayah?"

He certainly wasn't treating us like prisoners, but the whole thing stunk of something fishy. Or maybe that was his trousers, which—I wasn't imagining it, was I?—had a clump of dried seaweed stuck to one leg.

"I'll eat and drink when you answer my questions," I said. "Where's Kenté?"

He shrugged. "Who do you think is sailing?"

Keeping the knife between Nereus and me, I slid out of the bunk. My own clothes were still damp, so I found a bulky sweater in the locker and rolled up the cuffs. It reeked of smoke. Placing my Akhaian dagger beside my plate, I took a seat on the bench. The stranger gestured encouragingly.

I picked up a fork. "Are you a Black Dog? Do you mean to stop me getting to Valonikos?"

He tsk-ed with his tongue against his front teeth. "So untrusting."

"You look like a pirate. The last pirates I met tried to kill me."

He smiled. "Ayah, and didn't she send me to help you, Caroline Oresteia?"

An eerie feeling crawled down my neck. How did he know my name?

"Who sent you?" I said around a mouthful of omelet. Pepper and herbs were mixed in with the egg. It was delicious, or maybe I was just starved. "My mother? Do you work for the Bollards?"

As soon as the words were out of my mouth, I felt foolish. My mother was a member of a powerful house, but even she could not spirit a man onto a moving ship in the middle of the ocean. Was it possible he'd been following us the whole way from Siscema? Maybe the Bollards had an informant stationed among the Black Dogs. Something like that would be very typical of them.

I mulled this over as I lifted my mug. The coffee was dark and strong, the way Pa made it. Thinking about him made tears prickle my eyes. I saw Nereus watching me and faked a cough.

"Too hot," I rasped, looking at my plate until I had control of myself again.

Annoyingly, the man who called himself Nereus was right. With hot coffee and eggs in my stomach, I felt almost normal. For the first time, I let myself wonder if Fee might still be alive. She hadn't resurfaced, but after all, frogmen could breathe underwater. And it would be just like Fee to want to stay behind and protect *Cormorant*. I felt silly not to have thought of that yesterday.

"Me, I'm here because I owe a debt," Nereus said. "And because I missed the taste of rum. Never go three hundred years without rum, girl." He slapped his knee. "Now is that a piece of advice or what?"

I folded my arms over my chest, the oversized sleeves of my sweater drooping. "You can't expect me to believe you're three hundred years old. Who do you owe a debt?" I demanded. "Tamaré Bollard?"

"Bollard." He rolled the name over in his mouth and smiled. "Ayah, you might say I know the Bollards."

I squeezed my fist around the fork. If my mother felt the need to assign someone to shadow us, she might have picked a less annoying man. What did he mean, three hundred years without rum? I wasn't in the mood for fish stories. Didn't he realize the trouble we were in?

*Ayah, and didn't she send me to help you?*

Certainly I could stab him with the fork. Or bludgeon him with the frying pan. Or throw him overboard. On the other hand, it was possible he really was on our side. He'd had ample chance to murder me in my sleep, if that was what he wanted. He clearly had a different game.

I pushed my plate back. "Well, I can't say as I trust you. I don't like people who won't give straight answers."

"In my day," he said, "the girls was less prickly-like."

"Bully for them," I said over my shoulder. Grabbing Daria's hand, I tugged her up from the bench. Just because I'd decided not to kill him—for now—didn't mean I was going to leave her alone with him. "Come on."

We climbed the ladder to the deck. As the hatch creaked open, the wind whipped my hair into my face. For one disoriented moment, all I saw was ocean. My throat began to close. Never in my whole life had I not been able to see land. Kenté had mistakenly sailed too far. We would be lost at sea.

Then I spotted the blurry line of Enantios Isle off the starboard side and exhaled in relief. We were sailing north-northwest, on a broad reach with the wind over my right shoulder. The stormy night had given way to a fine, fresh morning. Kenté sat at the tiller, her braids looking fuzzy and windblown.

"Trouble always does seem to find us." I jerked my head at Nereus, who wandered down the deck, hands in his pockets. "You didn't happen to see where he came from?"

"Just looked up and there he was," Kenté said. "He offered me a swig off a very filthy rum bottle, which I declined, then said he was looking for you. He's not a shadowman, if that's what you were wondering." Her lip twisted. "He did be scaring the shit out of me when I saw him though," she added grimly.

I knew the feeling. "Black Dog, you reckon?" I studied him from afar, fingers drumming on my knife hilt.

She shook her head. "I don't know what he is."

Nereus lifted Daria by the waist and set her on the railing. "There you are, pet."

"Don't do that, she'll fall!" I snapped, striding over. "Daria, get down from there."

"I don't want to."

My heart flipped over, for something about the way she turned her neck just then reminded me of Markos. I glared at Nereus. "She's the Emparch's daughter," I told him. "The last of her line."

"No, I'm not." She refused to look at me. I remembered how Nereus had said all might not be lost, and I realized what had happened. He was putting ideas into her head.

"Markos is dead," I said bluntly.

Nereus squinted at me. "So sure, are you?"

My voice came out strangled. "The Black Dogs burned eleven wherries because he *might* have been aboard." And they'd murdered his parents and brother, but I didn't want to say that in front of Daria.

He shrugged. "I wouldn't want to be giving up on a friend so quick."

Feeling my control slipping away, I stormed off. He didn't

know anything about what I'd been through. How *dare* he say that to me? I yanked open the hatch to the cargo hold. Down in the belly of the cutter, away from their eyes, I finally felt like I could breathe. For several minutes I stood swallowing, fists clenched, until the burning in my eyes subsided.

Dusty light streamed through the portholes. I wrinkled my nose. Belowdecks, this whole cutter smelled like feet. Captain Diric Melanos had kept a spotless ship, but I was not inclined to think much of his crew's personal hygiene. The cargo hold was unlocked, the key dangling from a hook nearby.

I peeked inside.

And grinned for the first time in what felt like years. All manner of items overflowed the shelves, stuffed in higgledy-piggledy with seemingly no regard to their value. A stack of broken china rested beside a pouch, from which foreign gold coins spilled. There were jeweled necklaces and rolled-up carpets, pistols and paintings. One box was crammed entirely with silver talents. A locker in the back corner contained rows of muskets, many more than we'd been smuggling for Lord Peregrine.

I supposed everything in that hold was mine now. And it wasn't even like I'd stolen it. It was mine legally, by order of the Margravina, thanks to my letter of marque.

Opening the lid of an ornate carved chest, I lifted out bolt after bolt of lavish brocade. Underneath were fancy clothes, folded in paper. None of them were cut to fit a lady. I didn't care—they were better than the smelly garments I'd found in *Vix*'s lockers.

I buttoned the smallest waistcoat over a shirt of fine linen.

Over this I wound a red-flecked scarf, tucking it down the shirt like a cravat. I set a three-cornered hat on my head, and buckled a tooled leather belt around my waist.

For the first time, I felt like the master of a privateering ship. So this was how it felt to be Thisbe Brixton, walking the decks of her wherry. Like a woman who knew who she was.

Like a captain.

On the belt I hung my matched pistols. Sliding one out, I turned it over and over. Light sparked off the handle as I admired the mountain lion whose tail curled around the underside. A master metalworker must have made those pistols. They were much too expensive for the likes of me.

Of course they were. They had been meant for an Emparch.

The corners of my eyes stung, but I refused to let the tears come back. I let the lid of the chest slam shut and secured the door to the hold, pocketing the key. Climbing on deck, I opened my mouth to take in deep gulps of the fresh salt air.

Nereus, leaning on the rail, saw me emerge, but wisely chose to leave me alone. Daria jumped up to tag along after me. Her eyes seizing on my tricorn hat, she stuck out her bottom lip. "I want a pirate hat!"

"Stop that. Ladies don't pout."

"What would you know about it?" She pouted some more.

"Privateers don't pout either. That's what we are. We're privateers." I slid the flattened dog-eared scroll out from the inner pocket of my waistcoat. "This letter says we can take a prize. And so we have."

"So a privateer is a pirate with a letter?" She didn't look impressed.

Since she was more or less correct, I didn't have anything to say to that.

Daria's eyes widened at the sight of my matched pistols. "Where'd you get those?" She reached out to touch the cat's gemstone eyes, and her face grew wistful. "That's the mark of the mountain lion."

"Markos said it was the symbol of Akhaia."

"Sort of. It's the crest of the royal family. The Emparchy."

An uneasy feeling fluttered through me. "What?"

"Only a member of the family may wear the mountain lion. Or a highly placed warrior. Like a bodyguard or a general. Someone the Emparch wants to honor."

I traced the lion's lean body. "He never ought to have given them to me."

"He knew what he was about. My brother likes you." She followed me up the deck. "I saw you kissing."

"Daria. Your brother . . ." I swallowed. Saying his name would have felt too real. "Your brother is almost certainly dead."

"Markos promised we'd be together in Valonikos." She lifted her chin. "He always keeps his promises. Nereus said—"

"Nereus is an exceedingly suspicious character who hasn't even told us who he is." I glared at him. "Don't listen to him. He wasn't there."

Nereus rested one hand casually on the rail. "Tell me, girl who knows so much, why haven't you hoisted the topsail?"

"Because last night we were close-hauled, in foul weather." And because I was scared, though I would never admit that. I wasn't comfortable with *Victorianos*. We were already carrying more canvas than I was used to, even without the topsail. "It wouldn't have done us any good."

Nereus grinned, and I realized I'd passed a test. A square sail is no use when tacking. "Now that we've the wind behind us," he said, "there's no reason not to unfurl that topsail. We might do with a jib too, just for the fun of it. Give her her head."

I looked at the sky. It was clear except for horsetail clouds high up, which usually meant bad weather would hold off for at least a day or so.

"Let's do it," I decided, feeling bold.

"Now listen. This ship is a cutter," he said. "I mark her a little under seventy feet long on deck, eighty-five if you be counting that bowsprit. Ayah, not much bigger than your wherry, but with three times the sail. You'll see she carries much of her canvas forrard. Mark where the mast is stepped."

I glanced sharply at him—I didn't remember mentioning the wherry.

The cutter's mast was mounted far back, almost amidships. A wherry carries one large sail on a mast that sits in her bow. This ship carried a mainsail, a square topsail above that, plus a jib and a staysail that fastened to the long bowsprit. There was room for a third sail forward of the mast, a jib topsail of some kind, and maybe even a fourth.

"Ayah, on a fair day, this is the fastest little ship on the Inner

Sea," Nereus said, as if he'd heard my thoughts. "She were built to fly."

I watched, shading my eyes, as he nimbly scrambled up the mast to unfurl the topsail. We could use someone of his expertise. I'd just have to keep a close eye on him.

With the topsail raised and a second triangular sail billowing out in front of the bowsprit, *Victorianos* seemed to lift a little. She dove ahead, plowing across the next swell with a wave of white foam. She had "a bone in her teeth," as the sailormen said.

Something creaked loudly. I jumped, my shoulders betraying my surprise. With four times the number of sails that *Cormorant* had, this ship certainly made more noise.

"Think of it as her talking to you," Nereus said, noting my unease.

That ship had dogged me up and down the river, ever since Hespera's Watch. I didn't particularly care if it talked to me. It was not the ship I loved.

"Now, you see? Out here in the open sea, the Black Dogs ain't got a ship what can touch her for speed. Feel how she goes!" Grasping one of the stays, he pulled himself up onto the pin rail. "You wouldn't want to be missing this."

It *was* grand. In the sunlight and sparkle of the spray, in the rightness of how *Vix* pitched along, I could almost forget about yesterday.

Almost.

I leaned over the rail. The day makes us too eager to forget the horrors of night. In the sunshine the drakon seemed like a dream, but something else tunneled along inches below the water. Something slick and gray and—

"Look!" I cried. "Dolphins!"

One sprang up, sun glinting on its slippery back. Daria clapped her hands. There were more creatures, I realized, than just the dolphins. Fish of many colors popped in and out of the waves as they raced the ship.

"See how the fish leap alongside us." I pointed. "So many. They must admire how she moves."

Nereus only laughed. "Is that what you think this is?"

Annoyed, I went back to take the tiller from Kenté so she might catch some sleep. I wished he would stop talking in riddles.

Daria plopped down beside me. "What are we going to do next?"

Her hair was a ratted mess, and the beginning of a sunburn splashed her cheeks. Her cheerfulness worried me. From what Markos had told me of his life in the palace, her mother had likely been a vague, distant figure. I understood her lack of grief on that count. But she clearly believed her big brother could do anything, and now she'd convinced herself of his escape. How much would it crush her when her hope was shattered?

"Now we drink." Nereus winked, drawing a brown bottle from inside his vest. Kenté was right. It looked as if it had been in a shipwreck, the label water stained and half-gone. He took a chug off the bottle.

I rolled my eyes. "Isn't it a bit early for that?"

He passed the bottle to Daria, but I snatched it out of his hands. "She's eight!"

"Ah." He threw her a nod. "I tried, girlie." Stowing the rum bottle, he ambled up the deck with the rolling gait of a man long accustomed to being at sea.

Daria fidgeted on the seat, an obstinate expression on her face. Finally I sighed. "Fine. Go with him. Just don't stray out of my sight."

Later that afternoon, as we sailed along in the shadow of the barrier island's cliffs, Kenté slid onto the bench beside me. Her striped dress was still wrinkled, but her face was damp. She looked much refreshed.

"How are you holding up?" she asked.

I told her my hopes about Fee. "Perhaps," I said, "even now, she's sailing up the Hanu River on *Cormorant*."

"Perhaps." She pursed her lips, staring into her lap. "Caro . . ." She hesitated. "What about Markos?"

I squeezed the tiller until my bones hurt. "What about him?"

"You didn't tell me he kissed you."

"I don't want to talk about it."

"You were very handsome in that dress. You know, the one you wore when he danced with you at our house. Do you reckon that's when he started to like you?"

I was about to say she hadn't been there when we danced, but then I remembered she could make herself invisible. She was wrong about Markos though. He'd wanted to kiss me long before he ever saw me in a dress.

Secretly I was glad I hadn't lingered to see him run through with a cutlass or shot full of bullet holes. If that made me a coward,

I didn't care. Images flashed unbidden through my mind. Markos crumpled on the floor. Blood clotted in black curls. Blue eyes staring.

*Stop.* I pressed my fingers to my temples. Not thinking of him at all was the better way.

But I could not do that, so I focused on the last time I saw him. A boy with two swords, facing a staircase. I closed my eyes and froze him in that moment.

"Anyway," Kenté went on. "Perhaps it's as Nereus says. Perhaps there's a chance."

I exhaled in a huff. "Oh, not you too."

She shrugged one shoulder. "It's just that he says it like he knows something."

Farther up the deck, Nereus entertained Daria by fashioning things out of a rope end. Pa used to do that when I was little. My eyes blurred.

"Well, he doesn't," I said gruffly. "How could he?"

Hope was only going to make it hurt more.

Nereus whistled. "Ship ho!"

The vessel lay anchored off Enantios Isle. Her masts were bare, her square sails stowed away. They must have seen us approach, for a white signal banner unrolled and began to climb the flag halyards.

"White flag." I squinted at the ship. "Whoever it is, they want to parley with us."

"What if it's the Black Dogs?" Kenté cried. "It might be a trick."

"Look sharp," said Nereus. The muscles under his mermaid tattoo tightened as he gripped the rail. "And be ready to run."

The ship was a lovely three-masted bark with good lines. Her paint marked her as the *Antelope* of Iantiporos. Under the blue and gold of Kynthessa, she flew her own pennant. The wind had wrapped it around a rope, where it flapped halfheartedly. The bark was obviously a merchant ship, although four small cannons were mounted on her deck.

The breeze flipped the pennant over. I gasped.

A cask, crested by three stars.

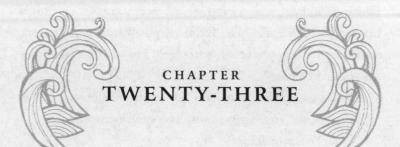

# CHAPTER
# TWENTY-THREE

I waited alone at the port rail as *Antelope*'s dinghy rowed across. I wasn't about to let the Bollards lay eyes on Daria until I was sure they could be trusted.

When I saw who sat in the boat, rowed by a lone crewman, I almost wished we'd run for it. She wore a drapey gold tunic under a short cape, fastened at the shoulder with a Bollard brooch. Sun glinted on her earrings as she stood, grasping the ladder we'd tossed over the side. Indeed only Ma could maintain such an air of detached authority while ascending a wobbly rope ladder.

"I suppose you have an explanation for how you managed to acquire a cutter of this expense and quality," she said, climbing over the rail. "Especially as it seems to me this one greatly resembles the ship I heard Diric Melanos was sailing recently."

Another girl might have embraced her mother. We eyed each other like wary cats circling.

"What are you doing all the way out here?" I blurted.

"As it happens, looking for you," she said. "I went to visit the Oracle in Iantiporos. She told me we'd meet you here." She tilted her head, studying me. "The Emparch was with you in Siscema, wasn't he? It's why you acted so strangely. He was the courier boy who came to dinner."

"No." I took a step backward. My mother had consulted an oracle about *me*? The expense must have been astronomical.

"Caro. You can tell me."

"I don't believe you," I whispered.

She smiled, showing all her white teeth. "I knew you wouldn't."

The crewman finished stowing the oars. I would have recognized him instantly if he hadn't been wearing a woolen cap pulled down low. I knew his every mannerism. I knew his broad shoulders and the strong grip of his suntanned hands as he climbed the rope ladder.

"Pa!" I flung myself at him the moment he cleared the rail.

"Caro! What's the meaning of this?" He released me, but kept a hold on my shoulders. "Where's Fee? Where's *Cormorant*?"

"I'm sorry." I didn't have the courage to watch his stricken face when he realized what I had done. "I'm so sorry." I buried myself in his jacket, finally letting the tears flow.

"Caro—" He lifted my chin. "Caro, d'you mean she's sunk? Where's Fee?"

"Oh!" I hiccupped. "Not sunk. I had to leave *Cormorant* in Casteria. The Black Dogs—I couldn't get back to her. And Fee jumped overboard to save us. I—don't know what happened to her."

"I never did sail with a crewman scrappier than Fee," Pa said, though his eyes remained troubled. "I wouldn't count her out."

"I for one would like to know about the cutter," Ma said. "And the Emparch."

Pa curled his arm protectively around my shoulders. "Will you just leave off for a minute? Can you not see she's upset?"

I knew he was distressed too. Fee had crewed with us for years. She and Pa were a team, and *Cormorant* was our home.

"Look here, Nick, I came all the way out here—"

"The Emparch isn't here," I said. They both turned as one. "Not anymore." My throat tightened. "Markos—the Emparch—he's dead."

"No, he's not." Ma shook her head. "The Black Dogs are trying to ransom him back to his relations in Valonikos."

She said something else, but I didn't hear.

"Oh," I said stupidly.

Markos. *Alive.* I couldn't let myself believe her. It wasn't as easy as that.

Ma and Pa went on talking, their voices an incomprehensible buzz. I put a hand to my forehead and tried to breathe.

Markos.

"Are you sure?" I finally managed, so much later that they both looked at me, confused. "The last time I saw him, he was fighting off ten pirates." I swallowed down tears. "He traded his own life for his sister's." The rest of the long story spilled out between choked sobs.

Pa pulled me against his rough wool coat. I closed my eyes,

relaxing into the familiar homey smell of his clothes. "I might've known you'd open that box," he said. "You're an Oresteia, all right."

"She is that," Ma muttered under her breath. "A Bollard has more sense."

I lifted my head. "But how do you know about—about Markos?"

"A courier came to our premises in Iantiporos with a letter. He'd ridden all night through that storm," Ma said. "The letter was to go via fast packet to Valonikos. It bore the name Diric Melanos. They might have put it on a ship straightaway and sent it on, had I not at that very moment walked into our offices."

"Let me see it."

She handed it over, and I skimmed the contents. It was as she said. Captain Melanos had sent a ransom note to Markos's relatives.

I lowered the letter. "But the Black Dogs tried to kill him."

"People like the Black Dogs sell themselves to the highest bidder." By the flare of her nostrils, it was easy to see what Ma thought of that. "A man like Melanos is thinking of Valonikos. Of how it's said that in the Free City, gold flows like the river. He wonders, what sort of family will shelter a deposed Emparch? And how much might they be willing to pay?"

"Konto Theucinian hired them to kill Markos," I said. "Won't he be mad when he finds out they didn't?"

"Likely greed clouds their judgment. Why get paid once when you can get paid twice?" Her mouth twisted. "I know Diric Melanos. That's what he'll be thinking."

"You know him?" This was something I hadn't heard before.

"We've met. I'll tell you this much, he'll be sorry he ever dared touch my daughter."

"Your *daughter*." Pa shook his head. "But you were willing to hand the boy right into those Theucinians' hands."

"I told you, nothing had been decided yet." Ma held her jaw stiffly. "We were only discussing our options. As it happens, the dice have fallen the other way. You can afford to have your high-and-mighty principles, Nick. I can't. Bollard Company must maintain our relationships—"

"With usurpers and murderers," Pa grumbled.

"Emparchs, kings, and Margravinas rise and fall, but trade goes on. The current carries us all. You know that. I can't take sides. This Emparch isn't one of ours."

"Yes, yes, because you're either a Bollard or you're nothing. Don't I know it." Pa rubbed the stubble on his chin. "Ayah, I know enough about *that* anyway."

I had a horrible thought. "What if this letter is a lie?" My voice wavered. "What if they only mean to cheat Markos's family?"

Ma rested her hand on my shoulder. "If it's a trap, we'll find out soon enough."

"What do you mean?"

"Like I said." The jewel in her nose twinkled as she smiled. "The dice have fallen the other way. We're going to rescue your Emparch."

I studied her face. As an accomplished negotiator, she could easily conceal a lie. But Pa seemed to trust her. "In that case," I said slowly, "there's someone you should meet."

Kenté, Nereus, and Daria emerged through the hatch.

"I have the honor of being Lady Daria Andela," the girl said in a small but formal voice. The ragged hem of her nightgown waved in the wind.

"Your Grace." Ma bowed.

"Andela?" I asked, surprised. "That's your name? Is that Markos's name too?" All at once I remembered the man who'd attacked us in the safe house in Siscema. *You have the Andela look about you, to be sure.*

"Whyever wouldn't it be?" Daria narrowed her eyes. "Are you saying you don't know his name?"

I felt a little sheepish. "He never said."

"If you don't even know a boy's name," she said with a saucy lift of her chin, "*I* think you haven't any business going around ki—"

"Shush," I said loudly over her, but Pa gave me a suspicious look anyhow.

Ma whistled at Kenté. "Well, your parents will certainly be happy to hear you're not murdered in a ditch somewhere. Whatever were you thinking, running off like that?" She spotted Nereus, and her voice changed. "Identify yourself at once, sir. For if you figured in my daughter's story, I do not recall it."

"You," Pa said hoarsely, the color draining from his face.

Nereus flashed him a grin. "Surely you didn't think she'd be left to fight alone."

"I—No." Pa glanced at me, then quickly away. He seemed troubled. "It's just—You ain't who I expected."

"The current carries us all as it will," Nereus said. "As your folk are wont to say. Ain't that right?"

I looked back and forth between them, bewildered. So *Pa* had been responsible for sending Nereus. But how—

Sudden understanding flooded through me. *The god at the bottom of the river.*

Somehow I knew that was the answer. It explained everything: how Nereus had mysteriously appeared on *Vix*, his secretive manner, and the cryptic references to being three hundred years old. Nereus had mentioned the Bollards, but thinking back, he'd never actually admitted he knew Ma.

"Pa—" I began, eager to hear the whole story.

Abruptly he shook his head, glancing sideways at my mother. "Not here. Not now."

To my annoyance, he refused to say anything further. Nereus volunteered to stay and guard *Vix* while Kenté, Daria, and I rowed across to the *Antelope*, which meant I was prevented from questioning him about it either. Not that he was capable of giving a straight answer.

We ate dinner in the comfort of the Bollard ship's well-appointed cabins, where Ma's cook had prepared pasta and clams in a delicate wine sauce. I practically shoveled it into my mouth.

Ma spread a chart on the captain's table, pinning it down with a brass paperweight engraved with the Bollard crest.

"That's it." I put my finger on the map. "Katabata Island."

"You're certain that's what they said?" Ma's eyes flickered up at me.

"Positive." I thought back to that night under the dock. "One of the Black Dogs said he voted to go back to Katabata."

"I know that island. There's an abandoned fort with a harbor due north—here." *Antelope*'s captain, a solid man with long side whiskers, spoke. "Likely that's where they're holed up. It's only a few hours' sail from here. We could come upon them in the dark. Surprise them."

"No," I said, and they all looked at me. "The shadowman, remember?"

Ma twisted one corner of her mouth, watching me with speculation. I suppose she wasn't used to me speaking up. "We'll attack at sunup, then."

Kenté froze with a forkful of pasta halfway to her lips. She gave an almost unreadable shake of her head.

"Dawn might be cutting it too close," I said. "Noon is when he'll be weakest. The brightest part of the day." At my mother's curious look, I added, "Markos told me lots about shadowmen."

Markos. It was strange, daring to hope. For the first time, I started to believe I really might see him again.

It was after sundown when we rowed back to *Vix*. Kenté stared out into the dark, her arm around Daria, whose head kept nodding. I pulled my right oar to turn the dinghy toward *Vix*'s lantern. Just two days ago we'd been on the run from that cutter, but tomorrow I would be sailing her into battle. Restless anticipation danced in my stomach.

As I rowed under *Antelope*'s high stern, voices stilled my oars. Lamplight spilled out between the curtains on the windows many feet above us. I held my breath.

"You can't really be meaning to let her keep that ship."

"It's her choice, Tamaré," Pa said. "She were given a letter of marque from the Margravina. She's authorized to capture a prize."

"She's not of age."

"A letter of marque is a letter of marque." I listened to the familiar rise and fall of Pa's voice. Strange that I'd spent so many days wondering if I would ever see him again. "It's her ship. Nereus'll help her with the sailing."

In the excitement of the battle plans, I'd forgotten Pa's enigmatic exchange with Nereus. *You ain't who I expected.* Desperate for answers, I strained to hear more.

"Of course you won't tell me where you know him from." Ma sighed. "Oh, go on with you. You'll do as you please, just as you always have." A wistful note crept under the stubbornness in her voice. "I know I gave you the keeping of her, but she's still my daughter."

"Of course I know that," he murmured. "You come to bed now, sweet girl."

I rowed hastily away from the window, because, really, who wants to hear *that*?

After settling Daria in her bunk, I found Kenté sitting cross-legged on the forward hatch cover. I might have missed her in the dark, had she not been muttering out loud at a necklace. I recognized it from the chest in the cargo hold, which she'd been poking around earlier today while I sailed. Around her feet were strewn several other pendants and lockets. At least one was broken.

"What are you doing?"

"Trying to put a little piece of night into this locket." She flung aside the bauble, wiping her sweaty forehead. "What does it look like I'm doing?"

I deliberately didn't answer that question, because it looked like she was talking to an inanimate object.

"Kenté, why don't you just tell your parents you want to go to the Academy in Trikkaia?"

"They say I'm their last and only hope." She sighed. "You know how upset they were about Toby." Kenté's brother was a professor of mathematics, which wasn't a very Bollard thing to be.

"I wonder if you're afraid—" I halted. "I didn't mean afraid."

"Of course I am. Caro—" She bit her lip, turning the locket over in her hands. "Do you think I'm doing the right thing? This magic . . . it's all about darkness and trickery." Somehow I knew she was thinking of Cleandros, who had betrayed his Emparch. "Perhaps it's something we're not meant to play with."

I remembered what Markos had said the night we met. "I think it's what's in a person's heart that makes them evil. Magic is just a skill. A tool."

She nodded, though she didn't look quite convinced. "This is going to sound stupid, but . . . I'm scared to leave home. Because if I'm not this"—she fingered the brooch that pinned her woolen wrap, which was stamped with the cask and stars—"then who am I? If I'm not this, who might I become?"

I didn't have an answer for that. Leaving her to her experimentation, I wandered up the deck. The sky seemed bigger out here, like a blanket draped over us. The night sounds of *Vix*—creaking planks, sloshing waves, the taut twang of rope—were achingly similar to *Cormorant*'s, yet there was an emptiness I could not place at first. Then I realized. There were no frogs or crickets. No sounds of small things.

I leaned my elbows on the rail. Beneath me the still black water stirred.

An eyelid popped open.

I stumbled back. The eye was the size of my head. It shone in the lantern light, inches below the water. Something was down there, under the cutter.

Something big. Something *alive*.

"Ayah, you noticed, did you?" Nereus sat on a barrel, the lit end of his pipe glowing orange. "She's been following you for days."

He couldn't mean this was the very same drakon that had kept pace with *Vix* in the dark of night, during the storm—could he? Then I remembered that day on the Hanu River, when Fee had hissed at something in the water. "*Her*," Fee had said over and over.

"Why would a drakon follow me?" My mouth was dry.

"Ah," he said. "You are used to the river. The sea be deeper. Darker. Full of secrets. The sea, she keeps the things she takes. The deeps be littered with the bones of ships and cities. Ayah, and men. Know you the tale of Arisbe Andela?"

"Amassia That Was Lost." The story Markos and I had spoken of. It seemed hard to believe that was only three days ago. Then something else struck me. "Arisbe *Andela*?"

"Ayah, that were her name."

"That's funny," I said. "It's Markos and Daria's name too." So Markos had been telling the truth when he said the legend was based on the history of his ancestors. How odd to think of Markos, of all people, being descended from a pirate princess.

Nereus tapped his pipe. "Arisbe had a brother called Nemros."

"The Marauder. Pa used to tell me that one too. The most fearsome pirate ever to sail the Inner Sea."

"Ayah, that's the fellow. Old Nemros, now, there were three things he loved. Sailing, and the fire of battle."

"That's two things," I said.

"Don't interrupt. The third was . . ." Something in his voice called to mind lazy summer afternoons, long past. "Fun," he said finally. "The dance of the fiddle. The taste of wine and rum and women." He puffed his pipe. "On that fateful last day, the sea god told Nemros she meant to take her revenge. He heeded her warning and took to his ship, where he rode out the storm. When the sun broke through the clouds on the third morning, no sign of his family's island was to be seen. No white towers. No pear trees. The sea had swallowed Amassia. Now what was he to do? For he were a man without a country. So Nemros, he went to her."

"Who?"

"Why, she who lies beneath. Who else?" Resting his pipe on his knee, he continued. "But the ocean were a fast one, she were, for she offered him a bargain. 'Take your sister's place,' she said. 'Serve me as she should have, and I shall make you the scourge of these seas. I shall give you a ship faster than the wind itself, and greater wealth in gold than you can possibly imagine. Serve me unto death, ayah, and beyond. Then and only then shall you have your family's city back.'"

"But Amassia is lost," I said. "It sank under the ocean. No one ever saw it again."

"Ah, I told you she were a fast one." He waggled his finger at me. "She didn't say *when*, now did she? The pirate Nemros became her servant. He sank ships and sacked cities on her command. And, oh yes, he became rich and famous beyond his wildest dreams." He paused. "But he never again was free. He never again had a home."

"I don't get it. What does any of that have to do with the drakon?"

"Nothing." He laughed, while I struggled to resist the temptation to knock him off the gods-bedamned barrel. "But there are some sailormen who say the drakon is nothing more or less than your fate coming for you."

There was one more thing I had to say. "Nereus." I hesitated. "You said he served her beyond death. Do you mean—"

He raised his hand to cut me off. "Speak no more, love. For I won't answer."

I wondered if that wasn't answer enough.

# CHAPTER
# TWENTY-FOUR

I stood on *Antelope*'s deck, squinting into the rising sun. Above me a square sail unrolled, and the second mate bellowed out orders, as sailors scurried to make fast the ropes. A man lugging a cart full of cannonballs pushed past me, jogging my elbow.

"What do you mean, we're not to fight?" I demanded.

"Caro, be reasonable," Ma said. "Remember, you said yourself it may be a trap. They want Daria and they want their cutter back." With her implacable face, she had never resembled a classical bronze statue more. "And I daresay they are not so enamored of you after all this."

"Pa—"

He dug his hands into his pockets. "Maybe it's best we do as your mother says. I know you can fight, but we must think of the girl."

I looked across at *Vix*, lit up by the morning glare on the water. As Nereus hauled on the halyard, her gaff climbed to the peak. She wanted battle. It was what she was built for. She pulled at her moorings like a horse rearing against the reins.

"*Vix* is faster than *Antelope*," I said. "She has more guns."

"She is also smaller," Ma said. "And you're not an experienced captain."

She and Pa shared a glance, while I bit back my frustration. Of all times, they chose *now* to be in accord. Further attempts to get my way by playing them off each other were easily routed. I rowed splashily back to *Vix*, cursing under my breath.

As Nereus gave me a hand up from the rope ladder, Kenté hopped off the hatch cover. "What's wrong?" she cried. I must've looked particularly murderous.

"We're not going to be in the fight," I spat out. "Six four-pounders, we have. That's two more than *Antelope*. Gods *damn* me." I paced the deck. "I mean, who do they think's been fighting the Black Dogs this whole time? They don't even know Markos." Kenté opened her mouth, no doubt to point out that Ma had met him in Siscema. "It's *different*. You know it's different."

"An unfortunate turn of circumstance." Nereus stared at the horizon. "For has she not canvas and powder and shot? Is she not built to blow holes in any ship that dare oppose her, and the gods damn them for trying?" He inhaled the salty air. "This is a day for battle."

He understood. I wanted to crash through the waves, swift as the wind itself. I wanted to ram shot into the cannons and watch that cursed *Alektor* explode in splinters.

"We're to sail around behind the island and wait at a rendez-vous point for *Antelope*," I said. "Ma will send up three bursts on the gun." I curled my hands into fists. "When it's *safe*."

I knew nothing of safe anymore.

Just before noon we reached the island. I anchored *Vix* off the wooded shore, while *Antelope* sailed around to launch her attack on the Black Dogs' fort. Absently I picked at my lip as I listened to the distant rumble of cannons and the occasional crack of a musket echoing across the water.

"And five makes eleven." Kenté surveyed the dice on the deck. "I've won again."

We had only been playing an hour, and I'd already lost two silver talents to her and one to Daria, who sat cross-legged beside Nereus. Her black hair hung in two complicated braids down her back. I suspected she liked both of them more than me, Kenté because she could plait hair and Nereus because he let her do whatever she wanted. I didn't mind. All I cared about right now was the battle. And Markos.

How could they game while the cannons boomed? I was too jumpy to sit. My lip began to bleed, the rusty metal taste only setting me more on edge.

"The water's so choppy." Kenté glanced over her shoulder. "It's making me nervous. It doesn't *look* like a storm's coming. The sky is perfectly clear."

The waves did look rough. I wondered if the drakon was weaving back and forth beneath them, her undulating body churning the water. Though I didn't see her, I sensed she was close.

I leaped to my feet. "I can't bear it." Gripping the handles of my twin pistols, I strode up and down. "What's taking so long?"

Just because I was angry at my parents didn't mean I wanted anything to happen to them. The shoreline was maddeningly still. If the Black Dogs had scouts lurking in the trees, I couldn't see them, for the island was heavily wooded. Anyhow, there was nowhere from which to launch a boat—this side of Katabata Island was a wall of rocks ten feet high, sloping straight into the ocean.

A gun rolled like thunder, causing my shoulders to jump.

"You need to find something to occupy yourself." Kenté shook the dice cup. I noticed she wore three lockets of varying lengths around her neck.

Pulling out both pistols, I decided to teach myself how to spin them, the way I'd seen rough men do to show off in taverns. I flipped the right one around on my thumb, and it dropped to the deck with a clatter.

Kenté winced. "Something *else*."

I fumbled, dropping the pistol again. That's when I realized. "The guns have stopped."

Ten minutes went by. Then twenty. Then an hour. And then I knew.

*Antelope* wasn't coming.

I made my choice. "Run up the main and the staysail. Run out the guns." I was fairly sure that was something people said.

"Best be cautious," Nereus warned as he tied off the halyards. I wondered if he knew something we didn't.

"All I care about right now is whether you know how to load those cannons!" I snapped.

He grinned, showing the gap in his teeth. "Ayah, I know."

We sailed around the corner of the island. Kenté gasped.

*Hespera's Watch*, was all I could think, because that's what it looked like: smoke and fire and barrels bobbing on the water. Both *Alektor* and *Antelope* listed far over on their sides, and wreckage was scattered everywhere. *Alektor* had a gaping hole in her hull.

Myself, I had a gaping hole in my heart.

We sailed closer. The Black Dogs' fort squatted on a rocky hill above the harbor, surrounded by a wall of spiky logs. The left side was partially collapsed, but not from today's fight, for tangled vines grew over it. A stone tower rose up on the other side, once perhaps a lighthouse or a watchtower. Sunlight reflected off a cannon at the top, but no one seemed to be manning it—and no wonder, because the tower didn't look very stable. Part of it lay in a steaming pile.

Daria curled into Kenté's skirts. I let go of the tiller and drifted to the rail, everything but my parents forgotten. I squinted at the floating hulk of the Bollard ship. Her ragged sails trailed in the water and flames licked up her hull.

Not a single person, alive or dead, was in sight.

"We should have been in that fight!" My voice broke. "The Black Dogs didn't have a ship that could touch *Vix*."

"Didn't need one." Nereus nodded at the fort. "Artillery on that tower. That be a thirty-six pounder. And mark the long nines on the palisade."

"They can't have killed everybody!"

"I think not." He pointed to the smoking wreckage. "The boats. Look."

All of *Antelope*'s boats had been launched, and *Alektor*'s too. But I saw none among the bobbing flotsam, nor any pieces of them. No planks. No oars.

I swallowed. "What does it mean?"

Nereus spat over the rail. "Nothing good. Likely they been taken prisoner. Inside the fort."

"It could be the other way around," I suggested. "Perhaps the Bollards took the men from *Alektor* prisoner. Perhaps they rowed ashore of their own accord to attack the fort from on land."

"Hear you the sounds of fighting?"

We all fell silent. I heard the slap of waves against wood. The crackle of fire. The wind rustling the trees. "No," I whispered, and with that word went my hopes.

"We best come about." Nereus turned away from the smoking ships.

"And just leave them?"

"*Alektor* didn't sink that bark. The guns on the fort did. You want to sit here in their range? That's begging for death."

"I don't care! We have to try." Everything that mattered was on that island. We were so close. I pressed my fingers to my temples to calm the shaking inside me.

"Sail!" a small voice cried. Daria scrambled onto the foot of the mast. "Look, there's a sail!"

The new vessel was sleek, with white canvas billowing before her one mast and cannons glinting shiny black in the sun. At this distance I could not read her name, but I knew her. She was the sloop *Conthar*.

The wherrymen were here.

"Quick!" I screamed. "Before they fire!"

Kenté stopped waving her arms. "Why would they fire?"

"They're here for *Vix*, remember? Run down below and get a white flag. If you can't find one, a bedsheet, as fast as you ever can."

I ran the sheet up to the crosstrees of the mast and waited, squeezing the rail so hard my bones ached.

As *Conthar* drew closer, Thisbe Brixton's voice rang clear across the water. "Hold! I said hold your fire, you cursed mangy lot! That's Oresteia's girl."

After we retreated south of the island, *Conthar* sent two boats across, and we met at *Vix*'s long table for a war council. It was strange to see all those wherrymen crammed into the belly of the cutter, after two days with just the four of us. The cabin smelled of mud and pipe smoke. My throat swelled, for that only made me miss Pa more.

They weren't all men. Three of them were frogmen and four were women. I knew Thisbe Brixton, and the sharp-nosed woman beside her had to be her first mate. They looked like the only fighters among the women. The others were wherrymen's wives, I supposed, left homeless in the attack at Hespera's Watch.

"Wait a minute," a man with long yellow hair said, after I explained the circumstances that had led us here. "I come to sink this ship. I come for that alone. Well?" He turned to the others. "Oresteia's daughter has this cutter, and half of those Black Dogs must surely be dead." He gave me a speculative look. "Though it do seem to me that a slip of a girl got no use for a smuggling cutter."

"D'you want to see the letter of marque?" I pulled it out of my waistcoat, tossing it on the table.

"Go back to Siscema," he told me. "Gather a ransom offer. If they're alive, the Bollards will surely pay."

"Nicandros Oresteia is in there too, or are you forgetting he's one of you?" I snapped.

"We belong to the river. I don't like it out here." He looked at Captain Krantor. "*You* know what I be speaking of. I say Nick Oresteia made his choice twenty years ago when he went and got mixed up with that woman. Them Bollards ain't like us." He spat on the floor. I bristled at that, but surely the Black Dogs had left worse on *Vix*'s planks. "Let them rescue him. Myself, I don't want no part in this."

I put my hand on my pistol. I didn't always see eye to eye with the Bollards, but I wasn't going to let them be insulted by the likes of *him*.

He leaned back in his chair. "The girl don't look like Nick. For that matter, how do we even be knowing she's his?"

I lunged across the table and struck him in the face with my gun. Blood burst out of his nose, spraying everywhere. My rage pounded in my ears. Outside a wave slammed angrily against the porthole, water sluicing down the glass. Dimly I felt Nereus and Captain Krantor grab my arms and haul me back.

Thisbe Brixton laughed. "Oh, I don't know, Dinos. She seems plenty like Nick to me, don't she?"

The yellow-haired wherryman pinched his nose, muttering a steady stream of curse words.

Perry Krantor stood, and the wherrymen fell into a respectful hush.

"I don't care about Akhaia's succession," he said. "The river, he run through Akhaia and Kynthessa and he don't much care who rules the land. And nor do I, for I belong to the river."

Every eye in the room was on him. I held my breath. "But I don't like that this new Emparch sends the Black Dogs to burn our boats." He gestured at the crushed parchment. "I don't like this business with the letter of marque. It was blackmail from the start."

The old man stroked his beard. "I reckon we're already in this, like it or not. I don't go with Caro because I care which man becomes Emparch of Akhaia. I go for Nick." He nodded at me, and my eyes suddenly swelled with tears. "And for my *Jolly Girl.*"

"All well and good for you," muttered another man. "But I have a family. Those Dogs bested the Bollard ship. You want to take that fort with a couple of kids, that's your right, Krantor. I vote we go home."

Thisbe Brixton folded her arms behind her head, her long braid winding down from under a knit cap. "Don't go lumping the rest of us in with you, Hathor. You wouldn't know a fight if it bit you in the ass." She winked at me. "I'll take my chances with these girls. Nick was my friend when plenty of you thought a woman got no call to captain a wherry. *I* remember my friends."

Everyone began to shout at once. My heart sank. It had been a lovely speech, but it hadn't been enough. Pa was in that fort. Each minute we wasted out here, they might be hurting him or Ma. They might change their minds and decide to kill Markos.

There must be something I could say to get through to the wherrymen. Something to make them listen.

I sucked in a breath, remembering the old man from the toll boat, back at Gallos Bridge. How he'd shown me the pistol in his overcoat. *We looks after our own.* And then I had it.

"Hey!" I yelled. They kept arguing. "Hey!"

I whipped my Akhaian dagger through the air. It stuck, wobbling, in the center of the table. That got their attention. I climbed onto a chair.

"I have something to say to the wherrymen. And women," I called out, catching Captain Brixton's eye. "I be Caroline Oresteia, mate of *Cormorant* and now captain of *Victorianos.*" The words felt strange in my mouth, and yet they were true. I fixed my eyes on the yellow-haired wherryman. "And anyone who thinks otherwise may try to take her if he likes.

"I had many opportunities to speak to Markos Andela," I went on, "him who would be rightful Emparch of Akhaia, before he were taken by the Black Dogs." I had lapsed into riverfolk cant. I thought Pa would have approved. "He regretted that folk died on his account, but he wanted to make restitution. He meant to repay everyone who lost property at Hespera's Watch.

"Markos is a good man," I said, daring to feel a trickle of hope. They were listening. "And my pa is a good man. I ain't asking for you to do any more than he would do for you. And oh yes, he would! Didn't he bail you out of the lockup that time, Hathor?" I spotted another man in the crowd. "And weren't he the one who helped you scrape and paint *Daisy?* And of course I need not mention that Oresteias and Krantors been running together since the days of the blockades. We looks after our own. I'm going to save my pa, on *Vix*," I announced, "and anyone who wishes may sail with me."

"Ayah!" *Daisy*'s captain shouted. "We may not be fighters, armed to the teeth with muskets and cannons, but we be free wherrymen. Let's let those Dogs know we won't be burned out!"

"Speak for yourselves." I raised my voice over the clamor. "*Vix* has enough guns for the lot of you, and we don't mind sharing 'em."

With the cheer that followed, I knew I'd won.

"Captain Krantor," I called, rummaging in my pocket. I pulled out the key to the cargo hold and tossed it over the crew's heads. "Open up the hold, if you please."

The old man caught it, throwing me a teasing salute. "Ayah, Oresteia."

As the wherrymen distributed and loaded the muskets, Captain Brixton beckoned me over. "Who is that?" She nodded at Nereus.

"His name is Nereus." I wasn't sure what to say. "We . . . met him in Casteria."

"Hmm." She watched him over the top of her pocket flask. "That one has the look about him, to be sure. Someone's finger on him."

"You mean the god?" I asked. She'd just confirmed my suspicions.

"Sure, and doesn't a fish know when a shark comes to eat him?"

Sometimes I hated the gods. Certainly everyone associated

with them talked in circles in a way I found most irritating. "So he's a shark?"

"Is that what I said?" She grinned. "Pay me no mind."

Nereus joined us, leaning on the table. He inclined his head toward Thisbe Brixton. "Cousin," he said respectfully.

"Are you related?" I asked.

They exchanged amused glances, while I thought some more murderous thoughts about the gods.

"There's something about this island," Nereus mused, examining the chart spread on *Vix*'s table. "Almost, it seems familiar to me. I remember . . . that fort. Only it weren't so run-down then." He shook his head. "I don't know."

I leaned forward on my elbows. "Do you remember what you were doing? When you came to the island?"

"I . . ." Eyebrows furrowed, he traced the kidney-shaped island on the chart. "I were running rum. Yes. Long ago, time out of mind. But back then, they called it—"

"What?" Thisbe asked sharply.

"Never mind that," he said, eyes sparkling. "Jogged my memory, you have. Listen. In my day, there was a secret harbor on the east side of the island." He pressed his finger on a symbol. "Here."

I looked at it skeptically. "That's the marking for rocks."

"Looks like it, don't it? That's the brilliant thing about it. There's a spot, a deep spot, where a captain might slip between those rocks and anchor in a safe hidden cove." He grinned. "If he or she knew the place."

"Do you?" Kenté asked. "Know the place?"

He winked. "What do you say? Want to rescue an Emparch?"

As Nereus steered *Vix* toward his hidden harbor, I readied myself for battle. Beside me, Thisbe Brixton rammed shot down the flower-engraved gun I'd so admired, while I loaded my own dueling pistols.

"How did you come to be here anyway?" I asked her.

"Our tale is short enough." She set the pistol on the table, uncorking her flask. "We hunted up the Kars for those Black Dogs, only to hear we missed 'em by three days. So we makes to turn around and go back south. The god in the river were with us, sure enough, for just as we rounded into Siscema, we come upon a Bollard ship. The captain said she'd seen your pa. And surprised we were too, for the last we seen of him were in the lockup in Hespera's Watch."

She took a swallow. "So I ask where Nick is. 'Gone down the coast chasing after them Black Dogs,' says she. 'Black Dogs!' says I. 'For ain't that who we been following this whole time?' Half a day out from Iantiporos, one of our frogmen spotted your sails. And so here we are."

"Is it true, what you said?" I asked. "About folk being down on you for owning your own wherry? My great-grandma captained our wherry."

"I expect she sailed with her husband as first mate, or her son. I got no men on my crew, see." She grinned at her shipmate. "Ayah, and what use have I for men?"

My cheeks burned. I hadn't known that, though it made sense.

"You aren't to take any notice of Dinos. He's a stupid man if all he can see is . . . Well." She tapped the table. "You got your pa's eyes and his reddish hair. And what's more, you got the look of your grandma Oresteia around your face. You won't be remembering her, but I knew her when I were a girl. She were a Callinikos of Gallos before she married, and you don't get more riverlands than that."

"Oh, I wasn't upset about what he said," I lied. "I just didn't like the way his face looked." After we finished laughing, I added, "But thank you."

Folding a gold scarf into a headband, I tied it around my hair. Daria hugged her knees, alternately watching me and staring at the frogmen as if they might bite. Over my waistcoat and shirt I strapped a leather chestplate and gauntlets, tightening the buckle to the smallest hole.

Kenté sat quietly, rolling her lockets between her fingertips.

I set a hand on her shoulder. "What is it?"

"Just worried," she said. "What if something goes wrong?"

"It won't."

Thisbe Brixton's mate stopped sharpening her cutlass and looked up at me. "The gods do be in the habit of testing folk who say things like that."

The god at the bottom of the river was supposed to be the god of my ancestors. He was supposed to speak to us in the language of small things. Well, I was tired of waiting around for him to notice me. I'd been waiting my whole life.

Maybe I was done with gods. Maybe from here on out, I was helping myself.

I slammed my dagger into its sheath. "Let them do their worst."

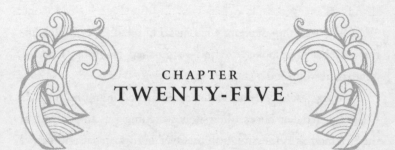

# CHAPTER
# TWENTY-FIVE

Thisbe Brixton wriggled forward on her elbows. "I count three men."

I peered through the thick underbrush, the dampness of the earth seeping into my knees. Captain Brixton gave me a nod, and we slithered back to the wherrymen, who crouched in the forest.

"Reckon there's no better time than now." Nereus leaned against a tree trunk, arms crossed. "They'll be taking a breather after that fight. If we be lucky, they're getting into the drink. They won't expect us."

I drew a deep breath. "Right. We'll take the back door, but no one go any farther." Looking at my cousin, I said, "Kenté is our scout."

The wherryman called Dinos gave me a sour glance. "Ayah?

And what makes you think that bit of skirt will be any use?" I knew he thought I was a piece of skirt too. He just didn't want to say it to my face because I was very well armed.

Kenté turned. "The fact that I can become invisible at will?"

"That 'bit of skirt' is a shadowman." I matched his rude tone. "Who do you think defeated the Black Dogs at Casteria and captured their cutter?"

Kenté swallowed a laugh at that outright falsehood.

"Current carry us," one of the men whispered.

Using the dense trees as cover, we crept closer to the fort. It wasn't nearly as impressive from this side. Plants grew in the cracks between stones, and the roof was thick with moss and weeds, with many shingles missing.

Either the Black Dogs didn't know their island could be taken from the southeast or they thought no one else knew. Armed with muskets from *Vix*'s hold, the wherrymen made quick work of the guards at the back door. On a table near their crumpled bodies, a deck of cards lay fanned out between stacks of trinkets and silver coins. Broken bottles littered the ground.

My gaze lingered on the dead men. Perhaps they had friends or family who would be watching the horizon, waiting for them to come home. I tightened my hands on my guns, hardening my heart.

Inside the fort, a lone man stood at the end of the torch-lit corridor. Kenté's fingers moved at her throat, and she disappeared, right in the middle of the afternoon. One of the wherrymen let out a choked gasp.

"Do not fight," Kenté's voice sang out, echoing off the stone walls. "For I am an untrained shadowman. I shall do something stupid and most likely explosive if you lay hands on me. Put down your weapons." She reappeared, pistol pressed to the pirate's temple. "Please."

The man immediately dropped his gun.

I rolled my eyes. "Please?"

The Black Dogs' headquarters was a mess. Never had I seen so many fine things dashed about in careless disarray: a golden goblet rolled into a corner and forgotten, a jeweled collar flung lopsided around the neck of a bottle of ale. I silently judged Captain Diric Melanos and his men for leaving their plunder scattered all over like that.

"Well done," I whispered to Kenté. "I didn't know if the necklace would work."

"And after you made that outrageous speech about how I defeated the Black Dogs and stole their ship! I see you have little faith in me."

"Seems to me I have a lot of faith," I muttered. "Since I made that speech in the first place."

"I knew it would work." She twirled a locket on its chain. "I tested them last night."

"Someone who doesn't want the Bollards to know her secret ought to avoid doing show-offy things like playing with magic right on the deck where anyone might see."

She put on an innocent look. "The sailor standing watch on *Antelope* fell asleep."

I shook my head. "You *better* not do that to me."

The sound of men's voices ahead made Thisbe Brixton signal for quiet. Presently we came upon the source of the noise—a great round chamber one level below us. Perhaps it had once been a formal dining room, for at one end was a raised dais. Flattening myself against the staircase wall, I glimpsed Ma and Pa sitting on the floor with *Antelope*'s crew. A wave of relief made my insides weak. But we weren't out of this yet. The prisoners were surrounded by Black Dogs.

"There's twenty men down there," Dinos whispered.

"More like forty." Thisbe cuffed him on the back of the head. "Can't you count?"

Captain Krantor jerked his pistol toward the stairs. "Saw you the Emparch?"

"He's not there," I whispered, nerves causing my pulse to hammer hot.

"Likely they got him locked up by himself," he said. "Leave this lot to us. You go find him." He turned to Nereus. "Reckon you're a man who'd be good in a fight. You with us or what?"

Nereus's fingers twitched on his knife. "I go with the girl." His nostrils flared, as if he could somehow smell battle.

"Figured as much," the old man said, wiping sweat from his sun-spotted forehead. "Now. We surround 'em on all sides. Once I'm in position, I'll sing out a signal. You lot sing back. Ready?"

Kenté eyed the arched ceiling of the great room, tugging her necklaces from under her dress. "I'm going to need two for this."

I held my breath. But it wasn't like what had happened when

she tried the same trick in Casteria. The great room went dark, as if a giant hand in a black glove had snuffed out the lanterns. More than that, Kenté's magic blotted the light from the windows and doors. The wherrymen crept in one by one, feeling their way down the curved staircase.

"Strike a match, you Dogs!" I thought that was Diric Melanos.

"It's not working!" one of his crew yelped in panic.

"Loooooooow bridge!" a voice boomed from across the room. It was Perry Krantor, calling out as the wherrymen do when they come to a bridge on the river.

"What was that?" The Black Dogs fell into a hush. I heard the ring of steel and the rustle of clothing as they drew their weapons.

Other voices called out in answer. "Low bridge!" The voices seemed to come from all around the room, echoing off the stone walls. "Loooow-ow-ow-ow." A shiver ran through me. It was an eerie sound.

"It's that shadowman!" someone yelled.

"No, it's the shades of them wherrymen come to haunt us," one of the Black Dogs cried. "Told you, I did! We shouldn't have done it."

I smiled. No—they shouldn't have.

A man began to pray out loud, while another fired a pistol. Several men commenced to yell at the one who had shot the gun.

Over the clamor I heard a familiar laugh. "That you, Perry?" It was Pa, who knew no one else from here to Ndanna would choose that for a war cry. No one except wherrymen.

"Ayah. How be you, Nick?"

"Well enough," Pa said, "once you put a pistol in my hand."

Kenté's fingers moved and the darkness whisked up, like a blanket being shaken out. It hit the ceiling and burst. All the little pieces of it flew into the nooks and crannies of the room.

And then the fight began.

One of the wherrymen tossed Pa a pistol and a bag of shot. He caught it. Lifting his eyes to the top of the stairs, he saw me. A long moment passed between us. He raised his hand in a salute, loaded the pistol, and jumped into the fight.

Hesitant as I was to abandon my parents, the wherrymen's attack was a spectacular diversion. I nodded to Nereus and Kenté, and we slipped down the corridor. As we hurried deeper into the fort, the smells of smoke and sea lay thick on the air. None of us spoke. My concern for Markos sat on my chest like a heavy stone.

From an open door on the right side of the hall came the clinking of glass. Nereus ducked into the room, and I heard a cry, followed by an unpleasant crunch.

Nereus held the Black Dog's arm twisted at an unnatural angle behind his back. A puddle of spilled ale seeped into the carpet. It was *Alektor*'s captain, Philemon, though his lip was bloodied. He wore a long gilt-trimmed coat, which I recognized at once as the jacket I had so admired on Markos.

"One silver talent," Nereus drawled, running the edge of his knife down Philemon's neck, "if you tell me where the Emparch's being held."

"Are you joking?" the man spat.

Nereus laughed. "'Course I'm joking. Tell me, and you might not get my knife through your eye. Can't make promises though."

"I—I don't know about any Emparch," he stammered.

"Liar!" My heart pounded a frantic beat. "You're wearing his coat." And he looked awful in it, with his arms stuffed into the sleeves like sausages. He was broader and shorter than Markos. "If you hurt him, I swear I'll kill you."

"He killed six of our men!" Philemon struggled in Nereus's hold. "Good, able-bodied seamen, they was. You're gods-damned right I hurt him!"

"Where is he?" I pressed my pistol into his neck.

"Perhaps we took his fingers off. An Emparch don't need fingers, do he?"

I schooled my face into stillness, refusing to let him know how his words upset me.

The blood in Philemon's mouth gurgled as he laughed. "Perhaps I cut his eyes out and gave them to the gulls to feast on. Guess he ain't so pretty now."

Nereus dug the blade into his cheek. "Shut up, you. The Emparch. Now."

Philemon glared, blood trickling down into his beard. Then he nodded toward the end of the corridor. "The tower," he growled. "But you're too late. It collapsed, and the stairs is broken. Whole bloody thing's coming down." He leered at me, showing a chipped tooth. "All you'll find down there is a corpse, girl!"

I swallowed down my rage. They had left him in there to die.

"I'll go with you," Kenté said.

"You heard him." I loaded my pistol. "It's not safe. Ma'll murder me if anything happens to you."

"Oh, and she won't mind at all if something happens to *you*."

I laid a hand on her sleeve. "Stay with Nereus and keep an eye on this fellow in case he's lying. I'll be right back."

She squeezed my arm in return. "Current carry you."

The ruined tower creaked and trembled. Somewhere tiny crumbs of mortar and stone trickled down the wall, and the air was thick with dust. Stepping cautiously through the door, I tested the first stair. It didn't seem like it was about to drop out from under me.

Bracing myself on the wall, I took the curved staircase one step at a time. The ghostly moan of metal made me squeeze my eyes shut. My pistol shook in my hand. The staircase descended much farther than I had thought possible. Surely I'd gone right down into the hill itself by now.

Something fell with a tremendous crash, causing the whole tower to quake. My legs went out from under me. For a long terrifying minute I huddled on the steps, clinging to the stone. I bit back a whimper. Markos was down there. He might be trapped under a fallen stone. He might be hurt. I forced myself to go on.

The stairs ended in a fifteen-foot drop into darkness. I gasped, scrambling back to safe ground. My heart raced as I flattened myself against the wall. I'd almost gone over.

The room below was not totally dark. A flicker of lamplight dimly illuminated the pit. I leaned over the edge, cold sweat prickling my neck.

Sitting in an inch-deep puddle of water was a chair. And tied to it with many thick turns of rope was the one person I'd never expected to see alive again.

"Markos!"

He squinted up at me. "Caro?"

His left eye was blackened, and a cut on his chin had spilled a thick trail of blood down his shirt. Other than that, except for his hair looking greasy, he seemed more or less unharmed. I was so relieved to see him that all I could do was grin helplessly.

He grinned back, which looked truly gruesome what with the state of his face. "Nice hat."

A moth-eaten tapestry hung on the tower wall. Unwinding a length of heavy brocade from the rod, I gripped it in both hands, took a deep breath, and swung. Halfway down, the tapestry tore and I fell the last few feet, landing with a splash.

Markos twisted against the ropes. "I heard the cannons outside and hoped it might be you. Where's Daria?"

"You mustn't think much of me, if you think I'd bring your sister into a place like this." I sliced through his bindings, careful to hold the dagger well away from his wrists. "She's safe on the ship."

He winced, sucking in a breath.

"What's wrong?" I cried in alarm. "I didn't cut you?"

"My hands," he managed. "I can't feel them."

I knelt before him, pressing his hands between mine. They were limp and cold. I slapped and chafed the skin until he gasped in pain.

"Gods." He rocked forward. "It's just pins and needles, but it hurts like a . . . Well, I can't say that in the presence of a lady."

"You don't mean you're counting *me* as a lady."

I was suddenly too aware of his breath on my hair. The last time we were together, I'd kissed him as if I was never going to see him again. Well, that was cursed awkward now. I dropped his hands and scrambled back.

He got slowly to his feet, stretching each leg in turn. I inhaled sharply. The crusted blood on his shirt wasn't from his chin. His left ear was a scabbed mess. It was the one, I queasily realized, where he'd worn the garnet earring. That jewel was missing.

He saw me looking. "Yes, well, I would say you should see the other fellow, but unfortunately I admit I got the worst of it."

"It was ten to one!" My hand hovered near his ear.

"More like twenty, once the men from *Alektor* arrived. Please don't touch it." He swatted me away. "It's finally stopped bleeding. I'd like to keep it that way. Who's out there firing cannons? When the tower got hit the first time, that's when the stones started to fall. The Black Dogs all ran out and never came back."

"It was the Bollards. Wait, the *first?*" Concerned, I asked, "How many times did they hit this tower?"

"I counted three. You brought the Bollards? You didn't even know I was alive." His left knee buckled and he clutched his side, as if he had a cramp. "Ow!"

"The Black Dogs tried to swindle the Theucinians." I offered him my arm. "They want to ransom you back to your family in Valonikos, or maybe they were just going to collect the money and then kill you. Only they hired a Bollard ship as courier, so Ma found out about it."

I gave him the brief version of what had befallen us since we parted, secretly enjoying the warmth of his body as he leaned on me for support.

"How typical," he said when I was finished. "You were stealing pirate ships and having adventures while I was tied to a chair. I was forced to concoct all manner of fancies to pass the time. I admit most of them involved you."

"Markos Andela—" I began sternly, to cover my blushing.

"How do you know that name? Daria, I suppose." He gave me a rakish smile. "Well, I'm not entirely sure I should allow you to take such liberties."

"That's funny," I said. "You talking about taking liberties. Stop flirting with me. This tower's going to collapse on our heads."

"You have a plan for getting out of here, don't you?"

I shrugged. "The way we came?"

"You jumped down from a doorway fifteen feet up in the air," he said, "with the help of a tapestry that is now torn and no doubt will not bear our weight."

"We can climb—"

"I can't," he said hoarsely, pinching the bridge of his nose with one shaking hand. All at once I realized he was embarrassed. "I'm sorry. It's—I'm—I don't have the strength."

"Markos, are you sure you're all right?"

"I could use some water," he rasped, his face as white as *Vix*'s paint. I hastily handed over my belt flask, and he gulped the whole thing down. "They left me tied to that chair for so long I was beginning to think I was going to die here." He wiped his mouth. "I'd like a bath and a shirt that isn't covered in blood. But I suppose that can wait."

I eyed him doubtfully, wondering what he wasn't telling me.

"I daresay there aren't any handholds anyway," I said, to make him feel better. "If only Kenté and Nereus were here." Unfortunately I'd left them at the end of that long corridor and come ahead on my own. That, I knew now, had probably been stupid.

I turned in a circle. By the light of the lone guttering lantern, I saw that the cavernous room was full of water, parts of it much deeper than the puddle we stood in.

"Why's the floor all wet?"

"There was a retaining wall outside," Markos said. "To keep the sea back. But—"

"The Bollards probably blew it to bits," I finished. "I expect when high tide comes, this whole room will be underwater. Well then, we'll just have to wait. When the water rises, it will lift us to the opening."

The tower moaned ominously, and he flinched. "Before the ceiling collapses on us?"

A stone fell, landing with a splash. I didn't much like the idea of being crushed under the tower when it came down. I was further annoyed that it might be Bollard cannonballs that indirectly ended up killing me. How long until Kenté and Nereus came looking for us? I hoped they would be in time.

"I don't like this," Markos said over the creak of the burdened rafters. "There's another door, of course. The one all the Black Dogs ran out of. Over there." He gestured across the pool. "At the bottom of the steps."

"What steps?"

"They're underwater now. We're standing on some kind of platform." He nodded out at the circular room. "They were using this tower as a storeroom to keep treasure in, I daresay. There were all sorts of interesting things, before . . ."

A set of stone steps led downward, disappearing into the murky water. I now saw that crates and barrels bobbed in the corners of the room. If Markos's chair had not been on this platform, he would have drowned before I reached him. He would already be dead. It wasn't only my wet feet that made me shiver.

"The sea's coming in!" Panic clutched at my throat. I'd lived all my life on the water. This was *not* how I died. "The tower's going to fall and trap us."

"Can't you do something?" Markos asked. "With your magic."

"You know I don't have any magic." I swallowed. "I would've thought you'd be polite enough not to rub it in."

"You haven't figured it out yet?" He raised his voice over the trickling pebbles. "Listen. Caro. You told me there was a god in the river. That spoke to the wherrymen."

"There is. But not to me. We've been through this, Markos."

"Well, obviously," he said. "Because your god isn't in the river. It's in the sea."

# CHAPTER
# TWENTY-SIX

"No." A cold feeling trickled through me.

*The day your fate comes for you, you'll know.*

Images flashed through my head. Seagulls watching me with beady eyes. Dolphins and fish racing alongside *Vix*. The drakon. My strange dreams.

It wasn't possible. Pressing my fingers to my temples, I tried to shut it out.

The pig man on his houseboat. *She a bigger, deeper god. The one who steers you. He don't be fighting her.* And Nereus. *Ayah, and didn't she send me to help you, Caroline Oresteia?* Finally I understood what he'd been trying to tell me, with that story about Arisbe Andela.

"On the Neck. The fog." Markos gripped my wrist. "I tried to tell you at the time, but you didn't believe me. Caro, I couldn't see a thing in that fog. Not those posts, or the cliffs. Not our own mast. Even Fee couldn't see."

"No." I yanked my arm away. "It wasn't that bad. It couldn't have been. I could see . . ."

"Right through it," he said. "I'm telling you, it was magic."

I shook my head. "The weather behaves oddly sometimes. That doesn't mean—"

"Isn't it strange that a fog happens to come up just when the Black Dogs were about to overtake us? You told me yourself, the Neck is saltwater."

Light sparkled on the seawater, taunting me. "That's not how it happened," I whispered.

"Oh really? What about the drakon? That's what Fee saw, that night on the river, isn't it? It *has* been following you. Caro, it's you. Don't you see?" His eyes shone earnestly. "The god's been calling to you all along. You were just so busy listening for small things, you missed the biggest thing of all."

A shower of stones tumbled down from the ceiling. Markos turned to the broken staircase. "We should yell for help. Maybe Kenté can find a rope or—"

"Wait," I said.

I pulled off my boots and let them drop. My bare toes curling on the slick stone, I took one tentative step. Nothing felt different. I took another, until I stood at the top of the underwater stairs, bubbles swirling encouragingly around my feet.

Biting my lip, I hesitated, as Markos watched me with a sympathetic look.

In truth, I was afraid. The sea wasn't a friendly god, content to simply guide wherrymen from port to port. She sank islands and smashed cities. *The sea, she keeps the things she takes. The deeps be littered with the bones of ships and cities. Ayah, and men.*

Who might I become, the moment I touched the water? If Markos had guessed correctly about me, everything I knew was wrong. Everything was changed. I drew a deep breath and walked into the sea.

The water gently lifted my clothing. Light from the nearby lantern rippled and danced on the surface. Plunging my hands in, I turned them palm upward and offered myself up to the sea.

I took another step.

Standing waist deep on the submerged stairs, I felt foolish and secretly relieved. The hem of my shirt floated around my stomach. Markos was wrong. There wasn't anything special here. I spun around to tell him so.

Then I saw it.

A wave turned over—small at first, a trickle of a wake on the surface of the water. Rolling out from where I stood, it grew into a frothy white line.

The wave began to break. Another followed, turning over and over, faster and faster. The breakers crashed against the walls, and I gasped as the spray flew over me.

A silvery fish jumped, then a second and a third. The splashes plinked like music. Almost, I might have reached out and touched them. My mouth dropped open. I felt the tide as it sucked against me, but this wasn't any natural tide. It pulled at something buried deep inside me.

Something I almost remembered.

A rumbling voice whispered my name. The wave broke over me, and I surged into it, my toes lifting off the stone. I could feel the sea outside the tower—infinite, roaring, and dizzyingly deep. Trailing my hands through the foam, I marveled at how sensitive they were. I felt a thousand tiny individual bubbles and each movement of the waves as they danced a wild rhythm.

Something clammy and wet trailed against my face. Dazed, I reached up.

I wore a crown of dark green seaweed. Pulling an errant strand away, I stared at it between my fingers.

"How?" I yelled over the churning water, as I drifted slowly down, my toes once more touching the step. I laughed. "How did I not know?"

My eyes stung, and not from the saltwater. All those years hoping. Being jealous of Pa and Fee. Wondering if I belonged.

There had never been anything wrong with me. I *did* belong. Just not to the river.

I looked up at Markos, my throat almost closing on the words. "How did you see it and not me?"

"Sometimes," he said with a wistful half smile, "we need others to see the good in us before we can see it in ourselves."

He waded down the stairs, struggling against the weight of his wet clothes. When he reached me, he circled my waist with his arm. I buried my face in his neck, breathing him in. He smelled of salt and blood and Markos.

He hissed sharply, pressing a hand to his side.

"What is it?" I asked.

"Nothing."

"You *are* hurt," I said. "I should've expected it. Just like a boy."

"It's not bad," he said between tightened lips. "Let's go."

"In case you've forgotten, we're trapped."

"Caro, look." He turned me around.

Only moments ago I had stood waist deep on the steps, but now the water sloshed around my ankles. Opposite us, a door loomed in the wet stone wall. What had been a great lake was rapidly becoming a puddle. The receding tide had littered the room with detritus—overturned chests and crates, a layer of slimy sand, and bits of broken shells.

Just my luck, to be chosen by a god who was a bloody show-off.

We splashed down the tunnel. As it turned out, it led to a small beachside training yard filled with weapon racks, one of which had been knocked over by the waves. Markos grabbed a sword off the wet sand, and we ran into the fort. I tried to draw a map in my head of those twisting corridors, but it was hopeless. Picking a direction, I crossed my fingers that it was the right one.

Markos's hands settled on my waist as we peeked around a corner, causing all my senses to skitter and jump.

"If you're going to kiss," Kenté said from behind us, "I suppose I can look away."

I whirled. "We're not going to—Why would we do that?"

"No?" She tilted her head toward Markos. "Ah well, lost opportunities."

He immediately let go of me, the ear that wasn't covered in blood turning pink.

"What are you doing here?" I asked to cover my own embarrassment. Part of me missed the warmth of his hands.

"Looking for you, of course. You didn't answer when I called down the stairs."

We found Nereus leaning casually against the wall, picking his teeth with his knife. Philemon's wrists were bound with strips of what had once been his own trousers. He looked very much like he wished to be elsewhere.

Removing a piece of seaweed from my hair, Nereus twirled it between his fingers. "Crowned, I see."

"Oh, you know about that little display, do you?" I raised my eyebrows. "You might have told me."

"You speak as if it were a secret."

"It was to me, since certain of my allies are most irritatingly given to talking in riddles." I narrowed my eyes at him. "That's who you meant when you said you were sent. She sent you. The god."

"She who lies beneath."

I stared him down. "And who are you, that you can be called up by a god? Tell me the truth. Are you a shade? Are you . . . dead?"

He winked at me. "Not today."

"Are you Nemros the Marauder?" I demanded.

The edges of his eyes crinkled. "I have been many men and gone by many names."

"How many lives have you served her?"

"One. A thousand."

"Do you mean one or do you mean a thousand?"

"Yes." He grinned.

"That's not an answer. Doesn't it bother you?" I asked. "Don't you want to be free?"

"If I wasn't serving her, where would I be? Dead, that's where. Free or dead's no choice at all. I like the smell of the sea on a fine day. The feel of the spray. The taste of the rum." He shuddered. "I'll do whatever she asks of me, if it'll keep me out of the bottom of the ocean, or worse—gods forbid—under the ground. Now." He inhaled. "I smell a fight."

Markos stepped up. "Wait." He eyed Philemon, then punched him hard on the jaw. The pirate collapsed on the floor.

"Ow." Markos winced, shaking out his hand.

I raised my eyebrows. "That wasn't very honorable."

"Yes, well, let's just say I've come around to your point of view," he said. Leaning over the man, he drew himself up regally. "Also, I would like my coat back."

Nereus slashed the ties at the pirate's wrists, shoving the knife against his throat. "You heard your Emparch."

Philemon struggled out of the coat, muttering curses under his breath.

Markos sniffed it before putting it on, his nose wrinkling. "This has been a very trying week for my clothes." He straightened the collar. "Let's go."

As we burst into the great room, we discovered the battle had been won without us. Holding my breath, I took a frantic accounting of the men and women still standing—Pa, Ma, Captain Krantor, Captain Brixton and her mate, and many more, including *Antelope*'s captain.

I exhaled in shaky relief.

Pa and Captain Krantor stared down at something on the floor, hats clutched in their hands. It was the body of the wherryman Hathor, lying beside three other wherrymen and two more from *Antelope*'s crew. I swallowed. He was the one who had not wanted to come because he had a family.

"Current carry you," I whispered. For the first time in my life, I felt strange saying the words. It was a riverlands expression. I wasn't certain it belonged to me anymore.

Pa's shirt was missing a sleeve. I realized it was tied around Ma's arm in a makeshift sling. She seemed all right, despite the smudge of blood on her cheek. Certainly she was bossing people around with great energy.

"I'll worry about that," Ma shouted to one of the *Antelope*'s crewmen, gesturing with her good hand. "You worry about clearing that gods-damned cellar. You might as well carry up anything valuable while you're at it, for they won't get much use out of it where they're going, will they?"

Behind me, Markos laughed.

"What's so funny?"

"All this time I was thinking you got it from your father," he said.

I shot him a dirty look, but my lips couldn't help twitching into a smile.

It was late afternoon when the Bollards and wherrymen rounded up the remnants of the Black Dogs and brought them down to the beach, placing them in a makeshift pen by the stockade. Never one to let a profit slip by her, Ma had found several items she liked among the pirates' stash. Those were stacked on what was left of the dock. By the time the last beams of sunset slanted over the harbor, lighting up the bobbing wreckage with an orange glow, every corner of the fort had been swept. All the pirates were accounted for.

Except one.

The shadowman Cleandros had disappeared. Pa hauled Diric Melanos out by the neck and flung him down. "Reckon I know three different harbor masters and a magistrate who'd like to get their hands on this filth."

I stood over him with my pistol. "Where's the shadowman?"

"Fat lot of help he were to us." Melanos spat on the sand. His fine coat was torn and his hat missing. "Buggered off during the battle, didn't he? The bloody coward. Told him we was going to kill the boy, just after we got the money, is all. He still wouldn't shut up about it. Good riddance, says I. You can't trust a shadowman."

Myself, I was surprised Captain Melanos hadn't ended up with a bullet hole in him during the battle. I suppose the wherrymen were content to watch him hang.

As we waited on the beach for Nereus and the wherrymen to bring *Vix* around, Ma reeled off instructions.

"Make for our offices in Iantiporos," she said to me, spelling the name of the street so I would remember it. "Send a message to Bolaji. Tell him to have two ships meet us here in full haste."

"Aren't you coming?" I asked.

She shook her head. "I'm staying with my crew. We'll try to salvage what we can of the ship. Reckon your pa will stick around too." She gestured to her injured arm. "He's got some misguided notion that I need taking care of. Anyway it seems to me you've proved yourself on that cutter."

"They don't know me in Iantiporos," I said, suddenly uncertain. "What if—?"

She unpinned the brooch from her doublet, pressing it into my hand. "Bring Kenté with you. And show them this."

Pa stood alone on the beach, fumbling with an alchemical match. I waded through the sand to stand beside him, curling my arm through his. His worn overcoat smelled like home.

Leaning on his shoulder, I took in the beach, the bobbing shipwrecks, and the sunset. Out there the sea rose and fell in a lulling rhythm. Farther down the sand, Thisbe Brixton was passing a flask among the other wherrymen. Their straggling voices rose in the chorus of a very rude song.

Seeing her struck a memory. She had recognized Nereus. *Sure, and doesn't a fish know when a shark comes to eat him?* An even more chilling thought followed on its heels.

Pa knew him too.

*You*, he had whispered, back when they came face-to-face on *Vix*. Cold suspicion trickled through me.

"Pa," I began cautiously. "You said the day my fate came for me, I would know."

He turned toward the sea, puffing on his pipe. "Ayah," he said slowly. His eyes looked troubled. "So I did."

"Is it true that *all* the Oresteias were favored of the god in the river? There weren't any of them who"—I braced myself—"who were, I don't know, something else? Something different?"

Markos ambled up the beach, shading his eyes into the setting sun. *Vix* was coming around the point, her sails billowing white against the sky. At the sight of her, something struggled to rise within me.

"Listen, Caro," Pa said, a thickness in his voice, and my heart wanted to shatter. His throat bobbed. "There's something I need to tell you."

Suddenly I didn't want to hear it. Not yet. I pulled free, shoving my hands in my pockets, and ran to catch up with Markos.

Halfway down the beach, I paused to look back at Pa. His shoulders drooped, and I was acutely aware of the lines on his face. He'd known the truth all along. I was certain of it. Emotion clawed at me, but I shoved it bitterly away. I didn't *want* to listen to him. How many lies had he told me?

We rowed out to *Vix*, where Daria leaned over the rail, waving frantically while one of the wherrymen's wives struggled to keep her from falling overboard.

"Markos!" she shrieked as he climbed the ladder, in a manner completely unbefitting an Emparch's daughter.

"Little badger!" He dropped to his knees on the deck, gathering her up. She buried her face in his chest.

Some things are not what you expect, like the most arrogant boy in the world crying into the shoulder of his eight-year-old sister's nightgown. Kenté and I exchanged glances, turning away to give them privacy.

Descending into the darkness of *Vix*'s cabin, I unbuckled my heavy belt and dropped it in a heap on the bench. Now that everything was quiet again, I didn't know what to do. I wished *Vix* had a cozy red-checkered tablecloth and a familiar bunk heaped with blankets. I wished Fee was there making tea.

My eyes filled with tears. I didn't recognize my life anymore.

The hatch creaked. "It's much bigger than *Cormorant*, isn't it?"

I closed my eyes against his voice.

Boots scuffed on the floor as Markos stepped down from the last rung of the ladder. With only the lone lantern, I couldn't see his face. "Oh," he said. "I forgot—"

I swallowed. "It's fine."

"Like hell it is. You told me she was your home," he said. "You told me when a sailor loves a ship, it hits you so hard you can't breathe."

For once he had called the wherry "she" and not "it." Somehow that made the lump in my throat more painful.

"It's done." I whirled away from him.

"Caroline, I'm sorry." He followed me, holding himself stiffly. "I'm ever so sorry. It's my fault. You let her go for me."

"For Daria," I corrected, biting my lip. A hot tear seared my cheek. "*You* jumped into the middle of a bunch of pirates all by yourself," I said to the wall. "I thought *you* were dead."

I felt him standing behind me. "Caro, Fee won't let anything happen to *Cormorant*."

"If she's alive," I whispered. Hope warred with despair inside my chest.

"I choose to believe that she is," he said. "And that *Cormorant* is still tied up at the Casteria docks. But I don't know. I . . . was unconscious when they carried me down to *Alektor*. When I woke, we were at sea." He set a tentative hand on my waist.

"What do you mean, unconscious?" I turned, almost whacking

my forehead on his chin. My heart reeled with alarm and something else as I examined his face. "What did they do to you? Did they torture you?"

He didn't say yes or no.

"But why?" I asked, taking his silence as a stupidly gallant attempt to protect me. "Did they want to know something?"

"No. They just . . . thought it was fun."

I grabbed his chin, turning his face toward the light. Besides the black eye, he had a mottled purple bruise along his jawline, crested by a long scab. But his left ear was the worst of it.

"*Markos*." I stared in horror. "I think part of your ear is missing."

"Can we go back to a minute ago?" he rasped. "I don't want to talk about it."

"Sit *down*." I shoved him into a chair.

"I admit I was thinking about kissing you." He sighed. "I've changed my mind."

I fetched a bowl of water and the cleanest piece of cloth I could find. Dipping the rag in the bowl, I lifted it to his earlobe.

"Ow!" He flinched away.

"I haven't even touched you yet. Stop being a baby."

"I wish you wouldn't touch me at all. Please don't take offense, but I don't really see you as the gentle, nursing kind of girl."

"I can be if I want to be." I swiped the rag down his neck more roughly than I meant to.

"Again, *ouch*. No, you can't." He gritted his teeth. "You're the throwing-knives-and-shooting-pistols kind."

I dipped the cloth in the water. Even in the dim light, his ear looked infected. He'd have to see a physician when we got to Ian-tiporos. As I cleaned the wounds on his face and neck, he dug his fingernails into his palms.

"Take off your shirt," I ordered, half-afraid to see how badly he was hurt.

He smiled, tipping the chair back. "Are you flirting with me?"

"I admit I was thinking about it," I said saucily, lifting my eye-brows. "But I've changed my mind."

I reached across him to drop the rag into the bowl of bloody water. He put his hand over mine, trapping me.

We looked at each other.

Then Kenté dropped from the last rung of the ladder and said, "Caro, don't move. The shadowman's right behind you. With a pistol pointed at your head."

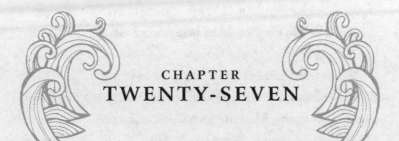

# CHAPTER
# TWENTY-SEVEN

The lantern whisked out, as if a shadow had detached itself from the ceiling and fallen upon it.

Without my pistols, I was helpless. A shot whistled over my head, and I hit the deck. Above me a locker exploded in a storm of splinters. Markos swore.

The light flickered back to life.

"You continue to be nothing but an aggravation, Miss Bollard." Cleandros stood a few feet away, the barrel of a long flintlock aimed straight at Kenté. "You aren't strong enough to overcome me."

She flung a broken locket to the floor. "Well, I'm going to keep trying."

He turned the pistol on me.

Of course, Markos immediately dove out of the chair and

threw himself between the shadowman and me. Because he was an idiot.

"Very chivalrous, my Lord," Cleandros said. "You know you can't stop me from killing her if I wish it."

Markos glared at him. "I think you mean Your Excellency." I suspected he was madder about being called the wrong title than getting shot at.

"I have half a mind to kill you too," Cleandros said. "But I think I'll take you to Valonikos for the reward after all, now that I don't have to split it with Melanos and his imbecile crew." He gestured to us all with the pistol. "Up on deck. Now."

I saw no choice but to obey. "Where'd he come from?" I whispered to Kenté as we climbed the ladder.

"He must have snuck on board during the battle. Saw him slinking around the deck in a mantle of shadows, so I followed him."

"Cease that chatter," Cleandros ordered, stepping through the hatch. He bowed to our borrowed crew. "Weapons down, if you please! Keep sailing. Just don't interfere."

Nereus set his knife on the deck. Daria's little hands trembled so hard that she dropped the rope ends she was holding, her eyes never leaving Markos. Nereus had been teaching her knots.

A pang of emotion hit me. She wasn't afraid for herself, but for her brother.

Markos threw an agonized glance over his shoulder at her. His hand barely moved, but Cleandros saw anyway.

He dug the muzzle of the pistol into Markos's back. "If you

touch that sword, your sister dies while you watch. Remove the belt."

"No."

Cleandros pointed the pistol at Daria. "Come, child. Over by your brother."

She obeyed, slipping her hand into Markos's. Bruises and cuts standing out on his pale face, he dropped his sword belt in a heap with the other weapons.

The shadowman waved us toward the bow of the cutter, past the forward hatch and the barrels stacked there. Glancing at the purple-clouded sky, I realized with dismay the sun had slipped below the horizon. He would only continue to gain in power.

"Since you are ignorant," Cleandros said, "I shall tell you about the children of the night. Some of us take strongly to the practice of lurking and hiding." He nodded at Kenté. "Others use the darkness to draw out men's deepest fears. But I have a great talent for the art of sleep and dreams. That's why His Excellency the Emparch prized me above all men in his inner circle."

As he spoke, my limbs grew slack. It would be so easy, I thought, to just give up.

"You may find yourself growing tired," Cleandros said. "Your mind becomes dim. In this state, the Emparch found, a mind becomes suggestive. Easily influenced." He smirked. "In a room with me, a whole council of men might find themselves agreeing with everything the Emparch said."

I struggled not to yawn. Even Kenté's eyelids fluttered.

Markos pinched his own arm. "My father trusted you. And you betrayed him."

"Your father didn't care for anyone who was beneath him. You of all people ought to know that. Not tired yet?"

Markos glared. Though he knew his father hadn't loved him, I could tell it angered him that Cleandros knew it too.

"Now," the shadowman said, "sit down on the deck."

I swayed on my feet. His tone was so friendly and reasonable.

"Markos," Kenté said. "Do not."

He blinked. "Isn't—that's—I know him. We're safe." He touched a hand to his forehead in bewilderment.

"He killed your mother." Kenté's glance darted between Markos and the shadowman. "He betrayed your family."

"I remember." Sounding unconvinced, he yawned. "I do."

It made me yawn too. I wondered why Kenté looked so overwrought. Myself, I felt quite at ease.

The shadowman waved a hand. "It won't work, you know." He gave Kenté an indulgent smile, like a parent amused by the antics of a small child. "Your power is but a flicker compared to mine."

"Markos!" she tried again. "Your brother. Cleandros killed him. Remember? Your *brother*."

"Loukas." His head dipped. "I—I'm just going to sit for a moment."

"No! You are going to stay standing." The words tumbled frantically out of her mouth. I wished she would slow down. "And you are going to remember why you want to fight this man!"

Markos's legs buckled under him, and he dropped to his knees. Distantly someone laughed.

I thought he had the right idea. "Got to rest," I mumbled, rubbing my eyes. "Only for a minute."

The shadowman's voice seemed to come through a thick fog. He turned to Kenté. "You may be able to resist me, you see. But your companions cannot."

Many things happened at once. Kenté reached for the sky. Markos and Daria disappeared. Nereus let out a ferocious war cry, yanking a knife from the back of his trousers, and sprang—not toward the shadowman but at me. Seizing my arm, he sliced my hand open. A flash of pain burned my palm.

"Ow!" I clutched my bleeding hand. "Why'd you—"

Then I realized. I was awake again. Blinking away my grogginess, I tried to refocus on what was happening.

Cleandros laughed at Kenté. "You think yourself powerful enough to hide them from *me*? The masters at the Academy will purge you of such childish overconfidence." He made an impatient gesture, as if brushing aside cobwebs.

And froze, sneering voice caught in his throat, when Markos and Daria did not reappear.

Turning to my cousin, he spat, "You have no training. You shouldn't be able to veil them from me. It's not possible!"

Before I could move to stop him, Cleandros aimed at the spot where they had vanished and pulled the trigger.

No one cried out. No blood spattered the deck. They simply weren't there.

He advanced on Kenté, ramming powder and shot down the pistol. "*Where are they?*"

I scrambled backward, dragging my cousin with me. My heel

hit the foot of the bowsprit and I stumbled, grabbing onto a stay for balance.

"I might've ransomed your cousin back to the Bollards," Cleandros told Kenté, anger curdling his voice. "But enough is enough. Let this be a lesson to you."

Behind him, Nereus lunged for the gun, but it was too late.

The shot struck me in the right side of my chest, red blood spraying out in a mist.

Pain—searing pain. My whole arm seized up. Spots danced in my eyes. My breath was uneven and raspy, as if I suddenly couldn't gulp in enough air. Blood matted my shirt and waistcoat. I staggered, slipping on the bowsprit. My hand loosened on the stay.

Time seemed to slow. I heard, as if from a great distance, my blood dripping on the deck. Below me, the sea rose and fell.

*There are some sailormen who say the drakon is nothing more or less than your fate coming for you.* If it was still down there, would it be drawn like a shark to my blood in the water? Was this my fate, to be gulped up by a sea beast like the *Nikanor* and her ill-fated crew?

No. Understanding flooded through me. The drakon belonged to the sea. And so did I. That same drakon had been following me since the river. As what—a protector? A guide? If I was right, the drakon would no more hurt me than cut off her own tail.

I let go of the stay—and dropped into the sea.

The shadowman laughed. Distantly I heard Kenté scream as I hit the water. I couldn't feel my right arm, and my legs were like limp dough. A wave sloshed over me, stirring the blood that clouded around me like spilled ink. I inhaled a gulping mouthful of ocean, salt stinging my nose.

I had been wrong. And my life would be the price for my mistake.

Then I heard her.

# CHAPTER
## TWENTY-EIGHT

"I greet you, sssssssister."

Something slippery but solid rose under me. I tangled the fingers of my good hand in the tuft that trailed from her back, which looked like feathers but felt like seaweed. Her neck was dotted with clumps of barnacles. With the last of my strength I tightened my knees around her body.

She burst forth from the waves like an explosion. She was beautiful.

Foam sprayed out from between the drakon's teeth as she swiveled her head. On *Vix*'s deck a wherryman stumbled backward, screaming. The scent of salt and snake dampened the air. Water streaming into my eyes, I fought to hang on.

"Show me our enemy!" she hissed.

I squeezed my eyes shut and pictured Cleandros, concentrating hard on his gilded robes and plain face. Shivering uncontrollably as I tasted blood in my mouth, I hoped somehow she could understand me.

"Ah! I smell him," the drakon declared. "The sandy grit of sleep. The sweet taste of darkness. I have eaten one of *you* before."

Cleandros turned to face her, and then it was as if the world went black. The shadowman vanished, and so did everything else—the sky, the rolling waves, and *Vix*.

I heard the drakon laugh. "Fool. The sea does not fear the dark."

She sprang, arcing out of the water like a rainbow, and I clung to her back as she flowed under me. She plucked the shadowman from the bowsprit with a bone-shaking crunch. Her sides convulsing under my legs, the drakon swallowed. With a splash her head hit the water on the other side of *Victorianos*'s bow.

The world plunged back into twilight, just in time for me to see the ocean rushing toward me. My stomach lurched and I took a last frantic breath.

I sank.

And sank.

I knew nothing.

After a long while, it came to me that I was not dead. I thought I might be breathing, or at least bubbles flowed out of my nose. I tried to keep count of the seconds as I drifted down, but it was like trying to grasp the wind in my hand.

I gave up and let myself float.

Beams of light shafted through the murky water, lending it a turquoise color. I couldn't see the source of the light, precisely. Maybe it was all around me.

How had I come to be here? I couldn't remember.

Something brushed my leg. I thrashed in panic, until I saw the yellow-and-black-striped body of a fish flitting away into the darkness. A second fish came to investigate, weaving about me.

I swatted at my billowing shirt, trying to see where I'd been shot. The bullet had torn a ragged chunk from my flesh. Hesitantly I touched the pale, clammy skin around the hole, too squeamish to stick my finger in it. No trail of blood curled through the water.

Perhaps I *was* dead. The colors of the sea and the fish reminded me of my dream about Mrs. Singer, the drowned wherryman's wife. Perhaps it had been a true dream, a foretelling of my own fate.

I closed my eyes, and when I opened them I was in a city.

I sat on top of a great tower, the ruins of ancient buildings spread out below me. Draped in seaweed and decorated with barnacles, some of the structures had toppled, the wooden beams that once formed their bones rotted away. The white stone remained, rounded smooth by time and water. Fish flitted in and out of the windows, and a hunk of bright coral grew in the middle of what had once been a road.

A whole city, at the bottom of the ocean.

Beside me stood a heron. I blinked in surprise. The heron didn't look as if it was worried about breathing any more than I was. It stood on the tower wall on one spindly leg, with the other one tucked up into its feathers. Its beady eyes held steady on me.

"I'm imagining this," I told it.

The heron spoke with a woman's voice. "Why do you think so?"

"Because I was shot in the heart. I'm either having fever dreams or I'm dead."

"Laughter. That isn't where your heart is."

"How would you know? You aren't human."

"Aren't I?" it asked. Which annoyed me, because obviously it was a heron.

"Don't you know what you are?" I demanded, bubbles tumbling out of my mouth.

"What do I look like to you?"

"A heron," I said.

"How odd. Laughter."

"Why do you do that—say 'laughter'? Why don't you just laugh?"

"I've been told my laugh unnerves humans." The heron swiveled on its leg, hopping toward me.

"What does it sound like?"

"Like a hurricane gale. Like a hundred knives." Her voice dropped to a hissing whisper. "Like a drowned man's dreams."

A drowned man's dreams. I thought again of the dreams I'd been having since the night I met Markos. Of the dead Mrs. Singer from the *Jenny* lying on a bed of coral, and all those strange, colorful fish. The fish had been like these.

"I know who you are," I said.

"We are both who we should be."

*She who lies beneath*, Nereus had called her. Her gulls had watched me, following me with round black eyes, since I was a child. She'd made a fog that only I could see through. Her drakon had protected me.

And I was hers.

"Why did you send me dreams about a dead woman?" I asked.

"I sent you dreams of this place. The dead woman is in *your* head."

"Is the heron in my head too? Why did you say it was odd?" As the sea lifted and twirled my hair, I clarified, "That I see a heron."

"A bird of both the sea and the riverlands," she said. "Maybe it's not so odd after all."

"Why did I never see you before today?"

"I could ask you the same question." The water swirled around me in a gentle caress. "There has never been a day of your life when I was not right here."

I gazed out over the crumbling rooftops. "What is this city?"

"The humans say it was lost," the heron said. "But they are wrong. It is where it has always been, a testament to the fact that those I claim belong to me. Arisbe Andela. Nemros the Marauder." Her voice dropped to a hiss. "*Caroline Oresteia.*"

I shivered, remembering how Nereus had said the sea keeps the things she takes.

The heron looked out at the city. "It's only the world that's changed." There was a certain wistfulness to her voice. She switched legs, and with them, the subject. "Who is he, that one you travel with?"

"Nereus?"

The heron made a scornful sound. "I know *him*. He is mine. As much a part of me as the reef and the seaweed and the swimming fish. I mean the other one."

"Markos. He's the true Emparch of Akhaia." If she didn't know about him already, I was reluctant to tell her too much. Nereus had warned me she was tricky.

"Laughter. I should have known. I smelled the stink of mountain air about him." I thought she would have wrinkled her nose, if she had one. "And yet there is something . . . Well. He is of no concern to me. As long as he who lies under the mountain still sleeps, as he has these past six hundred years."

"Why does Akhaia's god sleep?" I asked. "Why does he talk to no one but the oracles?"

I felt rather than saw her smile. It was a smile that suggested teeth, although I could not have said why or how. Herons don't have teeth. "Because he made the mistake of going to war against me. And lost."

"Does every god have a country?"

"Some have many cities and many countries. All cities that sit beside the sea are my cities. Valonikos. Iantiporos. Brizos." She lapsed into a brooding quiet. "Valonikos never belonged to *him*."

"Is that why Akhaia keeps losing pieces of its empire?" A fish was trying to swim into my hair. I resisted the urge to swat it. "Because its god sleeps?"

"Akhaia was once strong," she agreed. "It is lesser now. He licks his wounds and speaks to no one. He chooses no warriors. He cannot protect it."

"He needs six hundred years to lick his wounds?"

"It is but a moment to him."

"Do you?" I realized my question didn't make sense, and added, "Choose warriors?"

"Laughter," was all the heron said. I thought she winked, but it might have been a mote drifting through the cloudy water.

I wondered if she would ask me to make a bargain, like Nemros the Marauder. I wasn't certain I trusted her, or her bargains.

"Trust." She tilted her feathered head. "It matters not. You will serve me nonetheless."

"You got no call to be hearing the things in my head," I said. "The thoughts in my head are mine."

"They are mine, because you are mine," she said.

The thoughts in my head weren't particularly flattering at that moment. "Laughter. Always the humans think they can fight it. You can't." Her words were eerily like the pig man's. "It comes for you, slithering through the deep like my drakon. It always comes for you."

"What does?"

"Your fate."

Time stopped, or changed. The heron was gone. The city was gone. Alone I floated. Minutes went by, or days, or years, as I bobbed in endless blue nothing.

Something appeared above me. A pattern I almost remembered, though I had seen it long ago, time out of mind.

Sunlight, moving and shifting on the surface of the water. I cupped my hands and pulled toward it, my lungs burning. Bubbles rushed past me. Instincts taking over, every part of my body strove up, up, up—

My head burst through.

Much to my relief, the first thing I spotted was a beach. Sun sparkled on a line of breakers crashing on colorful, rounded pebbles, and there, on the horizon beyond, was a red-roofed city. I understood now how Jacari Bollard must have felt when he laid eyes on Ndanna.

The city was Valonikos.

I waded ashore, trousers clinging to my legs and shirt stained light pink where I'd been shot. My left foot squelched in a sand-filled boot. The other boot had gone missing. I was sure I looked like the most disreputable sailor ever to be washed up on Valonikos beach.

I shot the sea a sour look. "You might've left me a bit closer to civilization. And with both shoes."

Wet sand sucking at my bare foot, I limped toward the distant city. I made it about thirty feet before a breaker tumbled over and crashed on the beach, a brown speck visible in the churning foam. The wave receded, spitting out my right boot.

I stared at it.

The undertow seized the boot, which flopped over and began to slide down the sand.

Apparently this was the kind of thing that was going to happen now that a god was interfering in my life. I let out a whoop and chased my boot down the beach.

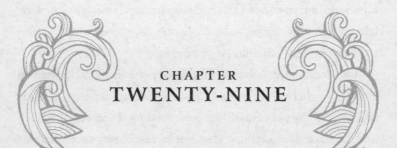

# CHAPTER
# TWENTY-NINE

*Vix* looked pretty tied up at the dock, but it wasn't the same as coming around the corner and seeing *Cormorant*. I didn't love her the way I'd described to Markos—she wasn't home. Even lying tamely in the harbor with her canvas strapped down, she was intimidating. I still hadn't forgotten all the times when the sight of her terrified me to the bones.

It was funny—her painted lettering still read "*Victorianos,*" as it always had, but I thought of her only as *Vix* now.

I limped up the plank, pausing to slide my hand along her polished rail. "All right, *Vix,*" I whispered. "So here we are."

A hatch slammed shut. I was unarmed, but both my hands flew to my waist out of instinct.

It was Markos.

He stood alone on deck, hand resting on the hilt of his sword. When he saw me, he froze. His eyes were sunken, reddened.

"Who are you?" he said flatly. "You aren't her. I don't believe it."

"I don't care." I stepped down, battered boots rubbing the raw blisters on my heels. "I've been walking for miles, and I'm sunburned. I have sand everywhere a person could possibly have sand on her body, and, yes, I do mean *everywhere*. And I'm starving."

He blocked me. "What did Caro do the first time I tried to kiss her?"

"You know what I did. We were both there," I exclaimed in exasperation. "Oh, I see. This is a test." I rolled my eyes. "I slapped you. And dumped a bucket of cold water on you."

He felt my salt-stiffened shirt. I hated how haunted his eyes looked. "You were shot. You went into the water. The drakon surely swallowed you up."

"She would never eat me."

"Then you drowned."

I whispered, "She would never let me drown."

Roughly he shoved aside the neckline of my shirt. Fingers splayed, he felt his way across my skin.

"What are you—?" Then I realized. Seizing his hand in mine, I brought it an inch lower, to the frayed hole in the right side of my shirt, under my collarbone. The sea had washed the matted blood away.

I stuck my finger through the rip in the fabric and waggled it. "All right?"

He let out a ragged breath. "Caro. I don't even—there's a scar.

But—it's all healed." The look he gave me was so intense it took me by surprise.

I rolled up my sleeve. "And here's where the Black Dogs shot me. The very night we met. As you ought to remember." I pushed past him. "Now, if you're finished manhandling me, can I come on my own ship? Need I mention I was recently shot?"

I fixed my shirt, wondering if he could hear how fast my heart raced. My ears burned. I had to put space between him and me, to restore things to their normal state. I swung through the hatch and onto the ladder.

"I thought you might be a shadowman. An assassin from the Theucinians." He pelted me with questions. "Where have you been? Why weren't you eaten by the drakon? And how did you get to Valonikos?"

I hopped down the last two rungs. The remnants of a meal were laid out on the table. "Don't know." I grabbed a block of cheese and bit right into it. I'd never been so hungry. "This is where I walked out of the sea," I said around a mouthful of cheese. "Just south of the city."

Markos stared at me, dazed. Or maybe he was just appalled by my table manners. "What do you mean, walked out of the sea? Not from *under* it?"

"Markos, I'm fine. She would never let harm come to me." I swallowed. It seemed strange to be speaking of such magical, personal things in conversation. We might as well be talking about the weather.

"You spoke to her."

I picked up a hunk of bread. "I don't want to talk about it."

"You really spoke to a god."

"*Markos.*"

"Are you alive or dead right now?" He looked at me as if I was not quite human.

"I feel alive. I'd rather not think any harder about it. Where is everyone?" I sucked in a sharp breath. "Nereus is still here, isn't he?" The terrible thought occurred to me that maybe his task was finished and the god in the sea had taken him back. I hadn't gotten to say good-bye.

"He took Daria to see the fish market. The Bollards have rooms above their offices here. That's where your parents are staying. And Kenté."

I dropped the butter knife with a clatter. "Markos, how stupid are you? You shouldn't be alone here!"

"I wanted to be alone. My cousin's wife insists on fussing over me incessantly. I came down here for quiet. To think."

"About what?"

He raised his eyebrows. "What do you think?" The silence that followed was both significant and awkward. He broke it by clearing his throat. "Would you like some ale?"

"I think not. I need water, and lots of it." My throat and skin felt tight and parched.

He reached across the table to refill my tin cup. I smiled. It was funny to see him pick up the jug and serve me—something he would never have done when we first met. I marveled at how comfortable it felt to be eating with him.

"What happened, back at the island?" I asked. "I don't understand how Kenté hid you from the shadowman. Are those meat pies?"

He pushed the tray at me. The pies were cold, but I hardly cared. "Actually she didn't. We were behind that stack of barrels on deck. When Nereus yelled, it woke me up just enough to remember we were in danger. I grabbed Daria and dove behind the barrels." His face colored. "Well, it was more like she grabbed me. I think he'd been concentrating on me, you see. It was the strangest thing. I was so confused."

"I know. I felt it too."

He went on. "It wasn't until Cleandros started shouting at Kenté that I realized he hadn't seen us hide. When we didn't reappear, he thought it meant she was more powerful than him. That's when he got angry and shot you."

As I ate and drank, he told me what had become of our allies. Five days had passed since I'd gone overboard. Nereus had taken *Vix* into Iantiporos, where Kenté visited the offices of Bollard Company. The Bollards had sent ships to retrieve the *Antelope*'s crew and transport the Black Dogs to the appropriate authorities. Pa and Ma took it upon themselves to make sure Markos and Daria reached Valonikos safely. Ma almost sent Kenté back to Siscema, only Daria pitched a fit and refused to sail without her. Meanwhile the wherrymen had bid them farewell and begun the journey back to Hespera's Watch on *Conthar*.

"Do you still have my things?" I asked.

"In the captain's cabin." He pushed back his chair. "I'll—"

I also stood. My heart pounded. "No, I'll get them."

The cabin had been cleaned, the bed made up with fresh sheets and blankets. I found my belt on a shelf. Sliding one of the pistols from its holster, I traced the mountain lion. Then I touched the brim of my three-cornered hat, sitting on the shelf beside it. They looked the same. But everything was changed.

I spun to find Markos leaning in the doorway. My eyes dropped to his jacket. It was the one he'd bought in Siscema, though the rest of his clothes were new. I longed to run my fingers down that gilt trim. It was a very attractive coat, especially on him.

"Still wearing it." He stretched like the lions on my Akhaian dueling pistols and grinned. "Would you like me to be Tarquin Meridios again?"

"Why would I?"

"Admit it, you found him handsome."

By all the gods, he was *flirting* with me, barely half an hour after I'd come back from the dead.

"There were things I wanted to say to you," I blurted out. "Not to Tarquin Meridios. You." My cheeks warmed. "But you were dead."

"I felt similarly," he said. "But then *you* were dead. Please, go on."

I was suddenly shy. "You first."

One side of his mouth twisted up. "Very well." Angling his eyes away from mine, he said, "I finally realized why it wouldn't have worked when I first tried to kiss you."

I crossed my arms. "Because I'm not the kind of girl who kisses boys she just met the day before yesterday?"

"No. Well, yes. That too." His voice was steady and serious. "All my life I expected people to respect me because I was the son of the Emparch. But you didn't. At first that made me mad. Infuriated me, really. You have no idea."

I had some idea.

"But now I know you better." Hesitantly he wound one of my curls around his finger. I didn't stop him. Emboldened, he brushed his hand over my hair. It tickled, but tiny fireworks lit up all over my body.

"Now I see." His voice dropped low. "You respect people who take care of other people. People who are bold. And brave. I couldn't figure it out at first. Why you thought more of common wherrymen than you did of me. You respect people because of the things they *do*. You were different from everyone I'd ever met. You knew what I did not—that it's the things we do that make us who we are."

I knew what I wanted to say, but I also knew what would happen if I said it. "Markos."

He braced himself in the doorway, trying so hard to appear casual that even I was nearly fooled.

"I think you're the bravest person I know." I stepped backward into the cabin.

"You're going to bed. Of course. You've been through a lot." He stuck his fingers in his hair. "I mean, you were dead. I'll just—"

I placed my hand on his shirt, spreading my fingers wide. The solid heat of him made me feel bold. "When you kissed me in Casteria, I didn't know if it meant anything."

His chest lurched under my fingers. "As if I would kiss someone like that and not mean something."

"Oh, wouldn't you?"

"Not," he said, clearing his throat, "like that."

"Perhaps you just wanted to kiss a girl before you died."

He raised his eyebrows. "Perhaps I didn't want to die without kissing *you*."

"That's what I just said."

"You know it isn't. Not at all." He whispered, "Can I please stay? I swear, I won't do anything."

He backed up, putting the length of the cabin between us, to prove his intentions. But the cabin was tiny and he was too tall for it. I felt his presence, a warm physical thing, taking up the whole room.

"Why do you say it like that?" I asked. "*You* won't do anything. When if we were to do anything, and I'm not saying we will, it would be the both of us doing it." I licked my lips. "Like, maybe *I* might want to do things. But then you talk like it's up to you and take me right out of it."

"I'm sor—*do* you?"

Realizing I'd gone slightly too far, I prepared to come about. "I don't know. Maybe."

"Are we talking about . . . I just want to make sure we're referring to the same kinds of . . . *things* here." Tension yawned between us. He stepped closer, as if there were a string connecting me and him, and I'd just tugged on it.

"Are there other kinds of things that happen between a girl and a boy?"

He gave me a sly grin. "Are you *asking*?"

I shoved him on the shoulder. "Shut up."

He kissed me.

A girl who, at the age of seventeen, captains a pirate cutter she seized as a prize ought not to let her head be turned by kisses, even if they are from a boy who is the rightful Emparch of a whole country. Particularly not if the girl knows embarrassing facts about said Emparch that should make him wholly unattractive. Such as, he doesn't know how to load a pistol or properly stow a sail, or in fact do anything of use except look good holding two swords at once.

I didn't care. Everything went right out of my head, except how greedy I was for his lips and his tongue, even if I did have to go up on tiptoe to reach them. He smelled and felt and tasted like Markos. I simply couldn't have been kissing anyone else.

It was all him. The silkiness of his hair as I finally twisted my fingers into it. The catch in his breath as he dragged his lips down my neck. We wrapped ourselves around each other until there was no space between us. Until I couldn't tell whose throbbing heartbeat I felt.

He laughed softly into my shoulder. "I can't believe this is happening."

"It's all right," I told him. "Tomorrow we can go back to not liking each other."

"You think we don't like each other?"

"I think I find you maddening." I tangled my fist in his shirt.

"Well. That's different."

His voice was irritatingly smug, so I kissed him some more to shut him up.

"It's most likely because," he said, breath tickling my neck, "we spent so much time on that damn boat together. That's all it is. A natural ... mmm ... thing," he finished absently as if he couldn't be bothered to think of the word. "Reaction," he said several moments later, kissing his way up my ear. So much later, in fact, I barely remembered what he was talking about.

"I agree," I said. "It's definitely nothing." I tried to climb him, wrapping my legs around his waist. His back bumped the wall, causing something on the shelf to shift and topple.

Eventually we found the bed, which wasn't hard even in the dark because the cabin was so small.

"Markos." I hesitated, unsure of what he would think. But it had to be said. "This isn't ... my first time. If that matters. Which it shouldn't. It's just—I thought you ought to know. In case—"

"Caro. You're talking too much."

Relief loosened the tension in my shoulders. "I almost expected you to make a rude remark about girls from the riverlands."

I felt him freeze. "I was a pompous ass when I said that."

I wasn't about to argue with that. "What do you want to do?" I whispered.

My heart hammered with unvoiced fear. I was scared he would come to his senses and remember that this was a terrible idea. That the two of us together was something like what happens when flint strikes steel.

"Take off more of your clothes," he said roughly, and that put paid to my worries.

His jacket hung from his left arm, where it had gotten stuck and we'd both forgotten about it. For my part, my hands were inside his gaping shirt. I'd always admired men's shoulders, and his were particularly fine from all that sword fighting. I wrapped my leg around his, my bare toes making a trail down his calf muscle. I hadn't ever imagined his weight pressing down on my body would feel so good.

"I meant, beyond that."

"I hadn't thought beyond that." He tugged lightly on one of my curls, watching it spring back into a corkscrew. "I love your hair." Casting his eyes down, he swallowed. "Caro . . . You know I can't promise you anything. I . . . just can't."

"What—what do you mean—'promise'?" I stammered.

"You know, marriage. An engagement. That kind of . . ." He trailed off. I saw him go a little dead behind the eyes, steeling himself for my reaction.

I shoved him back, propping myself up on my elbows. "As if I'd want that! I'm seventeen. I have more important things to do."

He regarded me with a strange half smile. "You're not like anyone else, are you?"

"And you're a liar, Markos. You said you hadn't thought beyond this. You thought enough to come up with that little speech, didn't you?" I flopped onto the pillow. "*Marriage*. I'm going to be a captain and a privateer. *I'm* going to be the terror of the seas. Whoever marries you will have to wear pretty dresses and go to parties and learn the names of a hundred boring politicians."

"Oh, pretty dresses. That sounds like torture." He whispered, "You're really all right with this?"

But I was. The thought of any more change was too much to bear. Just for once I wanted to do what I wanted and let fate go stuff itself.

"Why are you smiling?" I asked.

"Because," he said, "*finally* we're doing something I know how to do." He touched my linen undershirt. "Yes?"

"Yes," I said impatiently against his hair, trying to untangle his jacket from his left wrist. The buttons were caught

He fumbled with the ties at my waist. "Yes?" His hot breath tickled my ear.

I pushed up against him, and he grunted. "Yes." I kicked my underthings down the bed.

He wrestled off his own clothes, and I remembered I'd seen him almost naked that one time on Heron Water. I hadn't bothered to look very closely, because to be honest, I had not expected anything impressive.

Well. *That* had been a mistake. But it wasn't only his bare body that made me gasp. He was covered in purple bruises and wore a tight bandage around his ribs.

"Hush." He dipped to kiss my lips. "The physicians say I'm fine. It's only sore." We were pressed skin to skin. I felt him shaking, his breath an unsteady flutter in his chest. "Caro? Yes?" Catching his lower lip between his teeth, he waited for an answer.

"Why do you keep asking me?"

"Because." A line appeared between his eyes. The muscles in his arms were tense. "I made a mistake that other time. I don't want to do it again."

"Oh." I kissed him, but again he drew back. His lips slipped from mine, still stubbornly waiting. "Yes to everything," I said.

The serious look on his face nearly killed me. I couldn't figure out when he'd become so important in my life. It was like trying to name the moment you learned to breathe air. I tried to will myself to stop being nervous, but after all I liked him so much more than I had liked Akemé. So it wasn't the same.

I felt him all over my skin, even the places he wasn't touching. Curving my hands over the peeling sunburn on his shoulders, I thought my heart would burst out of my chest. Warm, his skin was so warm. And solid. And real.

A strange, hot hitch in my heart made me pull him close.

"I didn't think I would see you again," I whispered.

"I didn't think I'd see *you*." He buried his face in my neck, inhaling. "You shouldn't have come back for me. It was dangerous and stupid."

"That's me. Dangerous and stupid." I grinned, and that banished the possibility of tears.

What he did next banished them even further.

# CHAPTER
# THIRTY

A wherryman's voice carries. It is both a blessing and a curse.

For us it was a blessing, because I heard Pa before he even stepped onto the dock. I flung off Markos's arm, crawling to the porthole. It was my parents, sure enough. Kenté trailed behind them and Daria skipped between, wearing a flowered dress and a man's hat.

"You have to get out!"

Markos began throwing on clothes. "I thought riverfolk didn't have notions about their daughters' purity."

"They don't. Well, not my parents anyway." I added, "I think."

He tucked his wrinkled shirt into his trousers. "Wonderful."

"Ma might. But what can she possibly say about it? She took up with Pa, and they aren't married." I tried to scoop my hair together into something that didn't resemble a bird's nest. "It's just embarrassing."

There wasn't much space in the cabin, so we kept bumping elbows and knees while we dressed, which somehow felt more intimate than what we'd done last night.

"It could be worse," Markos said. "If we were in Akhaia I'd probably have to face your father at dawn."

I stared blankly.

"A duel," he explained, straightening his jacket. "How do I look?"

I smirked. "Your trousers are open."

He swore.

"If Pa thought you'd hurt me, he wouldn't bother to fight a duel with you. He'd just shoot you." I buckled my belt. "Pretend we're just eating breakfast together."

"Which doesn't sound at all suspicious." He trailed a finger down my cheek.

A thrill shot through me at his gentle touch, but I pretended it hadn't affected me. I unlocked the cabin door, and we climbed out into the common room. I was still wriggling into my boots.

He caught my hand. "How far away were your parents?"

"The end of the dock."

Before I could ask why, he swung me against the wall and kissed me. I couldn't help running my hands up around his neck. His skin was warm, and he smelled like me. We smelled like each other, I suppose, an appealing mix of sand and sweat and sleep. And probably other things that my parents, being neither stupid nor inexperienced, would recognize.

I couldn't bring myself to push him away. His lips were soft and his tongue strong and lazy. He gripped a handful of my shirt at the small of my back. I wanted to crawl inside his jacket and stay there all morning.

"We have to stop," he said, pressing me against the full length of his body. And then, no matter how much I felt like melting into him, I stepped aside. One of us had to halt this madness.

It felt so strange, after all I'd been through, to be accountable to parents again. I heard footsteps overhead and the hatch cover shifting.

Daria was the first down the ladder. Markos grabbed her from behind, lifting her. "Little badger."

She squealed, but I knew she loved it. Tapping him on the nose, she said, "You look happy again. I'm ever so glad."

"Hush, monster." He tweaked her hat, and my heart flip-flopped. Seeing Markos being a good brother made him even more handsome. "What in the world are you wearing on your head?"

"My pirate hat. Nereus got it for me." She peered at me from under its skewed brim. "It's just like Caro's."

My parents and Kenté came down the ladder, and suddenly it was all noise and hugging and everyone talking at once. Pa's gaze jumped from me to Markos and then back to me. I knew he wasn't fooled by the three feet of space between us.

"But how'd you find out I'm not dead?" I asked.

Ma went briskly to the stove and began to pour coffee. "Nereus told us this morning."

"Nereus? I didn't—when did Nereus—?"

Ma raised her eyebrows. "I don't suppose you heard him."

I couldn't look at any of them. An awkward quiet fell over everyone except Daria, who was still talking about her hat. My face burning, I wished I'd stayed dead at the bottom of the sea.

Pa clapped a hand on Markos's shoulder. "Perhaps you'll come along to the market with me to fetch some fresh bread." I almost choked on my coffee. From his voice, I knew it wasn't a request.

Markos knew it too. I held my breath, remembering how rude he could be if he thought his honor was being insulted, but he only said, "Yes, sir."

They left and then, laying a finger aside her nose, Kenté whisked Daria up on deck. Just like her to make herself scarce when someone else was getting in trouble.

I was alone with my mother. "Why didn't Nereus come back with you?"

"He spoke enthusiastically of seeking out a certain tavern. I didn't have the heart to tell him it's been closed these many years, since I was a girl. And the building was quite falling down, even then." She frowned. "I wonder how long it's been since he sailed out of this harbor, that he didn't know."

Her piercing glinted as she wrinkled her nose. "Probably I'm meant to be giving you the woman's side of this talk right now." She stared into her coffee mug. "Be responsible, mind your reputation, come to me if you've any questions, and so on. But let's just skip it, if you don't mind. You're grown, and it's not my business." She sighed. "I know I've never been very motherly."

"You do *not* have to start now." My cheeks were hot. If I had any questions about sex, she would assuredly be the second to last person in the world I would ask. "Really, it's fine."

"He seems nice enough. But, Caro, don't let it get too serious. People always like to think they can overcome having different backgrounds." She shook her head, and I sensed she wasn't just talking about Markos and me. "It isn't so easy."

I didn't want to think about that right now. "I wonder what Pa's doing to Markos?"

"Putting the fear of the gods into him, I expect." Ma tapped the table. "Now. This morning I suggest we visit some of the finer shops in the garment district—you've nothing to wear. Tychon Hypatos is a councilman, and a friend of the Archon. He and his wife are wealthy people. You can't go up there looking like a ship-wrecked scalawag."

"I would like new clothes." I paused. "I want a jacket with gilt trim. And more waistcoats like this one. And a pair of fine leather boots."

"Dresses," she said flatly, in her bargaining table voice.

"No dresses," I countered.

She cleared her throat. "Sometimes I wish I'd been around when you were a little girl. When I might've bought you pretty things. Braided your hair." She shifted uncomfortably in her chair. "Things that mothers do."

I saw her as if for the first time. Responsibility had put crinkled lines around her eyes, and her faith in her family made her tall and strong. Was it too late for the kind of love Pa and I had? Maybe we were both too prickly and stubborn. I could respect her though.

"All right," I said. "Dresses. But no stays."

She cracked a wry smile. "I suppose that's what I get."

"Ma," I began. Glancing down into my coffee, I gathered my words. "I should've trusted you. I'm sorry."

"All forgotten." She waved a hand. "You're like Nick, that's all. Depending on no one but the river."

"No," I said hoarsely. "Not the river."

"Ayah?" To my surprise she grinned. "Is that the way of it? I'd begun to suspect. You know, Jacari Bollard himself was chosen by she who lies beneath. And he discovered a trade route that changed the world. Maybe you're more Bollard than you think, eh?"

"Oh." Her words had reminded me. I dug in my pocket. "I forgot. You can have this back. I never did get to use it." I laid her Bollard brooch on the table. The morning sun glinted on the raised gold stars.

She pushed it back at me. "Keep it. You never know—you might need it someday."

Turning the brooch over in my hands, I wondered. Was I Bollard or Oresteia? Both? I rather liked to think I was something else entirely. Something new. I tucked the pin into my pocket. Maybe we can leave things behind, yet still hang on to the best parts of them. The parts that matter.

We went up to Market Street, where I commissioned a new wardrobe, paid for with the pouch of silver talents I'd discovered in *Vix*'s hold. I stood squirming in my underthings while the shop girls drew tapes around my breasts and hips. My best gown was to be green silk, with a black pattern. The seamstress draped the fabric around me, as Ma nodded in approval.

I didn't see Markos again until that afternoon.

Tychon Hypatos's house was a sprawling estate, set back off the road and surrounded by a garden of sculpted trees. I came up the shell-lined walk to see Antidoros Peregrine sweeping the front door shut behind him. He wore a wide-brimmed hat low over his face.

I bobbed my head. "Lord Peregrine."

"Miss Oresteia," he said with a tip of his hat as he passed me.

I did not waste any time barging into the sitting room. "What are you up to?"

Markos looked up from a book. "I don't know what you mean."

"That was Antidoros Peregrine going out the door." He opened his mouth to deny it, but I cut him off. "And don't you dare say it wasn't. I recognized him even with the hat. Why are you having meetings with notorious Akhaian rebels?"

"If you must know, he's the one who came to Valonikos to meet with me. He wants me to see the way they do things here. Did you know their Archon *and* their council are all elected by the citizens?"

"So?"

"So Peregrine believes we might be able to make a new Akhaia, one founded on modern principles. He thinks I could help his cause."

"He thinks you're a political opportunity!"

He snapped the book shut. "Perhaps he just wants what's best for Akhaia." I caught a glimpse of the title printed on the cover of the thin volume. *A Declaration of Principles: Being a Manifesto Concerning the Incontestable Rights of the People.* "I thought this would please you."

"You ought to be careful, is all," I muttered. "You know he didn't like your father."

"He didn't *agree* with my father," he corrected me. "Did you know I was never allowed to read this?" He gestured to the book. "My father ordered all copies burned. Peregrine has some compelling arguments, particularly regarding political power consolidated in the hands of the—"

"Oh? You think this Archon doesn't have power?" I demanded. "All men with power take advantage. Doesn't matter if they're born or elected."

"You're being protective of me." He grinned. "It's sweet."

The room was open on one side. Markos crossed the tile floor, parting the gauzy curtains to walk onto the balcony. The red roofs of Valonikos spread out beneath us like a lady's skirts. The Free City was similar in architecture to Iantiporos and Casteria and the other seaside cities that had once been part of the Akhaian Emparchy. They all shared the same white columns, square pastel-painted buildings, and roof gardens with potted trees. Beyond the city, the sea stretched to the horizon, decorated with white dots—the sails of ships going in and out of the harbor.

"I was not," I grumbled. "It's just you don't even sound like yourself. You told me you don't trust Lord Peregrine."

"That's not—"

"That is exactly what you said. Now you're just going to let him come waltzing in and put all these ideas in your head. It's not *you*."

"I suppose I'm meant to have all my beliefs—my whole life—already mapped out before I'm even twenty? That's hypocritical, isn't it? Coming from you."

"What do you mean by that?"

He raised his eyebrows. "I mean two weeks ago you knew you were going to be a wherryman for the rest of your life."

I couldn't argue with that. "I didn't say it was a bad thing." I drew my finger along the balcony railing. "I only think you should be cautious."

"When we first met Peregrine," he said quietly, "he called my mother by her given name. It made me angry."

"I couldn't tell," I said sarcastically.

"He wasn't being presumptuous." He sighed. "He knew her, better than most people. Apparently they were great friends at court, many years ago, before she married. I wish I'd known. I wish—" He shook his head. "I didn't know enough about my family."

I slid my hand on top of his, squeezing it. He squeezed back.

"My cousin Konto hates this city," he said. "He wants to have it back."

"How do you know?"

"The Theucinians are imperialists. I know how they think. Konto means to have me back too. Or dead. I don't mean to let him take me." His gaze took in the tiled rooftops and whitewashed balconies. "I've decided I don't mean to let him take either of us."

"Markos, what—?"

His eyes were alight with something I couldn't name. "This is a beautiful city. I feel a peace here." He leaned on the railing. "I feel as if I could be someone I like, in this city."

"If Lord Peregrine gets his way—" I began.

"He doesn't use his title anymore."

"Just the same. If he gets his way, Akhaia mightn't need an Emparch at all. Did you think of that? In a modern Akhaia, they wouldn't need you."

"No," he said, and instead of looking angry, I thought he looked exhilarated. "They wouldn't."

"That doesn't bother you?"

He shrugged. "The world is always changing."

"I didn't think *you*, of all people, would want that."

The breeze shifted his black hair. "I don't know what I want anymore. The world is so much bigger than I thought. And, Caro, the funniest part is—" He laughed. "I think it's a good thing."

Hearing Markos talk like that was certainly a surprise. I couldn't exactly pinpoint why it made me so uneasy. It wasn't that I begrudged him his excitement about Antidoros Peregrine's ideas, but why did everything have to be changing so alarmingly fast, including Markos? I desperately wished for a moment to catch my breath.

An even greater surprise came the next day, when a wherry sailed into Valonikos harbor. She was not the newest wherry, nor the fastest. Her paint was scratched and gouged, marred with bullet holes, and her black sails much faded from the sun. A frogman stood on her cockpit seat, waving.

"Fee!" was all I could manage before my throat closed.

Pa jumped aboard, rocking the wherry. He grinned at Fee, and I saw the relief in his eyes. "Well, I reckon there's a story here." He ran a hand over *Cormorant*'s warm planks. "Caro, what have you done to my gods-bedamned paint job?"

That was all he said for a long time. He wandered up the deck, setting his hand on the boom and stroking the mast. I watched him trace a coil of rope and caress the brass portholes.

"Fee, how?" I took her slippery hands, spinning her in a circle. I couldn't stop laughing. Or was I crying?

"Frogs fall," she said. "Frogs swim. Webbed feet."

"How did you escape from the Black Dogs? How'd you get *Cormorant* back?"

"Dark. Quiet. Water. Docks. Waited. Waited. Waited. *Cormorant*. Crept. Leaped. Man. Knife. Throat." It was the most words I'd ever heard out of her at once. "Sailed."

Fee's eyes widened. I turned to see Nereus leaning on the boom behind me, hands in his pockets.

"Cousin." He gave her a theatrical bow.

We sent a runner up to Tychon Hypatos's house, and eventually Markos and Daria joined us. Markos showed his sister around the deck, regaling her with stories of our narrow escapes in the riverlands. Even Ma came down for a while. We all squeezed around the table and dined on meat pies and fresh fish from the market. Then, one by one, the others left and it was only me, Pa, and Fee. Just like always.

But not quite.

*Cormorant*'s cabin seemed cramped now in the homey lantern

light. I trailed my hands over the shining wood of her cupboards, bunks, and shelves, lingering on the red-and-white-checkered tablecloth.

Had I really lived in her? It seemed like something that had happened years ago. An uncomfortable feeling. Swallowing hard against the lump in my throat, I climbed up to my favorite spot on the cabin roof.

"Ayah, so here we are." The deck creaked as Pa joined me. "They all gone up to Iphis Street. I be reading your ma's mind. She's thinking, 'If I get that young man a crown, then what might he do for the Bollards?'" He shrugged. "Don't care for all that myself. Give me a good heavy load and a steady wind."

He looked at me. "So then, this is where it ends for us. You and me."

Tears burned my eyes. "Pa, don't say that."

"I've wronged you, keeping my silence." He took a shuddering breath, staring down at his callused hands. "But now I've got to say my piece and hope you'll forgive your old pa." The sunset breeze stirred the graying hair around his face. "I knew you weren't meant for the river."

I dared not breathe.

"It were a long time ago. You must've been three or four. I was sailing up the channel when, don't you know, the weather turned as bad as bad can get. The waves near swamped us. I took a reef, then another. Weren't no help. I reckon that's the closest I've come to being drowned. And then . . . *she* was there. With a voice like the deepest fathoms." He shivered. "Like a wild thing."

"Like a hundred knives," I whispered.

Pa nodded. "Just so. 'I ain't one of yours,' I said. 'I belong to the one who lies under the river, and you well know it. Though I won't say no to your help.'

"'Know this. I'll never harm you, Nick Orestcia,' she said, 'and that you have as a promise. For I owe you a debt. Keep her safe for me.'

"I looked up and my heart near dropped out of my chest. You were sitting on the lee side, wet to the knees, for we was riding that low in the water. Every time a swell came, it dunked you to the waist, but you just laughed. 'Course I panicked. I yelled at you to come down into the cockpit. Then I heard her.

"'As if I would ever let her fall,' she said. And just like that, she was gone."

He sighed. "I never even told your ma. Guess I'm just an old fool. I reckoned maybe if I didn't say it out loud . . ."

I wiped my face with my sleeve. "I thought the god in the river didn't want me." Now I was sobbing in earnest. "I called his name so many times and he never—he never answered me."

"Hush, girlie." He wrapped me in his arms. "You were never unwanted. The truth is, the sea loved you from the moment you were born."

"But it's all wrong." I sniffed. "I'm supposed to be on *Cormorant*. This isn't what was meant to happen." I dug my face into his sweater. "I was supposed to be with you."

Trailing his fingers down my cheek, he said gently, "No." He kissed the top of my head. "I knew the minute you took that letter of marque. Knew it was your fate coming for you. That cutter is a beauty. You mind what I taught you and take good care of her now."

"But I love *Cormorant*." I pressed my palm flat on her warm cabin roof. "That ship doesn't mean anything to me."

He smoothed my hair. "Sometimes we have to let the past go before we can see our future sitting there in front of us."

I closed my eyes. "She's pretty and fast but she's not . . . home. She never, ever will be." I rested my cheek on his shoulder, breathing in the muddy, familiar scent of his clothes.

"Stop crying now." He slung his arm around my waist. "Don't you have more Emparchs to be rescuing?"

I laughed, even as I sniffled.

"Be careful," he warned. "I fear she'll ask more of you than he's ever asked of me."

"Thisbe Brixton said she was a fish and Nereus was a shark, come to eat her. But surely they must be friends. Surely the god of the river and the god of the sea—"

"Cousins, at most. Allies, sometimes." He gazed out at the horizon where, beyond the city walls, the sea waited in the night. "But friends? No."

He went belowdecks, leaving me alone. Through the open window, I heard his voice rising and falling. Pa always talked to Fee just the same as he did to everyone else. He didn't much mind when she didn't talk back.

I sat on the cabin roof past midnight, knees curled to my chest. One last night watch, feeling everything. The noises of her tackle creaking and clacking. The swirl of water against her hull. The singing of tiny frogs under the docks. Only when I unfolded my stiff legs did I realize what I'd been doing was memorizing, because this was it.

The last time this would be home.

CHAPTER
**THIRTY-ONE**

Three days later Tychon Hypatos and his wife threw a grand party
for Markos at their house. Fortunately my new dress was finished
that very morning. Pressed and wrapped in paper, it was carried
down to *Vix* by a shopgirl who stared bug-eyed at Nereus's tattoos.

The party was like nothing I'd seen before, even at Bollard
House. The courtyard was strung with floating paper lanterns.
Piles of grapes and cheese spilled down the middle of the long
tables. There were even sculptures made of food, which seemed
very silly to me.

I could tell Markos's aunt—or cousin, or whatever relation she
was to him—didn't like me. As she stared at me in the receiving
line, I had the distinct feeling she knew exactly what we were
doing when he slipped down to *Vix* at night.

As if it was *her* business.

She nodded politely as she welcomed Nereus, Kenté, and me, though I knew she considered us a lot of rough scalawags. I discovered Daria, in a stiff pink dress, sulking by the dessert table. There was no one her age at the party, and Markos had abandoned her to discuss politics. Kenté took her for a turn on the dance floor to cheer her up, while Nereus and I hid in a dim corner behind a tower made of fruit.

"Nereus—" I hesitated. "Now that you're done helping me, what happens to you?"

"Oh, I doubt I'm finished with that." Long sleeves covered his tattoos, but his gap-toothed grin still made him look disreputable. "Because *you* ain't finished. Not even close."

"I would ask what you mean by that, but you won't tell me anyway."

"You're learning." He winked, downing his first glass of wine. He had four—two in his hands, two on the table.

"Will you sail with me?" I hoped he would say yes. "As first mate on *Vix*? Really, you should be captain. No men will want to sail under me."

"Ayah? I don't know about that." He drew a crumpled piece of paper from his pocket.

It was a printed leaflet. A tale—highly embellished—about a girl who stole a pirate ship, who folk were calling the Rose of the Coast. I wished I'd done half the things it said I'd done. The caricaturist had drawn me with a feathery plume in my hat. I resolved to get one immediately.

"But this is mostly nonsense." I lowered the paper. "I don't in any way resemble a rose."

"Your hair is reddish."

"This is the stupidest thing I've ever seen." I tossed the pamphlet onto the table. He smoothed it, tucking it back in his pocket.

I might have questioned him further, had not Tychon Hypatos and another man chosen that moment to invade our corner.

"Aha! Miss Oresteia. I had quite given up hope of finding you. I have here a man who greatly wishes to meet you." Hypatos gestured with a flourish. "This is Basil Maki, the Kynthessan Consul. Representative of the Margravina."

The man bowed. "Current carry you, as your folk are wont to say."

"Oh good," I said. "Are you the one to talk to about the ten silver talents I was promised?"

"You don't waste any words, do you, Miss Oresteia?"

"Captain Oresteia," I corrected. "My contract said I was to deliver the box and its contents to Valonikos."

"The contents I see," he said with a smile. "Have you presented them to the dock inspector?"

"Seems to me that's a lawyer's answer."

"Alas, I am a lawyer." He bowed again. "Or I was, before the Margravina elevated me to my position."

"I suppose Markos could go present himself to the dock inspector," I said. "If that would get me ten talents."

His eyebrows lifted practically into his hairline, I guess because I'd spoken so familiarly of the true Emparch of Akhaia. "I ought to inform you that the Black Dogs have petitioned me for the return of their property," he said. "Of course, it is a jurisdictional issue now, since the ship in question is outside the boundaries of Kynthessa."

I didn't understand half his words. "I was a privateer. A letter of marque gives me leave to take a prize. I know my rights."

He tilted his goblet toward me. "Nevertheless, the Black Dogs are claiming you stole a cutter from them."

I smiled. "I did."

"From what I've heard, the Margravina isn't necessarily, ahem, what one might call pleased with the way things were handled."

"Then she oughtn't to have given that kind of power to *me*."

"Miss Oresteia, you should know that overconfidence doesn't usually impress me in the very young. And you are just a seventeen-year-old girl." Maki stroked his thin beard. "Nevertheless. Your legal claim to the ship is perfectly valid. I'm rather disinclined to grant the Black Dogs a hearing. But it may not matter."

"How's that?"

"Captain Diric Melanos, the man who made the petition, has quite vanished from the custody of the law."

My hand froze with my glass halfway to my lips. "You mean escaped?"

"Doubtful, seeing as he left behind a puddle of his own blood."

I was about to question him further, when Markos joined us.

"I have the honor of being Markos Andela," he said, extending his hand. I stared, for I'd never heard him introduce himself by that name, only by title. I suspected it was Peregrine's influence.

He looked—well, he looked wonderful. There was no getting around it, though I wouldn't dare say so out loud. He already had a big enough opinion of himself. He wore a formal coat with tails, crisp lace falling from the collar and cuffs, and his blue silk cravat had a pattern of lions on it. Had he gotten taller? He'd always been tall. It must be the way he carried himself tonight. He looked like an Emparch from head to toe.

"That dress is very dashing," Markos said after the Consul excused himself. "Although I don't understand your hair." He examined it dubiously, as if it was a nest of coiled snakes. Which, admittedly, was what it looked like.

"Kenté did it."

"It's pretty. But it's not really you. I like your hair when it's . . . big. And springy. And red."

"It's always red!" I snapped. None of those other things sounded like compliments.

"So prickly. I like that." His lips brushed my ear. "Always know this," he whispered. "I like a hundred things about you, and only one of them is how you look in a dress."

He certainly proved it later that evening when he dragged me into the empty library.

His lips crashing against mine, he pressed me into a bookshelf. I slid my hand under his collar to feel his hot skin. With the other I gripped his coat, tugging him closer.

"I miss you," he said hoarsely, kissing my neck. "You drive me mad. I miss you."

"Well? Which is it?"

He laughed. Our lips met again, slowly this time, tongues tangling. Something inside my chest twisted. He made me want things. And he made me scared of wanting them. I gently smoothed a lock of hair behind his ear.

He grabbed my hand. "No, don't—"

It was the one with the missing earlobe. The scarred new skin was shiny and red.

"Oh, honestly," I said. "I saw it when it looked much worse than this."

"It's ugly." He turned away. "I hate it."

"Markos, have you been wearing your hair over your ear all this time we've been in Valonikos? So no one will see? You are the vainest, most—" I stopped, recognizing the stormy look on his face. His body had gone rigid.

I put my hand on his cheek, turning him back. "I already told you, I think you're the bravest"—I was going to say "boy," but I sensed somehow that wasn't right for this moment—"the bravest man I know." I kissed him. "I like a hundred things about you, and be assured one of them was *not* that half of your left ear."

That finally got him to laugh. Our next kiss was so deep, it made me ache, and not just in the usual places.

"Caro, this dress has entirely too many buttons."

I pried his fingers off my back. "I know. Which is why it's staying on. Anyhow, I reckon I'm going. I can't bear another four hours of this party."

He knocked his forehead against the bookshelf and moaned. "Stay."

"*You* stay." I wriggled out of his grasp. "All these people came here to meet you." I kissed him softly. "I don't mind. Truly."

"Indeed, Peregrine is probably combing the party for me at this very moment," he admitted.

"See you later." I squeezed his hand before I went.

I had one more thing to do before I sought my bed in the captain's cabin on *Vix*.

My cousin sat in a pool of red silk, her back to *Vix*'s mast. Her hair was braided in rows and fixed in an intricate knot at the top of her head. I'd hardly gotten a chance to talk to Kenté in Valonikos. I suspected the Bollards were keeping her on a close leash, given her previous disappearing act.

There was a peace about the harbor at night. I dropped to the deck, resting my elbows on my knees. Absently I pressed one palm flat on the wood, as I used to do on *Cormorant*. The stored-up warmth from the day seeped into my hand.

"My parents are coming tomorrow, on a packet from Siscema." Kenté leaned her head against the mast, closing her eyes. "I don't know what to do."

"Yes, you do," I said. She opened one eye to squint at me. "Of course you do. The way I figure, you can slink back to Siscema with your parents. Or . . ." I nodded at the ship berthed across from us. "That's the *Olivios*. She sails up the Kars on the morning tide. To Doukas and ports beyond. To Trikkaia."

She said nothing.

I pulled a pouch from my pocket and set it on the deck with a clink. "Here."

"I don't need your money."

"Ayah, perhaps not under usual circumstances. But perhaps you do," I said softly. "For this."

"I can't." She took the pouch, turning it over and over in her hands.

"It's one thing not to know your fate," I said. "But you been hiding from yours, and I reckon you know it. You told me we're all calling out to the world and magic is the world calling back." My eyes stung, I knew not whether for her or for me. "Well, the world is calling to you."

"I'm afraid I'll never go to the Academy. And I'm afraid I *will* go. I'm mightily sick of being afraid of everything." She traced the inlaid cask and stars on her brooch. "But I don't know how to say good-bye."

"So don't *say* good-bye. Just go! What if everything that happened to Markos and Pa and me . . ." My voice broke. "What if that was my fate? What if this—all of it—was only about one thing? Getting me to *this* place, at *this* time. Kenté, maybe you're supposed to be right here. On this dock." I pointed. "Across from that ship. Tonight. What if this is your fate? What if you miss it? You have to—"

I turned. The moon still shone down on the Valonikos docks, draping the corners in shadows. The *Olivios* still creaked quietly at anchor.

But Kenté was gone.

"Good luck," I whispered.

The next morning I slipped out early, for I had errands to run.

First I visited the business district, where the buildings were freshly whitewashed and had pots of pink flowers out front. Then, jingling the coins in my pocket, I wandered toward the docks.

"Caro!" Markos jogged to catch up.

I waited. "I thought you'd be spending the day with your admirers."

"I needed to get away. Nereus said you'd gone out." He looked at me and laughed.

"What's so funny?"

"Your jacket." He tapped the gilt trim. "It's just like mine."

I pretended to be offended. "It is *not*. It's bottle green. Yours is blue."

He fell in beside me, and we walked in companionable silence. I snuck sidelong glances at him. He wore a snowy new shirt, but the cravat he had left dangling. I didn't think the old Markos would have appeared in public looking so sloppy.

"Caro, I like this city," he said, hands in pockets, as we threaded through the bustle of the market. A man jostled his shoulder, but he didn't snap or demand an apology. Almost, I thought he might have shoved back a little. "I like all the commotion. All the ships. I like that it's proud of being free."

"Markos . . ." I hesitated, unwilling to spoil his fun. "Should you be walking around the docks like this? Isn't your cousin Konto likely to send more mercenaries? Or assassins?"

"I'll hire bodyguards." He shrugged. "But for now I like walking around by myself. I've never done it before."

I shook my head. Just like him to get excited about something silly like that. Spotting a food stand, I tugged his sleeve. "Let's get some fish in a cone."

"Fish in a what?"

"A cone. There's a place on this street sells the best fish in a cone on the River Kars."

He stared at me blankly.

I'd forgotten I had to explain the simplest things to him. "Fried in bread crumbs and served in a cone of paper."

He looked extremely skeptical, but that went away ten minutes later. We walked up the street, our mouths full of flaking, hot fish.

Markos licked the grease off his fingers. "You should've made it like this on the wherry."

"I can't. They fry it in a vat of boiling fat."

He made a face. "Sorry I asked."

I halted, noticing a shop on the corner, and wiped my hands on my trousers. The sign read Argyrus & Sons, and underneath in smaller letters, Valonikos–Siscema.

A bell rang as I pushed through the door. The girl at the front desk looked up from her paperwork.

"This is Argyrus and Sons?" I asked. "The salvagers?"

"We are as the sign claims," she agreed. She wore a blue-and-white-striped shirtwaist tucked into trousers. Her face and arms were tanned golden, and her brown hair twisted into a loose bun at the base of her neck. I liked the look of her, a working girl like me.

"Is Finion Argyrus here?"

"He's in Hespera's Watch on a job," she said briskly. "I'm Docia Argyrus. The daughter. How can I be of help to you?"

"Current carry you," I said. "I didn't know there was a daughter."

Eyes narrowing, she crossed her arms. "It didn't fit on the sign."

"I'm Caroline Oresteia," I began, drawing a bag of coin from my pocket.

"The girl pirate." She examined me head to toe. "Didn't think to meet you. Interesting."

"Privateer," I corrected. "I took a prize recently. The cutter *Victoriano*s."

"I know her."

"In her hold she had a chest of silver talents." I dropped the bag on the table. "I am given to understand that your firm be overseeing the salvage of *Jolly Girl* and the other wherries as were lost at Hespera's Watch. I want to pay."

She glanced at Markos. If she guessed who he was, she didn't say.

"Additionally," I said, as she got out a pen to write down my instructions, "can you please include in the letter that in the cases of these four men"—I spelled out the names of the wherrymen who had died at the Black Dogs' fort—"I wish to pay ten talents to each man's wife or heir."

"On top of the other costs?"

"Ayah."

Her pen paused. "That's an awful lot of coin."

"Basil Maki is representing me in this matter. He's the Kynthessan Consul. So be sure to go to him if you need more money."

After we left the shop, Markos refused to speak to me for three whole blocks. "I told you I wanted to do that," he said in a growl.

"You haven't the coin. I have." I grabbed his arm, forcing him to stop. "I wouldn't have *Vix* if it wasn't for you. So in a way, it's your money too."

"It isn't," he said sourly. "While you stole that ship and rescued my sister, I was unconscious and tied up."

"Ayah, well, not everyone can be good at everything." I grinned. "You know what I mean. If I hadn't met you, none of this would have happened."

"I have been thinking that myself," he admitted. "About how thankful I am that I was fated to meet you."

"It was luck." Even as I said it, I knew it to be a lie.

"You still believe that, after all this? Think of everyone who helped save Daria and me. All the people we met along the way. The wherrymen, the Bollards, even Nereus. They all have one thing in common."

Me.

This whole time I'd been thinking I was in Markos's story, but maybe I'd had it backward. Maybe he was in mine. I heard the heron's leering whisper in my head. *Laughter.*

"Caro." Markos reached for my hand. "I want you to stay. With me."

Panicked, I tugged away. My thoughts raced in confusion as I looked somewhere, everywhere—anywhere but at him.

"Not like *that.*" He let me go. "Wait. That didn't come out right."

"You better not have meant it like that." I strode down the cobblestones, my emotions bubbling and boiling in a way I found distinctly unpleasant.

"Well, I didn't. Will you stop?" He chased me down the street. "Caro, I *didn't*. If only because if I did, you'd probably slap me. Again." He took a breath. "Let me finish."

"You said when we . . ." I was too embarrassed to continue. "You said there'd be none of that talk."

"I know," he said quietly. "But some things have to be said."

I stopped to face him. "I don't want you to change my life."

He squinted down at me in the noon sunlight. "It's a bit too late for that, isn't it?"

I remembered what Pa had said. *Sometimes we have to let the past go before we can see our future sitting there in front of us.*

The world had changed. We could not go back.

"But I've been thinking, a fast cutter has to be of some use to me. I mean, us. I mean . . ." Markos gathered his words. "What I mean to say is, since you're not going back to the river, I wish you would sail out of Valonikos. You can be a privateer. For me. I know I don't have an army, or a fleet." He shrugged. "But I have to start somewhere."

He extended his hand, as working men do to seal a bargain.

I took it. His fingers were warm in my grip. Lowering my voice so no one else on the street would hear, I said, "Markos Andela, Emparch of Akhaia. Lord of et cetera, et cetera. I will always be your friend. I will sail for you." I held up my free hand in warning. "Not for Akhaia. For you."

He did not kiss me, opting to stay at handshake's length. I could tell he felt it too—the moment demanded a certain solemnity.

"Well." He cleared his throat. "That's settled, then."

For the longest time we stood in the street, grinning stupidly at each other, the fresh wind off the sea flapping our clothes. I slid my hand out of his and started walking, along the boardwalk that led past the warehouses to the maze of docks. Markos strolled beside me, close enough that his sleeve brushed mine.

"So, do you have any ideas about what we can do with a cutter?" he asked.

We rounded the corner of the warehouse. "I don't—"

I halted halfway through my sentence. Suddenly I couldn't breathe. It was like being shot with a flintlock pistol all over again. It was like being punched in the heart.

"What?" Markos said, distantly. But I barely heard him.

Everything had stopped. I was mesmerized by the crisp edges of her bundled-up sails, standing against the blue sky. Her wood and paint shone. Her rigging and stays were all delicacy and grace. The curve of her hull, the shape of her overlapping planks, seemed to me just about perfect. But it was somehow more than that. I felt her essence.

A surge of thrilling music went through me. And I smiled.

Because that's when I saw *Vix*.

# ACKNOWLEDGMENTS

When I began writing this story, I had a feeling it was the one. I was right, but nevertheless it's been a long four years from that first draft to this book. The biggest thanks are due to my agent, Susan Hawk, for her enthusiastic support of this book. Thank you to my editor, Cat Onder, who read this manuscript three days after it was submitted. I like to think that means it went to the editor who loved it most. Also a huge thank-you to all the amazing people at both Bloomsbury and the Bent Agency.

Thank you to my friends and family, who were subjected to long monologues about publishing that probably weren't very interesting—and extra special thanks to those of you who read early versions of the book. Shout-out to NBA Twitter, an A+ group of people whose unbridled enthusiasm for my writing during my blogging days gave me the confidence to finally go for it. It may seem weird, but it turns out there's actually some overlap between YA readers and basketball fans—thanks to all you Twitter friends who were some of the earliest readers of this book! A particular thank-you to Laura Walker and Sarah Moon, the founding members of Team Book in the World. Without Laura cheering me on as my very first beta reader, I don't know if I would've made it all the way to the end of draft two. Guys! Look! It's a book! In the world!

It's funny how things work out. I just realized I have to thank Chris Paul. If you hadn't left New Orleans, I probably would never have quit blogging. In a bizarre way, this book exists because of you.

Thank you to my dad, who inspired a lifelong love of fantasy by reading *The Hobbit* out loud to me when I was little. (Someday I'll write a Swords and Horses one.) To my mom, who, when this book was out on submission, told me to visualize my dream book deal and say, "Things are always working out for me." They did work out! To my brother, Bryan, for spotting all the geeky references in the book.

Thank you to Michael, my sweetie, especially for all the weeks when I was on deadline during revisions and completely ignored him. Somehow the house didn't become buried in trash and dishes, and all the cats survived, and I am pretty sure those things had nothing to do with me. I love you!

This book is dedicated to the memory of my grandmother, Barbara Proops, who never laughed when eight-year-old me said

I was going to be a writer. I'm glad I was able to call her and say I'd sold my book. Unfortunately she never got to read it.

And finally, this book would not exist without Arthur Ransome's Swallows and Amazons books and Stan Rogers's music. To go forward, sometimes you have to go back. I went back to the folk songs and the sailing adventures I loved, the ones that inspired a girl with dreams of being a pirate. The girl grew up and the dreams turned into this book.